FIDDLER'S GHOST

FIDDLER'S GHOST

A NOVEL BY

MITCH JAYNE

WILDSTONE MEDIA

Book design by Diana Jayne

Publisher's Cataloging-In-Publication Data
(Prepared by The Donohue Group, Inc.)

Jayne, Mitch.
   Fiddler's ghost : a novel / by Mitch Jayne. — 1st ed.

   p. ; cm.

   ISBN-13: 978-1-882467-45-7
   ISBN-10: 1-882467-45-0

1. Ghost stories. 2. Fiddlers—Fiction. 3. Ozark Mountains—Nineteen fifties—Fiction. I. Title.

PS3610.A96 F53 2007
813/.54

Foreword

OOKS, I THINK, are kind of like movies: a means of letting your mind find new ways to look at a world you thought you knew. They only ask for a few hours of "suspend our disbelief" imagination from the "what if?" part of us—our curious chunk of brain, seeking possibilities. They have this in common with music, especially violin music, which is the most mysterious time-traveler of all.

If you need to know about me, I'm an old time-traveler who hopes when you read this book, you will find a ghost in the next fiddle you hear, and believe in strange stuff. That's what fiddles and books are for.

Prologue

OME PEOPLE CAN really tell a ghost story. Charles Dickens, for one, did it so well that people who didn't even believe in ghosts realized reading about his inspirational ones, that this world we think we might know could indeed be just the tip of an unknown iceberg.

I don't compare myself with Dickens, but we do have two things in common: a firm belief in the goodwill of Christmas and a faith that tells us that we can take some comfort believing in an existence beyond our own.

After so many years, I've finally become brave enough to tell my story about a ghost, an old violinist as real to me today as he was fifty-five years ago when I first met him. When he first made his presence known, he was so real, my wife Lacey gave him a nickname. She thought if she gave him a rustic name like Hiram, then we wouldn't believe in him and he'd leave and go haunt somebody who would be properly impressed.

For a long time, I was uneasy about writing this remembrance of our musical ghost. I remembered a quote from Frank Zappa or someone of his generation; "Writing about music is like dancing about architecture." With that, I realized I had an even more daunting simile to face: "Writing about ghosts is like whistling about the hereafter."

My children, though they didn't believe everything Lacey and I told them while they were growing up, believed our story of Hiram. And still do.

They have sat around the fireplace on long winter nights and heard us tell about him, seen me puff on his old pipe and listened to their mom and oldest sister play tunes on his fiddle that Hiram composed.

In the event that any of us Clarks should forget anything and on the chance that the supernatural might touch you too, here goes.

I, Stephen J. Clark, age seventy-eight and still reasonably sound of mind, as much as old retired schoolteachers are expected to be, and body pushing hard on elderly, am as sort of a piece of my will going to tell the story of Hiram, the fiddler ghost of Blessing Creek and bequeath it to you.

Hiram, wish me luck!

Chapter One

N THE AUTUMN OF 1951, I DECIDED TO become a schoolteacher. I was bored with my education and had nearly four years of college behind me, courtesy of Uncle Sam, whom I served in the Navy. I wasn't a very good student for Uncle Sam's money, which I was currently spending at the University of Missouri at Columbia, mainly because I couldn't seem to seek the proper goals. I was twenty-three and with 175 hours of wildly assorted college credits, I didn't seem fitted for any sort of profession. I was wearing the patience of the college down, along with my welcome at the Veterans Administration.

What I had accomplished was to take a little of each interesting subject like English Literature, or welding, or art classes, or logic, or archery, and the list went on, to the despair of my advisor. I still wasn't even near a degree and had a serious need to make some money.

The best part of my education came in my second year—

meeting Lacey Donnelly, a stunning girl from the Ozarks. As a result of my brain-stun of falling in love at first sight, on our fourth date I asked her to marry me. Lacey amazed me by simply saying: "That sounds like a good idea." It obviously wouldn't have sounded that way to most young women, but Lacey was never like most young women. She always operated on instinct. When I met her, she had just graduated with honors from the same university I was beating my head against.

She had a Bachelor of Arts degree in music and was the most curious, open-minded and outspoken woman I had ever met. Best of all, Lacey talked with an unbelievable comfort that Ozark people have with words, and she used expressions like, "My grandpa owned a fair scope of land," and "Athletes can sure be teejus company." I loved to listen to her tell a story, and when I went to Springfield to meet her parents, I understood where her ease of speech and storytelling came from. The Donnellys were keepers of a southern culture that stays with a family as faithfully as features, wherever they go. Lacey's mom, Vera, still called her "Alacia" when telling a childhood story. Her dad, Rabon, used words like "nineteen-and-forty-one" for dates and "abundance" instead of plenty. They had approved of me and despite reservations they might have had, accepted without question that Lacey and I had decided to marry. We married on their porch the summer of 1949.

The Donnellys were a family that always knew what needed to be done and did it, and they were a good inspiration for me. God knows, I had found little enough to light a fire, so far, in academia.

2

Two years later, Lacey was five months pregnant, and I needed a job worse than a degree. My advisor, a fine tweedy man who told me with a clank of his pipe on his Yale ashtray—there to prove he was a misplaced Ivy League man, "Clark, if you don't know what you want to do, then teach, man, teach."

I might still be bumbling around campus in a matching tweed jacket, pipe in teeth, advising another generation myself, except for two marvels: Lacey's pregnancy and a note on the bulletin board at the student union, which turned my advisor's words, however jokingly said, into sense.

Under the heading of Teaching Positions, I read:

> *Medley Springs Township, Burke County, Missouri*
> *Needs an applicant for Indian Glade rural school*
> *on Blessing Creek*
> *(grades one through eight)*
> *No degree necessary.*
> *Male or female.*
> –Contact *Walt Bangert, Supt., Medley Springs Courthouse*

The note also included a phone number for Walt Bangert's office. Although it wasn't exactly a trumpet call to startle me into action, I found something about it very attractive.

The name Indian Glade was wonderful, as was the name of the creek, and the town Medley Springs sounded like a place where I'd hear a variety of little tunes played by a waterfall, like wind chimes. Then there was the name Walt Bangert, not Walter, just a simple barbershop Walt. I'd always been a soft touch for

3

names and had given a lot more time than I probably had to spare, poring over maps of Missouri looking for great sounding places like *Pull Tight* and *Lookout*—named for things other than people.

I stole the note and drove to the housing unit off campus, where Uncle Sam had been boarding me for years. It was a jumble of Quonset huts, rebuilt barracks, trailers, with clotheslines and children everywhere. As I drove, I observed abandoned tricycles in the middle of weed-cracked sidewalks. I glanced at all the old but shiny cars and the cute hand-painted lettering on mailboxes emblazoned with things like *Dun Rovin* or *Belly Acres* and each bearing the family name with little boards hanging underneath enumerating the names of their kids like a rifleman's medal. I glimpsed at all the neatly competitive lawns and knew the whole place looked like a concentration camp for the middle class.

I drove slowly down the street to our cellblock, ignoring the fifteen-miles-per-hour signs. I didn't drive the speed limit; a speed bump would put the transmission right up in the seat next to me. So I drove five miles an hour, urging the old Plymouth to live through another year of road-salt rust. The Plymouth was a 1941 model, whose previous owner had babied it through the war, and I intended to make it last long enough to get us out of that place, which every day more resembled limbo.

LACEY WAS IRONING a shirt, her red hair damp and clinging to her neck and forehead; the place was an oven. From the cubicle next door, yells and screeches of the neighbor kids playing poke-the-eye or some such, came through with great fidelity.

Lacey, though five months pregnant, wasn't much bigger than when I first met her. However, she had begun to show signs of the coming responsibility of motherhood—like a tendency to worry whether the neighborhood kids were busy setting each other on fire and eventually our tiny apartment. I was even more concerned with the ruckus: how two-year-olds might turn her against the prospect of having a child of our own.

"Lacey," I said, taking away her iron and speaking loudly to override the miniature soap opera next door, "how would you like to move to lovely, tinkling-sounding Medley Springs, Missouri in the beautiful Ozarks?"

Her green eyes narrowed and I could see she was in no mood for dumb questions. "To do what?" she asked.

"To live in the cool woods, teach the children of Indian Glade School and work for a fine old man named Walt."

"Sounds good, I'll pack. When do we leave?"

"Well, first I'll have to ask Walt," I admitted, "he doesn't know about this yet."

I handed Lacey the purloined notice and went to get some quarters from our piggy bank. I went across the street to the Veterans Co-op to use a pay phone and call Medley Springs. It was surprisingly easy to get the school superintendent's office, and good old Walt was not only in, he answered the phone.

Yes, he said, the job was still open. Yes, my credentials sounded fine. Why, he asked, didn't I drive down tomorrow and present myself to the board of directors of the school.

After I hung up the phone, I yelled, "Why indeed!"

Exhilarated, I raced home to tell Lacey and unsurprisingly,

5

she was more fired up than I was. "Watching somebody get an education," she had once remarked, "is about as exciting as watching somebody fishing. I keep hoping for a strike." I liked her analogy, since from the day I had met her, I had been waiting for a strike and I now felt the line humming.

WE TOOK THE rest of the day organizing for the trip. It included such mind bogglers as trying to get my transcript from the dean's office, picking up an application for a teacher's certificate, and getting a Missouri highway map showing us just exactly where Medley Springs might be found. Somehow, we managed it all. Even though I wouldn't be certified for some weeks, we had enough ammunition to prove that I was reasonably sane, honorably discharged from the service and presumably educated enough to teach the first eight grades of a rural school.

We left the next day at daylight since the drive would take us about three hours, and the old Plymouth did better when the air was cool. I also wanted to show up suited, tied, and spiffy, before Walt could give the job to some wan-matron with flat heels and a degree from some Ozark Teacher's College.

The trip was beautiful, Lacey and I felt like two kids skipping school as we crossed over the Missouri river at Jefferson City and left the flatlands, heading for the Ozarks. The highway turned into a long, idyllic roller-coaster road, crossing little creeks and twisting its way through lush foothill farms and tiny towns with little ivory steeples poking up through tree-lined streets, indicating churches we couldn't see but knew were up there on the speckled hillsides. Going south, the hills grew and swelled trying their best to become mountains and live up to their names, but they were incredibly old and worn down like hound's teeth.

Every minute's change in scenery captivated and held me: the incredible endlessness of old woods where Osage Indians had once roamed, set their traps, fished and made their hunting camps. Although I had fished and trapped, too, I was a flatlander; I grew up near Mark Twain's hometown where creeks are muddy and farmland is as flat and unexciting as a Presbyterian revival. But here, clear rushing streams were like some magical transformation of water into wine, if not something better. Lacey delighted in the drive because it was like coming home for her, and I had only been south of the Missouri River a couple of times before, to meet her folks and later marry her.

WE PULLED INTO the little village of Medley Springs about nine o'clock. It was a pretty place, sort of run down and gauzy with age but still making an attempt to look hospitable with its EAT signs and homely awnings across storefronts. Huge elms and oaks shaded the lawn around the courthouse where Walt had his office. Lacey sat thankfully on a bench eating an ice-cream cone from the drugstore while I went to find him.

Walt Bangert, seated at an old oak table in the middle of his office had a rolled up paper in one hand, swatting flies. I felt like I had gone back in time; my visual impression was of Clarence Darrow at the Scopes trial—suspenders, huge trousers, a gray lock of hair hanging down and a rolled up newspaper instead of a fan. The tall windows of the room were open, and I remember thinking Walt was very likely going to put in most of his day

7

killing flies.

Introducing myself, I showed him my credentials. He looked them over amiably, making grunting noises of approval and occasionally swatting an imprudent fly. Waving me to a chair, he turned around to a file cabinet of Civil War vintage, and after some rustling of papers, came up with what he told me was a standard school contract, which I would have to have signed by the three members of the Indian Glade School Board. He signed it with a great flourish that seemed to give him considerable satisfaction.

"Now there's not much money in that deestrict," he informed me solemnly. "The number of chirren is down and that's what sets the revenue, don't you see. Scholar-days is what establishes the revenue for a school deestrict."

I expressed my ignorance and thought it was a good time to tell him I didn't have any grasp of the job at hand, since it was my first one teaching. Walt was more than willing to oblige me with information. He said he had taught for twenty years before applying for the job of superintendent and by going to summer school had amassed 160 college credits so that he could move up in his profession. I was encouraged; I, at least as a matter of record, was more educated than the superintendent of schools for Burke County.

He was a fine old man without an ounce of self-importance or pedantry. He handed me a teacher's manual with a batch of literature from the State Board of Education and said it would lay out the ground rules—the written ones at least. The unwritten ones he said I would have to figure out as I went along—

having mostly to do with satisfying the parents and the school board.

"Incidentally," I said, "when do I meet with the school board? Will they come here to interview me?"

Walt gave a good, rich chuckle; I could tell he wasn't trying to belittle me in any way, it was just a pleasant way in which older men react to a naiveté they remember in themselves. "Well, most giner'ly, Mr. Clark," he said kindly, "we don't have what you'd call a interview. You just go out there, see these folks one at a time, and let them size you up. You see, they're farm people. Myrtle Summers will be cannin' about now. She's the treasurer and I'd suggest you see her first, as the polite thing to do. You'll be having to see her every month to get your warrant, so it's a good thing to get off on the right foot, don't you see."

"What is a warrant?" I asked, thinking the only ones I'd ever heard of were the arrest kind.

"Why, that's how you get paid each month. You take Myrtle your attendance records to show how many scholars was there for how many days of school, so she can send it in to me. You see that lets me bill the state for half of the expenses to the deestrict. Then you take your warrant down to the county clerk—old Porky Johnson's office down the hall here—and they'll give you your check."

I could see I was entering a brand new world of finance, and that reminded me to ask how much I could expect to earn at Indian Glade.

"Well now," replied Walt, "that's a matter to be settled between you and the school board, naturally. The last teacher got two-hundred-and-twenty-five dollars a month, which I admit wasn't much wages, but it's all they could pay, there being a poverty of scholars in that deestrict." He looked a little embarrassed but continued, "That's why the school hasn't contracted for a teacher. Most schools had their teacher by the end of June, but Indian Glade hadn't the money to hire for what most teachers wants these days, and they got left out. Money's scarce down on Blessing Creek."

He was straightforward, and I didn't really care about the "poverty of scholars." Although I might be the last hired, lowest paid teacher in the county, I would at least be out of college and making a living for our soon-to-be family. Whatever injury my ego might suffer, I wouldn't have to go back to the veteran housing every night and listen to lawn mowers, Hank William records, or children shrieking, seeing how much the puppy could take.

We spent nearly an hour talking, I was absorbing as much wisdom as I had questions for, as well as getting directions to the people I had to see.

The day was getting hot when I left the courthouse, and Lacey was fanning herself with a limp *Medley Springs News*.

"I was looking for a place to live," she said. "What's the verdict?"

"So far, so good," I told her.

WE WENT TO the car, me carrying an armload of instructional materials and my hand-drawn map. We started out of town in the direction of Blessing Creek, while I described my job interview.

Lacey asked, "How much money will they pay or will we have to trade out in chickens and pigs?"

I told her what the top dollar was, and it didn't dismay her any more than it had me. We were young and newly married and almost anything seemed possible. I said I'd learned some new words; Walt called children in the Indian Glade School District either "chirren" or "scholars," and district was pronounced "deestrict."

"Shucks," said Lacey, "I knew that."

AS WALT HAD predicted, we found Myrtle Summers canning. A widow in her seventies, she lived with her son and daughter-in-law, and it was evident she ruled the roost. Sonny, as she called her son, was out seeing about their cattle, and his wife Min—a worn-looking creature who looked to be in her fifties—served coffee while Myrtle looked us over. The old lady seemed to spend more time talking to Lacey than me.

Lacey was wearing a simple but pretty dress and wore stockings on that scalding day and had said it was her "schoolteacher's wife look." She looked modest and charming. Myrtle gave her looks of approval and with some sort of second sight particular to people who have been there, done that, she asked Lacey when the baby was due. Lacey told her December, and the rest of the interview was a cinch. Afterwards, questions Myrtle asked me were of much more a family nature than anything scholastic, and when she saw Walt's signature, she only glanced cursorily at my credentials.

"Of course, we do like to look at a person's bill," she said

11

startling me—I thought she meant my nose for a moment. "But generally we hire by findin' out what a teacher's like. We haven't had much luck with men teachers."

I tried to look apologetic.

After a suitable amount of cross-examination asking what my father did (he owned a hardware store in Hannibal), where Lacey's folks lived (at the edge of Springfield), and so on, she signed my "bill" and sent us toward the creek to look for Jeff Farley, who also served as a member of the board.

FARLEY'S PLACE WAS several miles up the creek off a branching dirt road. The road came up through the car's floorboard in the form of dust settling on everything—the seats, the dashboard, Lacey and me. The old car lurched and rolled, making loud scraping noises whenever the rocky backbone of the road's hump clawed at one part or another of the underside, but we finally managed to pull to the top of a rise and find his house.

When I got out of the car, there were two little blonde children in the yard, a boy who looked to be about four years old, and a little girl perhaps a year younger. They were making a rock castle and scarcely seemed to notice the car until I stopped the motor and got out.

"Hello," I said. They both looked up at me gravely with doll-like, china-blue eyes. Other children began to appear immediately. From around the corner of the house came a girl of perhaps twelve, carrying a two-year-old on her hip like a Swahili mother. I just hoped to God that it wasn't hers. A boy, who looked to be in his teens, appeared in the doorway and behind him a middle-aged woman with a baby in her arms. It was obvious, on the scholar-attendance basis, the Farleys were the hope of Indian Glade school district.

Mrs. Farley was a well of hospitality. "Git out! Git out!" she said. I thought at first she was telling us to leave, but then I realized she was telling Lacey to get out of the car and come into the house. I had a lot to learn about the language, which became even more apparent by the moment.

"I'm Sadie Farley and Jeffrey's in the hay with our oldest boy, Cleavis. —Was you wantin' to see him?"

"I've come to see him about the school," I told her. "I'm applying for the teaching job."

The effect of this on the assembled children was wonderful. Never have I been stared at more analytically by so many pairs of Nordic eyes and for a moment, I felt like a freak in a Swedish sideshow.

"Why chirren, here's your new teacher," exclaimed Mrs. Farley proudly. "Now Jeffrey'll be so tickled, I can't tell you. Irene there, run to the field and tell Daddy the new teacher's come."

What a good sign, I thought.

While Lacey talked to Mrs. Farley, I used the opportunity to become acquainted with the children. To my amazement the first question Mrs. Farley asked Lacey was when the baby was due. Either Ozark women had x-ray vision or Myrtle Summers had a telephone and used it.

The Farley children were polite; the four-year-old took my hand and trustingly showed me the details of the castle he and his sister were making, and the twelve-year-old girl shyly informed

13

me that she was going to be a nurse when she grew up.

Shortly thereafter, Jeff Farley arrived with his son close behind. The eldest boy was fourteen and shook hands solemnly like a man, and both of them tipped their straw hats to Lacey.

A stocky, straw-blonde man in his forties, Jeff Farley had a fine open face and big grin. His hands were huge, freckled with sun, and when we shook hands, mine hurt for five minutes afterward. I didn't care, they were glad to see us—worried as they'd been for a teacher.

After he signed my "bill" without looking at it, Jeff was insistent that we stay for dinner, but I was impatient to end the suspense. I still had to see Soames Black, President of the Indian Glade School Board. The title was somehow intimidating and I was nervous wondering what Soames would be like. Not a bit put off by my suit jacket and tie, which I'm sure he thought was fitting for a job seeker, Jeff was aware of my discomfort and how much I wanted to get my business settled.

"Well now, you and the missus will come up and eat with us one day soon," he stated. "We don't have much else, but we eat good around here."

I could believe him just from the quantity of noise and manure that emanated from a hundred assorted ducks, chickens, turkeys, and hogs that ambled about the yard seeming very much at home. Behind the wood-shingled house, which must have been bursting at the seams when all the Farleys were in it at once, was a monstrous garden rusting under the August sun. It looked to be half an acre of corn, squash, beans, tomatoes, and God knew what else.

14

The smallness of the house, in proportion to the number of children, intrigued me. It reminded me of my Uncle Ed's joke about a farmer who had "screwed himself out of a place to sit." But all the children looked healthy, and the family seemed as happy as a litter of puppies.

"Now, Soames Black is kind of a stately man," said Jeff while lighting an old curved pipe and puffing it thoughtfully, "but don't let that fool you. At heart he's common as groceries, and his word's as good as his handshake."

As we were leaving, all nine of the Farleys surrounded the car with considerable racket and fuss, and then waved to us as we drove out of the driveway. I was pleased and much relieved by our welcome at the Farleys and now had only the president of the board to face.

"Stately," Jeff had described him; I pictured a portly old man in a blue suit with a gold watch chain and spectacles. My father had described one of his uncles as being *stately*, and I remembered seeing a picture of him looking just like that. It was all the more impressive since Jeff said Soames Black was the man who made all the final decisions in school matters and had been president of the board for longer than I had been alive.

I managed to get our car down their rocky driveway without rupturing the oil pan, and we turned again down the creek road that Jeff said would take us to the Black farm. It was cooler near the creek where pawpaws hung over the road; their enormous oval leaves covered with so much dust, I hardly recognized them. The creek was a pretty little thing: sluggish with summer drought but doing its best to look cheerful as it tinkled over riffles and

15

swirled in translucent pools. It made me want desperately to stop the car, strip to my skin and wade into its coolness up to my neck. Lacey looked longingly at it, too, but we were dressed for appearance and knew better than to dwell on the idea.

When we had gotten married, we had lost the crowd, taken off for a local quarry and both plunged in, wedding clothes in wads on the bank. But now we were responsible adults—job seekers, and creek wading was out of the question.

Lacey was in good humor. "So much for keeping secrets down here," she chuckled. "Those two women probably know if it's going to be a boy or a girl."

I agreed.

Around a curve, green clusters of bloodroot hugged under the cool shade where columbine decorated the bluff, and we came upon Soames Black's ramshackle farm. It stood on a low rolling hill across from Blessing Creek, which we had to ford to reach the house. The cool rippling water against the tires was tantalizing.

Lacey sighed, "Whether you get the job or not, we're hitting this creek on the way back. Even the baby's feet are burning."

She'd read my mind.

SOAMES BLACK'S HOUSE was incredible. A barn was nearby, in addition to a chicken house, a bunch of hog pens, machinery sheds, and a dozen other buildings scattered around the hill. The house sat perched on top of the hill like an old hen set on eggs. Built of oak logs beginning to bulge ominously at its bottom corners, the old two-story building sat looking across bluffs from

16

windows that were more patches than glass. The tin roof had long since turned to rusty brown, and the broad front porch sagged crazily in the middle. Two gigantic white oak trees shaded the sparse yard, while chickens scratched busily at what some time or another had been grass. Big black and tan hounds, at least half a dozen, raised their heads and watched us approach. One stood up and bawled halfheartedly at our car, but it wore him out and he lay back down in the shade. Soames Black was working on an ancient tractor under the sparse shade of a tin-roofed machine shed that adjoined the barn. The barn, bursting with hay, looked even more likely to settle under its load than the house.

Soames was a fine-looking old man with a face like an Indian except for his huge walrus mustache, which was snow white and matched his beetling eyebrows. He wore a great flop-brimmed straw hat and underneath, his piercing blue eyes peered kindly at us. He obviously thought we were lost. Wiping his hands on a rag, he approached and then doffed his hat to Lacey.

"Howdy folks," he said amiably. "Hot, ain't it?" He fanned his neck-length silver hair away from his face and looked anxiously at Lacey, who was obviously burning up. "You'ns git out and set in the shade a spell. The little lady looks like she could use a dram of cold well water."

I realized I was going to have to alter my definition of stateliness if this gentle old man was an example.

When I had explained our reason for being there, he chuckled warmly.

"Why, I'd about give ye up," he told me. "I'd got afraid that

17

the chirren wouldn't have no schoolmaster, late as it is. Now you two come to the house and have a cold drink of somp'nother. We'll set on the porch in the breeze if they are sich a thing."

I heaved a sigh of relief as we walked up the path to the house among fluttering chickens. Interested hounds rose to sniff respectfully at our legs and wag their massive tails. It was apparent the old man was honest in his welcome and openhearted with his feelings, and we couldn't help but feel accepted already.

Soames' wife came to the screen door with a tired dishtowel in one hand. She was spindly-looking despite her alarmingly protruding stomach. For a moment the crazy thought that she might be pregnant crossed my mind, but it didn't last long. She was at least sixty-five with a sad, wan face and wispy white hair that had escaped from whatever hairdo she had attempted that morning.

"Come in off the gallery," she told us. "Hit's a way cooler in the house."

Since Soames didn't show any sign of introducing us, I took the liberty. "I'm Steve Clark, and this is my wife Lacey. I'm applying for the teaching job."

The old woman was as mournful as Soames had been enthusiastic. "Ain't hardly enough chirren to keep school no more," she said looking at me doubtfully. "Folks don't stay in this ol' rocky hill country if they kin hep it. They all want a fine big car, and they move up to the city. Used to be we'd have twenty-five or more scholars over to Indian Glade schoolhouse. Used to have big doin's over there, back before ever'body left out. Course, I ain't well enough to go to nothin' no ways. You'ns wants some

18

ice tea?"

During her long speech, the old woman's expression never changed. With the exception of her first and last sentences, her attention was directed to the floor. Both Lacey and I accepted her offer, and Mrs. Black shuffled off to the kitchen, while I took the occasion to look around their living room. Lacey, riveted to one spot was doing the same.

Never in my life have I seen anything like the décor of that house. In one of the few open spaces sat a gigantic Stromberg-Carlson radio with a front like a church organ. Beside it was the most raddled old upholstered chair I had ever seen, with big tufts of stuffing exploding from every crevice and a spring plainly visible through the worn-out material of the seat. There was another chair on the opposite side that had lost an arm in some encounter and sat on a brick in lieu of a leg for one of its corners. There was an old treadle sewing machine table next to it, piled high with odds and ends of automobile parts, tractor parts, and shotgun shells. Beside it were shoes in the middle of repairs of some kind, cans of paint, and bottles of nuts and bolts.

A huge old fireplace took up most of the west wall and on either side of it, the corner space was interesting, to say the least. The sagging logs had burst their notches at the bottom and the spaces were stuffed with rags, old newspapers, and apparently whatever came to hand, all in order to keep the elements out. On the mantelpiece, or what Lacey called a fireboard, there was a collection of the same sorts of things the sewing machine held, only more of it. This included a tractor piston—complete with rod, an oil can, two or three bottles full of different kinds of

19

liquids, a picture of somebody lying in a coffin, and a fruit jar with some sort of used human organ—God knows what—floating in alcohol. Among other items, there were scattered boxes of bolts, washers, a doorknob set with a porcelain handle, and an old Seth Thomas clock with one hand.

The north wall featured an elderly Sears and Roebuck secretary piled with seed catalogs supporting a precariously balanced kerosene lamp. The secretary's writing desk held a load of papers, bills, letters, circulars, and other pieces of correspondence, all held down by a rock, carburetor and some sort of horseshoe. Starting at the secretary, I noticed strung along the wall, suspended from nails, a series of traps. Most of them looked ancient and were of every size and description: Old Victor No. 2s rusting away, beaver, mink and coon sets, wolf traps, Conibear traps for muskrat—everything needed for any sort of trap line. Above them, nailed to the logs were displays of deer antlers, some with hair still clinging to the bleached triangle of skull.

Overhead, kerosene lanterns hung everywhere, rusty wire hooks suspending them from the oak beams of the ceiling. There was a splayfooted Charter Oak stove and its crazy zigzag stovepipe somehow found its way to the flue by the kitchen door. Best of all, in the center of the room, a completely disassembled four-cylinder Ford tractor engine sitting on a few layers of oily newspaper.

The room was a museum of defunct machinery and the odds and ends of the Black family existence. Most impressive was the cleared debris; it was evident that someone had carefully swept everything into corners so that the center area (excluding tractor engine) was "shipshape" for living, but nothing would be lost to future sorting in case a bolt came up short.

"My old woman," remarked Soames gently, "has a tewmer, and she ain't felt just right of late," he added in explanation, "she's under a doctor."

When Soames invited us to "take a cheer," Lacey and I sat down in a couple of high-backed hickory ones with hand-woven seats. It would have been sacrilege to sit in their two ancient, overstuffed crippled ones, where I imagined Mr. Black and his missus had probably listened to *Lum and Abner* and *The Grand Ole Opry* back in the Depression days when radios depended on batteries.

Soames was the sort of mountain man I have since learned a lot about; he had captured us and wanted to keep us around a while, to see how we were made. He was in no hurry to complete the school contract. He probably thought it would be a breach of etiquette.

The Blacks interested both of us, and when Mrs. Black brought in tea, Lacey started a conversation, which made the old lady light up like a bulb. It seems Mrs. Black was under the constant care of doctors. I caught only slim bits of the conversation while passing the time with Soames and wasn't a bit surprised to hear her ask Lacey when the baby was due.

Virgie, (I was to learn her name later, Soames just called her "Mother") was evidently a confirmed hypochondriac who had finally come up with a "chewmer," as she called it, and it was the most important thing in her life. She wouldn't have parted with it for the world.

21

Soames went on talking about the neighborhood and about my scholars. "Now you've met the Farleys, and you can see they are good hands to turn out chirren. The Pulvers and the Cartwrights," he informed me, "they're old residenters like me, borned and raised on the creek. The Terrill clan is from up around Bee Branch, but they're good folks, kindly fanatical about church. They have two chirren. The McClellans moved here two year ago from Michigan. They're quare folks in a way but hard workers, and they pull like a team. They have five chirren, and they look to pup again about deer season."

I decided to get comfortable with my stately school board president. "Mr. Black, could I take off my suit coat and tie?"

"I never could see," he said solemnly, "why a man had to wear a neck rag to do a job of work. You make yourself comfortable, son."

From there on it was an easy slide; we talked about fox hunting, coon hunting, discussed guns, bee trees and trap lines—all of which I luckily knew something about—and we touched very little on education. I told him I would do the best I could with the Indian Glade pupils, and he believed me.

When it came to signing the contract, the old man did a very touching thing; he got out an old bank receipt and carefully copied his signature from it, holding his tongue out and squinting closely at the letters he had learned to write. He also said something I will never forget.

He asked diffidently, "Mr. Clark," you think you'll need to use a hickory much?"

I was appalled at his suggestion and assured him I would never

22

strike a child for any reason.

He nodded over his signature. "I'm not an educated man," he said, mildly, "but I believe that you can't learn a critter anything, man or beast, by whacking its backside. That's not the end you're after, seems to me."

We were engaged in this important exchange when their two sons arrived; one was a big, curly-headed boy of twenty with hair as black as tar and the other a redheaded young man, sunburned from the hayfield, with eyes as blue and friendly as his father's were. The redhead had a black and blue spot under his eye the size of a teacup and an injured hand wrapped in a rag.

Soames introduced them in turn. "This here's my boy Vance and the crippled-up one's Carney."

We shook hands. Carney, grinning, gave me his left one.

"I tell 'em and I tell 'em," said Mrs. Black dolefully, "but they go over to town and git to caperin' around and come home all tore up."

"Now Mother," said Soames.

"Well, it's the God's truth," continued Mrs. Black, "you cain't tell 'em nothing. I told Carney, I says, 'Carney, you go to foolin' with them Antioch boys, you're goin' to git your plow cleaned in the gravels,' but nobody listens to Mother."

"Now Mother," said Soames.

"Well, it's gospel truth," declared Mrs. Black, directing her speech to the floor, or perhaps to the disemboweled engine lying in the middle of it. "'Them Antioch boys don't fight, they jist kill and drag out,' I says. 'You go a'struttin' and draggin' your wing over yonder,' I says, 'and they'll bring you home on a shutter.'"

Carney was embarrassed. His brother, however, found his mother's lecture entertaining. He sat down, or rather threw himself into one of the overstuffed chairs that responded with an alarming cloud of dust and debris.

"Hell, he jist got blindsided, Ma," said Vance. "That biggest Adams boy come up behind him after he knocked Fletcher Tibbs down and caught him a lucky one. But by God, I fetched Homer one with a pool cue. Give him a knob on his head you could set on to milk."

"Now boys," said Soames with dignity, "this here is the new schoolmaster. Don't be a blackguardin' and tellin' your brags in front of his little wife. I don't aim fer 'em to think the Black family wears a hard name."

Carney grinned at me. "Them Antioch boys brought it on 'emselves, teacher," he said sheepishly. "Me and Vance was jist a' funnin' around, but them Adamses, and Tibbses is mean-natured as copperheads."

I couldn't really listen, someone had actually called me teacher; I really was one, my now official contract said so.

The Blacks invited us to stay for supper, but I begged off. I told Soames our next problem was to find a place to live, and we needed to start looking.

"Well now," said the old man, "you'll want to be near the school I reckon. They ain't too many places around here that the pack rats ain't took over. But they ain't nobody on the old Decker place, is there Mother?"

Mrs. Black looked forlornly at my shoes, or perhaps at a stray

24

tractor part and said, "Nobody there, or likely to be."

She didn't elaborate; I had a picture of burst plumbing—or lack of it, a leaking roof and floor joists riddled with termites.

"Hit's a real purty place," said Soames, "about a mile below the schoolhouse. I'd figger Gib Decker'd rent it cheap, jist to have somebody keep it up. A house don't thrive empty."

Lacey was hopeful. "Does it have plumbing?" She had enjoyed a privy as much as she could stand when she was a child and was thinking of the baby on the way.

"Why, I believe they's a raggler bathroom," said Soames, "with a commode and all sich as that. It wouldn't be too fancy, I reckon."

I was curious: "Is the place very big? We don't have much furniture."

"Why don't you'ns go down there and have a look at it," Soames suggested practically. "It might suit you and then it might not."

I asked, "Where would I find Gib Decker?"

"He has a little old grocery store in Medley," said Carney, "right across from the post office. He wouldn't keer for you lookin' the place over. Hit ain't locked."

I had known Lacey's parents long enough to understand that *he wouldn't care for* meant that Gib Decker wouldn't mind if we inspected his house.

"How about it, Lacey?" I asked. "Want to look at it while we're here?"

"I think we ought to," she said, "and we could look at the schoolhouse while we're at it."

"You'll need a key to the padlock," said Soames. "Mother,

what's went with the keys to the schoolhouse? Seems to me I had 'em hung up sommers."

There followed one of the damnedest searches Lacey and I had ever witnessed. The Blacks, having no use for keys in the first place, had no idea where such an item would be kept, and their ideas were varied and considerable. Vance rummaged through drawers full of junk, while Carney inspected all the nails in the walls, which had clothing of every description hanging from them: hats, coats, overalls, even a pair of hip boots for running a trap line. Soames favored the back porch for a hunting ground, and the old house quivered to the sound of washtubs, harnesses and other household gear hitting the floor as he searched among the likely pegs lining the porch wall. Mrs. Black left for the kitchen to "pilfer around," as she put it, among the pots and pans.

Falling into the spirit of things, Lacey and I joined in, directed by Carney, who suggested likely places to look. We searched in corners stacked with rifles, shotguns, saucers filled with small change, .22 shells, loose grains of corn, and pocket lint.

We learned more about their house than we could have in twenty visits. In lieu of closets—apparently nonexistent—nails in the walls provided *all* the storage. Small wonder, with all the horizontal space occupied. The variety of things went from a miniature metal crosscut saw for cutting small pieces of something, to an ornate old mandolin of ancient vintage—deep bellied with a staggering amount of mother of pearl inlay on the peg head and fret board. In any other house, I thought, this would be a work of art on display, but I found it hanging under a rain slicker.

Lacey and I would occasionally find a bunch of keys and cry *"Found!"* only to discover, when one of the Blacks arrived, that they belonged to a car they had traded some years before, or to a forgotten gate lock made necessary by some neighbor with a penchant for rustling, or grandpa's key to the old smokehouse, or a bunch of keys they'd bought along with a box of contents at some auction—with no locks to accompany any of them. It was a spirited search, and the Blacks found items they hadn't known they'd lost. They were turning out all the drawers, emptying most of the shelves, and raising more dust than a rodeo.

Soames finally found the keys in the kitchen, hidden behind woven strings of garlic along with "leather britches" (beans), red peppers, dill and fennel that festooned the ceiling beams. The keys, fastened to a big wooden paddle, had SCOOLHOUSE written plainly on it.

IT TOOK US a while to say good-bye. The Blacks were insistent that we stay for supper, but we begged off on the basis that I had to turn in my signed contract, find a place to live, and drive back to Columbia for our furniture and belongings.

All four of them saw us to the car. Mrs. Black, with her hands clasped under her apron, bent her head and peered at the ground next to the passenger side window to speak to Lacey. "Now that old house may not suit you," she said. "The last folks lived there claimed it weren't natural."

"Now Mother," said Soames.

"Well, it's gospel truth, Soames," she told him, lifting her

27

head up slightly, "them Wickhams didn't stay there but a month. Said they was somebody else livin' right in there with 'em that they couldn't see, but they could hear them a-prowlin' about of a night."

"Old woman talk," Soames said, followed by spitting his tobacco juice at a grasshopper and hitting it.

"Well, I wouldn't feel right, not tellin' it," his wife replied looking directly in the car window at Lacey and me. "And they's more than one says the same thing. Gib Decker wouldn't live there. His chirren wouldn't live there. Nobody he ever rented out to, taken to that old house. And Soames, you mind Mistress Clark is in the family way." This last said with an almost comical roll of her eyes upward.

Lacey's eyes crinkled in a beginning grin.

"Gib has a fine big house in town," explained Soames patiently, "and them two boys has married women that's sceered of the woods so bad that a hoot owl hollerin'd give 'em the fantods."

Lacey was fascinated; she liked mysterious things and had a good Irish appreciation for the occult. "You mean the house is haunted?"

"I ain't sayin' it is, and I ain't sayin' it ain't," said Mrs. Black, pursing her mouth at her husband. "But all's I know is, folks who've lived there don't take to the place. Now I've said my say. You'uns go ahead and look it over if you've a mind to. But you don't want to see anything to cause you to mark the baby."

Carney scoffed at the idea of anything so ridiculous. "They ain't nothin' in that old house but a bunch of pack rats or maybe flyin' squirrels. You take and leave a house empty a spell, the varmints move in. I wouldn't doubt they's a generation of possums been raised under the kitchen floor down there."

Vance nodded in agreement.

"Old Shad Wickham," continued Carney, "was skeered of hisself and I wouldn't confidence him noways. Ain't nothin' the matter with that old house."

WE FINALLY GOT our good-byes said, and I was so full of exhilaration, I could hardly contain myself.

"We did it, Lacey!" I shouted as we drove back toward the creek. "I'm a schoolteacher, by God!"

"How about getting our feet wet, teacher?"

We stopped at the ford and paddled about like children, splashing cool water on each other until we were both thoroughly disreputable-looking. Neither of us cared.

"When they named this Blessing Creek," said Lacey thankfully, "they were being modest."

I felt like an enthusiastic kid. "Let's look at the schoolhouse."

It was my first job, and I couldn't stand the suspense. I wanted to see my workroom and Lacey understood. She generally did when it came to me.

Chapter Two

E FOLLOWED THE ROAD BY THE CREEK, winding in and out of patches of sun and shade. The car was like an oven, but we were cool from the creek and didn't mind. Bluebirds flitted across the road while cardinals made scarlet streaks among the grapevines that lined it. Giant sycamores met in arches over the creek and road; it was a green tunnel with quilt-like pieces of sunlight and shadow. The air hummed with the buzzing of summer.

The road to the schoolhouse wasn't much more than an overgrown cart track leading off into the woods but with the aid of Soames' directions, we found it. No one had traveled the road in a long time; mullein stalks, high as the car roof, grew in its center and wild crabapples dragged at our fenders. We left the low pasture ground and entered the woods to the sound of locusts louder than the car engine. Jouncing from side to side in ancient wagon ruts, we saw the Indian Glade schoolhouse up ahead.

The old building sat basking in the sun in the middle of an acre of hit and miss clearing, its whitewashed boards flaking in the heat. It was a small schoolhouse, perhaps twenty-four by forty feet with a tin roof much the worse for rust and a little bell cupola with slatted sides poking up into a sky as blue as childhood. On the side we approached driving up, there was a wall of windows—the old-time sash type—all of them eight feet high. Mud daubers worked busily at roof eaves, and heat rose in waves from the packed earth around a big concrete porch.

I parked the car alongside the schoolhouse and, with key in hand, stepped out admiring my new domain. Lacey with her innate Ozark sense of custom, let me go up the cracked steps and open the door by myself. The door was in a little alcove, the sides carved with hundreds of names gouged out of the willing wood with pocketknives. Some young scholar years ago, probably either a sober churchgoer or a convict by now, had carefully inscribed, *Schoolteachers is sons of bitches all.* Several coats of paint since had not changed that old opinion.

I turned the key in the corroded padlock, released the hasp and opened the door. Inside, the smell was immediate and memorable—floor oil and chalk, dust and books, the smell of schoolrooms in any age. There was a quality of stopped time—a mixture of wood polish and old books and erasers. Red wasps hummed under the high ceiling of tongue and groove oak, while mud daubers hovered next to their clumpy dwellings on bookcases behind the teacher's desk. Row upon row, little desks marched toward the monstrous table behind where I would sit and be a teacher. Each desk had a hinged top and inkwell, the small seats looked

31

like miniature church pews, and there was a massive Charter Oak stove as big as a blacksmith's forge that stood in the middle of the room. The stovepipe climbed almost to the ceiling and turned at a right angle, where it disappeared into the flue behind my throne. The windows, blue with age, were as distorted as the heat waves rising from the schoolyard.

Lacey had followed quietly. "How do you like your workshop, teacher?"

"It's wonderful. It's the most wonderful workshop I've ever seen."

We went through books in the library, carefully trying to avoid the red wasps. Some of the books were so old, their backs were ruined and silverfish had taken them on for a diet. McGuffey's Readers and old blue-backed spellers were falling apart and smelled like old family scrapbooks. There were some amazing books—a leather-bound copy of *Toilers of the Sea* by Victor Hugo, *The Mill on the Floss*, *Anthony Adverse*, and *Gulliver's Travels*.

The arithmetic books, none newer than 1930 and some much older, were both funny and appalling. To test Lacey's knowledge, I picked a sample and recited from one of the relics: "If Jonathan has three apples and elects to share them with four friends, how shall he divide them?"

"Steve, I can't identify with Jonathan, give me a cute name, like Buford."

"Spelled B-E-A-U-F-O-R-T?" I suggested.

WE SPENT nearly an hour going over the place. We inspected a rusty pump over an ancient cistern and managed to raise a splash of tepid water. We investigated the boys and girls' privies, which were warped and spider-woven, but clean. We climbed the creaking ladder to the school bell and rang it, alarming a great number of barn swallows that had built big mud nests in the belfry. They flew frantically over our heads, abandoning what they probably had thought had been their retirement home.

In the schoolyard, we found a set of sturdy handmade swings and a merry-go-round that screeched and howled when we tried to ride it. As if run over by a steamroller, the schoolyard was packed and smooth, and the pathways of a thousand kids' feet marked the bases of a ball field over-grown with broom sedge and crabgrass.

Touching her stomach in empathy, Lacey said, "I think I'd like our child to go to school here with all the long-ago little ones."

For a moment we stood motionless, thinking about the future. I put my ear on her stomach and said, "You get that kid?"

We didn't need to say anything more, and I regretfully locked the old door.

We sat for a moment in silence in the car, looking back at the schoolhouse. Turning the car around in the scorching schoolyard and heading back to Blessing Creek, I was ready for my job and understood I had as much to learn as any pupil I would ever teach.

LOOKING BACK FIFTY-FIVE years later, I still appreciate the stillness of that little glade—the grasshoppers rattling in the sparse grass, the summer sky and the stillness of the woods around that modest place where teachers and students had come and gone for fifty years before me.

In that old schoolhouse, I had sensed generation after generation who had lived through the wonder of childhood. For the first time I had come very close to discovering something about myself I had never known before. Perhaps, I saw the first glimpse into some of the things Hiram would teach me: things are never meant to last long, and what counts is remembering their reality and passing them on to caring others.

Chapter Three

T WAS MID-AFTERNOON WHEN WE bounced back over the bumpy road from the schoolhouse and descended to the creek again. In my eagerness to tour the old schoolhouse, I had left the old Plymouth parked in the sun. It was like a hot box in a prisoner of war camp and dust was everywhere; it seeped through the floorboards and floated in through the open windows to settle on everything. We wore a thin layer of it like makeup on our hands and faces; it was a taste in our mouths. I don't think either of us paid the discomfort much attention. I felt like Balboa discovering the Pacific from his peak in Darien and Madame Curie hovering over glowing Petri dishes. I felt larger than life. I had a school; I was going to teach the little ones to learn, help form their lives, shape their minds. Without even seeing them, I knew what their faces would look like and pictured the wonders I would do. I have never been as drunk as I was on that first sober day I became a teacher.

Following Soames' directions, I turned onto the road that followed Blessing Creek and headed west. Where the road narrowed not much wider than a path, I drove slowly; on Lacey's side, brush hugged the car so tightly that she had to roll up the window to keep branches from whipping across her face. On our left, the creek wasn't very wide but the riffles, cool and shadowy under sycamores and cottonwoods, made tempting noises as we passed. We stopped once to navigate a turn where granite rocks cropped up and became part of the road, and a wave of some woodsy aroma filled the old car with a sweetness that was nearly overpowering.

"Honeysuckle," said Lacey, "or maybe pawpaws."

Whatever it was, it was magical. We forgot the heat and dust and drove on along a bluff where water dripped, and little green plants clung to the gray walls of stone. All of a sudden, the road dipped, made a turn, and we were there.

I'll never forget our first look at that place. A hollow opened on our right and back in the brooding shade of walnut trees, stood a little two-story house, white as stone. It had an upper balcony, almost like a veranda, with French doors under a flat gable. At the lower level, the pillars of the front porch cloaked in ivy, formed a canopy over the entire opening. The shade of two enormous fir trees bracketed a narrow stone walk leading to the porch.

I pulled the Plymouth into the long driveway and shut off the engine. Silence rushed in, broken only by water-dripping notes of a wood thrush in the timber behind the house and the gurgling of a little spring branch winding its way along the drive.

The grass was high and rank in the yard, and the entire place smelled damp and cool with shade. It was a place of enchantment.

Lacey sat staring at the house, her hands clutching her purse. "I think," she said carefully, "this is the best place for a house I've ever seen in my whole life."

My mind was racing when I said, "The lawn needs mowing." It was the most practical thing I could think of.

"Well then shoot, I guess it's out of the question," she said getting out of the car. "There's no one to take care of it. Look at the windows, not a curtain anywhere."

Gradually, I got out of the car and together we strolled up the stone walk. The coolness of the spring branch was almost visible, like the tingle of aftershave mixing with fog coming off dry ice, and the yard smelling of mint and catnip. Holding hands, we made our way to the porch steps and stood for a moment looking at our house. It had to be our house; we both felt as though we already lived here. We walked up the steps. Stopping at the door and twisting the handle, I swung the door inward to the creaking of un-oiled hinges. We stepped into a coolness as strange as it was refreshing. It was like going into my grandpa's springhouse where I had sneaked as a boy to watch watercress waving in the current that cooled the crocks of milk and butter.

We entered a little foyer, which I thought might have held a clothes tree, hat rack and an umbrella stand at one time. The white painted entryway had two snowy pillars of turned wood and beyond them, a central hallway and a dark walnut staircase ascending to the second floor. To the left of the hallway there

37

was a parlor and dining room, to the right, two bedrooms divided by a bathroom. Instinctively, Lacey moved left into the old-fashioned parlor: floors polished oak and the walls, plain pine boards, finished but never plastered. In front of us, a massive stone fireplace built of river rock, smooth and weathered by time, with a four-foot-square opening containing "dog iron" log holders and a wrought iron basket. Above its opening, a dark cherry wood mantle at least six-feet-long, and above it, padded hooks—about right, I thought, for a long rifle or shotgun to rest.

The only piece of furniture was an impressive ancient square grand piano sitting between two front windows with sunlight giving it a warm glow, lending a comfortable feel to the emptiness of the room.

Lacey walking over to it, admiringly laid a hand across the top. "My God, Steve, it's built entirely out of rosewood and must weigh a ton! I've seen it on guitar backs and fingerboards, but I've never seen a piano made entirely of rosewood."

She touched its ivory-yellowed keys, while I listened as she ran scales. It gave off-key sounds like a calliope, not unpleasant, just sounding like it might house a few mice.

THERE WERE TWO more posts between parlor and kitchen, probably a dining room, it was certainly big enough. The outline of a rug on the wooden floor showed where a table and chairs had once been.

The kitchen cabinets were unpainted cedar and an old-fashioned sink held two tubs of porcelain under a window that looked out onto a hollow through a view of bluegrass and apple trees loaded with glossy-green fruit.

Lacey leaned over the sink and laughing said, "Look at the pies hanging on those trees."

I smiled at the idea and at her. She was glowing like a candle.

Lacey let out a long sigh of pleasure at the sight of two pieces of furniture. One was an appliance, a great cook stove with a divided top; half the burners were for gas and the other side had circular iron panels for wood. The stove had chrome trim around the front and bottom, and high shelves beside an upper oven. Its china-blue porcelain glowing and its chrome gas fixtures gleaming as if former residents had polished it lovingly before they moved on. In the corner, a tall kitchen hutch made of maple that had two stained glass windows, a sliding porcelain tabletop, and a couple of big bins for flour and sugar, below. It wasn't hard to imagine all the many families over the years that used this making bread or rolling fish in cornmeal.

Downstairs the empty bedrooms were spacious, and the bathroom featured an old-fashioned bathtub on clawed legs. The toilet, probably installed about the time I was born, had an overhead zinc-lined wooden tank operated by a chain and both tank and toilet seat were oak. There was an old pedestal washbasin with brass faucets and above it an oak medicine cabinet with a splotchy mirror. The black and white tile floor was set in an octagonal pattern, and a little kerosene heater stood in the corner between stool and tub. The heater reminded me of the one of my youth, and I recalled it was the first thing my pop lit in the morning, even before coffee.

There was a curious lack of dust in the house, as if someone

39

had been busy with a vacuum cleaner or a dust mop, and the windows were clean. Although at the time, I didn't mention it to Lacey, it was almost as if we were expected in some way. The only indication the house had stood empty for so long was the accumulation of spider webs across the outside window facing, and the drifted leaves that lay against the back door from the previous fall.

Clomping upstairs eagerly as kids to see what was there, we stopped in wonder at the landing, railed except for entry space on either side. The second story was one big room, sunlight lighting it brightly, coming in through glassed French doors opening onto a leaf-strewn balcony.

The only piece of furniture was an awesome bed, and Lacey exclaimed, "My God, look at it!"

As if I could do anything else.

It was a huge old creation of the Victorian period, made of burled walnut with a headboard about eight feet high. A carved floral design ran from the head posts up to the top of the head of the bed; the whole thing topped with an intricately carved eagle, which spread its wings over the bed protectively. The four great bedposts were thick as wine kegs up to the level of the mattress and then tapered with the tops hand-turned into a series of graceful spindles that terminated in massive brass knobs.

Imposing as the bed was, however, I couldn't take my eyes from the feather tick laying on it. There, a little off center was an impression of a body form nearly as long as the mattress under the tick.

"Somebody's been sleeping in MY BED," I bellowed in a Papa

40

Bear voice. My neck hairs were prickling.

The house was silently empty. Except for the impression of a human shape so apparently fresh on the soft surface of the feather bed, there were no signs of life. There were no cigarette ashes, no scuffs on the polished floor where someone might have pulled off boots, no dust to pick up footprints and not even a whiff of a human memory, like perfume or tobacco, old sweat, or leather.

"Whoever moved the bed here must have just rested a minute," Lacey said warily. "But can you imagine Gib Decker or anybody leaving a bed like this, just sitting here? It ought to be in the Smithsonian."

I had a very strange feeling about the bed and the indentation in it, but I kept it to myself. It could wait. The only way I could see how the bed had ended up in this room was that it must have been hoisted up from outside and brought in through the French doors.

We looked at the space across the railed landing and saw what closets the downstairs bedrooms lacked were plentiful here. With the exception of a window seat, nearly the entire west wall was a continuous row of cabinets eight feet high and four deep, some shelved and some with wooden bars for hanging clothes. There was enough space in the room for another bed or a table for a workroom, to go along with all the storage space.

Lacey paced the room measuring, and her eyes returned to the massive bed on the other side of the stairwell. "Is this our bed?" she asked tentatively. "It's an awfully big room, big as the house. We don't have a rug big enough for a fourth of it."

I eyed the bed thinking it would be like sleeping in Henry the

Eighth's, lacking only the dark curtains of that time. I was still young enough to think of a bed as more of an athletic playground than a museum piece.

"Let's think about it," I said. "This whole upstairs is too big to furnish. It's a long way from the bathroom, and you're going to have a problem with stairs before long."

In my mind the bed, while it might be fine-looking, was about as inviting and romantic as a whaleboat. We left the whole thing to the future and went over the rest of the house as meticulously as we could.

There was a half cellar underneath, full of fruit jars and shelves piled with odds and ends such as paint buckets and usual basement junk. The electrical wiring was old, but respectable, and I was surprised there was any at all.

Every room had a ceiling fixture and one wall receptacle, no more, no less, and the wall switch, in every case, was a circular type that turned like a bakelite dial on my mother's old iron. The electricity came in from a pole on the road to another pole in the yard, which held an old-time transformer, the kind that resets with a hand tripper. I remembered growing up with the same kind and whenever my mother overloaded the circuits in our old house, Pop would go out outside with a long gig pole with a hook and pull the lever over to reconnect us.

A screened in back porch ran the length of the house with an old porch swing at one end. Lacey had to try it, and it squeaked miserably but with its old-fashioned oilcloth cushions, it was homey and comfortable. I sat down beside her, looking out onto an orchard with grassy fields and a spring branch.

42

Just a few yards from the porch, we investigated a little stone springhouse. Lined with moss as soft as velvet, it had a shallow concrete receptacle for milk jars. The well pump, fairly modern, sat in a corner, safe from the winter cold.

We prowled about the place for an hour or better, making sure of our first instinctual feelings. Both of us wanted to live in that house so badly; I was afraid I'd really do something dumb, like overlooking some aspect of the place that we'd find impossible to live with later. My mind didn't really access anything but the mechanics of it all.

There was a big square Warm Morning stove in the back of the center hall that could heat the lower bedrooms. The cooking range and fireplace would amply heat the kitchen, and the parlor that we'd make our living room. There was no telephone, but it seemed an easily solved problem. We decided we could have one put in the kitchen.

We were like newlyweds, tramping happily around the fenced property. There was a woodshed surprisingly piled with what looked like a winter's worth of dry and solid firewood, some cut short for the stoves. There was also an old outbuilding that was sort of a tool shed that had a feed storage room with a covered area, which could serve as a garage for the car.

I was satisfied. "I think this is it, Lacey. We'd better go talk to Gib Decker before he changes his mind."

"He won't change his mind," she answered tranquilly. "This is our house. Let's go get our stuff and find out what they use for doctors down here."

She was right, of course.

WE BACKED slowly out of the driveway, gazing longingly at the long white house we didn't want to leave. The drive back to Medley Springs didn't seem to take very long. Both of us excited, we spent the time talking about what we needed to do over the next few days. We did an inventory of what we had to move: a refrigerator, a bunch of furniture we had either made or bought at auctions, and a lot of pictures and paintings. We kept thinking of things we had and picking out places to put them in the house. Lacey tried to imagine how to relocate the old bed, as if it were already her own.

"It won't fit downstairs," I told her. "The ceilings are too low for it."

"You're right, Steve, it sort of belongs upstairs. I got a feeling about it, didn't you?"

"It must belong there," I replied, dodging the last question, "or Gib Decker would have moved it. Who would own a bed like that and not want it in their own house? Besides, it must be worth a bundle of money."

"Steve, I don't know what we could put up there with it that would look right. It would make our chest of drawers and nightstand look ridiculous." She pondered the problem. "I expect we'd better sleep downstairs," she decided, "and leave the upstairs for company."

Although neither of us could know it then, we already had company.

Chapter Four

E HAD NO PROBLEM RENTING THE house. Gib Decker was a kindly, squat little caricature of a small town storekeeper, complete with apron, bald fringe and pencil behind one ear. He'd inherited the Blessing Creek house, he told us, from his grandmother's side of the family, and it had always been something of a white elephant, so far out in the "jilikins" as he called it.

Gib was jocular, unassuming and plainspoken, hardly what I had come to expect of a landlord, and he loved to talk. He said he liked the old place but his wife wouldn't live that far from town, and his children were grown and gone—a married one in the service, the other off at college. He said he didn't want to rent to some family of woodcutters, who would have the yard full of cars up on blocks and turn the place into a dump. Consequently, the house had stood empty for a year and he only occasionally found time to see about it. He asked if fifty dollars a month would be excessive rent and he even would pay the electric bill.

Even in 1951, fifty-dollars a month was pretty cheap for rent. I was startled and said so.

Gib was adamant: "You're just who I've been a-lookin' for, young folks with a guaranteed job and enough education to not be superstitious and back woodsy."

I asked what superstition had to do with it.

"Well," said Gib while polishing his bifocals on his apron, "the last folks I rented that house to, was a preacher and his wife from down around Winona, and they stayed less than a month. He claimed he felt a call to go to Arkansas and take care of a flock down there, but I heard from the neighbors that the two of them were uneasy about the house. Claimed somebody was prowlin' around in there."

Lacey was interested. "Did they actually see anybody?"

"Well, yes and no," said Gib smiling at her. "The preacher's wife, she claimed she caught a glimpse of some old feller with a white beard settin' at the piano, peckin' with one finger like a kid would do. But when she called her man to see him, there wasn't nobody there. Them people was Pentecosts though, and they see and hear things most of us don't. Y'all aren't Pentecosts, are you?"

I laughed. "Lacey and I haven't picked a church yet, but neither one of us would be very spooky about that sort of stuff. We love your old house," and added, "and we'll do our best to take care of it."

"Well," said Gib, "the old place will fall in a pile if nobody lives there and keeps it up, but I d'ruther let it set and rot down as to let somebody like the Burdeys live there. I think you folks will like it fine."

"Who are the Burdeys?" asked Lacey.

"Oh, I reckon you'll find that out soon enough," said Gib. "They'll be your nearest neighbors up the creek. They'll come a-borrowin' as soon as they know you're there."

I didn't have much mind room for this, being more concerned with Lacey and the baby. "We need to find a good baby doctor, Mr. Decker. Lacey is going to have ours in a few months. Can you recommend anyone?"

His eyes crinkled with delight. "A baby! My God in heaven that's wonderful you two and just what that house was made for! And this town has Doc Brant, the best baby doctor in the Ozarks!"

His enthusiasm was so genuine, Lacey and I laughed with the fun of it—another piece of this day when everything happened right. It got better.

"I'll call the telephone office and get somebody out there to string you a line in a day or two," said our new landlord, and from under the counter, he whipped out his phone book. In a moment, he had given us a name and directions to the doctor's office, and we called and made an appointment.

I wrote Gib a check for the first month's rent. After a stop at the courthouse to introduce Lacey to Walt and turn in my contract, we headed back to Columbia. Gib had said he would see to getting our electricity turned on while we were gone and have a bottle of propane sent out for the stove. He even said that he would have a phone put in for us, and we could "deal with the details later." Though that didn't fit my experience with bureaucracy, there was something very solid and trustworthy about Gib Decker, a man who could get things done. That, together with my enthusiasm about getting my first real full-time job, made me ready to believe that in the Ozarks a person might do anything.

THE TRIP HOME was a cinch. Lacey and I talked the miles away and we arrived at our soon-to-be-memory duplex after dark, ready to start packing. Weariness prevailed, but we still packed things in our sleep.

The next morning, energized with the excitement of our move, I didn't realize we would be the best part of a day loading our belongings into a rental truck; I hadn't thought we had that much furniture. We had plenty of help from neighbors, who like us had visions of getting enough education to get jobs. By that evening everybody was excited about my new one and those who had known us for so long, toasted us with numerous bottles and wishes for our success.

Everyone but Lacey got a little tipsy, and we all hugged each other. Almost everybody had children, from babies to kids already in school, and Lacey and I had ended up babysitting for just about everybody. Thinking about our baby on the way made it even more poignant for us having to say good-bye to the little kids, who couldn't figure out what was happening. Neighbors and acquaintances had all promised reunions, but somehow we knew we weren't likely to see these fellow travelers again.

We slept that night at a neighbor's house and took off the following morning after sunrise. It didn't seem fair to be so excited about something we couldn't share with anyone else. Lacey drove the old Plymouth and I herded a heavy, exasperating rental truck toward Medley Springs. Now and then, we waved to each other like conspirators who had rescued each other from kidnappers. About halfway there, we stopped in Westphalia and ate sandwiches and grinned like kids who had stolen sweet corn from a field.

WE MADE IT to our new house before noon. Sure enough, Gib had turned on the electricity and outside were two shiny propane tanks waiting for hookup to the range in the kitchen. Against everything I knew about Ma Bell, a skinny, sunburned man was running a phone line to the house from our light pole, just in time for us to tell him we wanted a wall phone in the kitchen. He was cheerfully drilling away at the house wall when we took our first items into the kitchen—the salt and peppershaker. Lacey's folks had told us that salt and pepper should be the first things to go into a new house; it was an Ozark superstition that was supposed to guarantee good living. According to old-timers, we should have also taken in a loaf of bread, but I couldn't find the box it was in and was too impatient to hunt for it.

We were wrestling with a dresser when Soames Black, accompanied by Carney and Vance, drove up in a log truck. They voluntarily came to help and it was extraordinary what those two rawboned lads could do with furniture. Carney with his one good hand could lift more than I could with two and among the five of us, we had our little household set up in an hour's time. Soames helped unload books and with great reverence handed them to

Lacey to put in our homemade bookcases, while the boys strong-armed the refrigerator into the kitchen.

Soames got involved with our books. "Hit's a God's wonder," he said respectfully, "that anybody could put all them words side by side and make 'em tally out that-a-way. Jist look at all the thinkin' that has went into all these here books." As he said it, he was gently thumbing through a copy of James Joyce's *Ulysses*, which about did Lacey in.

The only items we put upstairs were Lacey's musical instruments, her cello, guitar, and mandolin—plus a few boxes of odds and ends and winter clothes that wouldn't fit in the tiny closets downstairs. It seems that the people who built houses back at the turn of the century didn't believe in closets much and the cabinets upstairs, built under the eaves, were a stroke of genius.

Downstairs, I hung my old Winchester 94 shotgun over the mantle where it looked right at home and stacked my fishing rods in a corner of the living room. Both Lacey and I were anxious to put our own stamp on the place, as if we were staking out a claim. We set up our homely Montgomery Ward bed in the front bedroom and then figured out ways to run extension cords throughout the house so that we'd have enough light to read by in all the rooms.

Our belongings intrigued the Black boys. They examined Lacey's Silvertone High-Fidelity radio and record player as if they'd never seen one, which probably they hadn't. It had been a first anniversary present from Lacey's parents, who had bought it from a dealer that specialized in up-to-date sound. At the time, high fidelity was a new technology, and we were thrilled to be able to hear records amplified through big speakers. Lacey, a thorough musician, had been collecting rare and obscure 78 r.p.m. records since she was a kid.

Seeing the boys' interest, Lacey had them set the cabinet beside the hearth. She guessed wisely and played them an old 78 record of Irish music. They listened intently to the skirling of the fiddle, but at the first roar of the Irish bodhráns, those great hand-held drums played with beaters that looked like turkey leg bones, the two of them gave a shout and struck into a jig. The boys were magnificent to watch. In Lacey's family, everybody was Irish, musical, and could jig, but the incredible grace it gave to long-legged men in overalls was always new to me. I came from a place where men danced—if they danced at all—like people pumping well water and they sweated doing it. But Carney and Vance strutted like roosters and moved on their toes; the music fit them like something skintight, while their legs twisted and flew to a tune that was old when Dublin was a young town. Even old Soames stopped to watch his sons show their skill, patting his hands to the drum's heartbeat. When the tune ended, they went back to work with a new respect for the Clark's "house plunder," as they called it.

They all gave special attention to any item they considered machinery: my old pump gun, the sewing machine, the kitchen mixer, and Lacey's Webster wire recorder she'd acquired at the university, and they eyed my typewriter warily. My pop, Jack, had given us a set of kitchen knives for Christmas the year before, and the boys hefted each one for balance and sharpness. Carney took out a pocket whetstone and worked on one that

51

didn't suit him, saying the blade was "as dull as a widder-woman's axe," and he plainly was appalled at my laxity.

Lacey made a pot of coffee, and by some sort of deft magic, managed to prepare lunch for all of us. She, flushed and delighted at our new house, seemed to know what was in every box. Like a sleight of hand trick, pictures went up on the bare walls, rugs spread, and our meager furniture landed where it belonged. By the same curious method: ice coolers emptied, and the refrigerator was full of food, shelves of the old stove were stacked with spices and the kitchen cabinets with groceries. This all done before I could figure out what box held toilet paper, or what bag contained light bulbs. I think it's called a woman's touch, but for me it was particularly Lacey's own way of making useable choices, which sustained our life flow.

Somewhere in the middle of all our milling about, the phone man—named Lennis—came in to install the wall phone in the kitchen and joined us for a sandwich. He knew the Blacks, and they visited a while before Soames put the boys back to work, but it was obvious Lennis wanted to get right to business. He was a long-legged, lantern-jawed young fellow, dark as an Indian. When I complimented his fast work, he smiled with a set of teeth as white as paint.

"Gib Decker's a right good customer," he said, "and he told us you'uns had a baby a'comin." He held the receiver up so I could hear the dial tone. "Can your little lady reach this here all right?"

Lacey nodded and he continued, "Now this here's a party line, so if you pick it up and somebody's a'talkin, wait a bit and try again. If'n it's a emergency just holler at 'em and tell 'em you need the line. Yun's party line folkses' names is writ on that sticker onto your phone book."

He handed me a phone book, which felt more like a thin book of verse.

"If yun's want to call any partyliners, you'uns have to dial '9' first." He paused for breath and looked at me quizzically as if waiting for a question. I could see Lennis was into details. When I didn't ask one, he continued, "Now if'n yuns needs to call away from here, dial '0' and Mistress Simpson'll get yuns an outside line."

Lacey and I thanked him and offered him some ice tea, which he solemnly drank in one swallow; it was almost as if it were part of his contract. I wrote him a check, handed it to him, and he shook hands with us both.

"Now dial '0' and ask fer Lennis if yun's needs hep, and Mistress Simpson'll run me to ground."

We assured him we would and watched him walk stork-like to his truck.

"Now there's a man who makes English interesting," I said.

"Mistress Simpson," said Lacey gravely, "had better have long legs if she aims to run Lennis to ground."

We had to admit the phone was comforting, making us able to connect to the world outside and a useful way to deal with remoteness.

The greatest favor the Blacks performed that day was to return our rental truck. Those boys loved to drive, and when I mentioned that Lacey and I would have to take the truck back to the nearest big town driving in tandem, they volunteered. Carney said he needed to go anyway, after a tractor part, and his brother could follow in the truck. Vance told me in a whispered aside that what Carney needed was "gravels fer his goose"—an expression I only learned about later; Carney wanted to get laid. I had actually thought Carney was after a load of gravel.

The three of them left around two o'clock; Carney driving the rental truck—that I hoped to never see again—and carrying a blank check to take care of the mileage on the truck. It was the first time I had ever signed a blank check, but there was something about the Black family that inspired that sort of thing. Totally worn out, Lacey and I still had a few things to un-box and put away.

WE WERE UNPACKING the last of the dishes when the Burdeys arrived: a Papa Troll, a Mama Troll and a Troll Junior. They were the family from up the creek, and Gib Decker's description of them didn't begin to do justice.

Clive Burdey was a little man shaped like a pear, with tobacco stained teeth and a stubbly sand-colored beard about two or three days old. He had only three fingers on his right hand and two on his left; he gesticulated constantly like an addled crawdad. He came, "goddamit-to-hell," he announced, to welcome us to the neighborhood. As Lacey and I were to learn, this cuss word expression fit everything to Clive and had no rancor in it. He expressed it the same sort of way my pop would say "By George."

His wife was even shorter than Clive; she was composed of great rolls of fat that shook like a pile of tires. The third member

54

of the family was in his forties, wore dirty overalls and had an eye that wandered about, oblivious to its mate. Clive introduced his family warmly.

"I'm Clive Burdey and this here's my wife, Beulah Lou-Lou, and my son Travis T."

Beulah Lou-Lou had popping blue eyes and her gray hair was tethered into a greasy ponytail above her bulging neck. She had about the same amount of whiskers as Clive, except hers were white and grew mostly from warts. Travis T. was one of the most weaselly-looking humans I had ever seen, with a sizeable un-healed gash across his nose and cheek that gave him a sort of pirate look. He shook hands sullenly, his good eye peering about for what I could only imagine to be an escape route in case we were hostile.

The truck the Burdeys arrived in was the most leprous old pickup I had ever seen. I later learned that Clive had bought it from a cousin who had obtained it for next to nothing from a chemical company where he worked. The body was a network of scaling yellow paint that had pitted and sloughed away until it resembled a diseased old leaf. Whatever chemicals it had hauled had eaten away at the fenders and bed, until it looked as if only the remaining paint held it together. Later I also found out that whenever they parked it for five minutes, great patches of paint would fall off and leave sign that the Trolls had been there. At the time of their first visit, the door on the driver's side was inoperable due to an internal collapse, and the Trolls had to get out on the passenger side. This complicated things considerably; Beulah Lou-Lou, who generally rode in the middle, unloaded herself by a series of scooting movements, much like a heavy barrel of something.

Beulah Lou-Lou looked us over with drunken good-nature, her eyes beaming with cheer. She held a fifth of "Cabin Still" in one hand and a small bottle of Coca-Cola in the other. "Would you'uns keer fer a drink?"

Lacey and I declined. The temperature in the truck must have been well over a hundred, and just the sight of those two tepid bottles would have made a fly throw up. "Well," said Beulah Lou-Lou with a solemn attempt at manners, "would you'uns keer if I had one?"

Lacey assured her it would be fine with us.

Beulah Lou-Lou tilted the whiskey bottle, drank three or four noisy glugs and reduced the amount in the bottle by at least half. She set the bottle down in the driveway and pulled the cap off her Coke bottle, from which she took a dainty sip and informed us, "I jist cain't drink that shit straight."

"We come up to see if we could hep to git you'uns settled in," said Clive amiably. "That's what neighbors is for, I always say."

I assured him that we were in good shape. I said the Blacks had helped us move in and the heavy work was done.

Relief glowed from his face. "Well, goddamit-to-hell, I told Beulah Lou-Lou we should have got here sooner but she had to feed the peegs and then of course the damned old peekup wouldn't start, and we had to poosh it."

I looked uneasily at the truck popping dime-sized flakes of paint off in the heat of the sun, like a tree shedding leaves. Travis T. picked at the paint with an idle finger.

"Will it start now?" I asked Clive conversationally.

"Oh, hail yes," said Clive. "I'd jist went and let the water in the batt'ry git down. Why that son-of-a-beetch will start the coldest day of the year. Hit ain't much fer looks but it runs like a sheep's nose in the wintertime."

I thought what a fitting metaphor.

The real purpose of the Trolls visit was to borrow a gallon of gasoline so they could make a beer run to Medley Springs. Clive carried a "cipherin' hose" for such purpose, and Travis T. siphoned a bottle full from the Plymouth. This occasioned a seizure of retching, spitting and spraying—which apparently he was used to.

He was able to pour gas into the old truck with little trouble, since it had no gas cap. I noticed gasoline leaked out the bottom of the tank about as fast as it went in. Clive told me there was a "big son-of-a-beetch rock" in his driveway, which he was "goddamit-to-hell a'laying off to dig out one of these days" that had caused the leak.

When they left, Lacey and I finally got to laugh after having held back as long as we could. "Beulah Lou-Lou," she told me, "is a name I can't handle. One of those goddamit-to-hell names, once you get started on you can't turn loose of the son-of-a-beech."

I was as slaphappy as she was. "'Travesty' is a perfect name for that boy. Did you hear Pa Troll tell me there had always been a travesty in every generation of his family?"

Around four o'clock, Lacey made us a couple of badly needed martinis and put an extra olive in hers. "I jist cain't drink this shit straight," she explained formally.

BY THE TIME it began to get dark, we were worn out but moved in. We made the bed, and almost everything was in place. Most of the clutter of packing paper, cardboard boxes and twine, we piled on the back porch, out of sight. We had all our clothes hanging in closets or stacked in drawers, and our kitchen clock was ticking comfortably on the shelf above the stove. The little house was beginning to seem very much like home.

Not wanting to be finished quite yet, I prowled around arranging things before supper and heard Lacey say, "I'm going to call Mama and tell her we're settled."

I walked into the kitchen and said, "Good idea, I'm going to fix myself another a drink. Say hello to Mistress Simpson for me."

After talking with her mother, she said she heard the line click a couple of times. "Probably," as she put it, "our partyliners checking in. One of them had a radio on so loud I heard either Bill Monroe or Kitty Wells."

"Monroe sings higher than you can whistle," I explained. "Kitty Wells whines—more like some country girl being twisted through a knot hole."

"Thanks for the music lesson, Teach, but anyway we'll have to watch what we say. Our party line is the school board."

"Uh-oh. I hope your mother talked nice."

"Nicer than Dad," she said cheerfully, "he wanted to know when you're going to get off your skinny ass, and get a real job."

Whipporwills started calling behind the house, and a tree frog grated away somewhere on the front porch, giving a homey sound to the place. Moths batted against the porch light, and I turned it out so they wouldn't beat themselves to death. I don't think at any time in my life I have ever felt more comfortable or at home as I did that first evening in our new house. I hadn't strung an antenna for the radio yet, so Lacey put on her favorite EP record of Vivaldi's "Four Seasons" and went into the kitchen to fix supper. The sight of Lacey fixing our first meal on that ancient stove and listening to the picture-creating Vivaldi was like reliving something that had happened a hundred times before.

Marrying Lacey was marrying music, and I listened through her ears for the first time to melodies I'd liked instinctively but never understood. My mother and pop's favorite music had been tunes like "Red Sails In The Sunset" and "Harbor Lights," and they hadn't even owned a piano.

Lacey fried pork chops with milk gravy and biscuits. I remember because it was homelike to warm up the kitchen with the oven. I remember wondering if the old house liked the smell of her cooking. Such was the magic of a new place where somehow we already seemed to belong.

By nine-thirty, we were exhausted. Turning out the lights, except for a little table lamp in the bathroom, we went to bed. It took me a while to get to sleep—one of those things that happens when I get too tired to stay awake. My mind kept racing around like a hamster on a wheel; I was thinking about the school, the Blacks, the Trolls and all the new variables I would learn to live with.

I have no idea when I finally went to sleep, last thing I remember was a hoot owl down on the creek doing his night conversation. Ozark folks say hoot owls ask each other a question, *"Who cooks fer you . . . who cooks fer you-all?"* They engage in the most outlandish chatter in the world. They laugh, whoop, and make sounds like two old men playing checkers, cackling with glee over some woodsy happening or other. It is a wonderful sound to go to sleep to, a wild sound as comforting as the hypnotic calling of the whippoorwills.

Chapter Five

REMEMBER VERY WELL WAKING UP.
I'd been having a dream about living in the
house in the little town where I grew up. I was
a child; my mother and father were arguing,
and I was listening from the top of the stairs to find out how
adults did that sort of thing. My father was pacing the floor, and
his creaking footsteps were louder than what they were saying.

Suddenly, I was awake taking in the sharp sensations of a
strange house. However, the footsteps of my dream continued—
they were right over my head. Lacey continued sleeping, her deep
breathing almost a snore. For several minutes, I lay there trying
to separate the footsteps from my dream world and remember
where I was; there was enough moonlight in the room to put it
all together in my mind, and I felt my way out of bed as quietly as
I could.

I don't think I've ever been paranoid, but I come from a family of hunters. My Uncle Matt once told me, "A gun ain't no

good if it ain't loaded or you can't reach it," a lesson he had learned while relieving himself on a deer stand.

Before I was even quite sure of what I was hearing, I had my hand on my old Stevens .22, which I had stood from long habit, by the head of the bed. The footsteps continued overhead: not loud, more like bare feet. The floor creaked under them, measuring the progress of whoever was walking. I slipped quietly out of the room into the hallway patched with bluish moonlight. With my first step on the old staircase, the worn oak boards creaked under my weight, a sound I had never noticed in the daytime. The sound of the walker upstairs, continued. I moved over to the wall side of the staircase, placing my bare feet where the steps had better support. One step at a time, I moved upward, the hair prickling on my arms. I had no more idea what I was going to do when I got up there than I had about the source of the sounds.

There was a light switch at the top of the stairs; when abreast of it, I turned it on and stepped onto the upper floor with .22 cocked and ready to intimidate.

There was no one there. The moonlight came through the French doors and illuminated more than the hall light; I could see everything plainly. The great bed was empty and except for a few boxes full of crumpled newspaper scattered about the floor, the room was empty. I looked under the bed, then into the series of closets under the eaves, throwing the doors open suddenly and leveling the .22 like some kind of commando storming a building. I opened the French doors and inspected the balcony; it was as innocent as the room had been.

62

Downstairs, Lacey sleepily called, "What are you doing up there?"

"I heard something!" I hollered back, while I un-cocked the Stevens and padded back down the stairs. It suddenly occurred to me that I had completed the whole episode as naked as Adam, and I felt sheepish.

Instantly curious, Lacey asked, "What do you think you heard?"

"I don't *think* I heard anything," I said a bit tersely. "I heard somebody walking upstairs."

"Maybe a coon on the roof?" she guessed hopefully. "Flying squirrels under the eaves?"

"Good God, Lacey, maybe we're sharing the house with a raccoon the size of a bear!" The memory of the floorboards squeaking under man-sized footsteps was too strong. I didn't buy the concept, but certainly could not explain it any other way.

She yawned. "Well, come back to bed and as long as we're awake, why don't we take our minds off noises and such. Just snuggle and maybe celebrate our bed."

I was determined to push intruders to the back of my mind. I got into bed chuckling, "Did you really say *celebrate our bed?*"

"My husband's a schoolteacher, he talks funny."

FIFTEEN MINUTES LATER the footsteps began again. For a moment neither one of us had much inclination to stop what we were doing, but there had been no way to ignore the creaking footsteps over our heads.

"Our two-hundred-pound coon is back," I whispered.

Lacey was looking up at me wide-eyed, an instant believer, realizing like Sherlock Holmes that when the possible has been eliminated, you had better start working on the impossible for answers.

"Does this mean the place is haunted?" she asked calmly, but in a very irritated voice.

"All I know is I've gone over the upstairs a foot at a time, there isn't anybody up there."

So we went up together, Lacey in her summer bathrobe, myself still as naked as an egg.

"Is there somebody up here?" I asked inanely at the top of the stairs.

Lacey stopped behind me; I could feel her heart beating as she pressed against me. Frozen in an attitude of listening, my heart was making twice as much noise as hers. We stood very still, waiting at the side of the bed for something to make an appearance. Nothing did.

After a few moments, I said, "Lacey, I feel ridiculous. If there is somebody up here, they're seeing a lot more of me than I'd want to show to strangers."

My statement was strictly a front; I was scared and didn't want her to know. Clinking chains and moans are movie stuff and insignificant when compared to the sound of footsteps creaking with no one to creak them. I repeated my speech just as stupidly as before. There was still nobody up there.

Lacey, who is nothing if not thorough, started turning over boxes in the closets and rummaged through their contents. We searched under the bed again, the balcony and under the eaves.

The great bedroom was empty except for us.

A faint prickle of sound came from downstairs and both of us froze, my blood turned to ice. There was a sound worse than creaking at the edge of my hearing; someone or something was rustling around in the kitchen and opening drawers.

I have never been more frightened in my life. My entire body surface erupted into goose bumps, and Lacey clung to me tight.

"Where's your gun?" she whispered.

I realized abruptly that I had been completely stupid through this last trip upstairs. The .22 was propped in the corner by our bed and my shotgun was hanging unloaded on the old pegs over the fireplace. I didn't even have a pocketknife, since I didn't have a pocket to put one in; I felt defenseless.

"Stay here," I ordered.

I took the steps three at a time down to the bedroom. With one hand, I snatched up my weapon and with the other, managed to put on a pair of shorts. Armed again and feeling less vulnerable, I peeked cautiously into the dining/kitchen area. There was no one there.

"Come on down, Lacey, and get the shotgun from the fireplace! The shells are in my desk drawer."

Coming down very carefully, not sure whether I'd cornered somebody or not, she felt around for a light switch and turned it on—something I hadn't thought of. While I held off the unseen with my .22, she loaded the shotgun.

For some reason or another, there is usually nothing quite as reassuring as the chink-chink sound of a shell entering the chamber of a twelve-gauge in some circumstance when you need it, like maybe facing up to a wild boar, or a rapist, or whatever dark threat you have in mind. In this case, however, it didn't give me a bit of comfort because I had a very uneasy feeling about the source of our noises. Either our house was haunted, or we were the victims of some practical joke too elaborate to be practical. My inclinations were toward the joke-side, given that the other side was beyond belief. We were new in the neighborhood and could be an easy mark for a gag. But for the life of me, I couldn't think of any reason why the ailing Mrs. Black would set us up for a gag by hinting of "things that weren't natural." And, why would Gib Decker, anxious to rent his old house, want to frighten us off before we were even settled in? Carney and Vance might play some games with us, but I couldn't picture either of them being clever enough to make any charade work.

Lacey used a shotgun reasonably well; it gave me some confidence seeing her carrying it over her arm. Together we worked the house over, searching every room, every closet and every conceivable hiding place. I got the flashlight and went down to the cellar. The beam showed nothing but empty Mason jars and junk, while Lacey stood guard at the top of the stairs. The night was warm, but I was in a cold sweat. There was no one in the house but us, at least, no person.

WE WERE NOW thoroughly awake. I brewed a small pot of coffee, and we sat at the kitchen table trying to apply reason to the unreasonable.

"A poltergeist?" I suggested.

"Maybe, but don't they throw things and break dishes and do

hateful stuff? This one just pads around at least."

I considered: "And rummages through drawers, which reminds me, did you check any of the drawers to see what was missing?"

I was instantly sorry I had said it. What sprang to mind from my youth filled with horror movies was a drawer opening eerily by itself and a butcher knife being withdrawn. The thought made me physically ill. I got up and went through the drawers below the sink, one by one. There was nothing out of place, and the knives—*thank God*—were all where they belonged.

"Okay," said Lacey, "it's got to be some kind of joke. Sort of a ritual trick they play on a new schoolteacher. They've probably worked on this one all day while we were going to get our furniture, and they're sitting outside somewhere chortling at us. Just a little rural Ozark humor, Steve."

"Okay," I said carefully, in case anyone was listening, "let's do a you-asked-for-it gag on them. Hand me the shotgun."

"Steve, don't hurt anybody. They're just having some fun with the new kids on the block."

"Fine," I said grimly, grabbing the twelve-gauge, "but the gag stops here. I need some sleep."

I went into the bedroom, pulled on a pair of jeans and slipped into my old moccasins. I went out the front door and into the front yard carrying my shotgun across my arm, and with the flash-light hooked over my hand that held the pumping mechanism, I shined a beam into the blackness.

"All right, you guys!" I shouted into the velvety summer night.

The tree frogs, whippoorwills, and crickets hushed instantly. I was standing in a silence as thick as syrup, while moths batted at the porch light with a dry smacking of wings: there was no movement or sound anywhere else. I fired the shotgun, very carefully aiming at backgrounds I could see in the flashlight's beam. I shot a tree to the west of the house and into the spring branch on the east where water leaped up into the light like a geyser, then to the north where an apple tree shed its fruit in the hail of buckshot, and finally to the south where the moonlit road made its curve into the drive.

The roar of the twelve-gauge was deafening but satisfying. It shocked away all the ghostly feelings that had taken over what I thought was my reasonably analytical mind. "GAME'S OVER! I didn't shoot to hurt anybody, but for God's sake, GO HOME, and let's all get some sleep!" I felt much better.

The silence of the night slid back in; a whippoorwill that hadn't paid attention, started calling again from up the hollow where I had whacked the apple tree. I waited for the sound of a car engine starting, or at least the sound of someone breaking their way through the brush. There was nothing. Gradually, frogs, crickets, and other night insects forgot my ultimatum and got back to the business of night.

Back in the house, I felt like a fool for going out into the yard in the pitch darkness and shooting at nothing.

"I hope you didn't hit anybody, Steve."

"I took great pains not to, but I hope to Christ I scared the hell out of whoever took that much trouble to scare us."

Thoughtfully, Lacey refilled my coffee cup and poured some bourbon from a fifth of Hiram Walker. "Let's go over this bit by bit," she said being analytical. "We have footsteps upstairs clomping around and drawers being opened and shut."

I answered a bit disconcerted, "That could have been done by just about anybody who could install a complete sound effects system in the walls."

"Come on, how about a crack team of specially trained midgets who all disappear into secret panels?"

"Lacey, seriously, what if somebody just doesn't want us to live here? What if they don't want anybody to live here and they're trying to make their point very subtly without using violence?"

"Name somebody who doesn't want us here for some reason, Steve. Everybody we've met wants a schoolteacher desperately. Gib Decker wants to rent the house; the Trolls are overjoyed to have neighbors to borrow from; the Blacks helped us move in. We haven't offended or hurt anybody in any way, so why would anyone go to all that trouble to set up some big, elaborate trick to scare us away?"

"I don't know," I said after taking a sip from my bourbon flavored coffee. "All I know is that I'm supposed to be a responsible adult, and I just got through firing four loads of buckshot at nothing because somebody or something scared me skinny. I feel dumb as bait, and I don't like to feel dumb. I'm a schoolteacher for God's sake!"

Lacey stirred her coffee and asked carefully, "Do you believe in the supernatural?"

"Oh hell, Lacey, you know me better than to ask that. I don't have any way to believe or disbelieve that kind of thing. It seems to me we just have to go with facts because that's all we have to trust. I find it pretty hard to predicate my life on things that go bump in the night."

"You're probably right, Steve, but I have sort of a feeling about this house. I had it when we first looked at it. Not a bad feeling, actually—just the impression that somebody already lived here. No dust on the floor, no cobwebs in the corners, and no wasps' nests on the ceiling . . . somebody's keeping house."

I heard what she was saying but only marginally, my mind now occupied with watching something so totally unreal that I felt my blood slowly congealing like Jell-O. In the upholstered chair seat next to Lacey, where I had been staring absently, a change was taking place. The seat cover wrinkled slowly and was pulled taut in places, as if by some invisible weight. My skin crawled with horror. I found it impossible to speak.

Lacey had no idea what was happening when she said, "If there really is a ghost in this house, I think we ought to get acquainted. It's his place as much as ours, I suppose. Let's call him–it . . . " and she looked around and her eyes fastened on the whiskey bottle, "Hiram, like some old codger relative, and learn to live with him."

"Lacey," I said very carefully, "I don't want to scare you, but Hiram just sat down next to you."

70

Chapter Six

T TWENTY-ONE, LACEY WAS SMALL, redheaded, and impetuous with a young person's strong sense of right and wrong. She never told lies, or believed them from other people and was always deeply hurt when somebody told her one. I know she was capable of fear but not when it involved a threat to herself, her territory, or me. Lacey had gotten an education more thorough and disciplined than mine. She had an Irish temper that didn't suffer fools, charlatans or stupid things that disturb the tranquility of a useful life. I'd seen her cry at movies, while reading a book, or witnessing the death of a small thing that didn't have a chance against the odds of nature, but Lacey was the most mature human I had ever met. That's one of the reasons why I married her; I loved what I saw in her. From the moment we first met, we both had an immediate sense of teaming up.

When she saw the impression of a bodiless bottom on a chair that belonged to her—in her kitchen, which she had just mopped, scrubbed, and made her own, in a house she had just put her stamp on—Lacey lost her temper.

"Okay, Hiram," she said to the empty chair, "let's get the rules straight. We live here now and if you want to stay here, fine, but your butt print is giving me the willies. Who are you anyway?"

It was an amazing speech directed at the chair, and I looked at her in astonishment, wondering if both of us were potential mental patients. We watched as the indent in the seat cover shifted slightly.

The only thing that kept me from wetting my pants was that I was too spooked to do anything that physical. Lacey, on the other hand, had her dander up at the invisible *Hiram.*

"What the hell's the matter with you?" she demanded angrily. "Can't you say something? What do you want? We're good people. Show us something besides your ass print. Why were you rummaging in our kitchen drawers?"

We were quiet for a moment, listening for any sound. I was hearing the ticking of the kitchen clock and Lacey drawing a deep breath. In the next instant, as she exhaled, the impossible happened.

From the chair across from us came a very small voice, "I was hopin' one of you smoked a pipe, and I could borrow the loan of it."

It was a human voice but apologetic and very thin, like someone who hadn't spoken for a long time and wasn't sure anybody would bother to listen. It had a particularly rich southern flavor despite its wispiness. I was prepared for almost anything, but

72

not a voice from the unseen.

"I am very sorry to have bothered you," the voice said, sounding like a bee in a jug, "but your music seems to have called me here."

Lacey, now given something to identify with, was instantly solicitous and spoke to the bodiless voice as calmly as if someone were actually sitting in the empty chair. "How about a cigarette, Hiram? Steve smokes cigarettes."

The disembodied voice cleared its invisible throat and said very politely, "I was always partial to the smell of pipe tobacco. I'm not really much of a smoker but I did enjoy an occasional pipe."

The voice was becoming slightly stronger, sounding less like a bee in a jug; I could make out the words more plainly, as if someone were approaching from a distant silence into the present. The voice had an antique quality, not so much in its southern flavor but more in the careful way the words were manicured, as if the speaker had taken a course in elocution.

"Who are you?" I asked, intensely aware that I was sitting there like a dummy listening to my wife and something weird having a conversation.

"I do not know," replied the voice. "I am not right sure I have ever known. You called me *Hiram*—am I a Hiram?"

"I had to call you something," said Lacey. "Are you haunting this house for some reason?"

The voice was perplexed and hesitating. "I am not sure what hauntin' is. I'm afraid I just go where I am placed, and I do not comprehend the places. I have been here before, but this time, perhaps the music . . ." and then the voice trailed off, "I do not recall, really."

Lacey and I turned our heads and stared at each other. Then she turned to face the empty chair and said, "The music? You mean you heard the music on the High Fidelity this afternoon?"

The voice when it came again was even more apologetic. "I am not familiar with a high fidelity. It must sound much like a violin. But I thought I heard music in my dream and came home. This is sort of home for me . . . I think. I hope I haven't offended too much by my presence?"

"Offended?" I exploded. "You've scared us half to death. In fact, I'm sitting here right now wondering if my heart is going to stop. Can't you let us see you?"

"I don't know," said the empty chair. "I do not seem to have a great deal of control over that. It's only lately that I have begun to make the floor squeak . . . or . . . actually feel the things I try to touch."

Lacey was intrigued and asked almost shyly, "Could I touch you?" I started to reach out and grab her hands, but controlled myself.

"I don't know," answered Hiram anxiously. "But you are certainly welcome to try. I am not sure I am real though, and it worries me that I might not have any clothes on . . . I don't want to embarrass you. You are the first people who have spoken to me in some time."

Lacey, bless her heart, laughed, making my goose bumps fade. "Reach out your hand to me, Hiram," she said, "and we'll try it."

74

Nothing happened that I could see, but Lacey, feeling about in midair, contacted something. Her hand closed around an oval of nothingness and her face drained of color.

"He's actually here," she gasped.

It was as if everything we had been through before was some sort of kid's game that we had elected to play in the middle of the night, not expecting results.

Defensively, I reached out and put my hand next to hers. It was a very strange sensation. I was touching a hand with fingers, knuckles, and skin textured like leather binding on an old book and all the more eerie because there was no temperature to the skin, neither cold nor warm, as if I was touching the hand of a mummy. Having gone that far, I reached past Lacey's small hand, past the circle of her fingers, where I could clearly see the chair seat and the wall behind it, and I felt Hiram's arm. Shockingly, if one could say that about a situation that had already gone beyond mind-boggling, there was some sort of clothing on the nonexistent arm.

"You have clothes on," I informed Hiram.

"I am certainly glad of that," the ghost said in a relieved voice. "I tried very hard to concentrate on puttin' somethin' on, but it is hard work to imagine things. Sometimes it works and sometimes it doesn't."

Lacey asked gently, "Do you think you could let us see you? It would probably help us a lot."

Hiram sounded very helpless, as if he were a bee going back into the jug again. "It's beyond me, I am afraid the process isn't mine, apparently. I have appeared at times when I did not want

75

to at all and when I try to hardest, I sometimes feel myself fadin' into sort of nothin'ness, I suppose you'd say."

Remembering Gib Decker's story, she asked, "Did you play the piano for Mrs. Wickham? The Wickhams said you had a white beard and played with one finger."

"I do not remember about the piano," said Hiram, "and I cannot see myself. I don't remember much about things, you see. Things come and go . . . in sort of ribbons."

There was a great urgency in my mind to see what Hiram looked like, but an almost equal horror at trying to discern his outlines Braille-fashion with my hands. The gentle voice cracked seemingly with disuse and age; it was disarming. The arm I felt was as no larger than my own.

"I suppose you can see us all right," I said.

"Oh, yes," he answered eagerly, "I see you very well. You are a handsome pair indeed." He gave a little "ahem" of embarrassment as if he might have gone beyond propriety.

Lacey asked, "But why can't we see you?"

"I do not know," answered Hiram sadly. "I do not know much of anythin' really and what I do remember, sometimes gets all mixed up with somethin' else 'til I'm worse off than I was before. Not only do I not know who I am . . . I do not even know *why* I am."

Lacey asked again shyly, "Would you mind if I felt your face?"

"Not at all," said Hiram mildly, "if I have got such a thing."

The thought jolted her, but Lacey was not one to back out of things once she'd started them. "If you used to smoke a pipe," she said sensibly, "and you can talk, you'd have to have a mouth,

I'd think."

She ran her hand above mine to the invisible sleeve and, very gently and carefully, felt of absolutely nothing. It reminded me of Helen Keller who could form a picture of someone's features by touch alone. What made our situation so strange was that Lacey looked like she was gesturing incongruously at a wall.

"You do have a beard," she said, sounding ecstatic, "a nice long one. Feel it, Steve, it's as real as anything."

Good God! I thought. But I, too, put my hand tentatively next to hers. Incredibly, there was a great cascade of curly hair in front of my fingers, though I could see nothing more than the peeling paint of the kitchen wall with a lighter space where the last residents had taken down a picture. I jerked my hand back hurriedly as if I had committed a personal affront.

But Lacey continued to explore the invisible face. "Why, Hiram, your face is fine. You have a nice big nose and very bushy eyebrows, and you are all crinkled around your eyes."

"That's because I was afraid you might stick your finger in one," said Hiram apologetically. "Most of the time it would not bother me, I think, but I feel very solid just now."

"Oh, I'm sorry!" said Lacey alarmed. "I was trying to be so careful. Has anyone else ever, you know—felt of your face?"

"I do not think so," said Hiram thoughtfully. "Whatever it is that I am, I don't seem to engender much contact. People are afraid of me."

It was a statement that at any other time would have had me in hysterics. My goose pimples were just beginning to crawl back into their burrows when I managed to ask, "When was the last

77

time you actually, ah, appeared?"

He replied sounding thoughtful, "I wish you wouldn't ask me about time, you see that is what I am afraid I am lost in. The faces all mingle about and the clothin' changes. One day someone rides a horse by the house and the next, drives up in a metal machine that does not need a horse. I know I could probably puzzle things out better if I did not dream quite so much, but I keep driftin' like a ship that has slipped anchor somehow and fetch up against places I do not recognize. I do seem to recognize this place now and then . . ." and he paused and sounded embarrassed at this discourse, which didn't answer anything.

"So you recognize the house?" Lacey asked. I knew she was trying to pinpoint the era Hiram came from, remembering that Gib Decker had told us the house was built in 1904.

Hiram was perplexed. "I recognize where the house is," he said, "but houses have always been pretty much alike."

"Then you've lived in more than one?" I asked quickly.

"If this can be called livin'," said the old man with what I thought was a touch of humor. "I've lived in several. I seem to go with the bed, somehow . . . but cannot remember why."

So that was it, the huge four-poster upstairs.

Lacey was feeling the ghost's hand when she did a very gentle thing; she held it and then patted it as you might do to a very old person or a sick one.

"How very strange that feels," said Hiram. "No one has touched me for so long—I had forgotten what human contact was like. My mind seems to be stronger somehow with your kind touch."

"Can you remember anything at all about the bed?" she asked. "Maybe we could help you to remember who you are—or who you were. If you're a ghost," she added apologetically.

Hiram's voice was stronger and he spoke with an anxious note of urgency. "I'll try, but I'm afraid I may leave you at any moment, madam. I'm beginnin' to drift again . . ."

Lacey flinched and withdrew her hand involuntarily. "I'm sorry," she said, afraid she'd hurt his feelings, "but you're starting to feel like a balloon with the air going out."

"I am sorry, too . . ." said the voice becoming more and more like a bee in a jug again. "I don't seem to have any control over these things. Is it all right if I come back and speak to you again, if I am allowed?"

"Be our guest." I told him wondering if I meant it and then thought quickly to add, "I'll hang a little bell at the head of the big bed we don't use and you can ring it when you're here."

"You're very kind," replied the voice as thin as a distant violin. "Good-bye."

"*Good-bye*," said Lacey and I simultaneously.

THE SILENCE THAT followed was humbling. Gradually the night sounds came in: katydids, tree frogs, and a million courting insects filled the air with their trilling and down at the creek, bullfrogs took up their music again, like distant kettledrums. The shiny seat cover of the chair became rounded and smooth as risen dough.

After a minute, Lacey asked, "Where do you suppose he went?"

79

The events of that strange night were so exhausting to two people already exhausted; I didn't trust either my brain or my senses. "He's someplace in the Milky Way," I told her, "or maybe back in time a hundred years, scaring somebody else. On the other hand, he may be upstairs in bed."

Carrying the flashlight, we went up stairs timidly as if we were trying not to wake a baby. The counterpane, quilt and two pillows that Lacey had furnished the bed with were as smooth as new snow. The silent walnut eagle's wings brooded over nothing, and the giant bedposts looked like tree trunks. We could simply feel the room was empty.

THE IDEA OF going to sleep was ridiculous; we went back down to the kitchen and made another pot of coffee. The more we talked about what had taken place in this room, the calmer and more able we became to apply some sort of weird rationale to something that was completely irrational.

"Good God, Lacey, if Hiram's a ghost, it means there really is an afterlife."

For some reason that overpowering fact hadn't occurred to either of us earlier. We had been taking one thing at a time. It was very hard to consider beliefs or philosophical aspects of the world when we were touching evidence of another one for the first time.

"I forgot to ask him about God," said Lacey. "I can't *believe* I could forget to ask about anything as important as that."

"Well, Lacey, he didn't bring it up. Everything we did ask him seemed to confuse him. My God, I actually told that *thing—Hiram,*

I would put a bell at the head of the bed so he could sign in. I think I'm losing my mind."

"But just think about it. We've actually felt a ghost and talked to one. We know there wasn't any trick. *We touched him.* We have done something nobody else has ever done, at least as far as we know. We've been exposed to the fourth dimension, maybe another world—*maybe another universe.*"

I shivered. "Lacey, let's get out of this place. I don't understand what we've just been through, but I don't think I could stand doing it on a regular basis. I don't think we could live here with that *thing* coming and going all the time. As a matter of fact, I'm not sure my hackles will ever lie down again."

Lacey poured me an extra shot of whiskey and filled my coffee cup again. "*Hey, whoa!*" she cautioned, a finger on my lips. "All we'd have to do—if it comes to that . . . is get rid of the bed. You heard what he said about it. For some reason it's his connection with the house, like those old stories about ghosts hanging around buried treasure or something." She looked at me gravely, "Steve, I'm not giving up this house because of anybody or anything I can learn to deal with, let alone a piece of furniture!"

I tried to give her concept some sensible consideration. We could move the bed someplace, and perhaps Hiram would go with it—haunt somebody else. "Okay, Lacey, the bed goes. I don't know where, but we'll find a place for it. Gib Decker can put it in his basement or sell it or something."

I had a feeling I knew what she was going to say next.

"On the other hand, we have just experienced something I bet

81

anybody we know would have given anything to see," she said.

"We didn't *see* anything," I reminded her grimly, "we just felt something and heard something—and my skin still feels like a plucked chicken."

"But doesn't it make you feel like Einstein, knowing something that nobody else knows? That there can be life after death?" she asked reasonably.

"*Life?*" I answered incredulously. "You call zooming in and out of some other dimension and not even remembering who or what you were—*life?* I think we're both having a nightmare, and I'm ready to wake up now. Please."

"Listen, I was as scared as you were," she pleaded, "but I couldn't help but feel sorry for him. He's lost, and he doesn't know where he belongs."

"Lacey, you weren't as scared as I was. I just happen to be able to pretend coping with total panic sometimes. It would never have occurred to me to call him Hiram off the top of my head, and see if he was touchable. Whatever world your Hiram is lost in is none of our business, and it scares me more than I can tell you."

"Yeah, but think of the possibilities, Steve, think about the things we could ask him if we could get him to remember what he was and where he's been. We could find out about God, and heaven, and reincarnation, and Christianity, and the occult, and all of those things people wonder about," her eyes lit up with the thought. "What if," she asked totally caught up in her flight of imagination, "*what if* we asked him what happens when people die? Or, if there are parallel universes?"

"Lacey, he didn't even know if he had a beard or any clothes on. How could you expect him to explain the infinite, if he didn't even know who he was in the first place?"

That gave her pause. "He's been out of contact with anybody," she explained. "Didn't you notice how strong his voice got when we touched him? I have a feeling that he needs people, and maybe we could help him find out who he is—or *was* and where he belongs. Besides, where did I come up with the name Hiram? Isn't that one of your great-great-uncle-or-other's name, or did I just make it up? Maybe it's a family thing and not part of the house at all."

"*Lacey, look,*" I told her holding up the whiskey bottle, "Hiram Walker ring a bell?" She looked sheepish for a second, and I took advantage of it. "See what this has you doing—making it up as you go along?"

The exhaustion and the whiskey got the better of me. I remember getting very philosophical and taking Lacey's reasoning very seriously. What I ended up doing was agreeing to keep the bed for a while, at least until such time as it became imperative to get rid of it.

I was so full of curiosity and bravery from being juiced up from the alcohol, coffee, and unreal amounts of adrenalin that I actually went up to the bedroom again to search through boxes until I found a strap of old sleighbells that had once belonged to my grandfather. I hung them from a nail near the head of the bed and shook them tentatively. They rang a comfortable jangle of sound, hollow and wintry.

"There now," I told her, "if Hiram keeps his word and an-

83

nounces himself, we'll know when he's in the house. If he shows up without ringing—he goes, the bed goes."

"And listen," said Lacey, having talked me into that much, "could you maybe get him a pipe and some tobacco? It's the only thing he asked for."

The idea struck me as hilarious: "Can you imagine somebody coming to visit us and seeing a pipe hanging in midair with smoke puffing out of it? Good Lord, Lacey!"

"Well, at least you'd know where he was," she said with practicality.

Despite myself, another cold shiver rippled up my back, "*Yes,* at least we'd *know* where he was. Now listen, you realize we can't say a word about this to anybody. If anyone finds out that we think we have a ghost, my job will disappear like Hiram did. These people didn't hire a medium to teach their kids book learning."

Lacey nodded. "I think Mrs. Black already has an idea about Hiram, she doesn't need any more encouragement."

"Okay then, maybe the discovery of the century, but it's just between you and me."

"You and me and *Hiram,*" corrected my wife.

84

Chapter Seven

N THOSE DAYS, I MUST CONFESS, I KEPT a journal. If it weren't for the journal's survival, despite everything that's happened to Lacey and me over the years, I'd be delving around in my mind for facts, names, and figures, like someone trying to remember the details of childhood. Even with the journal, it's still a little like that. I have to give my pop credit for my keeping a journal in the first place. He had always urged me to write things down, since as he put it, "Nobody learns as much as he learns from himself." On my twenty-first birthday, he presented me with two legal size volumes of blank lined pages that demanded filling as plainly as hollow teeth. It wasn't until Lacey and I moved to Blessing Creek that I started writing. Now after all these years, I depend on my journal to help tell my story of Hiram, and the people and children we came to know.

❖❖❖❖❖❖

The Journal

SUNDAY, AUGUST 19, 1951

GOT THE LAWN mowed at last, and what a job that was. The house looks neat and tidy as if someone had lived here all the time, which if you count Hiram, I suppose is a fact. There is still no sign of the old man returning to haunt us. I'm beginning to wonder if we hallucinated him, although, knowing our factual minds, I know we didn't. It's been ten days since the ghost's visit, and the memory gets less traumatic as time passes. Hell, if our old ghost has been around this long and meant harm, he'd be a neighborhood legend already.

I went to the Cartwright's house this morning and introduced myself. Mr. Cartwright owns a sawmill on one of the forks of Blessing Creek and is obviously a hard worker. His son is twelve and will be in the eighth grade. It's hard to imagine anybody that age being so strong; I saw him dragging oak 2x10s off the rollers and stacking them on a pile as if they were pine 2x4s. What am I supposed to do if I have to discipline one of these near-teenagers? They've all worked in timber for years and are as tough as leather. Luckily the ones I've met: the Farley boys and the oldest McClellan boy, whose name is Ruby (my God!) and Buck Smith, who is thirteen, are the only big boys I have. They are all good-natured and seem to look forward to school as a welcome relief from making a crop or cutting wood.

I have met every family now. The Pulvers have only one child, a lovely ten year old girl, who I suspect is spoiled silly. The other two Smith girls are eight and ten, both of them very serious-looking dark-eyed children with oval faces and hair so black they look like Indians. Following the teacher's guide, I have made up my grade schedule and am beginning to make sense of the rules for teaching eight grades at once. Lord help me.

❖

MONDAY, AUGUST 20, 1951

HOT ZIGGEDY DAMN! The baby doctor is great. Lacey's new obstetrician, Doc Brant, seems to live up to Gib Decker's description of him. His office is modest and like himself, reassuring. He told us the baby is fine. Doc is in his forties and looks somewhat weather-beaten, his office walls were full of children's drawings instead of the usual diplomas. I think most of the drawings were by his own kids, since he seems to have several. I take this as a good sign and so does Lacey, who was totally comfortable with him. Doc Brant asked her all sorts of questions and didn't mind me being there, even though I was a bit fidgety. He said for me being a first-time dad, I'd probably need more taking care of than Lacey, since she already knows what she is doing.

I felt so good about this first visit that I phoned Pop as soon as we got home to tell him everything is going well. I talked to him for fifteen minutes before he'd let me hang up. Ever since Mother died, Pop has wanted a grandchild to make up for her death, which hurt him so badly. I wish Mother could know about the baby. Now that we know about Hiram, maybe she does.

Okay, now to the money, because I'll have to figure it out sometime. Pop has insisted the hospital expense is going to be his present to us, but I'm going to make sure I can pay for everything myself. So far, our money looks like a drop in the bucket:

$325.00 from the job I worked at in college

$500.00 that Lacey's folks sent as a going away gift

$67.30 left from my last V.A. check after paying all the expenses of moving, rent, and wood for the fire-place, etcetera.

A total nest egg of $892.30—with a baby due in December! Now that's scary. If we can live on what we make from Indian Glade, we'll get by—barring breakdowns and all the other stuff that usually happens. I'm not going to worry too much right now. Lacey's fine, the baby's fine and life looks good on Blessing Creek.

❖

WEDNESDAY, AUGUST 22, 1951

TODAY I HAD my first teachers' meeting—of which I understand there will be more. It was held in the high school auditorium in Medley Springs with Walt Bangert presiding. There were some forty of us one-room schoolteachers from the forty districts in the county. This was also a book-buying spree, where each teacher orders workbooks for his classes: textbooks for the grades that use them and whatever teacher's aids he will need for a one-room school. I probably should have used *her* instead of *his* because women outnumber us three to one. Apparently, only ten men have decided to settle for the small pay of a rural teacher. I understand that several of them are actually preachers on the side, in order to make enough money to get along. From what I gathered from Walt Bangert's talk: one paints houses on weekends, one builds kitchen cabinets, and another one is helping in his wife's restaurant on Saturday and Sunday. I don't mean that Walt imparted this information; he just gave a cheerful and informative talk for first-timers like me—filled with ponderous jokes that the old-timers must have heard a number of times. Then he introduced the State Superintendent, a brisk young fellow half Walt's age, who gave us a rapid-fire speech about the future of the country being in our hands and how he was proud of those of us who had decided to join the most honorable profession, etcetera.

Walt turned us loose on the booksellers, or maybe it was the other way around. Luckily, I'd done my homework; I went through the school library and knew what books were needed. The conclusion being, I need everything. How the previous teacher had managed to pump any information less than ten years out of date into her classes, I have no idea since our moth-eaten library predates World War II. The maps are useless relics, and there are almost no textbooks dealing with Europe's post-war problems. There isn't even a world globe so I can show the little ones the world is round. Evidently, Myrtle, who's the keeper of the exchequer, is as tight-fisted as she thinks.

Walt advised me to buy what's needed. "Myrtle'll squall," he said kindly, "but Soames Black loves books, and the other member of your board has a raft of chirren in school and more pushin' to get in. He'll see you get your books."

On Saturday, I'll take my bill to Jeff Farley and try to explain what I've bought.

❖

THURSDAY, AUGUST 23, 1951
WE HAD THE School Board meeting. Myrtle nearly had a stroke

but I won; the books are due the day before school starts on the 27th. If they don't get here, I'd better be able to do a high wire act until they arrive. Lacey has the answer: just test them for a day or two to see what they already know. "This *deestrict* is too poor to teach them something twice," was her sensible comment.

❖

SATURDAY, AUGUST 25, 1951

ANOTHER VISIT FROM the Trolls—they arrived on foot, hooted at the house from the yard and woke me at just about daylight. I'm surprised they didn't throw rocks at the house to turn us out. I pulled on a pair of pants and went to see what they wanted.

The "son-of-a-beetchin'" pickup wouldn't start, and they had to go to town for the Saturday livestock sale, or they wouldn't have bothered me, said Clive. I threw on some clothes and told Lacey where I was bound, to either jumpstart, push or pull the old truck.

"See if they really live under a bridge," was Lacey's sleepy advice.

Loading my fragrant neighbors into the Plymouth, I headed up the creek to the Burdey place. As Gib Decker had surmised, there were a number of old cars in the yard and most of them perched on blocks, with several bellied-up like terrapins. Their house was an old tin roofed shack that managed to lean four or five ways at once. Most impressive was a missing windowpane, where a leghorn hen was perched facing out as if to show where she'd spent most of her time.

When I nosed the car up to the truck, Clive with a great show of authority, took over the jumper cables and proceeded to hook them up backwards. Thick blue smoke curled up from the truck's wiring after a moment, and to the surprise of no one, Clive had to reverse the connections. It seems this is a near daily occurrence since nobody commented much on it, barring their usual cussing, which they seem to save for their old wreck of a truck. Clive looked for all the world like a chipmunk trying to get nuts out of a knothole, when he had to climb back under the hood.

Beulah Lou-Lou stood back with arms folded and watched the drama unfold. The early sun catching her patches of silvery whiskers was very becoming to her. Travis T. had the job of hooking up wires where the ignition had once been, while Papa Troll held a screwdriver on the solenoid connections. Predictably enough, the truck groaned a couple of times and sputtered to life, spouting a cloud of noxious smoke that completely obscured everybody for a minute.

While he unhooked the jumper cables, Clive coughed and cursed the "peekup" and the general nature of mechanical things. I backed away a few yards, hoping it would keep running, which it did. All of them got in from the passenger side with Beulah Lou-Lou in the middle. When Travis T. slammed the door, a generous hunk of the outer door shell fell off, exposing little gears and rods that operated the window. Hoisting their beers and waving, the Trolls took off toward town and I followed, hanging back to avoid their dust, until I reached our driveway.

This afternoon they drove by the house, and I'm sure would have honked if the truck had a horn. Two thoroughly miserable-looking "peegs" staggered about in the bed of the truck, presumably headed for pork chop junction.

Gib Decker came by this afternoon to see if there was anything he could do to make us feel at home. He is a very nice man and anxious to have us comfortable. The mowed lawn pleased him a lot, as did the way Lacey had arranged the furniture. This time I asked him about the bed, on the chance that he might want it. Naturally, I didn't mention Hiram. Lacey wanted the whole history of the bed and quizzed Gib thoroughly about it— an effort that was pretty much wasted on him.

Gib had bought the bed from folks who had lived in the house some twenty years back, and where they had gotten it was anybody's guess. He said they didn't want to move it and for seventy-five dollars, it seemed a bargain. I did manage to get the name of the folks who had owned the bed but only after a considerable pause, during which Gib shuffled around in his mind for forgotten facts.

"Spencer," Gib finally announced. "That's the name, Tyler Spencer. I can't think of his wife's name. I think the bed came from her side of the family because she was the one hated to give it up. They were from somewheres in Tennessee."

That, so far, is all we have to go on to trace Hiram's connection to the bed, but I'll work on it.

MONDAY, AUGUST 27, 1951
SCHOOL STARTED TODAY, and I have to admit I'm totally worn out. All the kids arrived fairly early but not as early as Myrtle Summers, who was waiting when I unlocked the schoolhouse at seven this morning. I'd wanted to get there early and

92

prepare all of my bookwork, which is more considerable than complicated. The old lady was dressed in her best black dress, looking a lot like Poe's Raven or maybe a Blake etching and sat on the back bench by the water bucket. I got the feeling she was there to test me like a foreman looking over the shoulder of a worker on his first day of a job. She hardly said anything, but her displeasure with my book expenses was obvious, and her presence was overwhelming. She said she hadn't missed a first day of school in forty years, so I knew I wasn't being singled out for her particular attention. However, I wanted to get acquainted with my students on a less formal basis than quizzing them in front of a formidable old lady, who looked like death honing a scythe.

By eight o'clock, the students were all there, even though school doesn't officially begin until nine according to my instruction book. Added to the children I had already met, there were two new ones whose parents had just moved to a farm in the district. They are T.J. Terrill and his sister Franny. T.J. is eight and is a big, gap-toothed country boy with an enormous smile and a shock of red hair that looks like a fright wig. His sister is seven and with Cissie Smith and Austin McClellan, they'll make up my combination first and second grades.

I had doubts about arranging the seating, but I needn't have worried; the children did it for me. The older brothers and sisters, who knew about such things, arranged the little ones on the front row before finding for themselves the same seats, I guessed, from the year before. I just sort of let things happen naturally; if I have to shuffle them around later, I will. I have a great deal to learn about the order of things.

Mrs. Summers had taken care of the maintenance jobs on her own. She issued them to the bigger children who live near enough to take care of such things as floor sweeping, window washing, and taking care of the fires. Children interested in extra money, bid on these jobs. Old Myrtle, who watches out for the pennies, hires the ones she thinks can perform the work for the lowest dollar. Cleavis Farley is in charge of the stove, and Penny McClellan is the housekeeper. Oran Cartwright, who's father owns a sawmill, is in the best position to supply the woodpile. All this may change at midyear when bids will be submitted afresh and give everyone a chance to make extra money. It seems very democratic and sensible, and I'm glad the whole thing is in the hands of Myrtle Summer. I'd hate to begin teaching with any sort of favoritism on my part.

Promptly at nine o'clock, I rang the brass hand-bell that Myrtle had brought for me. It's old-fashioned, with a handle that must have been used by fifty teachers before me to get the attention of their pupils. The sound was strong and pleasant and had the mellowness of age. The children not already seated, came in from the swings and schoolyard. They took their seats with an anticipation that was catching; all of them sat and stared at their new teacher with curious eyes, and I stared back.

"My name is Mr. Clark," I told them and wrote it in large letters on the blackboard. "This is my first time teaching school." I sensed rather than heard a disapproving sniff from Myrtle, who thought I was leaving my flank open. "That means," I continued, "I'll need your help, especially from you older kids. We're

94

going to have a good time together, and I hope you're going to look forward to coming to school as if it was your own house, which it actually is. This place was built for kids."

The rest of the morning was a cinch. The children were eager to tell me their names, ages, and grades. Even the older boys, like Oran and Ruby McClellan, and Cleavis Farley, seemed to warm to the idea of somebody who wasn't afraid to admit he was a greenhorn. They naturally knew it anyway because in this little community nothing stays secret for very long. I'd wanted to begin with honesty and see what happened.

Myrtle left at noon recess after having established, I supposed, that I wasn't a child molester or a fraud, and I watched her long black figure disappear into the woods at the turn of the road.

Betty McClellan, age ten, is the older sister of Austin—who appears dumber than a fishing worm and spending his second year in the first grade. Betty asked me if we "was ready to take up books yet." I told her we had a few more minutes, and she looked me over in a calculating way ten-year-olds have. "They ain't no water drawed, Mr. Clark," she informed me.

"You mean there isn't any water drawn," I told her, and her eyes crinkled as if she thought I was teasing.

"That's what I just told ye," she said. "Most giner'ly, the little ones all gits to pull on the well rope. Could I tell 'em to commence?"

"If that's the custom, Betty," I said, "I'd be a fool to break it. Tell the little ones to pull away."

The drilled well, some hundred-feet deep, is Myrtle Summer's pride, since the school board only just paid for it last year. The top of the six-inch casing is a foot or so above ground, and it's capped with a bucket. The well bucket itself is a slender galvanized tube that goes down into the casing. A little trapdoor in the bottom of the tube allows it to fill, and then the kids pull it up hand-over-hand to dump it into the double-walled cooler that serves the school. In order to make the job reasonably easy, Soames Black and his sons have built a framework and pulley over the wellhead, and the children work like horses to pull up the rope, which has a huge knot on the end in case they should all lose their grasp at once and let the bucket fall.

If nothing else, I have found out two things of importance today: children in hot weather drink water like horses, and they think that drawing it out of a hundred-foot well in thirty-two pound buckets is fun.

I learned something else; the school has no electricity, and on dark days, we'll have to do tasks that do not require intense reading or close work. There are two big gas mantle lamps that pull up and down on ropes, and I have a feeling the lamps probably emit a total of maybe a hundred watts. I shudder at the thought of filling them in the wintertime when the stove is lit, but Cleavis Farley took care of this chore last year and says he fills them outside from a can of white gas that is always kept in the little tool shed. The shed also contains the snow shovels, sweeping compound, cans of floor polish, and a scythe—called a "brush hook" locally.

The children are very helpful and good-natured; they overlooked my ignorance of their one-room school with a politeness that apparently is part of their upbringing. I have a feeling they receive instructions at home to be hospitable and helpful to the schoolmaster, but I also have the feeling, they would do it anyway. I've never met people with such a mania for hospitality as these Ozark folks, and the children having grown up with it, reflect it themselves. They are shy and sometimes inarticulate, but they appreciate my efforts to get acquainted with them. At recess, Austin McClellan told me very seriously that his brother came home from the Solomon Islands with a "Japanese Winchester." I discovered in the Ozarks they refer to all rifles as Winchesters, as opposed to shotguns. I have a lot of this language to learn and evaluate before I try to teach them a better one. I wonder, for instance, whether Oran Cartwright's native tongue isn't superior to mine when he describes something. He complained that he and Ruby McClellan had traded .22 rifles fair and square, and now Ruby "wants to rue back his bargain." He also told me that the last teacher, an ancient lady named Mrs. Sawyer, had hung up a "pretty scenery" of George Washington sitting on his horse at Valley Forge, which accounts for the discolored square on the wall behind my desk. Irene Farley, who is twelve, told me that her little sister Mavis is "always out of pocket." T.J. Terrill said his father—named Bailey—whittled small figures out of cedar "to beguile the time."

I have a feeling I had better think twice before messing with a language so firmly entrenched in custom and antiquity. If, in teaching them to diagram a sentence, I must also teach them to abandon the beauty of a speech that so adequately describes things without diagrams, I'm afraid I'll do them more harm than good. On this first day of school, I learned a lot about how Ozark people say things and how they use nouns, verbs, and adjectives, interchangeably in a way that defies any use of the rulebook. Penny McClellan said Myrtle Summers told her it would rain in ten days according to the Farmer's Almanac, but she didn't "confidence that none." I also heard Buck Smith use a noun as a verb so believable that I'll repeat it: "My cousin conceits he can call up a turkey better'n me." Seeing the careful way Buck does everything, I bet his cousin is wrong. What an incredible amount I have to learn!

I let the children go home at two o'clock because I had so much organizing to do. The new textbooks and workbooks should arrive in the next day or so, and then I'll be able to assign a sensible amount of work for each grade, leaving me free to deal with one group at a time.

This is the secret to teaching eight grades at once: Parcel work out to various students in an age group and the teacher recites, or personally interviews a grade, while others study. I will recite the first and second grades, which I'll combine to make things easier. While they're learning their alphabet and numbers and learning to recognize short words, I'll have the third and fourth grades study for a test. The seventh and eighth grades, I'll combine for current events while the sixth grade, combined with my two fifth graders, will sit in and try to master the mysteries of fractions, long division, and decimals. This is the way it's done according to teachers I met at the convention. I imagine I'll think up some tricks of my own as I go along, but for right now, I'll tend to stick pretty well to what has worked before.

Whatever it is I'm doing, I think I like it. I'm looking forward to those scrubbed innocent faces in the morning, carrying their Hopalong Cassidy lunch buckets, and wearing their neat clothes that have been through lye soap and washboard until they smell like the essence of flannel. I hope to God my little throne won't ever give me some false sense of power, or if it does, that I will use it with some borrowed wisdom.

Chapter Eight

❖

WEDNESDAY, SEPTEMBER 5, 1951

 INTEND TO BE VERY CALM AND responsible about this. Hiram has come back and is possibly looking over my shoulder as I write, although I think he is probably too polite.

We had a fine, crashing thunderstorm this afternoon, and it delighted the children. They are seasoned country children used to the weather. They squealed and laughed, and the little ones hugged each other in mock fright as thunder shook the old building. The driving rain rattled like hail on the tin roof, making the place gloomy, so I lit the mantle lamps and between flashes of lightning, I read to them from *Tom Sawyer*. The wind gusted, hollowly ringing the old bell in the slatted belfry, and the rain made rivulets on the west side windows. We were all a fine and comfortable family in there, safe against the weather. While I was reading, T.J. Terrill went to sleep during the fence-painting episode and Buck Smith, who would make a good Tom Sawyer himself, wouldn't fill him in on what he had missed.

"Teacher norated it all out to us," he said, "and them that wanted to listen, *listened*. Don't be a-quizzin' me about it."

It hardly seemed fair since T. J.'s father takes him out at night to listen to the foxhounds, and that may be as important as anything he'll pick up from me. I think Mark Twain would have understood.

By three, the rain had stopped and everybody headed home, kicking through puddles and taking their own shortcuts. I loaded the old Plymouth with all of the little ones who wanted a ride, and I took them to their mailboxes, none of it being very much out of my way.

LACEY WAS WAITING for me on the porch. Someday I'll write an article, maybe for a magazine, and I'll describe the way Lacey handles facts in order, not importance.

"The electricity went off," she said, "and I can't find a bad one in the fuse box. Maybe it's the breaker on the light pole."

I told her I'd find the trouble.

"There's a leak in the roof upstairs," she continued, "dripping into the closets."

I told her I'd fix it.

She poured me a blessed glass of homemade wine, a present from Soames Black. It would have raised a corpse. I thanked her, took a sip and prepared to unwind.

"And Hiram's back," she said flatly. "He rang the bells around three. He's lying in bed upstairs, and you can see the print of his body as plain as anything."

My wine came mostly out my nose, and I looked at her with watering eyes while I cleaned myself up. *"He's back,"* I said numbly.

"That's what I just told you, sweetie," she said. "Did you remember to get his pipe and tobacco at Gib's?"

"Of course," I said after I had regained speech and a dab of dignity. "I got him a cherrywood pipe and some real aromatic stuff to smoke in it. That way we can tell where he is."

Now it seems incredible to me that I can sit writing about this knowing that anyone who might read it someday, won't believe a word of it. But whoever you are at whatever time you read this journal, I assure you that the things I'm about to write are the truth. Lacey is my witness and you couldn't want a better one.

I WENT UPSTAIRS with wine glass in hand and Lacey behind me. I observed Hiram's impression in the bedspread and said, "Hiram, are you awake?"

"Certainly," answered the small voice, "I am always awake except when I've dreamed myself off somewhere. This is a very nice quilt," he added shyly. "It reminds me of somethin', but I am not sure what."

Lacey was pleased. "It's a double wedding ring pattern my mother Vera made for us as a wedding present. Steve got you a pipe and some tobacco."

"Really?" said Hiram, and the impression on the quilt shifted to the side and became a bow-shaped depression at the edge of the mattress. It was the most disconcerting thing to watch, but I suppose I could get used to it in time, or maybe not.

102

I put the pipe, an envelope of Dutch shag, and a book of matches on the bed and waited for developments.

"That's very kind of you," said Hiram. "I hope I remember how to do this."

Although it sounds as strange as it looked, the pipe rose from the bed and levitated at an angle while invisible fingers opened the tobacco pouch. Lacey and I watched entranced; the pipe dipped itself and the coarse shag tamped itself down into the bowl. The pipe was stuck into an invisible point in space, which I can only assume was Hiram's mouth.

"I don't suppose you have a light?" he asked.

"I put matches by you," I replied. Hiram had never used book matches, and I made a mental note; *when were book matches invented?*

I lit a match and held it to the pipe. The smoke made an interesting globe behind the stem before it puffed out. I have never felt more fascinated by an ordinary process than I did this afternoon, staring at a pipe suspended in midair, as if I were a shill in a magician's act. Lacey, however, wasn't at all impressed.

"Hiram," she said, "why can't we see you? It's daylight and we know you're here."

"I do not know," said Hiram, "but after I left you the last time, I began to remember some things. I think it was because you had talked to me. No one has done that you see for . . . oh, the longest time."

I noticed Hiram's voice was much stronger now; the pipe seemed to have fortified him. Lacey and I looked at each other in wonder.

"I remembered about the piano," said Hiram, "and the woman you talked about."

"Mrs. Wickham," said Lacey, "the preacher's wife."

"Yes," said the ghost with mounting interest, "that must have been the one. I was just findin' that I was able to touch things, you see, and sat down to try the piano, just to see if I could actually make a sound, when in dashed this person shriekin' and brandishin' a broom. She frightened me out of my wits."

The incongruity of it was too much for Lacey and she laughed aloud. "Hiram, what do you suppose you did to her?"

"Why, I—I did nothin' to her," said the ghost bewildered.

"What Lacey means is," I said, "finding a strange man playing the piano in your living room might be something of a shock to a middle-aged lady." And added, "It would come as a shock to me."

The pipe puffing away in midair released a cloud of blue aromatic smoke and formed bubbles at its stem. Lacey looked at it thoughtfully and asked, "Why do you suppose she could see you, but we can't?"

"I have no idea," said Hiram sadly. "I suppose it was just time for me to be seen. Most of the time I just sort of feel like unoccupied space. Do you have any idea what it is like not being able to see yourself?"

I assured him that I didn't.

"Just bein' able to see the pipe I am holdin'," said Hiram, "and to watch the smoke billowin' out is a point of reference for me, and it makes me feel more real. You should try walkin' downstairs when you cannot see your feet."

104

I thought of something. "Hiram, would you mind very much if we weighed you? I think it would be a good idea if we all knew more about what's real here and what isn't."

Hiram answered, "I wouldn't object at all."

I went to the bathroom, got the scales from under the great projecting bathtub, and brought it upstairs.

"Stand on this," I instructed after I placed the scales on the floor by the bed.

"Shall I stand squarely in the middle of this apparatus?" asked Hiram as the pipe moved in my direction.

I told him yes, to stand on the rubber pad and waited for him to step onto the scales.

"I'm standin' in place," said Hiram cheerfully, puffing away on his pipe.

The scales registered absolutely nothing.

I was mystified. "Hiram, are you playing a joke on us? I know you have to weigh something. I've seen your impression on the bed. Are you really standing on the scale?"

Hiram was indignant. "Young man, your observations are your business. I am standin' on this contraption of yours as you asked. If it doesn't record my presence, it does not mean that I am not cooperatin' as best I can."

Since I could hear him, I wasn't much inclined to disagree, but I did put my hand out and felt for his foot. I quickly snatched my hand back; I had grasped an invisible shoe—another quantum jolt to my already taxed imagination. Hiram and his worn brogan were definitely on the scale, but the needle denied his existence.

105

Lacey was tapping her fingers against her teeth, something she does when she tries to puzzle something out, like a crossword puzzle or a forgotten recipe. "I'd think," she said, "that Isaac Newton would have loved to meet Hiram. Evidently, weight isn't the same thing as force or pressure."

"Lacey," I told her, "Hiram may *be* Isaac Newton for all we know."

Hiram, didn't make any comment, he was enjoying his pipe too much to be concerned with theories.

Another thought occurred to me. "Hiram, how do you get into the house?"

"Oh, different ways," said the ghost. "Sometimes if I am pretty solid, I open the door and walk in. Occasionally, I just come in through a wall or a window. Every now and then, I just sort of find myself here, and I don't know how I got in."

"Good God," I said.

My statement reminded Lacey to ask what she had forgotten to ask him previously. "Hiram, tell us about God."

"I beg your pardon?" replied the ghost.

"I mean, is there one?" she pressed.

Hiram puffed on his pipe, while Lacey and I stared expectantly at the smoke clouds. The answer to the universal question was taking a long time.

"I have not the slightest idea," said Hiram. "It's been a very long time since I considered that name, though I do remember hearin' a great deal about God at one time or another, but you will have to give me some time to think about it. I don't think I have ever met anyone called God . . . I'm sorry."

106

Lacey and I looked at each other dumbfounded because there was no one else to look at.

"Hiram," Lacey said seriously, "do you remember ever being alive? I mean like Steve and me."

"Oh, yes," he replied enthusiastically. "I think I have been alive like you two because sometimes when I watch the two of you together, I can remember bein' with someone I talked to a great deal and admired—just as you two seem to do with each other."

"Watch us when?" I asked in alarm. Somehow, the idea of an invisible spectator in the bedroom was even more disconcerting than watching a ghost blow smoke rings.

"Oh, dear," said Hiram anxiously, "I do not mean I have invaded your privacy, that is—your intimacy—in any way. I would never think of such a thing. It's just, given that I seem to be here a great deal, and you two are here now, and seemin'ly very kindly disposed toward me, I might watch you and remember whatever it is that I cannot remember."

Lacey was solicitous and said, "Hiram, don't worry about it. I'm sure you're a gentleman—or a gentle something. If being around us will help you remember things, you're welcome."

"Within reason," I added hastily. The thought of a ghost becoming acquainted with us in the bathroom disturbed the hell out of me.

Lacey however, had her own agenda and moved on to other questions: "Do you ever get hungry, or cold or too hot, or bark your shins on anything?"

Hiram seemed to ponder this. "Sometimes, I get impressions

107

of havin' been very hungry, but it's just a fleetin' thing. Mrs. Wickham, as I believe you called her, prepared a meal one day of sausages, buns, and a gravy that I could very nearly smell, and I wished very much that I could actually try some of it, but I was much too weak to make the effort. As to cold and heat, I can scarcely remember what they are, except I remember that they were both uncomfortable. As to barkin' my shins," he added almost apologetically, "I do not seem to have any."

Lacey was determined to get some concrete evidence. "What about heaven and hell?"

"Pardon me?" asked Hiram.

Lacey explained the concepts for him as carefully as she could. She sounded very much like my mother trying to explain the construction of a meatloaf to a new bride in the neighborhood. Lacey believes in simplicity. "Well, if you were a Christian," she said, "you would have believed that after you died you'd go to either heaven or hell, depending on your conduct and whether you'd been redeemed or not."

Hiram sounded perplexed when he answered, "If I remember correctly, redeemed means *bought back*. When one has borrowed on somethin', it must be redeemed I think, before you can own it once more. Or am I mistaken? I often am."

Lacey was encouraged. "You have it Hiram, you're remembering!" she exclaimed.

"But I'm very confused," said Hiram. "If one were redeemed, who borrowed on one in the first place? I thought the term referred to silver plates, watches and the like. I certainly don't remember anything of the kind ever happenin' to me."

108

"Well, you for sure didn't go to heaven or hell," said Lacey, "because you're here."

"What is the difference," asked Hiram anxiously, "between heaven and hell? Perhaps I went there in my travels."

"Don't you remember?" I asked exasperated. "You must have been brought up with some kind of religion. If you go to heaven, you become like an angel and rejoin all your loved ones and if you go to hell, you burn in an everlasting fire."

Hiram was speechless for a moment. "How do you expect me to know these things?" he asked despondently. "I do not even remember *who I* am or *what I* consist of from one moment to the next. It takes all of my concentration to hold this pipe, and you want me to give you answers when I do not even understand your questions."

The pipe shook back and forth as if Hiram had given up trying to communicate with us. But after an anxious moment of silence, his creaky old voice came back. "I don't mean to offend, but I think you're mistaken about your heaven and hell, unless for some reason I have missed them both. Who is in charge of these places?"

"Well, God is in charge of heaven and the devil–Satan is in charge of hell," said Lacey cautiously.

Hiram gave what sounded like a polite snort. "Madam, since I have no physical body, and it seems unlikely that I will get one again, what purpose would there be in puttin' me into an everlastin' fire, whatever my conduct? I could likely sit on your stove for a day without discomfort."

That gave us pause for thought.

"And as for heaven," continued Hiram thoughtfully, "just what would an angel be expected to do?"

Lacey wasn't about to field that one and looked at me.

"Nobody knows," I explained, "and that's why we're asking. They're supposed to have wings and crowns, play harps and sing God's praises all the time. At least that's the way I think it's supposed to be. It's in a book called the Bible."

"I remember now," said Hiram excitedly, "about a Bible. We had one I think, but I cannot remember just what I mean by *we*. I remember a huge book as big as your scales."

"Hiram!" exclaimed Lacey. "Your voice is fading again."

"I know," said Hiram. "I can't help it. I'm off to somewhere or another, I suppose. Maybe hell this time or heaven. I will try to keep track for you this time."

"Just try, Hiram," said Lacey urgently, "try to remember about where you've been and who you are. We'll be here."

"Take the pipe," said Hiram in a little hover-fly voice. I reached in time to take it from midair. "Good-bye. I will ask God if I meet him, about hell and angels for you."

Then he was gone as perceptibly as a person leaving a room and slamming the door after him, although the only evidence was the pipe still smoking in my hand. Some schoolteacher I am! Faced with a real intellectual responsibility, I feel as though I'd just tried to explain Sunday to a duck.

Chapter Nine

NOTHER VISIT FROM THE TROLLS this morning when it was very chilly, and of course, their old truck wouldn't start, and they had to tell me their (predictable) story. Clive said he and Travis T. had tried to roll it down the hill toward the creek, but since the only access to the controls is from the passenger side, it was awkward for them to be in the right place when it started. It took both of them pushing to get the old wreck moving and then neither one of them could catch up to get in. The truck unattended, picked its own course with both of the menfolks chasing, and I imagine, hollering for it to stop. Beulah Lou-Lou said she wasn't there when it happened and as she told Lacey, she "ain't a bit mechanical." It steered itself toward the decrepit old chicken house and carried the fence, chickens, and building on toward the hog pen, where the two "peegs" were waiting out their days in peaceful oblivion.

Travis T. managed to catch up with the truck just as it demolished the hog pen fence and for some reason or another, he jumped into the bed, as if he had thought he could drive it from there. The pigs got out of the way, but the truck pretty much made alterations to the hog house and Travis T., who upon impact, slid down the bed and knocked out the back window with his head. He doesn't look much different but the truck certainly does.

I don't know how long their truck will last if things keep going on this way, but I think it is indestructible. I pulled it back out of the hog pen with a length of log chain. Clive jump-started it, and the poor old thing roared to life like a new one, billowing clouds of blue smoke from every gap.

How the Trolls live, I have no idea, and I definitely don't want many details. Clive gets a disability check and he and Beulah Lou-Lou are old enough for some sort of pensions, I think. Travis T. occasionally helps somebody fix fence, or does odd chores for neighbors, but otherwise he is completely indigent as far as I know. Of course, they borrowed a gallon of gas to get to town and buy groceries. The Trolls' idea of groceries is a case of beer, a bottle of whiskey, a half-gallon of vodka, and three pork chops. That's all I saw on board when they stopped by to repay me for the gasoline.

NO SIGN OF Hiram since September 5th. It's like having a traveling salesman for a boarder; we never know when he'll show up again. Lacey and I discuss him frequently. Mrs. Black has asked us a lot of what I suppose she thinks are clever questions about how we like the house.

Yesterday after school, I went by their house to talk to Soames about a new liner for the stove in the schoolhouse and as Clive would say, she "fell to quizzin' me." "You'uns sleeps well of a night, I reckon," she said dolefully. "Some does and some doesn't in that old place."

It was a question if I ever heard one. I dodged it as best I could. "Sometimes the frogs and whippoorwills keep us awake," I said, "but we'll just have to get used to that."

It seemed like a good time to do a little investigating on my own. "Did you know the Spencers, who lived there back in the 1930s? The ones who owned the bed and the piano?"

"Oh my, yes," said Mrs. Black. "Soames and Tyler Spencer run a sawmill together back in them times. We was nearest neighbors to 'em and you could say our kids was raised up together. Spencer and Maudie lit a shuck for California when times got so hard, and we ain't heard from 'em since, except Maudie sent me a Christmas card once."

Having helped search for the schoolhouse keys, my next question seemed pointless, but I asked anyway, trying to be casual. "Some of my relatives moved to California, too. Do you know what town the Spencers moved to?"

Her answer surprised me. "I saved that card back in the bureau. It had a real purty mountain scenery, I believe. I forget what the backin' is, but I'll fetch it if you like."

I assured her I would really like to see it, and she waddled off into the bedroom trundling her stomach before her like a wheelbarrow. Having been in on one search in that house, I didn't have much confidence in her. But in a minute or so, she reap-

113

peared magically with an old postcard. On the front was a black and white picture of Mt. Shasta with snow-laden trees in the foreground. I turned it over to look at what Mrs. Black called the "backing," where Maudie had written her message. It was dated December 11, 1933, the return address, Summit City, California, and the message was in flowery script.

> Dear Virgie,
> Merry Xmas from all here. Tyler is working in timber. The boys, Boyce and Ervin and their families have moved out here with us. Hope all is well there.
> Best regards to all,
> Maudie

"By any chance, you wouldn't know what Mrs. Spencer's maiden name was?" I asked.

Virgie thought about that for a minute. "I believe her family name was Springfield, best I remember her family come from some'eres back East."

I'll have to try the name Springfield on Hiram next time and see if it rings a bell.

❖

THURSDAY, OCTOBER 4, 1951

THE DAYS ARE getting chilly in the mornings, although by noon, I let the fire go out in the schoolhouse stove. I sent the fourth and fifth graders out on a twig gathering tour, which is definitely a mixture of learning and pleasure. These kids know every tree in the woods, but their knowledge of botany is scanty, and I had them make leaf displays from various phyla.

I have never seen anything in my life like the colors in these Ozark woods. The maples along the creek are enough to take my breath away—great canopies of translucent gold and orange hanging over the road. The oaks are vivid red, the hickory leaves are bright gold and when the sumac leaves fall to the ground, they look like blood stains, as if someone had wounded a deer and the drops were scattered in the leaves.

This morning, when we were in the schoolyard at recess, a great skein of geese went over, honking and gabbling at each other or maybe at us. The sight of their wings winking in flashes of sunlight against an incredible October-blue was better than any lesson I taught today. I can't get the music of those goose voices out of my mind, a thousand chattering gypsies hurrying south. I wonder what poetry I can teach the students of Indian Glade that is any more lasting or impressive than what they already have heard.

The children are a joy, each a separate and definite entity and, like this journal, they are pages waiting to be filled. Every day I learn as much as I teach.

Buck Smith explained to me about the meaning of gums, and it has nothing to do with the kind you chew or chew with. They refer to the trunk of the gum tree, in which old ones are almost always hollow and are used to contain things. There are rabbit gums, which are traps the boys use to catch supper; bee gums, which are sections of log used to make hives; and gum cribs, which are cradles made from a half section of gum log with board ends.

They call cedar "sweet wood," and slippery elm is "piss elum," a word that causes them no embarrassment and it gave me a start when Oran Cartwright brought in a branch for the leaf collection and announced it.

I am going to have to make a list of all the language I'm learning. I have to teach these children how to speak and write well enough to get jobs and pass examinations, but I don't want to rearrange the way they talk, it is so pleasant to my ear. Their metaphors are so natural and interesting that I would rather listen to them than teach them a more new-fangled manner of speech.

Little Cissie Smith, who is eight, informed me gravely that her father "principally farms." I'm getting used to hearing these very grown-up words from children who are barely able to spell "cat."

T.J. told me yesterday that his father, Bailey and Jeff Farley had just sat around "squanderin' an opinion" for an hour while he was "waitin' within the truck" for a ride to school.

All the children refer to Mrs. Summers as "Mistress Summers" as if they were all Elizabethan courtiers, and Ruby asked me the other day how my mistress was, meaning Lacey I'm sure.

Cleavis was perplexed with a problem in long division last week and told me he "jist couldn't riddle it out," and he's also the one who told me that his four-year-old baby brother Jeff is "dauncy about his vittles," which I suppose means the child is particular. Where that word comes from I have no idea, but I'm going to order a better dictionary. I have a feeling these terms are

116

a great deal older than most of the trees that grow around the schoolyard.

I'm also finding out that words I think of as ordinary are unfit in Ozark speech. You just don't say "cock" and my pronunciation of "cock-a-doodle-doo" in one of their readers, convulsed the first and second graders. The older boys avoid "cock" by saying they "rooster back the hammer" when hunting squirrels. Penny McClellan was embarrassed tremendously when I asked her to point out Cape Cod on the map, and the entire school tittered (also a word I must avoid) because "cod" is a definite phallic term here. "John Hancock" got several snickers from the eighth grade history class and anyone named "Peter" is good for a giggle.

Probably my biggest single laugh came when I asked Cleavis and Ruby at recess if any of the ponds froze thick enough to play hockey. "Hockey" in the Ozarks refers only to feces, and Lord knows you're not supposed to play with the stuff. In addition, the word "bull" is considered crude, and these kids say "male ox" instead. Who knows what they would think if they had to spell "peacock," which would offend twice. The strangest part of this prudery is its anomalies: big black ants are "piss aints" to all the children. Ruby told me the other day that his dad wouldn't go to "a big city like Rahley to see a piss aint eat a bale of hay." Metaphors like that are not hurt a bit by the fact that the town's name is Rolla, and it's not a city at all.

The children are all doing well and seem to love school, which I don't think is a tribute to my teaching ability so much as the fact that school for farm children is really fun. They all seem to help each other family-style; they learn as much from each other as they do from me. What's the most fun, despite them all having something to do, is they eavesdrop on the other classes being recited and pick up a variety of knowledge that astounds me at times. The other day I had Ruby, Cleavis, Joey Farley and Oran at the blackboard for a competitive test in eighth grade arithmetic. They love that sort of thing; it brings out the ham in them to stand at their section of the blackboard and whip out an answer before the others can come up with it. The whole thing turns into a game, and I gave the four of them a reasonably complicated problem in long division. While they were struggling with it frantically and scrubbing out mistakes in great clouds of eraser dust, a small hand raised in the fourth grade. Sandra Pulver who was supposed to be involved with participles in her notebook, said, "Mr. Clark, I've got the answer," and sure enough she did. She had it worked out on the margin of her page. A quantum leap of four years in mathematics! I'm beginning to think a one-room school discovers early talent faster than parents ever could.

What pleases the children most is to choose sides and have a school-wide contest of some kind, which passes all age boundaries. Spelling bees are their favorites, and I give out words in proportion to their age group or grade, but the amount of fence jumping involved is wonderful. Twice this week, twelve-year-old Irene Farley spelled down the whole school. A lot of times they do not pronounce words the way they are spelled: *picture* being "pitcher," *terrible*—"turble," *yeast*—"east," *wheelbarrow*—"wheelbar." Sometimes a word I pronounce is a mystery to ev-

118

erybody and I sort it out a letter at a time. They find it hard to believe that *Missouri* ends with an *i* and that *soda* ends with an *a*, since they pronounce them the opposite way. They also reverse pillar and pillow, weary and worry, tar and tire, but these are all habits they can unlearn. The problem is that when they go home each day, they settle comfortably back into their "mother tongue," as Walt Bangert called it. I have to teach them all over again that *boil* should be pronounced as it's spelled, not "bile" as they've said it all their lives.

Some things I refuse to mess with. No child at Indian Glade ever says *I won't*. They all say "I'll not," which has a fine Shakespearian sound, as does *et* instead of *eaten*, which the British still seem to get away with, so why not my children. If I were to read to them from the words of Edmund Spenser, or Samuel Johnson, or even Chaucer, they would find the sounds of words more familiar than they do when I try to read anything more current. There is a mellifluous sound to the things they say and poetry in the way they say them. It makes the speech I grew up with seem barren in comparison. I can't see them all becoming radio announcers.

Sandra Pulver told me proudly that her Uncle Finus had "made a lawyer," which was a startling mental picture, but it expressed her thought.

It is interesting the way they use *for* in place of *because*. Last week, Cleavis said, "I know Pa'll do it, for he's not bad to lie," meaning that his dad would take him to the carnival in Rolla. It sounded a great deal more sedate than anything I would have said at his age. Little Cissie informed me "there's a generation of

119

fiddleback spiders in that tool shed," which was likely. Eleven-year-old Mildred Cartwright informed me soberly that her mother was "a master quilter because she had the sleight of it."

I try to write these things down as I hear them, and it isn't easy. Carrying a notebook around with me is out of the question, so I keep one at my desk. Usually, I memorize what they say and then later, when it appears that I'm doing lesson plans or grading, I jot down what I've heard. I don't ever want to embarrass the children or cause resentment.

Penny McClellan brought me a sack of apples and said that they had "lavishes" of them if "Mistress Clark" wanted to can some. Carolyn Smith reported that some "rogue" had "pilfered some gas out'n Daddy's truck," and Irene Farley told me shyly that she had "looked the workbook" but "couldn't find no remedy for this here numbers problem."

Like children everywhere, they're looking forward to Halloween, and they have the schoolhouse decorated becomingly with fall leaves, construction paper pumpkins and witches hats. My art courses in college are paying off. I can't help but wonder what they'd think of Hiram as a real Halloween ghost. I'm damn sure not going to try to find out.

Chapter Ten

❖

OCTOBER 15, 1951

ACEY AND I GOT A LETTER TODAY from Maudie Spencer, answering my letter in quiring about the bed. I had about given up on her since I sent it to an address nearly twenty years old. But fortunately, her husband Tyler Spencer owns a lumberyard in Summit City and is well known.

Lacey had the letter waiting for me when I got home from school and I read it over, looking for clues to our ghost. Lacey had already read it twice and had the dates down pat.

Maudie said the bed and square grand piano came from her grandmother Elizabeth Springfield, whose husband Benjamin died during The War Between the States—as she called it—at the battle of Missionary Ridge in 1863, leaving her to raise their two sons.

She said her grandmother Elizabeth died at the age of seventy in the bed and said her folks didn't like the ancient bed but they kept it, as well as the piano, for sentiment after her death. Maudie said she inherited the bed and piano after her father, Harlin passed away sometime in the early 1920s.

And now her letter gets interesting and I quote:

My husband Tyler and me tried sleeping in the bed but it never slept good for us some way or another. Tyler said he could imagine somebody a breathing, standing over the bed looking at us as if we were in somebody's way and said it gave him the crawlies. We never seen anything, but the old house we lived in back then popped and cracked on cold nights and there was a lot of noise we never could explain, although we figured pack rats was in the walls. Somehow we had it fixed in our minds that my grandma dying in that dark old bed was bad luck or some such foolishness. So we put it in the spare room that used to be our boys' room, who were all grown up by then.

When we moved from Tennessee up to the place on Blessing Creek, I had to fuss with Tyler over bringing that old piano and bed with us. I was real sentimental about them but he said we could get along very well without them. But anyway, I had my way and they came with us.

When we lived on Blessing, the grandkids would come stay with us during the summer. They'd play on that bed but never sleep in it. They claimed it was too spooky to sleep in. (They were just like their grandpa.)

When we were fixing to move out here to California in '32 so Tyler could work with his brother, he really put his foot down when it came to moving those two big old pieces of furniture. I had to agree with him since it was far to go in our old truck and we wouldn't have been able to pack much else. So we sold them to Mr. Decker for the food bill we owed him.

I'm glad you are now enjoying them. Hope this has answered your questions. I have all the old births and deaths in the family Bible which the first entry is in 1810 and the last is our grandchildren, of which we have five now. Remember us to Virgie and Soames and other of our old neighbors.

AFTER I READ the letter thoroughly, Lacey said, "If the old man, Benjamin Springfield, who died in the Civil War, is really Hiram, he's been dead for eighty-eight years now. If he were twenty when he died, that would make him over a hundred years old."

I had an argument for that. "But we don't know *how old* the bed is. It could be over two-hundred years old. Any number of people could have owned it before Elizabeth and Benjamin Springfield and anybody who could tell us, is dead. And one thing for certain, we know that *Elizabeth* isn't our ghost."

"I'm going on the fact that Mrs. Springfield died in the bed and that Hiram might just be Benjamin," said Lacey.

I reminded her that a lot of people could have died in the bed if it was two-hundred years old, and our ghost could be just about anybody. But I remembered to add, "Well, one thing we know for sure, our ghost was—is obviously, a southern gentleman."

"Steve, I think you're going to have to write to Mrs. Spencer again."

While she was talking, I was half listening; I was already constructing another letter to Maudie. We really needed to find out how old the bed was and if there were previous owners before Maudie's grandparents. Plus, just in case, I was going to ask if she knew her grandfather Benjamin's birth date. That way we could peg how old he was—on the slight chance that he was indeed our ghost.

Then Lacey had an idea. "Steve, maybe we can take the bed apart and look for a date. They used to put identifying marks on old furniture."

The thought of taking apart what was still apparently someone else's resting place, particularly Hiram's, gave me goose bumps.

"Let's think about that a while," I said. "Even scooting it out from the wall would take two really strong men, and I don't see you and me taking it apart. Meanwhile, I'll write to Mrs. Spencer again, and we'll find out all we can."

I could tell though, Lacey was hot on the trail and was already convinced. On the face of it, so far at least, it looks like our sometime guest could be Benjamin Springfield, deceased. Maybe when he comes back, we can ask him himself.

❖

NOVEMBER 1, 1951

HALLOWEEN HAS COME and gone. We had a big, funny Halloween party at the school last night, with dunking for apples, pin-the-tail-on-the-donkey and all sorts of scary games. The kids wore blindfolds and felt peeled grapes they were told wer eyeballs, and plates full of spaghetti they were told were worms. We all played charades and I think the older folks enjoyed these the most. Lacey, who remembers her own one-room school days, arranged the whole works and showed up dressed as a witch, wearing an old costume she had made when she was in high school. All the children had made their own costumes with a little help from home. The old schoolhouse rattled and shook with their shrieks and laughter as they dashed around in ghost costumes, which were numerous since sheets were plentiful. Owls, goblins, and miniature witches in construction paper hats were also in good number. Money being short in the neighborhood, there weren't any store-bought costumes, but Sandra Pulver did have a tinsel tiara to complete her fairy princess outfit made of curtain lace, and some of the little ones had masks from a store in Rolla.

Practically the whole neighborhood came, as they always do

125

for these functions. The adults were sitting on benches at the back and sides, laughing and visiting with each other and enjoying their children. The two old mantle lamps cast just about the right amount of spectral gloom for Halloween. On the bookshelves, Lacey had set lighted candles that flickered over everybody convincingly. The parents had made cupcakes, cakes and pies enough to stuff everybody.

The prize for best costume—judged by Soames Black and Mrs. Summers—was won by Austin McClellan, whose mother and sisters had dressed him up to look like a bat. He was covered in a dyed sheet with huge protruding cardboard ears and some carved wooden fangs that he was very proud of.

It was nearly ten o'clock before we wound up the party, and the three youngest Farleys—Mavis, Arley, and the baby—were asleep on blankets. We said good-bye to everyone at the door, feeling very good about the success of it all and very tired, too.

Last night the woods were pitch dark when I turned the mantel lamps off and locked the door. The big owls were calling everywhere, a very Halloween-ish sound. We drove home chattering and laughing about all the funny things said and done. I don't know about Lacey, but I was punch-drunk.

"I wonder why the Trolls didn't come?" Lacey questioned with good humor.

"Don't be silly," I told her. "The Trolls are what Halloween is all about—they do this every night."

"Speaking of what it's all about, if Hiram doesn't come home tonight, I'll never believe in Halloween again," she said.

126

SOMEHOW IT WASN'T quite as funny to me as it ought to have been. About the time we came to the mouth of the hollow where our house stood, we saw the light on the porch that I'd left on for us. What bothered me was there was also a light on upstairs in the balcony window, a thin, yellow light that wandered about as we stared at it.

"That's either Hiram or a burglar," I told Lacey, "and until I find out, you'd better stay in the car."

The light didn't go out when we turned into the drive; I pulled up slowly, turning the car lights off to see the nature of it better. It appeared to be our coal-oil lantern or some small flame, hardly larger than a candle. I had locked the doors for some reason, probably thinking that Halloween pranksters wouldn't go so far as to break in. As I fumbled for the key, I remembered that neither Vance nor Carney Black had been at the schoolhouse, and this was probably their gag. I felt more confident thinking that a couple of boys their age would be tempted to play a joke on the schoolmaster while we were gone because I also knew Soames Black was their father, and they wouldn't dare go too far with it.

"Is that you, boys?" I called.

"It's me," a voice called from the landing. "I couldn't ring the bells because you weren't here, so I decided to announce myself with a light." The pipe hung in midair, smoking away.

"Come on, Lacey," I called, "it's just Hiram."

Under the circumstances that might seem a little bizarre, but Hiram is preferable to a burglar and we expect him at odd times.

"Hiram!" exclaimed Lacey delightedly. She's actually become very fond of our ancient ghost and couldn't wait to read Maudie

127

Spencer's letter to him. "Come down here with us, we're going to have a drink."

"Well, I do not wish to intrude," said Hiram doubtfully, and then caught sight of Lacey in her costume. We were looking up at the top of the stairs and watching a cloud of smoke puffing out of nowhere, when we saw the pipe drop nearly to the floor.

I realized with a start that she must resemble someone from the 1800s, with her voluminous skirt and puffed sleeves all dyed black for the occasion and her black knitted shawl. Her long red hair tumbled down when she removed the witch's hat and it was very becoming.

"Why, young lady," said the ghost, descending the stairs, "for a moment there, I . . ."

"What, Hiram?" Lacey asked excitedly. "Did this old dress remind you of someone?"

"Why, I'm not sure," he said very slowly, "but you look very charmin'. People do not wear clothin' of that sort anymore, I think, and I seem to remember that sort of long gown bein' worn at some place in my travels."

"At some place in *time*, Hiram," she corrected. "We think we know something about who you are. Bring your pipe and sit down here with us, while I fix a drink for Steve and me."

Once again, I was treated to the sight of Hiram's invisible buttocks. He was sinking into a chair by the kitchen wall and the quite visible pipe standing on air a few feet from my face. It is a sight I don't think I will ever get used to.

"You figured out how to light the coal-oil lantern," I said, "so you must be pretty solid tonight. Plus, you remembered about

128

the matches, so your memory is getting better."

"Oh, I'm gettin' a little better at everythin'," said Hiram. "I went through the rooms turnin' the lights on and off, as I have watched you do with those little contraptions on the wall. That is a marvelous invention."

I said, "But if you're so solid, how did you manage to get in? I'd locked the door because it's Halloween."

"All Hallow's Eve," said Hiram wonderingly. "I have a memory of that too, somehow. But to answer your question," he added eagerly, "I find that I can become solid or un-solid pretty much at my choice now when I come here, and it is a great advantage."

Lacey brought our drinks and asked without thinking, "Hiram, would you care for anything?"

"I might just try a dram of somethin'," he said shyly. "Just to see if aught would come of it."

I was thunderstruck at his answer.

"What would you prefer?" asked Lacey in wonderment.

Hiram sounded perplexed. "Why, I don't know, havin' as far as I know, never drunk anythin', but at the same time I seem to remember how it's done. Perhaps a sip of what you are havin', please ma'am."

What we were having was some inexpensive bourbon, whose nature improved with Seven-Up. Lacey very carefully poured a tiny amount of it in a wineglass and started to add ice and soda when Hiram interjected.

"I'll drink it reverend, if you please, ma'am."

"Fine," said Lacey. "What's *reverend*?"

The ghost chuckled and the sound took me aback since his

129

voice had always been so distant and sad. Our Hiram was a stronger ghost than before and able to be amused.

"Why, pardon me, just as it is," he said. "I suppose the term, like me, is somewhat out of use."

Lacey poured more into the glass and handed it to him. The glass performed a balancing act as the pipe dropped to what I can only suppose was Hiram's lap. I could hardly wait to see what was going to happen to the liquor, whether it would form a long thin stream like something poured in the air or simply go splat on the kitchen floor. It did neither. It disappeared a little at a time into an invisible place in the air. It was such a tiny sip, I wasn't sure what I was seeing, but when the glass became upright, half of the shot was gone. Hiram was silent.

"Do you feel anything?" asked Lacey anxiously.

"Well," answered the old voice judiciously, "yes and no. I think you would describe it as a distant glow of some sort."

"Wonderful, Hiram!" I exclaimed. "That's what it's supposed to do. Try another!"

"I shall," said the voice, and this time he tipped the glass and drained it.

Now if this was an entity, I thought, who hadn't had a drink or needed one for that matter, in eighty-eight years, the results were due to be spectacular from this first one.

And then something marvelous happened; Hiram gave a gentle belch and for just a second we saw a slight, tenuous outline against the kitchen wall, as if someone had drawn it with smoke. It was the outline of a man's head and chest and went all the way out to the hand that held the glass. Then it was gone.

130

"Hiram," said Lacey gleefully, "you're starting to become real. We almost saw you."

"But I don't feel anythin' much," said Hiram. "I had hoped for more."

"Rome wasn't built in a day, Hiram," I told him. "We'll have to work on it. Lacey, get Mrs. Spencer's letter and read it to Hiram while he's definitely with us."

Lacey took the letter off the kitchen counter and began reading while Hiram puffed thoughtfully on his pipe. When she finished, she laid the letter on her lap, and we both eagerly leaned forward.

"Is there anything that sounds familiar?" asked Lacey.

"That part about the War Between the States," said Hiram thoughtfully, "sounds familiar. But I do not remember dyin', and I don't remember anyone named Elizabeth as far as I know."

"Well, I don't suppose anybody would want to remember dying," said Lacey encouragingly, "and you might just get the memory back a little at a time."

I agreed with her. "Listen Hiram, if you are this person she wrote about, you were in the army and you wore clothes. We know that because you had some on the first night we talked. Are there buttons on your coat?"

I thought that was a stroke of genius, but it drew a blank. Hiram it seems had no coat, merely a shirt with a collar. Lacey hadn't discovered this when feeling of his face because of his wide expanse of beard. With Hiram's permission, she made sure of this, while I felt a pant leg for a brocade stripe and even felt for a belt buckle. Neither was there. What Lacey did find was a pair of old-time "gallushes"—as she calls them—suspending his pants.

"Are these the only clothes you've ever had?" asked Lacey wistfully, very much wanting him to be the old man who had died at Missionary Ridge.

"I think so," said Hiram, "but those early days are hard to remember. Before I met you, I could not recollect anythin' at all, you see. I'm afraid I'm not of much help to you."

"Don't worry," said Lacey, patting his hand, "it will all come back. You're here for some purpose or another."

"By the way," said Hiram, whose voice was getting a little thick, "what name was I supposed to have when I was alive?"

"Why, Benjamin," said Lacey, "Benjamin Springfield."

The ghost was silent for a moment. "I like Hiram better," he said with a slight hiccup. "I feel like a Hiram."

Lacey and I grinned at each other.

"That's because we called you that," she said. "So obviously you'd like it. Nobody's called you anything in years."

"You know what I think?" asked Hiram amiably. "I think it is time for me to go upstairs and lie down a bit. I need to consider all of this."

"Hiram, are you feeling tipsy?" asked Lacey knowingly. She reached for his swaying glass, which he extended with great, though invisible, formality.

"As a matter of fact," answered the ghost, "I am. I think I need to lie down. I will bid you both a most pleasant goodevenin'."

Very carefully the pipe knocked itself out in the ashtray with perhaps one more knock than was necessary and went with just

132

a hit of a weave toward the staircase.

"*Good night Hiram,*" we both said and listened for the creak of feet on the stairs.

Lacey and I looked at each other and both broke into muffled laughter.

"Steve, I believe our ghost is schnockered."

Chapter Eleven

ACEY AND I HAD LEARNED NOT ONLY to put up with Hiram's presence, but also his absences when his wanderings called him away, whatever they might have been. It was a little like worrying about an aged relative flying to Hawaii, wondering if he'd land safely somewhere and whether he'd make it back. Oftentimes, Lacey would go upstairs to check for him several times a night, like someone, I told her, whose favorite hound had taken to the woods.

We each had our theories about his wanderings. I felt the old man was caught up in some strange time warp that carried him full circle, like a moon in its orbit and dumped him back in the same place, knowing no more than he had before. Why that orbit seemed to focus on the huge walnut bed, I didn't understand. Lacey thought he was looking for his wife on these excursions but didn't realize the fact himself.

Lacey's idea was more logical, if indeed Maudie's letter actually concerned Hiram. But then if he was the soldier who had lost his life at Chattanooga, and was on a pilgrimage to find his wife, why didn't he remember what he was looking for? Maybe he was like one of my children on the playground, tossing a marble to see if it would land near a lost one.

THE BABY WAS growing at a great rate, taking up more space than Lacey's clothes would allow, so she spent a lot of time at the sewing machine making maternity clothes. She was concerned with everybody else's babies, new puppies and anything else that had to do with birth, helplessness or just being small, and Hiram, who was neither small nor young, somehow captivated her in the same way. He was a new being to her, and she doted on him. Sometimes, when she'd be at the sewing machine and I'd be grading papers, she'd look up and hush me, as if I were the one making noise. She'd cock her head and listen for Hiram's bells or his footsteps creaking.

ONE NIGHT IN early November, when he'd been gone for a couple of days, a sudden snow blew straight out of the west. I would see the wind whirl clouds of it under the eaves whenever I went out to the back porch for wood. It was the week of deer season, and the snow was a blessing both for deer hunters and for me because I knew school would be called off for both. The two happening together meant missed days wouldn't be docked from my firm budget of pupil hours, which Myrtle Summers adhered to like glue.

"Missed days must be made up, Mr. Clark," she informed me

at warrant time. "If each scholar misses one day a month—that's sixteen scholar days a month. Hit totes up, Mr. Clark, hit totes up." She wanted the kids there even if they had diphtheria.

I love snow and my spirits were high that night; there was a five-inch snow on the ground and more coming down every minute, and the night sky was a perfect whorl of dime-sized flakes. When I poked my flashlight out the door, our car was a white mound with a diamond flash of bumper protruding, and the spring branch to the east, glittered slate-gray between mountainous banks. Lacey's birdfeeder was twice its height, looking like a Swiss chalet and the posts of the yard fence resembled a line of dark old men in white busbies, guarding the house. It was a definite storm, and I mind-snuggled the fact that there would be no school the next day.

I always had a lot to do, what with the woodpile, splitting kindling wood, taking out ashes, grading the kids' workbooks and preparing lesson plans at night. I remember sitting at the kitchen table with my stack of papers, while Lacey sat beside the fireplace reading a book in the living room. In the background, there was the soft music of a Mahler symphony accompanied by snapping wood settling in the fireplace.

We were interrupted by three loud knocks at the front door. With the deep snow making the road a trackless wilderness as impossible to navigate as a woodland swamp, we couldn't imagine anyone trying to drive, besides, it was after ten o'clock and all our neighbors were long in bed. As I got up and walked through the living room, Lacey and I looked at each other quizzically.

I went to the door, figuring somebody was in trouble and in

need of help; I hastened to turn on the porch light and open the door. There was no one there, apart from a line of fresh man-tracks that came up the drive and onto to the porch leading to the front door.

"Hiram?" I asked puzzled.

"I heard your music again and I've come to visit, if it is all right," said a rich southern voice in front of me. I became aware that I was seeing three patches of snow—one was on top of an invisible head and the other two on shoulder patches as thin and plain as epaulets that marked where he stood. As my eyes fo-cused I could see a patch of snow-beard and all sorts of zigzags of flakes up and down the invisible figure's length, which I sup-posed was snow caught in the folds of his clothing.

Lacey called from the living room, "Hiram! Where have you been? Get in here right now!" I knew she was going to be great with kids because she already sounded like my mother had years ago.

I closed the door behind us and said, "Let me brush off that snow, you must be freezing." It was an interesting experience, very gingerly done, since I could only make a rough guess as to where any of Hiram's areas were.

"Thank you," he said. "I am not at all cold, but I would hate to track snow in on Mistress Clark's floors."

As Lacey walked into the hallway, she said happily, "Oh, Hiram, I'm glad you're back!"

"If you would permit me your hand," said the ghost.

When she extended it, I had the rare privilege of seeing her hand kissed by a cluster of melting snowflakes.

137

Hiram noticed the protuberance of Lacey's stomach and reacted with great joy and enthusiasm to her general hugeness. "Mistress Clark!" he exclaimed. "You are to be blessed with a child I see. How wonderful for you both. God willin' I might get to see the little one. May I ask when the child might arrive?"

"Of course, Hiram," she said. "It's due sometime near Christmas. You could be our first babysitter."

"I beg your pardon?" said Hiram.

Lacey laughed realizing the term must sound as strange to him as it was familiar to us. "Someone who stays with the baby while Steve and I go to school functions and parties, and places where you shouldn't take a baby," she explained.

Hiram was amazed. "You mean you would not take the baby wherever you go?" And added doubtfully, "But, Mistress Clark, the feedin' and so forth. Wouldn't one have to be with the baby to nurse it?" It was obviously a delicate subject to Hiram.

"Oh, Hiram, don't you worry about that," she reassured him. "I can see I'll have to do a lot of explaining about having babies today, and bottle-feeding, and formula, and all those things. But you do remember about babies, don't you? You seem to be remembering more."

"I'm not all that sure of anythin'," replied Hiram in a cheerful voice, "but the music of your house speaks to me, Mistress Clark."

"Hiram, please call me Lacey. I know you come from a different time, but you'd make me feel so much more comfortable."

"Indeed, madam," he said, sounding a bit defensive. "It might be easier for you, but it does not seem easy for me to address you

138

as a child or a house servant. And besides, your husband might consider it a familiarity under his own roof."

"Hiram," said Lacey, "you have a lot to learn, my friend. Now come sit by the fire and I'll get your pipe and tobacco."

During this exchange, I had been furiously adding up evidence; it was the only way I knew how to take Hiram's measure each time he came home. When I had brushed off the snow, I knew he was a few inches taller than I was, and I had his bootprint in the snow to measure his footstep and the shape of his shoes. From his manners it was clear he wasn't a farm hand and perhaps had been an officer, commissioned or otherwise, if this was indeed Benjamin Springfield. I had a list of things to ask him but each time he left us, I'd realize that I had forgotten to ask him a number of things.

I pulled Lacey's rocker around to face the fire and invited Hiram to sit. I turned down the record player against his protests; Lacey insisted that we all needed to talk, and he could listen to music to his heart's content, later. While Lacey went upstairs to fetch the pipe and tobacco, I went to my journal and found the second letter I'd received from Maudie, who'd answered my request for details. While Lacey was upstairs, I quickly re-read the letter to myself.

Summit City, Calif. Oct. 29, 1951
Dear Mr. Clark,

    It's very nice of you to be so interested in the old family furniture. I will help any way I can to give you dates and

139

places from the family Bible. Here are the answers to your questions:

<u>Where did the bed come from and how old is it?</u>

Well, the bed, according to Grandma Bess, was new when she and Grandpa Benjamin got it. It was made for them as a wedding present from his parents when they was married in 1847. There is no record of who made it.

<u>What was Benjamin Springfield's birth date?</u>

According to the family Bible, Benjamin was born April 7, 1828, at Low Gap, Tennessee. His parents were Ezekiel and Evangeline Springfield who had migrated to Tennessee from Advance, North Carolina in 1826. According to Grandma Bess, Grandpa Benjamin was a tall, very gentle man, who was mostly known for his fiddle playing. Of course this wasn't all he done because Grandma said he was good with stock and a great hand to make and repair machinery and make fiddles and even gittars for people. He was also very kind to his colored who was all free Negro hands and servants. I guess his family was pretty well fixed and his daddy Ezekiel owned a pretty

big scope of land in Tennessee. Grandpa
Benjamin didn't believe in slavery and
wouldn't have had none without he heired
the colored, which he freed them and hired
them for pay.

Grandma Bess told Mother that when the
war came close to their home, Grandpa en-
listed in Col. William Bate's division when
he seen that he must fight for his own
farm. For many years Grandma kept a letter
from Grandpa's company commander telling
of Grandpa's death on the battlefield and
I wish I had it to send you but Mom misplaced it somewhere in her many moves. I
read it though, many times when I was a
child, trying to imagine what Grandpa had
been like. Grandpa was killed in what they
call the Battle of Missionary Ridge where
the Rebels was trying to hold off the Yankees. Some calls this the Battle of Lookout Mountain and you could look it up.
Anyway, the Confederate lines was overrun
by Yankees and Grandpa was killed trying
to protect the way into Chattanooga, which
they took anyway. Grandma told us children
many a story about Grandpa, which since
you seem interested, I'll tell you the one
about the piano.

Grandpa and Grandma was very fond of music and Grandpa Benjamin was always making or getting Grandma whatever musical instrument she had set her mind on. Well, when they lived at Low Gap, Grandma Bess took it in her head to have a piano. Of course the nearest place to find such a thing was plumb to Knoxville where there was a place that sold them. Grandpa Benjamin took the wagon and a couple of Negroes to help him and lit out. It was a three-day trip by steamboat and then they had to ferry back across the Tennessee River at a place called Crump's Landing. Well on the way back the ferry cable broke and the whole works would have went down the river but for the ferryman snubbing up the rope with his brake, which liked to turn them over against the bank and threw one of the colored men into the river. Grandma said that Grandpa yelled to him, "Tread water, Silas, I'll fetch you out as soon as I've seen to Bessie's piano!" It was a joke in the family for years and we'd recall it whenever one of us grandkids was in a pickle and needed help right away. The others would holler out "Tread water, Silas!"

That's all I can think of to help you
find out about the bed and piano, which
I'm certainly glad you and your wife are
enjoying. I wish you had Grandpa's old
fiddle which come down I guess from his
Grandpa and was worth a lot of money, but
we could never find it in Grandma's things.
My daddy Harlin said Grandpa Benjamin was
a master fiddler and made several of them
for other fiddlers and said he was a way
too modest to play in the contests they
used to have in the old days, for the few
he'd entered he'd always win. Daddy himself never played the fiddle after his
first wife died and he thought his fiddling was the cause of it. He wouldn't
touch one after that, and mostly played
gittar and banjo and mandolin. Daddy was a
good soul, but he did get his bill too deep
in the jar now and then.

But back to Grandpa Benjamin. There was
a lot of fiddlers that learned tunes Grandpa
Springfield made up himself, and I've heard
that people still play them, ones like
"Elizabeth's Waltz" and "Big Gap Reel" and
"Horse In The Corn."

Grandma Bess told my mother that he
would play things she liked, like "Missis-

143

sippi Sawyer," and "Leather Britches" and
"The Girl I Left Behind Me" but her favorite was an old one they'd play together—
"Believe Me If All Those Endearing Young
Charms." I'm not a bit musical so had none
of that to pass down to my kids, Boyce and
Ervin, and my husband Tyler says the piano
is in better hands, because in this family
we can't play nothing but the radio, ha-
ha. My it was pretty though.

The rest of the letter was full of reminiscences about her parents, particularly her father, Harlin, who I gathered was also a
good musician but more of a free spirit, and before his first wife
died, played mostly for gatherings at taverns. I wished she had
written more; she was a garrulous old lady, at least in print, and
I'd liked to have plumbed her memory. Meanwhile, I had some
ammunition to expend on Hiram and was very glad that he'd
come home, and that I had free time to quiz him extensively
about things.

LACEY CAME DOWNSTAIRS, and soon Hiram's empty chair
was rocking comfortably before the fireplace; clouds of luxuriant
smoke swirled above the invisible head. I sat on a stool by the
hearth and waited while Lacey fixed our guest a little whiskey
"reverend" in a wine glass. Hiram puffed furiously on his pipe.
Lacey returned and handed him the goblet; it lifted itself and
poured a sip into a place in the air. At last, I started reading

Maudie's letter aloud.

When I got to the part about Bess and the piano, the chair stopped. It was a little unnerving when the rocker ceased, but I kept on reading. When I got to the part about Benjamin's fiddle playing for Bess, the wine glass crashed to the hearth, and then came a frozen silence. Lacey and I sat startled, waiting.

The pipe rose shakily in the air, and Hiram sobbed a heart-rending, "*My God, my dear Bessie!* How could my mind have lost you? How could I have forgotten my life, my fiddle and my music?"

It was as if all of his history had tumbled out at once, from whatever dark closet ghosts keep memories. In an instant, Lacey was in tears and instinctively rose to find one of his hands and clasp both hers around it.

She tried her best to look into his un-seeable eyes. "Hiram, I'm so sorry—*oh, shit!*—can we help? I know the memories must be awful, but at least you have them now. Maybe your wife is stuck somewhere in time too and now you can find her."

"Time has taken her!" said Hiram in a stricken voice. "*Oh my dear God!* When I arrived tonight, it seemed fine to walk to the house with the snow all about me and the light of the windows yellow and friendly." His voice trembled and choked. "I turned to look at my footsteps in the snow and I realized it was me who had made them, and know that whatever I am, *I am somethin'.*" His voice seemed to rise above the chair. "But now I am worse than nothin', how could my creator allow me to forget my reasons for livin'? How could he let me forget my music and *my Bessie?*"

There was something so pathetic, so yearning in his old voice that I could understand Lacey's tears and would have probably shed some myself, except I was stunned. In the reading of Maudie's letter, Hiram had recovered the memory of God and his wife in a thunderclap of time.

I watched Lacey try to help the invisible old ghost back into his chair, which rocked with agitation for several minutes to his agonized groaning. I hadn't felt that sorry for anyone since my mother died, leaving my pop in a dazed and forlorn state I thought I would never see again. But Hiram's grief was so real, so heart breaking and untouchable, I realized that loss never gets any easier but only more bearable with time, and Hiram had never even received time's benefit. It seemed like the most ghastly injustice of all, and if God wasn't going to pay attention to this poor creature, I was determined that I would.

It was nearly a half hour before the furious rocking and moaning slowed and then stopped. Lacey had swept up the glass and replaced it with a cup of mulled wine.

Taking his forgotten pipe, she urged it into his hand. "Try this, Hiram, and let's see if talking will help some. Would it help to talk about Bessie? We'd like to know her."

It was the right thing to say, and Hiram took a sip of his wine and cleared his throat. "I played the violin back then," he began in a low wondering voice as if regaining his memory was in the experimental stage. "I first saw her when I was playin' for a dance. She was all of what the music meant to me . . . playful, light-footed, and frolicsome but as endearin' as all things beautiful. I loved her at sight as I love her still. There was deepness to her beauty with her soul peepin' out—a curiosity, and a sense of joy so contagious that it caught up my fiddle, and I played that night as joyfully as a wood sprite."

I pulled out my journal and tried to write, but I was so taken with the sound of his voice, I had to lay it aside. He must have talked for an hour, stopping only to sip his wine or pause to fill his pipe and puff it a time or two. Between pauses, I tended the fire and fixed Lacey some tea.

It was a condensed life story as Hiram told it but so much more a love story than anything else. Lacey sat entranced with the depth and reality of love in Hiram's words.

The plantation boy fiddler, who had brought Bessie into his life and tried to fulfill her dreams the way she fulfilled his, was the stuff of legend. He told of his farm nestled in mountains, his two boys and his hopes, but the story always returned to Bessie. Bessie and her zest for life, her singing at chores, her care for neighbors and her boundless enthusiasm for things childish and fun. Bessie, who encouraged his obsession for music, was the inspiration and love of his life, until he was plunged into nearly a century of ghostly nonexistence.

After a while, all of us were silently pensive; there was only the sound of crackling hickory logs, and the creak of his chair.

Eventually, I broke the quiet. "Hiram, do you remember when you died?"

I heard him give a deep sigh. "I am not sure. I remember somethin' happenin' to me, but it was more like when you cut yourself with a skinnin' knife and look down and think—*did I do that?*—as you watch the blood run. I do not remember pain or

147

dyin'. I can put it together in my head now, better than I ever have—although—I think I have pictured it a thousand times.

"There was a Yankee boy, much younger than me, comin' toward me through a mist that was as heavy as fog. There were great shiftin' clouds of mist that made me wonder what was real and what wasn't, and I could hear guns and cannons everywhere. I didn't know whether they were theirs or ours, but I could smell the powder-stink and see flashes in the fog like lightnin', and I know how my ears hurt with the noise.

"I remember how homesick I was, I missed Bessie, my two boys Harlin and Jacob and the quiet valley where my farm lay under the low gap. Most of the soldiers were just boys, and some of them were excited to be in uniform fightin' for the South—but I was thirty-five—all I could think of was I must get home to see about the corn pickin'. I'd come because I knew they needed me. . . . *I hated that war.* I missed my family, and I knew no matter how hard Bessie and Silas and my two boys would try, the farm needed my patience, my experience."

Lacey and I were spellbound.

He sighed remembering, puffing his pipe. "The day before, Sherman's divisions had made a frontal attack on our fortifications. I was listening to a picket tellin' me he had liked hearin' my fiddle playin' two nights before around a campfire. He was a lad from Jackson, who remembered every tune and was askin' me if I knew the 'Turkey In The Straw,' when a sniper ball took him in the neck. It was fired from *God knows* how far away, and the poor boy clutched his throat and fell into the fire. Wretched lad—he couldn't have been more than seventeen and had never gotten to do anythin' but follow a mule all of his life—his only fun, a fiddle and country dances. I dragged him out of the fire . . . but he was dead by then. All I could think of was my two sons and wonder if they too, would grow up to be soldiers and kill innocents who loved old fiddle tunes.

"I determined that very moment I would go home, even if I had to desert as soon as we held the way to Chattanooga. —The next mornin', here came Hooker in a heavy fog, with a force that outnumbered us three to one."

Hiram's voice had been dry and matter of fact, but I could now hear him strain. "The firin' had been hellacious and I heard an officer shout and tell us to leave the rifle pit we were holdin' and fall back, when this boy appeared in front of me out of the fog cloud. He was but a schoolboy, so young lookin' and scared to death, more afraid than even I. He had black hair, it was long and wet with sweat and fog, and I dream about that face some-times—it was a child's face with a look of death on it. He had his lower lip caught up between his teeth as if he couldn't make up his mind what he had to do. In an eyewink, I had my musket on him, but when I saw him over the sights, I couldn't pull the trigger. He looked like someone prayerful, like just a lost boy who has come upon a bear in a cave. I held my fire, and I reckon he shot me."

HIRAM'S VOICE WAS rising and falling as if he were relating the tale of an adventure that had happened to someone else. While the fire crackled, Lacey held his unseen hand. My mind took me back eighty-eight years to that Battle Above the Clouds,

149

which I had read about a long time ago. Hiram was the man who should have survived his meeting with the enemy, but he was a man who in conscience couldn't pull the trigger against a boy. *I thought, my God, was this how ghosts were created—through the injustice of things?*

We were silent; our old house groaned under the weight of snow, while hickory logs hissed and spat.

Lacey whispered, "Hiram stay with us. You're welcome here if this is where you belong."

"Perhaps I can stay now," Hiram sighed. "It seems to me that somehow I am drawn here for some purpose. I will try to stay if I won't discom-fit you too much."

We assured the old man that he would be no inconvenience at all.

"Where have you been, Hiram?" I asked. "Can you remember where you go when you're not here with us?"

"I'm not sure," said the ghost sadly. "I just get glimpses of things. It's like walkin' down a long road by a river, where you can stop if you like, sit under a tree, and if you wish, walk back the way you came and see the things you passed before. The river is always there, but until you young folks came here, I didn't walk back much. I just sort of wandered on down the stream, lookin' for my Bessie, I reckon."

Hiram set his cup down on the hearth. "Great God, Bessie's piano," he said softly.

Lacey and I sat motionless while the rocking chair gave a spasmodic tilt, and the pipe went off toward the old square grand piano in the shadows.

We watched as the lid rose and the bench slid away from the piano, over the polished floor. A marvelous thing happened—with one finger, Hiram began to pick out the melody of an old song—"Believe Me If All Those Endearing Young Charms." My mother used to sing the words to my sister and me, and Hiram knew the tune.

Gradually there came big rolling chords filling out the tune. It touched me to the quick. I knew from what depths of time it came, and what tender memories it must have had for our old visitor.

Magically, as Hiram played the chords, he became visible. Out of the darkness, there began to materialize a shape. Lacey clutched my hand excitedly. Beginning as a smoky outline, Hiram's form began to show itself; first as a ragged shimmering mist like dust motes gathering, then as a two-dimensional figure like a photographic negative turning into a tinted hologram, and suddenly he became three-dimensional and almost lifelike. I knew that Hiram couldn't really be there except in our minds.

It is very difficult to describe the unexplainable, but sitting on the piano bench was an old man dressed in a gray long-sleeved shirt and what looked like work pants with reddish suspenders that crossed over his back. His hair was long and white, and his beard tumbled in a cascade of curls over his breast. I remember with perfect clarity, he had a fine memorable face. He had a big nose that Lacey had described, great bushy, inquiring eyebrows and bright China-blue eyes that, despite the good-natured crinkles around them, showed an infinite sadness. On the keyboard, his hands were long and supple. If he had been an actual living person, I'd have placed him at around sixty. I remember wondering, *why would a ghost age? If Hiram had died at the age of thirty-five, it seems to me he should have been frozen in time at that age.*

Lacey, being matter-of-fact, said, "Hiram, we can *see* you now."

As he played the final notes on the keyboard, he turned his head towards her and asked absurdly, "Am I decently dressed?"

Lacey giggled. It was simply wonderful to see the author of that voice.

"You're fine, Hiram," I said. "Play some more."

The most remarkable thing about Hiram's appearance was, although we could see him clearly, there was translucence about his body that allowed us to also see the piano keys right through his middle and the wall behind him.

"That was Bessie's favorite song," he said smiling, "and she could sing, too. Every evenin' after supper, she would go to this old piano for a while and sing and play. I would sit near her and play the harmonies on my fiddle. The colored folks loved to hear us too, and they'd sit on the steps of the porch to listen."

I asked just to keep him thinking positive, "Whatever happened to your fiddle?"

To my dismay, he disappeared as he stood up.

His answer surprised us both.

"*Why* I suppose it is still in the bed, unless someone has rifled it," he said stunned. "I hadn't thought to look without thinkin' of Bessie to play for."

"*In the bed?*" said Lacey and I at the same time. We looked at each other in confusion.

152

Chapter Twelve

NE OF THE FIRST MAJOR CHORES I'D done the day after we moved into the house was move the feather tick and two side by side old mattresses and lay them on the balcony to air out. As I hefted them off the bed I noticed a dozen old hickory slats, most of which had been probably replaced by the Spencers. I remember Lacey and I looking the bed over carefully, admiring the way it was built, so I couldn't imagine there was a fiddle hidden in it.

Energized with his memory of the violin, Hiram said, "If you please, Mr. Clark, come up with me and we'll look. Mistress Clark should not climb the stairs again." He pronounced the last word "*stay-uz*" and Lacey grinned.

"Hiram! Forget that," she said. "I go up '*stay-uz*' every day to sweep and dust; it keeps me limber. If I've missed an entire fiddle, I want to see how."

I fetched an electric lantern and turning on the hall light,

Lacey and I went ahead of Hiram, so we wouldn't step on invisible heels.

"It will take two of us," Hiram said. "Bessie and I made this hidin' place ourselves in case our home was plundered by the Yankees. Even they wouldn't try to carry off somethin' this size."

Standing at the side of the bed and following his instructions, I grasped the big right hand head post by the lowest spindle with both hands, and I held it while Hiram apparently twisted the brass globe on top.

"Now turn it to the right," said Hiram.

To my amazement, the post revolved two inches in my hands on some invisible seam.

"Now lift upward!" said Hiram.

The entire spindle, along with a big flare of the huge keg-shaped post below it, came free. It took both of us to set it on the floor beside the bed.

"Ahhh," sighed the ghost.

From a smoothly padded pocket hollowed out of the post, the bottom of a violin case appeared. Lacey and I watched the case float through the air and then place itself on the mattress. Hiram opened the case, revealing a dark, gleaming body of the most beautiful violin I had ever seen. I heard Lacey's breath catch.

From a velvet niche in the inner lid, Hiram took out the bow, followed by the violin, which rose from its case.

"Ma'am, would you be so kind as to close the case for me?" Hiram requested.

As it floated in the air, the old violin was remarkably free of dust; its dark maple sides shone richly. "Thank you humbly Lord," said Hiram, "for leavin' me this much to love."

"Bring it downstairs," said Lacey. "That fiddle ought to be seen by candles and firelight. I feel ridiculous seeing it with this lantern."

The fiddle laid itself on the bed and Hiram and I put the post back, reversing the moves. Then, Lacey carrying the case under one arm, led the way downstairs while the fiddle and bow floated behind us. I was feeling a bit light headed from the mystifying events that had just taken place.

"THE STRINGS ARE useless," said Hiram gloomily. "I'm afraid to touch them after so long."

"Hiram, don't worry about it," Lacey told him. "The Ozarks abounds in fiddlers, and the town of Rolla has a music store. We'll find you some."

Hiram held the old violin and turned it sideways; firelight gleamed warmly on its curves.

"Was this the one you took to war?" I asked softly but somehow knew better.

"*Oh my, no!*" exclaimed the ghost. "I had several, like most fiddlers. Some like this one, soundin' better with classics or waltzes, and some that were brighter for reels and jigs, and some smoother for ballads. My eldest son Harlin's was of the latter sort, kind to a voice it accompanied and rich in tone. I made little Jacob's first fiddle to accommodate his size and bought others to suit him. The one I took in my pack to war was of my own makin', hardy maple and spruce and strongly made to withstand weather and travel. I played it around many a rainy tent and

155

camp fire."

Lacey's eyes had never left the old violin. She asked if she could hold and examine it. Hiram extended it into her hands.

Holding it up to the lamp by her chair, Lacey looked through an f-hole at the violin label and exclaimed, "Good God, Hiram! This is a Guarnerius from 1730! Where in the world did you find it?"

"I didn't," said Hiram pleased. "It was a gift from my father Ezekiel, who had received it from his father, old Cyrus Spring-field, who fought the British at Concord. He was a violinist—but my father and I were all around fiddlers. Granpa Cyrus said it was an old violin when he acquired it."

Lacey handed the violin back with care and reverence. "I saw one played in a symphony orchestra," she said almost shyly, "and once, I saw a Stradivarius in a museum, but I never thought I'd actually touch a real Guarnerius. It's sort of like touching you Hiram—hard to believe."

The ghost chuckled. "I am just so happy that unlike me, this glad creature survived the war, as it has survived others. Wars usually take the best we have, like the war that destroyed the library at Alexandria. Better a million warrin' idiots die, than one magnificent creation for mankind like that library, or even this small violin, made to bring joy and beauty to humans."

There was a moment's silence while Hiram turned the fiddle in his unseen hands. "Whoever won that war?" he asked mildly. "I've a great curiosity now that I remember my part in it. Was it all for naught in the end?"

I explained as best I could how the Civil War had turned out, wishing desperately I had paid more attention to details when taking my eighth grade history class through it. I told him that all the slaves were freed, but they, as well as the white Southerners, had a terrible time for many years afterward because of the period called the Reconstruction, which was pretty much a blot on the nation. I also told him about Lincoln's assassination and Lee's final surrender at Appomattox.

Hiram listened closely. When I said Lincoln had died just five days after the surrender, the old man grunted audibly.

"I lost my patience with Abe Lincoln," he said, "for he declared war on his own people, and wars are always unforgivable. But his belief in the Union was true, and he died for it just as we Sessesh died for ours. What a pity for so many to die for a freedom all humans should expect from each other."

What a strange feeling I got from his long statement, as if he had taken Lincoln as personally as a betraying relative.

"Hiram," Lacey asked gently, "why do you suppose you forgot everything for so long? When you came to us, you didn't even remember your wife or yourself or your music for that matter. You were so lost, you couldn't answer anything and now you're remembering the library at Alexandria."

We heard Hiram get up and begin to pace the room; our eyes followed the fiddle and bow he carried.

His voice was strong and clear. "I only know it was none of my doin'. Somethin' beyond my knowledge wiped my mind as clean as a window-light. Not right away though. After I died at the ridge, I went home again—for a spell at least—which I remember more of by the minute. It was the saddest part of this long non-existence I've somehow earned."

Apparently the old ghost was struggling with this memory. His voice broke, and we waited in silence. When he continued, it was painful to hear his effort. "I went—or was sent—back to my family for a while, hopin' that I could help, and thought perhaps Bessie and my sons would someday see me or feel my presence. But I found no one could hear me tryin' to communicate with them, not even through the music I so desperately wanted to pass on to my children—for it had been entrusted to me. I had betrayed that trust by goin' off to war—for whatever cause—and deprived them of their heritage."

Once again, he paused for composure. "I thought perhaps there was a purpose for this strange incarnation I found myself in, and that I might somehow be allowed to insert my thoughts into Jacob's head. He was my youngest and most receptive. He showed his affinity for music before he could talk, mesmerized by the dancin' of my fiddle bow when I would play a tune for him—his tiny hands imitatin' the movement. By the time he was twelve, he knew every tune I had learned and all that I had composed myself and taught him. He was my protégé; I invested my musical hopes in him."

The trembling old voice hesitated as if he was wondering if we would understand what he himself could not. "It was simply dreadful. —I couldn't even reach my Jacob. His brother Harlin was older but understood my death even less. He tried to act strong and do his part, but he hadn't the wisdom to help his brother or comfort his mother, for his mind was always wanderin' off to far places. In a way, he was as absent as I."

He was silent for a long time and when he did begin to speak again, his voice was tremulous with what seemed agony. "I got weaker with time and less able to be in one place. I only know that after a bit, I finally was just whisked off, blown like thistle-down, unaware of the passin' of days or months or even years."

"When did you come back to the bed?" I asked knowing that *why* wasn't a thing he could tell us.

"I have no idea," answered Hiram. "I found myself in it one night, and it was like wakin' up from a long sleep. There were children jumpin' up and down on me or rather—through me— since I had no substance back then. They weren't my children and I backed off to watch, wonderin' perhaps if they were my grandchildren. It was almost as if they were strangers who sensed my presence and were uneasy with it; I felt no kinship. Then, I was whisked away again. I think my hopes that I could someday contact my sons began to fade. I had no memory of my precious violin in its hidin' place—but that must have been what brought me there."

"You didn't know when Bessie died?" I asked as gently as I could. I was curious why the two spirits hadn't joined or at least met in their paths, if ghosts had paths.

Hiram shook his head sadly. "I don't understand about that. I have no idea where I was, or why I wasn't allowed to meet her somehow, somewhere."

"Hiram," I said carefully, "did you ever stop to think that maybe your death was a mistake and hers wasn't? She died in the bed an old lady, and you shouldn't have been killed at all. You must have been on a different wavelength."

"What might a 'wavelength' be?" asked Hiram with a sigh.

It took some describing and I didn't do it very well. Hiram hadn't the slightest knowledge of such terms, but Lacey got up and turned the radio on, then described how it worked—much to his amazement. He understood the telegraph since it had existed during his lifetime, but the idea of transmitting voices and music was beyond his comprehension.

Lacey took over. "Hiram, it's just one of the things since your time you'll love. Radio is an invention that radiates sound waves through air, kind of like pond ripples."

She was describing it better than I could, and I thought she could tell this to my students, too.

"Every sound sender is called a *station*," she continued, "which on a radio receiver is a different *wavelength*—so that senders don't interfere with each other," she explained, "and it might be that you and Bessie were separated in the same way. But, I'm afraid I don't understand a thing about the afterlife. Until we met you, we didn't much believe in one as a matter of fact."

"But these people on your 'radio,'" said Hiram, hopefully, "are they alive? Do the dead sometimes communicate?"

"Well, yes and no," she said carefully. "You can hear the voice of someone who has been dead a long time, but it's recorded— *imprinted electronically on a wire*. The person isn't actually there, just their voice."

"Just as I am not actually here," said Hiram, "at least, not like you two. I'm sort of a 'recorded' person, I suppose."

His simile wasn't that far off and I could see Lacey was pleased he was a quick study.

160

She thought a moment and then said something I thought was as intelligent an explanation as anything else we'd come up with, though it might not mean much to Hiram.

"Suppose Einstein was right," she said turning to me, "and time has no beginning or end—like a Möbius strip—and theoretically, every moment is still as much in existence as it ever was. And, let's suppose Hiram for some reason is making endless swings around that strip, trying to find a place to either get on or get off, but for some reason he doesn't fit into any given time. Perhaps his death was some sort of cosmic error, and he'll just have to wait until the proper time to slip himself or be slipped into someplace."

Hiram said, "I don't recognize the name of the person or the strip you mentioned, but I think I understand the idea of what you are sayin'. I am in a state of limbo."

I was excited with the idea. "Do you suppose his time is getting close, and that's why he's become so much stronger and has discovered his fiddle?"

If it embarrassed Hiram to have the two of us discussing him as if he weren't present, he didn't protest. By now perhaps he was used to it in his other dimension.

"I think that is why I let go before, when I felt things pullin' me away," said Hiram thoughtfully. "I always thought I might go somewhere I belonged. Now it seems to me for some reason this is where I'm goin' to end up anyway."

"Oh, Hiram, stay if you can," begged Lacey. "Maybe the time isn't too far away now."

"Yes—and sit down at the piano, Hiram," I added, "so we

161

can see you again."

He laid the fiddle and bow gently on top of the piano and the bench pulled itself in. He began playing very softly; the notes sounding like a fiddle tune. Suddenly he appeared, looking at us. "What do I look like?" asked the old man amiably. "I did not care before, but now I wonder how I used to look when a young man."

It took a bit of undoing fasteners, but I fetched the big mirror from the bathroom door, and I held it in front of him.

"Drat!" exclaimed Hiram, "my beard is as white as a badger and to my chest. I look like a renegade. And my wild hair! Bessie wouldn't know me if she ever does see me."

"Hiram, I'll cut your hair and trim your beard," said Lacey. "I cut Steve's all the time."

Hiram looked at my hair doubtfully, but his own reflection jarred him. He sat patiently, his hands tinkling with the piano keys, keeping him visible, while Lacey went to get scissors.

I was amused with the idea of Lacey actually cutting his hair. But there she was, coming back into the room, scissors in hand.

She trimmed his hair to his collar and carved his beard into a shape he said he'd worn in life. And, as Lacey worked, moving his head, his hands left the keyboard, yet, his image remained. It was as if her touch alone were enough to keep him visible.

It was fun to observe; I sat holding the mirror, while Lacey's scissors clipped his long locks and watched gray hair disappear like ash. When I felt along the floor, there wasn't anything there.

When she finished, I thought he looked very refined. I said, "Hiram, I have a feeling you had better stay out of sight as much as you can. We have a lot of drop-in company. If you think you can stay visible, we'll tell people you're my Uncle Hiram but showing up, on-again-off-again, isn't a human act in our time."

"Nor in mine," said Hiram. "No, no, my young friends, since I have no control of that, I'll hide from your guests. —If I might have some books to learn of your time and perhaps, be allowed to listen to your radio contraption, when no guests are here. But . . ." and he paused for a second and added a little wistfully, "do you think you can find strings and some bow hair, and perhaps resin, and a tail gut, in this day and age? I need to play my violin."

Lacey chuckled. "Hiram, the one thing that hasn't changed much since your time, is the violin. We even still use gut to fasten the tailpiece. I'll write everything down for Steve to pick up in Rolla after they plow the snow off the creek road. It's only twenty miles from here."

"Twenty miles!" said Hiram. "I couldn't ask Mr. Clark to make a day's trip, and alas I have no money for such a venture."

It was my turn to chuckle. "Hiram, doing anything for you isn't a venture, it's an *adventure*. Teach Lacey a tune on your fiddle, and we're well paid. Once I'm on the highway, I can make the trip in less than an hour. I'll explain the horseless carri . . ."

Hiram interrupted, "Mistress Clark, *do you* play the violin?"

"Not really," she told him cautiously, "but I know a little from music school, and the strings are tuned the same as my mandolin. Actually the cello was my recital instrument."

"The cello!" exclaimed Hiram delightedly. "The choir voice of the strings was how my father described it. We must play together my child! Do you also play, Stephen?"

I told him I didn't but that I loved music, and Lacey taught me to be a very appreciative listener.

We had another drink to celebrate his appearance. Finally seeing his features and experiencing his emotions gave him a new reality for us. Perhaps even more for me, since Lacey, from the moment she met him, had accepted whatever reality he dwelled in or came from.

It was as if Hiram were a real person; he had deep blue penetrating soulful eyes and a wide comfortable mouth with uneven teeth showing through his beard as he talked. He was thin with skin transparently pale, yet he seemed quite agile. His mind was now strong, compared to the one that had triggered the tiny voice we'd first heard in the kitchen.

"Hiram," said Lacey, as she was pouring him another cup of mulled wine, "why is it you can drink but you don't seem to need food?"

"I don't know," replied the old man. "I don't seem to need or hunger for it, and I cannot smell anythin' except for a pleasant sensation I get when you are cookin'. Perhaps if I were to eat somethin' solid, I would never pass through doors or walls."

That was something Lacey and I didn't even want to think about. But what a good and satisfying feeling it was to see Hiram seated on the piano bench, legs crossed, with cup in hand, as at home as he had been anywhere for eighty-eight years. With his new memory he fairly turned on and off like a lamp, telling of his farm, his music, his sons and his Bessie. His kind old face lit up with his memories and only saddened when he talked about the

164

war.

At the beginning, the South had let him farm because the Confederacy needed part of the food he raised. Fortunately, his sons were too young to go to war. But at last, when the fighting approached their home, he had to leave his family and the autumn corn in the field to go and do his part in what was now *his* war. Old Silas, the field-hand musician he had saved from the river, had walked with him to the wagon road and hugged him tearfully. Silas assured "Mista Ben" that the place would be there when he got back, "better'n new." But, Mista Ben never came home.

"I only called you Hiram to give you a name because you didn't have one," said Lacey gently, "would you rather we called you Benjamin?"

"No," said Hiram after a moment, "I'm not Benjamin Springfield anymore, and I like it that you made up a name for me. It was a piece of human kindness and made me believe I could belong somewhere. I'll be Hiram until, or if, I become Benjamin again, and I thank you."

It was the middle of the night and now there was over a foot of snow covering the ground. Lacey, exhausted and not willing to admit it, was like a kid playing with a new toy and I knew better than to try to get her to lie down.

Out of politeness, Hiram said, "It's time for you to rest, Mistress Clark."

We said our goodnights and I held my arm around Lacey as we walked to the bedroom to the sound of Hiram's creaking footsteps up the stairs. I'm sure the ghost had his new memories to ponder, and we had a lot to consider, hoping we were to have a part in his future, if there was such a term for a ghost.

Chapter Thirteen

NKNOWN TO LACEY AND ME, RUMORS about Hiram had been flying ever since Halloween. Carney and Vance Black, too old to enjoy the school party but still young enough to want to pull off some sort of trick, had indeed come by our house Halloween night to put the porch swing up on the rooftop or some such prank, but they had been arrested by the sight of lights winking on and off in the house. Since they knew we were at the schoolhouse, the two of them had sneaked up to the windows to see who was in the house. To their surprise, no one was turning lights off and on. However, what really startled Carney and Vance was the chance sight of Hiram's pipe floating in mid-air, smoking like a "tar kiln" as Carney told his mother. That seed fell on fertile ground, since Virgie Black believed thoroughly in "haints" and wore glass beads to ward off witches. Within a week, the news had penetrated the neighborhood. Lacey and I were clueless.

In the very short time that Hiram was gone after Halloween, the legend, even without fresh evidence, had grown to Ozark proportions; it was thought that blue lights were on upstairs in our house at night and imagined wailing and moaning had been added, heard when the moon was full.

I don't know if Lacey and I were naïve or just too wrapped up in our own lives—our ghost, her pregnancy, and my teaching— to worry about what the neighbors thought. But looking back on it, I realize that we had no conception of the furor we had going in that rural community.

AFTER HIRAM'S RETURN in that first early snow in November, I was so excited about his fiddle that I didn't wait for the snowplow to come the subsequent morning, and I followed a log truck's tracks to the highway. In the Ozarks, snows however deep only last a day or so, but I was impatient even with that and went to Rolla to get strings. Lacey had given me explicit directions, and I came back with a new set of lamb-gut strings, equivalent to the best ones of Hiram's time. The man at the music store assured me they were the finest old-time fiddle strings he had. He said they would "make a catalog fiddle sound like Ol' Yashi Hyfits." I hoped so; twenty-five dollars was a lot of money from our shrinking budget, but Lacey had insisted I get the best strings, rosin, tail gut and hank of horsehair for the bow. It was amply worth it to remember the look on her face when she first saw Hiram's old violin. A look that had reminded me, she was above all, a musical creature who had laid her career aside to take her chances, marry me and have our baby. This had to be an incredible adventure for her. Having a Guarnerius violin in the house, for Lacey, was a little like having Igor Stravinsky come for the weekend to talk music with Tchaikovsky. Her eyes were shining with a whole new world.

It was afternoon by the time I got groceries and slip-slid home over the creek road. I sat recovering from the slimy trip with a glass of wine and watched the invisible Hiram patiently remove one string at a time from the old violin. My mother used to say about Pop's tinkering, "He has the patience of Job," and watching the old violin repair itself, I understood what she meant.

For Lacey's benefit, Hiram talked while he worked, explaining as he removed each tuning peg, wiped and rosined it, about how these ancient violins survived the years. He reset the sound post, secured the new tailpiece and restrung the fiddle. At last, he adjusted the bridge and tightened the strings. Lacey laid her tuning fork beside him.

"These new strings will stretch and alter," he told her, "and I will ask you to re-tune it from time to time, Mistress Clark. I will be a while at re-hairin' this bow."

"Oh Lord, Hiram," Lacey protested. "What if I break something? It's so old."

Hiram chuckled; it was a comforting sound. "Why it was a hundred years older than me when I lived, Madam, but still must be tuned to be played. Rub the strings with your palm as you would your cello and maintain your 'A' with your nail."

I left to put on a pot of ham hock and beans and mix cornbread batter, while Hiram counted and laid out 150 horsehairs he told

169

us was the number to be stretched by the bow. From the kitchen, I could hear Lacey tentatively plunking the strings a little louder as she gained confidence. I tended the stoves and fireplace and "pottered" around longer than I needed, just enjoying the sound of their voices and the sight of the Guarnerius lying on Lacey's potbelly. I had finished taking the cornbread out of the oven when I heard "a-HA!" from Hiram. I stuck my head out the kitchen doorway to watch as the bow, floating in firelight, rubbed on a chunk of amber rosin.

"The fiddle please ma'am," I heard him say, and Lacey held it up with great care.

I forgot all thoughts of food when his bow touched the strings. Hiram became as visual as we'd ever seen him, his cheek against the chin rest, and his eyes squinted intently to capture the sound. As he drew the bow across each string, little chips of sound emerged—each requiring a minor adjustment of frog and tuning pegs. He looked over, smiled at us, and lit into a rollicking "The Girl I Left Behind Me."

Lacey was enchanted and gave a yelp of pure joy hearing the rich notes coming from the splendid violin that had been silent for so many years. I don't know what stunned me most, the dark old fiddle or the skill of the visible Hiram playing it, but what Lacey and I both saw, were tears running freely down his cheeks. That said it all for us; the old ghost had recovered his music and the wonder of it leaped from the strings like spring water.

It was nine o'clock in the evening before either of us ate a bite. Lacey at Hiram's urging, got out her guitar and accompanied him on tunes she knew. His joy of playing with her made his eyes sparkle and his hands dance. Later, she had me unearth her cello from upstairs, and she added rich harmonics to "Elizabeth's Waltz," which was so touching that the three of us sat silent a minute when it ended.

"If that won't bring Bessie to me," Hiram said quietly, "we aren't intended to meet again. It was the gift we gave to each other that has outlasted all others. But if we aren't so intended, why am I here?"

It was the question Lacey and I took to bed with us that night, listening to Hiram play upstairs by candle light. Lacey told me the names of some of the tunes she recognized: "Mississippi Sawyer," "Grey Eagle" and "Wagoner." She said the baby kept womb-time to the sprightly tunes and I half believed her. An unborn child while it grew its soul could do worse than get its musical inspiration from a fiddler ghost.

MEANWHILE, IN A few short days, Indian Glade grew its rumors and delved into its superstition bank. I wondered why we had so many visitors, but a future baby was so important, I just attributed it to custom and tried to remember to put the alcohol out of sight before visitors came. I'd also bought a pipe for myself—to blend with Hiram's aromatic tobacco scent that filled the house.

Hiram didn't help despite his very best intentions. For a while, he was surreptitious and careful, but he was not of this world, not used to people's habit of driving up without "hallooing the house," as the Trolls called it. His constant reading or recollecting of old fiddle tunes made him sometimes oblivious to our

171

world downstairs. His mind was so busy with recovering eighty-eight missing years, he would forget and make himself heard or felt at awkward times. Lacey and I did our best to cover up these accidents, but it wasn't easy.

One time, we warned the old man that the Farleys might stop by, and he put the fiddle away in a closet upstairs and began reading a Civil War history. Forgetting the Farleys had arrived, he came downstairs, book and pipe in hand, to argue what he considered inaccurate reporting. Luckily, our visitors had their backs to the stairway and didn't see the book and pipe descending the stairs, but they certainly caught Lacey's horrified gaze. With fluttering hands she motioned to warn the ghost that company had come. Lacey, in an adrenalin rush, pretended she had seen a spider on a chair and sprang to brush it off and step on it.

If all of the pack rats we reported—to explain our absent-minded ghost's creaking and thumping—had been living in the house, we would have had to move or buy a terrier. Lacey and I became proficient improvisational liars out of necessity, with no idea we were already wading through rumor.

One time, Lacey and I were having coffee with the three Summers; Myrtle was there ostensibly to find out why I thought the school needed electricity. While I was attempting to explain the importance of using visual aids through free films from the university, we heard a loud thump over our heads. Hiram, who had turned the bed into a library, knocked *Webster's Unabridged Dictionary* off the end of it—a book that weighed a good eight pounds.

Lacey was lightning quick. "Steve, I knew I piled those books too high. I'm afraid one has fallen off the bed."

The three Summers exchanged glances in what I could only interpret as a meaningful way. I hastily lit my pipe to account for the blue clouds of aromatic smoke that came wafting from upstairs and explained that Lacey and I had been going through our boxes of books up there.

Myrtle Summers decided to hold one of her polite but firm investigations. "Soames'es," she said, using a tidy Ozark expression which includes the whole family, "was up to see us a'Friday, and they said that you'ns was bothered with pack rats. Sonny, he knows how to trap 'em out fer you."

"You betch'ee," said Sonny grinning, "you just let me find out where they're a'gittin' in at, and I'll show ye how to get shed of them pack rats in a week's time. Soames said they was a'livin' upstairs."

"Oh, I have traps set," I said hurriedly, "it just takes time to find all their runways."

"Sonny, maybe you ought to look upstairs," commented Myrtle, "and see if Mr. Clark has the holes stoppered good."

"Oh, don't worry about the upstairs," I said, "the main problem with pack rats is the back porch." I had a mental picture of Hiram lying on the bed, smoking his pipe and reading *James Randall's Civil War and Reconstruction*—or whatever.

I was telling the truth about the pack rats. Whatever effect Hiram might have on his surroundings, neither mice nor pack rats were impressed with him, and we had as many as ever. I tried diligently to steer Sonny toward the back porch, but he was sly.

"Most giner'ly," he told me, "they come up through the walls.

Let me just make a check up under the eaves."

Before I could head him off, he was stomping up the stairs. Using whatever quickness of thought I had back in those days, I yelled, "I just sprayed poison up there Sonny, to kill wasps. One breath of that could make you sick. Hold your breath now."

It worked. Hiram would have hidden by this time, but Sonny it seemed was deathly afraid of unknown chemistry and reversed direction. Lacey looked at me gratefully.

"Well, I'll just wait 'til that pizen has wore off," he said with a sheepish look at his mother, "that stuff will eat yer brains out."

Myrtle's face showed disappointment.

After the Summers left, I had a talk with Hiram and Lacey. It was definitely time to head off trouble before the next batch arrived. Lacey suggested a thick rug to muffle Hiram's noises and footsteps. Hiram suggested a hidden string tied to his sleighbells, which could be pulled from downstairs when company arrived. I suggested that visitors be allowed to satisfy their curiosity by prearranged trips upstairs where they would find nothing but a smoothly made bed and some stored books. We decided to adopt all three plans.

WHO ACTUALLY SHOWED up next, however, were the Trolls. Clive and Travis T. walked into the yard and as was their style, yelled at the house until I came to the door.

"Howdy, Teacher," said Clive. "I thought I just seen you upstairs. You'ns got company?"

I hurriedly explained that I had just come from upstairs. Clive and Travis T. exchanged perplexed looks. From out in the yard

174

they had apparently seen Hiram's pipe and book in a haze of tobacco smoke, which gave his form a faint outline. At the same time that I had opened the door, Hiram had opened a balcony door in time to hear the Trolls shout. I cursed the luck but covered myself by changing the subject.

"What brings you by afoot?" I asked.

"Well, goddamit-to-hell," said Clive, "I had a accident with the son-of-a-beetch peekup." Whereupon followed one of their ghastly but funny stories.

It seems that while Travis T. was feeding the "peegs," Clive decided to start the truck after getting a roll of wire from their "barn." The ignition problem being what it was, Clive wired things together but had to crawl into the open hood to short out the solenoid, as per custom. The old wreck of an engine started instantly, of course, but Clive, having been a "leetle drunk" the night before, had left the truck in gear and off it went up the hill with Clive in its mouth.

"I thought about bailin' out," said Clive, "but I'us skeered I'd cut my foot off in the fan." As I watched his crawdad-gestures, I could understand why the Troll didn't want to lose any more parts.

Having decided to ride it out but with no way of knowing which course the truck would take, Clive hung on hoping their wreck would head for something soft, like a wire fence or some lilac bushes. But the truck, left to its own devices, picked a walnut tree a foot thick, hitting a little off center of the radiator (the bumper having fallen off the week before). The truck spit Clive out "like a sack of feed," as he put it and rolled him into some gooseberry bushes, then it emptied the contents of its split radiator on the ground, belched and died. Clive was covered with scratches; Travis T. remarked that his father "looked like he'd been tryin' to chase a fart through a kag of nails."

It was a good description.

I took the two Trolls to town, and at the junkyard they finally found a radiator that would fit. Clive was exceedingly jovial about the whole thing, especially after they'd stopped and cashed his disability check and bought a case of beer. By the time I had delivered my passengers with their load (and believe me, they were loaded), it was past lunchtime, and I was pretty aggravated with them, although I wouldn't have missed the episode for anything.

At the door, Beulah Lou-Lou was waiting for her family with a beer bottle in hand. I noticed she was holding herself stiffly upright as if lashed to a poker. When she greeted me, she turned her whole body along with her head, like a person in a cast. When I inquired if there was something wrong, she said she and Clive had gotten a trifle drunk the night before and in their tiny kitchen had attempted to dance to music from Travis T.'s mouthharp. "Clive," she said, "dashed me up agin' the warshin' machine and like to ru'rnt my back, and Clive says now I'm trussed up like a goddam turkey" She said she was treating her injury with whiskey—the sovereign remedy for all Troll ills—"follered with a beer rench," which meant a swallow to rinse it down.

THE TROLLS DURING that time did me a lot of good despite the inconvenience of being their nearest neighbors. It was pos-

176

sible to keep some sense of proportion about our other neighbors' lives when I glimpsed into the void the Trolls used for a life. They could read no books, had no interests to occupy them, no place to go but town, and they didn't know anything about food, which for most people is one dependable pleasure whatever their lifestyle. Papa Troll had told me that the one gourmet treat of his experience was a "pot of turnips with a hawk flung in there." It was only later I realized he was talking about a hock as in ham hock, which took the romance out of even that image. The Trolls, more than anyone else, made me feel very much a rich man in our little house by Blessing Creek.

Chapter Fourteen

URING THAT TIME, MY OLD PLYMOUTH, which had done such long and dutiful service, finally got too old to get me to school. I traded it for an army surplus Jeep; it was a wonderful little tractor of a vehicle that would go nearly anywhere. The kids loved it and walked to our house to get a ride to school. They piled on any horizontal surface inside or out, hanging onto anything available for the bumpy ride to the schoolhouse. The bigger boys rode on the front fenders with their shotguns and killed squirrels, when they could hit them, which was most of the time. We skinned the squirrels at first recess and they arrived, fried, in lunchboxes the next day. I didn't worry about allowing them to bring their guns to school, because from the school board standpoint, it was an accepted custom at Indian Glade.

IT WAS AT a reading of *A Christmas Carol* for the school play that the subject of Hiram was brought up, however obliquely,

178

and I was startled to realize that our secret was definitely out.

We were going to do a condensed version of Dickens' story and several parts were up for grabs. Penny McClellan and Irene Farley had both set their sights on the Mrs. Cratchit character, and there was a Mexican standoff going for the Scrooge part between Ruby McClellan and Oran Cartwright, each of whom saw Ebenezer as the plum part since they'd get to wear side-whiskers and powdered hair. Nobody wanted the Tiny Tim part, which I had to assign to Cissie Smith, who wanted to be a boy anyway, and the promise of using a real crutch was too much for her to resist. As I remember, I lured Buck Smith into the part of Scrooge's nephew with the promise of a top hat and a gold-headed cane to use in his role. I managed to get most of the Cratchit family organized; their lines were nominal and their ages pretty much left to the reader's imagination. Cleavis Farley made a good Bob Cratchit, and Joey Farley and T.J. Terrill were going to play the charity fund seekers because both admired the shortness of their lines.

That left a few odd characters such as the Ghost of Christmas Present to be filled in with the losers in the main contests and by my small supply of understudies. Obviously, all of them had to have some sort of walk-on part, even though it meant that I had to pad the Cratchit family to a point that would have bankrupted the original Bob.

Having explained the function of the ghost in the play, I awaited volunteers. Instead, I got questions. Betty McClellan raised her hand and asked the first. "Mr. Clark, do you believe in ghosts?" she asked in her small voice, and all of a sudden, I realized that the attention of the entire school was riveted on my answer.

The room was as quiet as an old abandoned church while they waited, and then I knew—because my children were never completely quiet—in that brief moment of silence, I made up my mind irrevocably concerning both Hiram and my kids. For whatever practical purposes, it made no sense to deny Hiram's existence or to lie to my students. The truth had to start somewhere and the schoolroom was a good place to begin.

"Yes I do," I admitted.

Not even raising her hand, Carolyn Smith demanded, "Have you ever seen one?"

"I am sure I have," I replied carefully, "but I'm *not* sure you would. You have to remember that seeing and believing isn't always the same thing. Lots of people see what they want to see— like you do when you read a book and you think you know what the people in the book look like."

Then the questions so long in coming began to come at me from every grade, polite but curious, and I was on my own. They were in a way the same questions that children ask about sex— not seeking complicated in-depth information but just enough answers to form their own opinions.

"What color is a ghost?"

"Do ghosts have hair?"

"Why would a person be a ghost instead of being in heaven?"

Now if there is one thing you learn as a teacher, it is to field questions judiciously, avoiding the fancy footwork that kids recognize from years of coping with adult word-games. Kids know adults seldom have all the answers, and they're quick to see flaws in reasoning, cover-ups and the bland wordy euphemisms with which we try to explain the unexplainable.

As best I could, picking my way as carefully as a man in a minefield, I tried to answer their questions. Ghosts, I told them, could be apparitions that only one person could see and there-fore, could only be described from that person's viewpoint, in which case a ghost could be any color, hairy or hairless, man or woman, young or old. I pointed out that no one I knew—except for one other person—had ever seen a ghost and that my seeing one was strictly a personal experience and hardly the sort of evi-dence you taught as fact.

My answer made the next question inevitable: "Has Mistress Clark also seen a ghost?"

Bravely casting Lacey's fate in with my own, I admitted that she had. That put the seal on it because most of the kids knew Lacey very well by this time, and regardless of what they thought of me, they had to look at a declaration from Lacey in a different light. With the children, Lacey was always gentle and interested and engagingly straightforward, and an answer from her was gen-erally treated as fact. Actually, I didn't have to go into the nature of ghosts very much after that. The kids were satisfied with my answers, and they didn't ask any more questions. I did tell them that since ghosts were pretty much in the eye of the beholder, not to make any judgmental leaps, which could get them in a lot of trouble with people who didn't believe in that sort of thing.

There was one benefit to my confession; the Ghost of Christ-mas Present was eagerly sought after by Betty McClellan. There

181

was another benefit, although I wasn't to know it until later, and that was that the children believed me, and I was to be very glad one day that I had earned their belief.

WHEN I GOT home, Lacey was in the kitchen and said she had another indication for me that Hiram was being regarded as more than a rumor. She said that Oran Cartwright senior had come by that morning with stove wood and questions regarding something Soames Black had noticed.

The morning after that deep snow when Hiram came home, it seemed that Soames Black had uncovered a mystery when he came up the creek road with a tractor and blade to clear the neighbors' driveways. Walking up to the house, Soames noticed tracks nearly buried in the snow. Since the tracks started near the driveway, he'd thought I must have walked out toward the road and then turned back, but on the porch, there was only one set of tracks pointing inward, which came from nowhere. Being an old trapper, Soames had thought this odd enough to try to puzzle out. Added to his other suspicions, this was real fodder for speculation.

I recalled when Soames had been here. "I remember, Lacey, when he came in that morning, he looked at my galoshes in the hall and then stared at my shoes. He asked me if we had company. Nothing gets by these old trackers."

"Steve, you haven't heard the half of it. I'd left the glasses where we had our drinks on the hearth, and Soames noticed there were three. He doesn't miss much, does he?"

"Nobody does around here, especially when they're looking

for it. Who did he tell about that?"

"Oran Senior, of course," she said emphatically, "after which, it became supper conversation for four or five families. You can bet everybody in the district has a theory about our haunted house and why we live here."

IT SOUNDS A little strange to describe it now so many years later, but the people of Indian Glade School District had a unique way of keeping track of each other. There were no locks on their doors simply because there was no need for them. They were a neighborhood of woodsmen, trackers and farmers, who understood the signs most of us have forgotten to notice.

I met Doyle Pulver at the grocery store one day and he said, "Sorry I missed you at the house yesterday. Hope you didn't need anything."

I was dumbfounded. I had dropped by the Pulver house to see how Sandra was doing with the flu, but no one was home, and I hadn't left any homework. No one had come by while I was there, and I couldn't figure out how he could have known I had stopped.

"Why, your tracks," he had said surprised in answer to my query. "I seen your tire tracks in the mud at the end of the driveway."

In time, I was destined to get used to that kind of observation and logic, but it had never occurred to me to look for tracks in my own driveway—so I supposed no one else did. If there was any difference in tire tracks, it hadn't come to my attention.

It was no wonder that nothing had ever gotten stolen in that neighborhood, as well as everyone knew his neighbor's "sign," much less that of a stranger. They knew what brand of cigarettes everybody smoked, who chewed Beech Nut tobacco, who shot a sixteen-gauge shotgun, who carried book matches from Matty's Grill in town, and so on. They could turn a footprint in a field into a hunting story and tell from a hound's track what it had been hunting and with whom. It was a whole new world for me, a Sherlock Holmes world where facts inferred from evidence are a matter of daily life.

Once I became used to the ways of the Indian Glade folks, I began to adapt them to my own life and have since wondered smugly why so many people never notice the obvious. In that winter of 1951, however, I knew less than anyone did and had a lot to learn. I had actually assumed I could keep our ghost a secret from everybody, just by not saying anything about him.

I TOLD LACEY about the question and answer session I had with the children. With what she had just told me, it had added up to quite a jolt.

"Steve," she said, sitting down across from me with her coffee cup, "I think we had better tell the neighbors something. This is getting out of hand."

We heard Hiram come creaking down stairs. He knocked timidly at the post in the entryway. "May I join you?" he asked politely.

I said, "I wish you would. Three heads are better than two.

Lacey thinks we ought to tell people you're here and let them work it out, since apparently most of them know about you already."

Hiram's familiar print settled into the chair beside me. "Well, not to contradict Mistress Clark, but I would advise against that course of action. If people are anythin' like what they were in my day, you would be subject to ridicule at the best and persecution at the worst for your trouble. What could you hope to gain?"

"I don't want to gain anything," I told them both, "I just don't want my school children to lose respect for me. I've never lied to them intentionally, and it's too late to start now. You have to admit believing in ghosts is hardly part of grade school curriculum."

"Maybe it ought to be," said Lacey mildly.

Hiram struck a light in midair and lit his hanging pipe. "If a ghost is what I am, you would be teachin' a fact, but I don't think you'd get much credit for it. I seem a great deal more substantial than any ghost I ever heard of. Perhaps I am not a ghost at all."

"But Hiram," Lacey asked, "what else could you be? You're dead, you're invisible, and you live in another dimension part of the time, and if your hanging around this house isn't a haunting, what would you call it?"

"I'm sure I don't know, Mistress Clark," said Hiram easily. "I suppose a ghost and spirit are one and the same. Yet, somehow I feel more like a spirit . . . sort of a misplaced purpose rather than person."

"Well, either way, it's a moot point in view of the problem we're facing," I said. "What Lacey had in mind is admitting to the school board and the parents that we definitely have a ghost—or whatever they want to call it, in our house or at least *we* think we do, which would probably be their opinion anyway. If we told them we had a ghost, at least it would put them on our side, and it would appear that we weren't trying to hide anything."

"Don't you see, Hiram," said Lacey earnestly, "they think that somehow we're in cahoots with you, which of course we are, but we're making it look like a conspiracy against the neighborhood, with all sorts of weird things going on, and they think we're keeping secrets. I believe we should tell them and put the ball in their court."

Our ghost was disconcerted. "What *ball* is that madam, and in what *court?*"

I explained the expression, since he probably had never played tennis.

I thought about Lacey's suggestion somewhat doubtfully and said, "I can see the angry villagers now, with their torches storming the castle."

I was instantly sorry for the metaphor because I thought I had to explain a little about movies to the old man. I had to keep remembering that almost everything we took for granted had been discovered or invented since his time. But fortunately, Hiram didn't question my metaphor.

"I mean all of them will have some plan for exorcizing Hiram," I told Lacey, "and we'll end up with spiritualists and mediums and God knows what variety of preachers trying to put Hiram to rest. And what's worse, I don't think they'd believe us, even if we had him recite his family history and play his fiddle at the

186

same time. They'd think we were trying to put one over on the community with some sort of un-teacher-like parlor tricks."

"I am afraid I've brought all this upon you," said the ghost sadly. "I cannot get used to being among people again, and I cannot remember to hide all of the time. My mind is so full of other matters. I was an indifferent soldier, too, I am afraid. My mind is always elsewhere."

"Never mind about that," said Lacey sympathetically, "you can't help being here. But I really think Steve and I should try to explain you to our neighbors. Tell them something, even if it's only to lead them off on the wrong track."

"Like what?" I asked, knowing that Lacey would make a poorer liar than Hiram made a soldier.

"Well," said Lacey, "what if we simply told everybody that we *thought* we had a haunted house and leave it up to them to figure out if we did or not?"

"What did you tell Oran and Mildred?" I asked.

"I just told them that every old house has some peculiar things about it, and ours was just a little more peculiar than others," she told me.

I thought that seemed sensible, so we decided, finally to let things go on as they were until the next big crisis and not borrow trouble. Hiram promised to remain as secretive as he was able. Lacey and I knew he carried the brunt of responsibility and we felt for the old man. We understood that unlike us, he really had no choices at all.

187

Chapter Fifteen

IRAM WAS BECOMING ACCUSTOMED TO human contact, and we had become as comfortable with him as he was with us. Always collecting concepts for later analysis, Lacey had made a list of things she wanted to ask him, and the ghost, who seemed to enjoy our company and conversation, tried his best to answer her.

Late one evening we were sitting in the living room, surrounded by the amber glow of the fireplace. Lacey was looking at her notes, while invisible Hiram sat across from us in the rocking chair on the other side of the hearth, pipe smoke billowing around him. I was watching his ghostly image while I sat on the hearth stool next to Lacey.

"Hiram did you go to school?" inquired Lacey.

He had a rich voice nowadays, and his gentle Tennessee accent was pleasant to the ear. "Oh, yes indeed, Mistress Clark, I attended the subscription school at the church house in Low

Gap"

"What's a subscription school?" I asked.

"Why, one where the parents of scholars paid a fee to keep a teacher for whatever time they could afford," said Hiram. "He would board with the families who hired him and eke out his livin' with farm work. We had many young men much like me, who would stay the winter with various neighbors and teach the children."

"What sort of things were you taught?" asked Lacey.

After a few moments, he answered. "I learned the same things as most children of my time, at least, farm children. We were taught to read and cipher and identify the states of the union along with their capitals and principal products. I went to the fee-school for seven years, learned to write a good clear hand and parse a sentence, and I was taught the proper use of grammatical principles. I learned enough about animal husbandry to begin farmin' and enough geometry to find the height of a buildin' or a tree."

"What did you read?" I asked curiously.

"Mostly the great writers, I expect you know them, for I have seen their titles in your library—Dickens, and Victor Hugo, Thoreau, and Emerson, Robert Louis Stevenson. We had a teacher in Latin and a singin' schoolmaster. Both of them came only at intervals, since those subjects were considered a luxury. As I remember, our young teachers were paid fifty-cents a day for the school, which was a huge sum in those days. The older ones, who taught penmanship and literature and the social arts, were in more demand and could ask a higher fee."

"What about religion?" Lacey asked.

"My parents were good churchgoers, and I grew up in what was called the Cumberland Methodist Church. We went to church at Low Gap on Sunday for both mornin' and evenin' services. There was always a big dinner, and we visited with my Uncle Buford and Aunt Ellie in the afternoon, for they lived nearby. The church was the only social life we had besides visitin' the neighbors. Bessie started coming to church with me, and we attended Sunday School together.

"Did you join the church?" I asked.

"Everyone did in those days, as soon as you were considered old enough to make the decision. Bessie and I were baptized together in Taney Creek. It was part and parcel of growin' up and we were both pretty young. I remember that I thought the ceremony very impressive."

Lacey said, "But Hiram when you first came to us, I asked you about God, and you didn't remember anything about religion at all. You said you had never met him, and you told us that *redeeming* was a pawn shop term."

"Both of those things were true," said Hiram, puffing away contentedly on his pipe. "I'd lost my memory, my child, not my intellect. I was never religious in my lifetime, I realize now—and perhaps that is why I am in the fix I'm in. I don't know. I always believed in God because it seemed an instinctual belief in everyone I knew. Who could observe the beauty around us and not be awe struck and thankful for a creator? Who could listen to music made by his creatures and not realize that music was the sweetest gift he could give us."

190

I could see our questions had awakened a thought machinery that had been running for eighty-eight years and wondered if we had opened a Pandora's Box. But Hiram, it seemed was just reminiscing.

His next sentence was more wistful than angry. "What foolishness humans do in His name. In my own church, they called the violin 'The Devil's Box' and in others forbade the harmony of human voices singin' to him. Imagine—music, the kindest and sweetest comfort given to our fellow creatures."

I stared at the place where Hiram was supposed to be, awestruck realizing I was listening to heresy from beyond the grave. It was an uncommonly disorienting feeling knowing that dying didn't provide any answers either, at least in Hiram's case.

His voice became placid. "It wasn't until I went off to the war that I really gave the concept of God a great deal of thought. I was a farmer and a fiddler, my business was renewin' life each year in my fields, cowsheds, and sheepfolds, and passin' on what I could of my musical heritage to whoever chose to listen. I never thought myself a philosopher."

Hiram paused to clank his pipe, and I handed him my penknife to clear the dottle. Lacey was looking over my arm at my scribbled notes, a sort of shorthand she was beginning to read better than I could. She nodded to indicate I was getting it all just as Hiram relit his pipe and continued telling us his thoughts.

"I found a great deal to quarrel with in this description of heavenly justice each day on picket duty or at night by the watch fires when I read the Bible that Bessie sent with me. It was too much like men puttin' words in God's mouth, somethin' I would

191

never presume to do. Wrathful vengeance, human sacrifice, jealousy, a need for worshipful obedience and praise, these are all mankind's traits, unthinkable in a creator who could envision a universe as wonderful and a world as workable as the one I lived in. I had always thought of God as nature, which I could understand."

"But Hiram," said Lacey interested, "I don't think nature could be God. I always thought nature was God's careful gift to us, an often-cruel science but a way to make the planet work. But nature can be horrible, random, and destructive, wiping out a species to make another work. Why would God do that? You seem as confused as anybody else."

"Undoubtedly," said Hiram, "but I wasn't long blamin' war on God, my dear lady. Only the nature of man, who apparently will never understand peace, would think of war as God-approved or inspired. I like your thought that he gave us nature to thin the herd, manipulate the elements and impress us mightily, while his goodness lies in minds and hopes and the search for perfection."

The old ghost's voice sounded almost like a chuckle. "You realize that these are the ravings of a nonentity, who most of the time cannot even see his own feet. I appear to be an accident in a world where most things go accordin' to plan. Why on earth would you want to listen to me?"

"Oh, c'mon Hiram," protested Lacey, "we're privileged to listen and besides, you're almost—*well*—fun to listen to when you talk about the time you lived. You're a hell of a lot less dry than history books."

"History books have very little humor," agreed Hiram cheerfully, "like the Bible, which it seems has none at all. I remembered wonderin' when readin' parts of it in camp, why God would give us such an important sense like humor and a dry book with no time for it."

"I get the feeling you're not a churchly ghost, Hiram." I told him while I continued scribbling.

"Not a dab's worth," said the old man, blowing a smoke ring above him. "Think I should be in hell for it—or heaven? What I had when I was alive, I have still and that is respect for a God I don't know. Respect for the unknowable, which accordin' to your questions, you feel I should have some expertise in. Well, I don't. Here I am lately boundin' about the universe like a pea in a whistle—if your theory is correct—and more ignorant of purpose than I was in life. At least life made some sense for me. I grew things and played my fiddle—both pleasant things to do, and I fathered two children—that was pleasant, too. I helped my neighbors, loved Bessie, and my music, and never faltered in my belief that these things were right and good. Never in my life did I strike a man or an animal in anger, and I was even unable to do so, to save my own life. I have been no better and no worse than other men, I suppose, so why should my present state be either reward or punishment?"

I was almost afraid to ask my next question. "Were you a Christian?"

"Young man," answered Hiram with dignity, "I liked the idea of Christ as who wouldn't, but couldn't help but notice that no one past His death ever followed His teachin's. How could they?

193

They went against the practical nature of mankind, and His followers botched things up the moment He died. But as I grew to think while on the battlefield among the dyin', only human bein's could conceive of a God who would allow His son to be butchered like this, to settle the score for human idiocy and greed we're born with. I decided then that if Christ had *lived* for me instead of dyin', I would be a Christian. So much I believed in the goodness of God."

Hiram's voice was sad when he continued. "People were no worse or better for that death than any other, since death doesn't prove anythin' as far as I can see, at least if you would care to use me as evidence. All of the Godly men of earth are dead, from Christ, to Buddha, to Mohammad, to Confucius, and you must read their words in musty rule-ridden tomes written by men whose doubtful translations always demand that you accept their version of truth and no other. I know nothin' of God, apparently, but I do know somethin' about men."

Lacey and I both looked at each other, speechless. When asked an opinion, Hiram was certainly no slouch at speaking his mind. My mind, however, was a mass of confusion. Like Lacey, I had hoped to gain at least a little universal knowledge to answer a few questions in my mind from someone who had seen the other side of death. It was a little horrifying to realize that if Hiram from the spirit world didn't know about God's intentions, human chances of doing it were questionable.

Lacey thought about something she had read in a magazine, one of those back-from-the-dead experiences. "Hiram," she asked carefully, "is it true that dying is like looking down at yourself from a place above?"

"Yes indeed, and so is being kicked in the head by a cow and lyin' in the straw of the cow shed for five minutes with your brains addled. In both cases, which I can vouch for — I can remember, leavin' my body and lookin' at it rather disinterestedly from a distance and wonderin' what this experience was all about. In the latter one, however, it didn't last long. One minute, I was observin' myself all bloody on my back with a mere child of a Union soldier staring at me in horror, and then I was caught up in some monstrous void of what I supposed was sleep—if, I supposed anythin'. It was very like being a dandelion puff caught up by the wind. A blind wind I think, which tried to set me down in places that didn't suit it and then picked me up and set me somewhere else."

"Didn't you feel the passage of time at all?" was my next question.

"I think not, and that's the most confusin' thing. Is what I saw in your mirror what I look like or only what I imagine I should look like and have suggested to you? I feel as if I should be very old."

"But Hiram," said Lacey, "we've seen you too, and you do have white hair and a white beard. Did you *suggest* that to us? If you did, it must have been your idea. Why would a ghost grow older?"

It was a good question and Hiram's answer was so touching, I believed him immediately.

"Well, I saw my dear Bessie growin' older, and I wanted desperately for us not to become anymore separated than we were.

I wanted us to become old together, and I set my mind to it when I was able. Until the last time I visited her before she died, I tried to imagine myself at her age, with the wrinkles of care and the white hair of time, and the wisdom that age is supposed to mellow one with. When she died, I didn't try anymore, and so I suppose I look the same as I did then."

"You keep saying *suggested*," said Lacey. "It makes me wonder if you're a figment of our imagination, or we're a figment of yours." She looked upset and Hiram noted this with alarm and set the rocker upright.

"My dear Mistress Lacey," he sputtered, "you must never doubt that you and your unborn are the ones livin' in reality. It is old Hiram who wanders about in a world of suggestion and dreams, takin' his strength from you young people. My dear child, if I could look like an angel with a harp for you, I would."

Lacey laughed and asked teasingly, "Could you look like a king?"

Bit by bit, line by line, a hologram began to appear immediately in an old leather chair beside the rocking chair. It was as if Hiram were an artist doing a painting in midair and things appeared as he thought to put them in—a flat beret, a gold chain, great puffed sleeves, a doublet fronted with gold embroidery, a great round face with a rim of beard, dark piggish eyes, and a mass of curling hair over a ruffled collar. It was Henry the Eighth or rather a Henry the Eighth of sorts, who wavered and faded in places as Hiram concentrated on others. Nonetheless, the monarch was there for a moment and then suddenly the hologram took life. He smiled and winked at Lacey then saluted her with a

196

fat, many-ringed hand, and instantly he disappeared.

"There, that's the only king I ever saw—from a book, I believe. My, that's hard work," he said with a sigh, which always astounded me that he could actually sound like someone living, breathing, but invisible.

"Hiram, he was wonderful!" declared Lacey. "He was almost real enough to touch."

"I don't think you could have touched him," said Hiram doubtfully, "for unlike me, there was no substance there, only a great concentration on my part. I'm not at all sure how it works, but I've entertained myself many times by creatin' company in this way."

"What else can you do?" asked Lacey, delighted that the conversation had turned away from religion.

"Well," said Hiram, "would you like to see Silas?"

"Sure," we responded.

"Well, I can remember him singin' 'Horse In The Corn.' I'll try that."

In front of the fireplace began to form an old black man of about sixty in rough work clothes. He was sitting on a wooden porch step, surrounded by black children. He had a gentle, good-natured face, and his wooly hair was mostly gray, his hands long and powerful. He was playing a crude handmade banjo and he was singing something the children found funny but we couldn't hear anything. The long-dead Silas raised his yellowish old eyes and grinned at Lacey and me. There were no teeth in his wrinkled face and as his grizzled head bobbed over the chorus, we could almost hear his feet stamping rhythm to the banjo.

It was the most amazing hallucination I had ever seen but not the least bit frightening. I don't know how long the shape was there but when it disappeared, it was very slowly, as if Hiram were holding onto the picture, loath to let old Silas slip away.

"My God," I said quietly, "he was so real! I'd know him again anywhere."

"People I knew are very real to me," explained the ghost with modesty, "unlike the king who I had to sort of put together from memory. There are times in your life when everything stands out clearly as if it is etched on your mind and you never forget that moment. Like this one . . . ."

Without warning, the fireplace suddenly filled with a mist so thick that all we could see was a dark flood of swirling smoke. I was so disoriented, I half rose and grabbed Lacey's arm. She and I were staring at a fog that began to flicker and flare like lightning and out of it walked a young soldier in a Union uniform, rifle at the ready. If the previous holograms had been suggestions of form and color, this one was a three-dimensional nightmare for clarity. I realized in that instant that we were seeing possibly the last thing that Benjamin Springfield had ever seen.

The boy's face was wet with fog and fear. His hands were white as bone, clasped around the wet stock of a Springfield rifle, and the bayonet glittered dully before our faces. I could almost smell him, the figure was so real. I have remembered every detail and still shudder to think of the button missing from his tunic, the cracking leather of his belt and ammunition pouch, the rain-shrunk webbing of his pack-straps against his drenched shirt. He moved toward us, his black-billed cap drawn low over startling blue eyes that looked as frightened as a rabbit's, and his lower lip was caught between his teeth in bloodless determination.

I heard an urgent and pitiful, "Oh" from Lacey, just as the boy's blue eyes widened and the whites showed all around his irises, his gun came in a rush to point toward Benjamin Springfield. I think if Hiram hadn't been so taken with his own thoughts, he never would have exposed Lacey to this apparition.

"*Stop it, Hiram!*" I shouted.

I grasped both of Lacey's hands and held them within my own and the vision disappeared instantly.

"Oh, my dear child," Hiram pleaded, "forgive me if you can. I was thinkin' of the war and wanted to show you the clearest picture of all, little thinkin' what it might do to a gentle lady like you. *My God*, what a thoughtless, heartless thing to show you."

Immediately, I could feel his hands over our own.

"It's all right, Hiram," Lacey said, recovering. "It was just so dreadful. I felt so sorry for that poor kid and then when I realized what he was going to do, I couldn't stand it. The worst thing of all—I think I've seen him before."

"Hiram," I said, still shaking from the emotion of it, "you should be ashamed of yourself. Don't you realize that we're fond of you? How could you let us watch someone shoot you?"

"I am so very sorry, my friends," said Hiram humbly. "I have done the unforgivable. I have spent too long alone and have forgotten the feelin's of people. Imaginin' Silas, I let my mind wander on toward the war and before I could realize what I was doin', I actually let you see that pointless horror, too."

199

I was getting my breath back and my sense of proportion, and what Lacey said about the hologram sank in. "Where could you have seen that boy? In a book?" I asked her. "A school book?"

Lacey didn't answer.

I felt Hiram's hand on my shoulder and only supposed he was looking over it.

"Maybe it wasn't so pointless," he said, sounding a little ponderous, "since birth and death are an endless chain beyond our grasp. Perhaps it's evidence that God is never finished with us, Mistress, and we are works in progress."

We were silent for a moment considering that awesome premise. An ember popped in the fireplace and Lacey flinched.

"I think Lacey might like to see something else to take her mind off your last picture," I said.

"Would you like to see Bessie?" Hiram asked softly. "Bessie is a very pleasant picture for me and perhaps I can atone for my thoughtlessness."

"I'd love to see Bessie," said Lacey quietly, "if it wouldn't be too painful for you."

"Oh my, no!" said Hiram. "She's a great comfort to me."

The ghost anxious to make amends, regained some of his enthusiasm. "Many times at night, when you are asleep, upstairs I re-create Bessie, watching different times of our lives together. Sometimes I can recall her clearly, and sometimes I have difficulty remembering her face and have to work at her for hours at a time in order to get her right."

Of course, although I had no way of knowing it then, it is easy to see why the neighbors back in that long-ago winter were seeing blue lights and other ghostly phenomena. Hiram was showing his own home movies upstairs.

Hiram set the pipe on the hearth, and I could feel the intensity of his concentration in my own head. What followed was as wonderful as the previous image had been dreadful. He was showing us the best he had to give, to make up for the worst.

The room became hazy and the fireplace transformed into one that must have been from Hiram's time. In the firebox were hanging pots of iron, and steam came in little puffs from beneath a jiggling pot lid. To the right, a bread oven lined with brick. The hearth was stacked with split wood and to the left, an ash bucket, a fire shovel, and tongs. Now in a corner of what had been our living room was a high kitchen safe of oak that held plates and serving dishes of blue stoneware. I saw above the fireboard, a long Kentucky rifle on pegs and lying beneath it, a fan of wild turkey feathers twisted into a hearth broom.

I got the feeling Hiram was constructing a painting as complete and subtle as a Vermeer. The image was in daylight and the sunlight crept through a winter window to make a square on an old stone floor, the light as soft and tangible as the people it shone upon. There in a rocking chair in the exact same spot where Hiram had been sitting, he imbued an image of Bessie nursing a baby.

She was a jewel of time and memory; we saw her through Hiram's eyes as she must have been long ago when his mind had captured her in a moment so intimate that it astounded me. She had long dark hair, which fell in soft waves about her pale, thoughtful face. She had a lovely profile with small nose, soft mouth, and down-swept lashes. She was concentrated on the child at her breast and looked to be about twenty, certainly at the height of her beauty despite work-reddened hands and a smudge on her cheek from tending the fire. She wore a light blue wrapper and around her shoulders was a knitted shawl that also enclosed the baby in a fold of deeper blue.

Lacey, sitting close beside me, was entranced with Bessie and the baby, a tiny, rose-cheeked mite of life whose little hand spread as far as it could reach to press the milk out of its mother's breast.

We were caught in Hiram's magic. It seemed so natural when the woman looked up to greet her husband coming in on this homey tableau. She showed us her deep blue eyes and smiled. This was the picture that our lonely old ghost had kept of his wife and now shared with us.

"She's beautiful," breathed Lacey, hardly daring to speak.

"Indeed she was, inside and out," Hiram said gently, his voice coming from behind us. "A kinder or more brighter-spirited lady never lived, I think. The baby was my first son, Harlin."

The figures began to fade and Hiram said, "She was brave, too, and always did what was best for the children. If she had married again, I would have understood I think and given her up gladly for her sake. But she chose to raise the boys alone—and became the source of strength for an entire generation of war-shattered families, colored and white."

Then the image began to gather again in the way it had before—the fireplace and ancient kitchen assembling was the same, but subtly different in the furnishing, and the light had shifted. On the mantle was a tintype of Hiram in his gray Confeder-

202

ate uniform. We knew him instantly, although his beard and moustache were short and dark.

Then we saw the children as Hiram let them form—his two teenage boys, gangly, and serious looking, with high cheekbones, and like their mother, their hair was black. They sat at a long table—a workbench in front of the fireplace, and while the youngest played careful notes on a fiddle, the bigger boy was writing with a quill pen on a sheet of paper, his hair hanging over his work. As we watched, the writer swept a lock out of his eyes with his sleeve, a gesture so real that I could scarcely believe the two weren't alive. The writer looked about fifteen, the fiddler maybe twelve.

Hiram's voice whispered, "Those are my boys, Harlin the oldest and Jacob. They are tryin' to preserve a tune of mine by transcribin' it to paper."

Then Bessie stepped into the picture and my heart nearly stopped at the sight of her. She was still lovely, but the heartbreak of years showed in every angle of her posture and in the lines of her face. Her hair was streaked becomingly gray but her eyes were as blue as ever. There was an aura of strength and patience about her and for a moment, I couldn't place the sinking feeling I had upon seeing her. Then I realized what life had done to her. From a soft and sensitive young woman whose face seemed to float lightly, graceful as a waltz, she had been forged into a strong and creative creature designed by nature to protect and nurture her young. In our last view her brows were gentle and questioning but now had become separated by fine lines of concentration, as if she had knitted them many times over problems only she could solve. There were lines around her mouth that time had furnished and deep crow's feet framed her stunning eyes, but she was every inch an incredible woman and time hadn't defeated her—at least as yet.

Lacey and I watched in silence; Bessie laughed and rumpled Jacob's hair in some unheard joke.

The image faded to the sound of crackling wood in our fireplace.

"Thank you, Hiram," whispered Lacey with tearful eyes, "for letting us see that. It must be very hard for you sometimes to be able to recall things so clearly."

Hiram sighed softly, "Oh no, Mistress Lacey, like music, it's God's gift and I'm thankful for it, the bitter with the sweet. But that last view of my children is almost too painful in a way that isn't clear to me yet. My reason tells me they must be long dead, but I have a sense of desolation about them, which I don't feel recallin' Bessie."

I couldn't make a meaningful comment, so I tried to take Hiram's mind in another direction. "I know it sounds stupid to ask an unanswerable question, but do you have any idea how you can make these images visible to us?"

"I don't know," admitted Hiram, "but I think it must have somethin' to do with my own determination to pass what I know on to you and Mistress Lacey. It is much simpler to create these scenes for you than it is to appear myself because you seem to see what I see. Since I have only lately seen myself, it's a little harder to concentrate on my own image, which I remembered very little of."

"Why just Lacey and me? Wouldn't other people be able to see these images you showed us?"

"I think it would depend a great deal on what they want to see," replied Hiram thoughtfully. "You must remember most people have no desire to see me—far from it! They must deny any evidence I exist, for then they would have to try to explain it. I do believe it would be far easier to blame my existence on the two of you, than on my own unfortunate state. In the superstitious minds of your neighbors, witchcraft would be more admissible than any amount of truth, and it is certainly more explainable."

"But Hiram," argued Lacey, "Steve and I aren't that much different from these people. Couldn't we at least try to let them see you and realize what you are?"

I pointed out, "What if they *can't see* him? If we announce the Clarks are going to prove to everybody that he exists, we'd become charlatans."

"Maybe we would," Lacey said determinedly, "but that's something we'll just have to find out. Hiram has no place else to go, and we're his only friends. This house is *his* place as much as ours."

"Unfortunately," I added, "it isn't even ours, Lacey. Gib Decker could evict us pretty quick if the neighbors didn't want us here. Most of them trade with him."

There was a short silence; then Lacey's face took on that stubborn look I knew so well.

"Steve," she said, "I've got the answer; let's buy this place from Gib Decker."

205

I was thunderstruck. Lacey, who was even more careful about money than me, was proposing to take on a mortgage in order to protect Hiram's waiting place.

"But Lacey," I said, being realistic, "I could lose my job or at least not be re-hired next year."

Lacey pointed out the obvious, "Wherever you work or teach, we have to *live* someplace," and added, "and we both love this old place and agree that we belong here—besides, Hiram needs us."

"My dear child," said the ghost haltingly, "I was here before you came, and I can survive on nothin'. I wouldn't hear of . . ."

"*Survive!*" exclaimed Lacey. "Why, you didn't even know who you were, dashing in and out of reality like you did, afraid to speak to people and with nobody to help you find yourself. You weren't surviving, Hiram, you were just sitting around this house fluttering like a candle about to go out. Now don't give me arguments, I'm not in the mood *damn-it*, I'm pregnant and have a short fuse."

"But Lacey," I protested, "even if Gib Decker will sell this place, how could we come up with the money?"

"You leave it to me," she said decisively. "When Uncle Bill died, he left me two thousand dollars, and Dad put it in the War Bonds when I was just a kid. It's bound to be more by now— enough for a down payment, anyway."

I had known about the money because Lacey doesn't deal in secrets. But it was her money, in trust for whatever might befall her. Lacey's Dad, although he liked me well enough, had made sure that if our young marriage didn't work out, his only daughter would be protected by money in the bank. I also knew Rabon Donnelly well enough to understand that when his daughter put her foot down, he didn't stand any more chance than Hiram and I. I didn't really have to think about it too long.

The little house was home to us and we had money enough to pay for the upcoming baby. I loved my work and the kids I taught, and I had grown uncommonly fond of our ghost, who sat nervously tapping his pipe against invisible teeth.

"If only," said the old man trembling enough that the pipe stem shook, "I were able to help."

Lacey spoke with determination. "Hiram, you just stay where you are and let us handle this. This is our home and we're going to live here, and you're going to stay here with us as long as you like. I'm going to have a baby, and our baby has to have a home. *Dat's it and dat's dat and dat's all, begorra!*"

Having said it, Lacey put her hand on her hip and gave us an Irish grin, beaming at us both as pleased as if the whole thing was settled.

And that, as she said, was that.

Chapter Sixteen

INETEEN-FIFTY, ACCORDING TO OLD-timers had been the driest year in fifty, and it seemed as if nature had determined to make up for her stinginess during the winter of 1951-'52 with as much saturation as she could fling at the Ozarks. From early November on, it alternately rained, sleeted, and snowed, with an occasional ice storm flung in for the novelty of it.

The schoolchildren of Indian Glade were the most determined scholars I had ever seen, and it's one of the high points of my life that school was the high point of theirs. I hasten to admit that I can take only partial credit for this dedication since most of the parents having had very little schooling themselves, urged their kids to attend every day they felt well enough. Well enough in most cases meant able to walk, and I taught on days when ten out of my sixteen pupils should have been home in bed with sniffles, fevers, and cold symptoms. Once or twice I had to take one of the kids home, spirit still willing but flesh reduced to feverish throwing up at recess.

In these cases, I would put Penny McClellan or Cleavis Farley or another of the older kids in charge until I returned. Faced with the responsibility of sitting at my desk and managing the duties of Mr. Clark, while I was gone, these temporary proctors showed without exception, extraordinary good sense. This was helped along by the fact that if no disturbances (except for the family ones, which were to be expected when big brother or sister was being "bossy") were reported upon my return, the kids got to decide how they wanted to spend the last hour of school. Since this was customarily a spelling bee, word game, or reading-aloud of a favorite story, it usually killed two birds with one "donick" as Soames Black would put it. What they liked to do was usually what I was there to teach them one way or another. It also strengthened my belief that self-discipline is very likely the only discipline that has any lasting qualities.

NOVEMBER 6, 1951

YESTERDAY IT WAS time for Lacey's twice-a-month visit to Doc Brant; I picked her up after school and we drove to his office. He said she was doing great, and I might as well get Santa Claus to deliver the baby since it's getting so close. He has made arrangements at the little Medley Springs hospital, which is a ten-room clinic the doctors around here financed and share.

Lacey insisted we stop at Gib's store and feel him out about buying the house. Gib was impressed with both Lacey's size and earnestness—she now weighs nearly as much as I do. She radiates a glow of Ozark confidence and determination that Doc Brant said, "comes with the package." Gib said he'd have to talk to his wife and kids and the bank, but I can tell he likes the idea of selling the place. He needs to enlarge his store and parking lot, and I watched his eyes light up when Lacey said we were interested.

❖

NOVEMBER 11, ARMISTICE DAY
TONIGHT GIB DECKER called after supper and said he had arrived at a reasonable price for the old place: six thousand dollars for the house (piano and bed thrown in) and forty acres, which includes all the frontage on Blessing Creek that bisects the property. Lacey amazed me by offering five, with two thousand dollars down and a mortgage note to Gib payable in quarterly installments. She sounded so confident; I knew she had talked to Vera and Rabon. Gib said he'd have to think about it, but somehow I know it will work.

It's a good feeling knowing we can own our own house, at least partially, and whatever happens to my teaching job, no one can dispossess us. Since Lacey is so set on this house, we decided to call Pop and ask him to come for Thanksgiving. With Vera and Rabon coming as well, we'll have everybody's opinion and advice, and they can all enjoy seeing Lacey with the next generation aboard.

But where to put Hiram—a cot in the Baby's room maybe? How will I explain that? Pop will of course bring his camper—

you can't get him to sleep anywhere else; he has it so full of Kamping Komfort stuff from his store.

❖

NOVEMBER 15, 1951

MRS. FARLEY IS having a baby shower for Lacey this weekend. She has been through this baby experience seven times and is a wealth of information and enthusiasm. Edith Farley is convinced in her own mind that "babies are half of your life." Although Lacey isn't very sure about that, she finds the fact that Edith has survived seven, very encouraging. I am not invited, this being a woman's ritual, but I'm sure my ears will burn. The way the weather has been, I'm glad we have the Jeep so I can drop her off and pick her up. Maybe Hiram and I can watch one of his "movies" while she's gone.

❖

NOVEMBER 18, 1951

WE CALLED LACEY'S folks and Pop, inviting them for Thanksgiving and everybody is coming. Vera has been anxious to come since August and told Rabon firmly that if he can't get away from his work for a couple of days to see the mother of their first grandchild, she would come on her own. Since Vera would have to learn how to drive his truck, Rabon pretended he was being railroaded, but Lacey knows he's as anxious to see us as Vera is. It's just that Rabon is always hip deep in a half-dozen projects and always feels he can't get away. Pop, of course, loves holidays but has the same problem with the store. He says he is bringing a bigger washing machine for Lacey and a vaporizer for the baby. Knowing Pop, I have a feeling it will take all of us to unload his truck. We're just glad they can all come and pray for some decent weather.

Lacey's baby shower went very well, I guess. All the neighborhood women showed up at the Farley house and brought something for our baby, which by the way, Doc Brant says he thinks will be a boy. I have no idea what he bases this on, but all the women say he's infallible; so they believe Lacey will have a boy too. Telepathy? A talkative nurse? Gossip? According to Lacey, they brought more blue stuff than pink (in the way of what they call Layette pink), I take it, in case we would maybe have twins, one of each. From the bulk of stuff they loaded into our Jeep, a layette is enough to get a kid through grade school. The diapers alone made a formidable pile and by the time the Jeep was loaded with swaddling stuff, snow suits, blankets, wrappers, caps, mittens, coverlets, baby photo books, toys, pacifiers, baby bottles, and crib pads, there was hardly room for Lacey and me. When we got home, I piled everything in the baby's room on a little crib that we'd bought but had never assembled until yesterday. The piled stuff has the effect of making the crib look pregnant, too. Lacey had painted the walls a bright, sunny yellow, and every time I look into the room, I'm hoping it will soon hold a cheerful little kid—boy or girl—who won't mind "haints" anymore than its folks.

NOVEMBER 25 —*Three days after Thanksgiving*
THANKSGIVING WAS A pretty amazing holiday with Lacey's folks coming from Springfield and my pop, Jack, from Hannibal, arriving on the day itself.

Previously, Lacey and I had talked the whole thing over with Hiram, since as our star boarder—sort of—we figured he should have some say about where everybody would sleep. It would look a little odd to put Lacey's folks on a rollaway downstairs, with the big four-poster bed upstairs. Hiram volunteered to give up his sleeping place. According to Hiram, it was all one to him—if he lay down in the baby's room, on the couch in the living room, or a pallet on the floor, as long as he could be someplace in the house. He even offered to stay in the basement since neither damp nor cold have any effect on him. We wouldn't hear of it, assuring him that his presence, even unseen, would be as important to our holiday as having our folks here. Hiram promised not to smoke in company or to play his violin; this last was a necessary precaution since Hiram, absentminded like many old people, has a tendency to live in the past and had already awakened us one night by playing "Dixie" on the fiddle, stamping his foot enthusiastically to the tune.

Rabon and Vera arrived the day before Thanksgiving and they love the house. Rabon is head of his own construction company and like most builders, he had to poke around, peck on walls and study the general soundness of the place with the skepticism all builders seem to have about other people's work.

Vera, wrapped up in her daughter's pregnancy, spent most of the time with Lacey in our warm kitchen discussing diapers, formulas, and names, while Rabon and I thumped around on floor joists and tested support beams for termites. I didn't mind doing it at all, knowing that Hiram was probably keeping just out of reach of us and enjoying himself hugely.

213

Wednesday evening I saw Hiram once at supper but no one else did, thank God. At least, I saw his print settle into the old leather chair in the living room as he sat down to watch and listen to the rest of us. I can only imagine the pleasure he got from our conversations, eighty-eight years beyond his own time. Rabon is a big, bluff, friendly man, good at what he does, and his political opinions centered mainly on "The people in government who don't know their ass from a hole in the ground." I don't suppose politics changes all that much over the years, and I must admit that it was fun to listen to Rabon castigating Truman with what would probably have been the same sort of arguments used in the days of James Buchanan, or Abe Lincoln for that matter. Lacey and I swapped amused glances from time to time, knowing that Hiram was paying close attention to our conversation, probably longing for a pipe of tobacco but loathe to miss a word. While my father-in-law was hitting his stride, which was his "white bread" opinion on colored people's effect on the workforce, I saw him wince and sit up straight.

"Now damn-it, Vera," Rabon said startled, "what did you kick me for?"

Lacey's mother smiled at him and cocked her head to make sure she was hearing him, since she's a little deaf on her left side. "I didn't kick you dear," she said calmly. "It must have been your conscience. You always blame colored people for everything that goes wrong."

"Well, somebody kicked me," said Rabon suspiciously glaring at his daughter.

Luckily I was out of range and therefore not suspect. Lacey

and I knew who had barked his shin, and it was all either of us could do to keep a straight face.

Though Lacey and I laughed about it later, I think that incident gave us a premonition that there is a change occurring in Hiram. Our ghost is establishing himself in the physical world, which he has been away from for so long and is now beginning to feel less helpless. It seems incongruous that the mild old man we are getting to know—that timorous, wispy spirit who had seemed to apologize for existing—has become the sort of entity that would kick a shin in order to express his invisible opinion. It both pleases and worries us; Hiram, new to corporeal existence, doesn't know his own strength.

POP ARRIVED THANKSGIVING morning, laden with packages and good will. Thanksgiving is typical of Pop's love for holidays. He arrived in his usual festive mood, and it was a cold and snowy day, which he has always considered necessary to the celebration of the season. He reminded me of Santa Claus, with all the gifts he brought: a cured ham, a whole smoked salmon, a huge fruit basket, a supply of rum, whiskey, wines, and beer that would have started a bar; a washing machine with the store's dolly to unload it, and a huge boxed-up playpen for the baby that when assembled, promises to be big as a duck blind. When that great red-faced symbol of good-nature entered our house, he represented a lot of things to be thankful for. Pop seemed to be in his prime, full of stories, enthusiasm and holiday spirit that instantly took in everybody, and he had the old house shaking with laughter in no time. The pungent aroma of his annual hot "Turkey Day" punch, mixed with the smell of the turkey browning in the oven, would have awakened the dead.

Hiram became so involved in our family activity, I was afraid one of us was going to run over him—and sure enough, Lacey, bustling all around between stove, refrigerator and dining table, actually bumped into the old ghost twice and had to pretend she was a little addled from smelling the punch. Hiram told us later that in his anxiety to be a part of our family gathering, he had had to twist, turn and sidestep so much in overseeing the kitchen that he finally went and sat in the wood box, where Pop, getting a log for the fireplace, nearly upset him.

Dinner was what Thanksgiving is supposed to be about— one of those amazing meals you're bound to feel guilty about if you think about little kids in Asia. But when Pop said the table grace, which was sort of a family custom, he didn't mention them. He said, "Thank the Lord for this food and don't forget to thank Pa Clark who wrung the hen's neck," and then he kissed his palm, patted his belly, and began to carve the turkey. I figured the Donnellys would get used to Pop's family rituals, having a few of their own.

Sometime after dinner, while we were recovering—the men drinking coffee and brandy in the living room, Lacey and her mom stacking up dishes for me to wash—I heard a car pull up in the driveway. When I went to the front door, I discovered it was Soames and Virgie Black, who said they were just stopping by briefly to meet our folks.

Soames was wearing his Sunday suit, and I don't recall what Virgie wore because the only memorable thing about her, besides her "chewmer," was her ability to enshroud any kind of gathering with sad cryptic comments about the shortness of life and the general unhealthiness of everybody she knew. Virgie and Myrtle were sisters under the skin—either of them could cast a pall over a wedding feast—Myrtle with her buzzard aspect, Virgie with her foreboding ways.

Within minutes of their arrival, Virgie announced, "Edith Farley wasn't no good." It's one of those Ozark expressions meaning that Edith wasn't well. Since Edith was also pregnant (as usual), Lacey was very concerned until it turned out that Edith merely had cold symptoms, but Mrs. Black's diagnosis was "prob'ly hippy-titus."

Pop wasn't interested in the dialogue; he and Soames had already found a common ground—bird hunting, and they were off on a discussion of shotguns, shot, and endless stories about bird dogs that hadn't suited them. Rabon, who wouldn't know a pointer from a setter, was following the conversation as best he could. The women were involved with female concerns, so I was the only one to hear Hiram whisper in my ear telling me that Virgie Black was *grimmer than a temperance lecture.*

You could forget that Virgie was really a good neighbor when, with her penchant for bad news, she lived up to Hiram's expectations.

"Them Smiths is gettin' that least girl a rabbit for Christmas," said Virgie complacently while stirring her tea, "and I just hope that child don't have to see a little bunny rabbit killed in front of her. Them with all them hounds."

In a minute or so, she topped herself. "I guess you'uns heard

217

about that Allen woman down on Bixby Branch, had that baby borned without no liver. Poor thing was as yeller as a gourd. They claim that Jess Allen's drinkin' was what done it. Deprived his own child of a liver that a way. He'd ort to be horsewhipped."

Next to my ear I heard, "*Good God-a-mighty!*" Hiram's breath smelled strongly of Pop's wine punch, obtained I expect by some sleight of hand. He actually slurred the words, "*That old woman'll cause Mistress Clark a miscarriage.*"

It was hard to ignore his comments, but impossible to return them. I sat spellbound, listening to that nattering old lady spread her depressing opinions, which I knew perfectly well Hiram wasn't going to put up with much longer and wondered what he would do.

"Now that's a pretty centerpiece," she observed sadly, glancing into the dining room. "You know, Elsie McCall made one sort of like that'n back endurin' the war, with leaves and turkey feathers, a punkin, and pilgrims, and all sich as that made out of wax and it caught itself afire from the candles some way and liked to burn the house down one night with all them babies asleep upstairs."

"What did you say, Steve?" asked Pop, who had overheard Hiram say "Damn!"

"Nothing," I said. "I just had a twinge in my shoulder." It was the truth; Hiram had grabbed my shoulder in lieu of Virgie's and pinched me hard.

"It puts me in mind of the time . . ." continued Mrs. Black, who decided to plumb the depths of her memory for holiday disasters, "when Calvin Forsyte put up a Christmas tree one year, and it was wet from the woods, and he didn't know nothing about 'lectric no way, and when he went to plug in a string of them lights onto it . . ."

The rest of the story is lost forever. At that point, Virgie's teacup turned over onto her crotch, and the old lady sprang up in the air like a quail hurtling out of a sorghum patch. Lacey and I commiserated, fetched towels and did our best to dry off the old lady—and the chair. We took pains to keep from looking at each other.

The incident served its purpose and shut Virgie's bad news mill down for the rest of their visit. The old lady knew *she* hadn't turned over her cup, but she couldn't come up with a likely alternative, so she just sat there and stared at her lap, pondering and occasionally muttering, "My crown in heaven!" It pretty well finished the Blacks' social trip and they left soon afterward.

I wonder if she will think to blame it on spirits and actually be right for once.

EARLY NEXT MORNING as my in-laws were almost ready to head back home, the Trolls arrived. Having told everybody a number of Troll stories, I offered to display them in action and invited the entire Burdey clan to come in for a drink. I knew they wouldn't offend Pop, and Lacey had told Vera and Rabon stories over the phone. Armed with their enthusiasm, I went out to welcome God-knew-what into our house.

Clive, Beulah Lou-Lou, and Travis T. were already enormously drunk, of course, and they'd brought with them a visiting Troll. All four of them were crammed into the cab of their old rotten truck, like pickles in a jar. With the strange predictability of Trolls, they had stopped by to introduce us to the visiting Troll. Travis T. had somehow gotten his two incisors knocked out and looked like a sullen vampire. The visitor was everything you'd want in a Troll to show the folks, a fat little man in what looked like an orange fright wig, with one arm off at the elbow, and with the startling name of *Pus*. The man had a set of bowlegs that were amazing and as Clive proudly put it, "They ain't no way Pus here could ever catch a peeg." I introduced everybody, fetched hot punch for the visitors and sat back to await developments. I hoped for great things from anyone called Pus and wasn't disappointed.

"I don't guess you'd want to tell Steve what Pus done on the way over here?" said Beulah Lou-Lou, beaming at Clive.

Clive hooted, while Pus looked both embarrassed and proud. "Why, goddamit-to-hell—*'scuse my French,*" said Clive, "we was comin' off the hill up there by Benny Wilson's pasture, and Pus says he's full and has to stop and relieve hisself—*'scuse me ladies*—so I stop and let him out and what does he do but walk over and water on Benny's electrical fence! Good Godamighty—*'scuse my French*—but it run up there to his works and knocked him flat. Pus hollers 'Holy SHIT cakes!' and grabbed a'holt of his tool like it's afire and liked to peed all over hisself.—*Beg pardon, little lady.*" (This last, directed at Vera.)

"I tried to look t'other way," said Beulah Lou-Lou demurely, "but when Pus went to hollerin' like a shoat in bob wire, I couldn't hep myself. I turned around, and there he was down in the road a'kickin' like a frog and hangin' onto his weeny."

The Trolls lived up to my stories wonderfully and were really

220

at their best, but their visit nearly turned into a disaster. As they were leaving, after an hour or so of Troll conversation, which was pretty much a shouting match after a drink or two; Pus decided to show us his dog, "Skippy," which he had tied in the back of the pickup. Skippy was a big, disgruntled-looking cur of a bluish color, with mismatched eyes, a bobtail and hair like steel wool—the least likely "Skippy," I could imagine. Although I didn't know it, Hiram followed me out to the truck to see the Trolls off, while everybody else stayed in the house, having probably thoroughly enjoyed the Trolls as much as they could stand.

Pus, in order to show off Skippy's fine points, let him out of the truck bed, and it was immediately obvious that here was a definitive Troll dog. Walking slightly out of plumb, the weird-looking animal sniffed at all of our legs suspiciously and decided to make a round of the truck, at which time, he ran into Hiram's invisible legs. Our ghost, being careful, had walked in footprints already made and only Lacey and I could figure out what happened next.

What followed was one of the most unlikely ballets ever witnessed by anybody, sober or drunk. Being totally wrecked by this time, the Trolls watched in stunned curiosity while the dog crashed stubbornly against the unseen obstacle, and backed off with bared teeth to try again. He couldn't see or smell Hiram, but he knew something was there, and he was determined to tackle it. Hiram had very little choice, unless he wanted to give himself away by making new tracks in the snow. He just stood his ground, grabbing the determined animal any way he could and throwing him back in the hope of discouraging him. The general effect was of an ill-shaped blue dog turning somersaults and snapping at absolutely nothing.

"Why, goddamit-to-hell Pus, Skippy's got the rabies!" said Clive with interest. "You best to knock him in the head."

Pus was too drunk to think this premise out. He watched his flying dog with wonder and some pride. "Look at that sum-bitch go!" he said as Hiram lifted the fool dog's chin with his foot and turned him over on his back.

"Why that thing's crazier than a box of assholes," said Travis T, staggering back a few feet to get perspective. "What the hail's he a'tryin' to do?"

"By God, Skippy's a-fixin' to fly," stated Pus happily, "and I never give but ten dollars fer him. Sum-bitch got more talent'n a circus midget."

Beulah Lou-Lou was convinced otherwise. "Shit, that's a runnin' fit!" she said. "I seen a hundred of 'em. That thing'll hurt somebody directly, you don't get a holt on him."

My only regret about the entire episode was that it ended too soon. Hiram, finally losing patience with Skippy, picked him up by the scruff of the neck and tail, and then bodily threw him into the pickup bed, an effect that nearly fulfilled Pus' statement about the dog trying to fly. The Trolls watched in stoned amazement as the wretched creature rose straight up, snapping and snarling at his unseen captor, and landed on his back in the truck. Travis T., being just drunk enough to do it, snapped the lead to the animal's collar and stood back with a pleased look, waiting, I suppose, for applause. Instead, Pus waded through the snow to Travis T. and hit him with a fine, flailing right hand punch—his only choice.

222

"Where in hell you get off a'catchin' Skippy up when he was just gettin' the hang of it?" demanded Pus.

"Well, shit-o-dear, I thought I was doin' you a favor," said Travis T., "but there ain't no way to 'commodate sich an old bastard as you."

At this point, both of them threw ill-aimed punches, which, missing their targets and balance, put both of them on their backs in the snow. Clive running to intervene, of course, fell himself and lay there like an overturned terrapin, waving his claws futilely, while the two men used him as handholds to get back on their feet. Beulah Lou-Lou took control of the situation; grabbing a skinny stick of stove wood from the pickup bed, she laid about her at anyone who looked liable to get up, giving the dog a lick for good measure when he showed signs of recovering from his flying lesson.

Beulah Lou-Lou said with clenched teeth (the few she had), "I swear to God, Clive Burdey, every time we get out of the house, you sons of bitches have to embarr's me in front of the neighbors. It'll get to where we don't have no place to go to socialize."

"What in hell are you whuppin' on me for?" asked Clive, waving his claws protesting. "I warn't doin' a damn thing besides tryin' to settle things down."

Beulah Lou-Lou landed a well-aimed whack with her stove billet, catching Clive at the funny bone.

"By God, there's going to be a little higher class in this family," she stated, "if I have to beat yun's balls off."

"Lay off, Ma," begged Travis T., "you're a' hittin' my sore arm."

By this time, he'd rolled over out of range, but Beulah Lou-Lou had fire in her eyes and had the distance figured. The only thing that saved Travis T. was that Beulah was too busy working on Pus' pudgy backside to give him her full attention.

"Olympus Burdey," she mouthed between smacks, "you goddamn bully, hittin' Travis T. when you know he's been hurt and ain't got strenth enough to pull a sick whore off a piss-pot. I'd ort to knock you simple!"

I was relieved to know Pus had a name not based on some grim infection.

"Leave off, Beulah Lou-Lou," the little man pleaded, rolling around in the snow to dodge the stick. "I never meant to hurt the boy, I just wanted to smack him a good 'un. You're abusin' a disabled man with that goddamn club!"

"Lord God, woman," said Clive, sobering up from the wet snow, "slack off afore you break a bone in somebody. They wasn't nobody hurt afore you commenced to frailin' us with that goddamn stove wood."

"You'uns get in that truck," said Beulah Lou-Lou shaking her weapon at the three prone men. "Thanks-Be-To-God-Day, and here you are a wallerin' in the snow like infi-dells!"

Finally, with all four of them in the pickup and the dazed Skippy in the back, they wobbled down the road to Medley Springs. Hiram was at my side, muttering apologies.

"I didn't know what else to do," said Hiram. "I shouldn't have come out here at all, I suppose, but I was curious, for the Burdeys are like no people I've ever seen before."

While I was reassuring him, I looked back at the front porch to see the whole family standing around in various stages of laughter.

"Who in the hell are you talking to?" asked Pop when he got his breath.

Luckily, everybody was far enough away to think that I was talking to myself. "Nobody, Pop," I said, "just mumbling over my crazy neighbors. Did you get to watch the fight scene?"

"Good God!" said Pop, "Was it the dog got them started into it?"

"Oh Lord, you saw how drunk they were," I told him, "and you saw them on a good behavior day. Wait until you see them when they're unruly."

Vera was so smitten with the episode that she sat down on the front steps and laughed til' she was done. I knew that the Skippy-fling would be retold for years to come.

Poor Hiram had to wait until all of us had gone back into the house before he could move, but he was a patient soul and didn't mind.

RABON AND VERA headed home shortly after the Troll visitation, and Hiram, knowing better, didn't come outside when we said our good-byes.

Pop, who was almost always pleased with the antics of various members of the human race, had enjoyed himself immensely. He hated to leave but he was a businessman and since Mother had died, he devoted himself to the store knowing he had to concentrate on something. He said good-bye to Lacey at the door, and I walked with him to his truck.

225

"Steve," he said, "when the baby comes, I want Lacey to have the best of care and it's on me."

"Don't worry about that Pop, babies have been born in a lot worse places than the Ozarks and we've got enough money."

"Money or lack of it, shouldn't be what a life hangs on, son. I have a great respect for life these days—any life." He had a speculative look, like someone searching for a word. "I know that somebody saved mine one time, back in the big war, and I wish I could have done that for your mom. I'd have died for her in a minute, but I guess it doesn't work that way." Pop clapped me on the shoulder and looked into my eyes fondly. "If I can do anything for this new life son, please let me . . . I owe for one." He smiled at his own words. "Maybe I'll pay up next time, if life gives us another chance."

"I'm pretty sure it does Pop," I told him very seriously. "I wish I could tell you how I know, but I can't. It just does."

Pop looked at me curiously and I think he sensed I wasn't just making conversation. He was a tough old bird used to making quick decisions that he could live with. "If you say so, son," he said.

We shook hands gravely and he said, "I like the way you're living and I like what you're doing. If you need anything, just give me a call."

"I will Pop and don't worry about your grandson, or granddaughter—as the case may be. We're in good hands."

"I'll be here," said Pop, "one way or another."

226

I REMEMBER THAT day as clearly as if it were on some sort of mental movie reel. Jack Clark was the sort of man who believed in every sort of celebration and threw himself bodily into holidays with a zeal that made my own growing up rich in an inherited sense of fun. On Fourth of July, he always bought armloads of fireworks and concocted cannons that blew tin cans to dizzying heights. He was fond of sparklers, skyrockets, and big spinning pinwheels that always set fire to a neighbor's lawn. Thanksgivings were always a bacchanal, and more than Mother could handle. There was always an abundance of food, booze, people, and a turkey the size of a blimp, and Pop wearing a pilgrim's hat that made him look like a parade float. New Year's Eve found him in his warmest bathrobe, out in the yard at midnight with a bugle from the First World War and a twelve-gauge shotgun, celebrating at midnight with the neighbors, whether they did or not.

"Cracker Jack," as his friends called him, saw to it on Mayday that the town always had a Maypole with crepe paper streamers and a bunch of kids to dance around it. On April first, Pop would plan the most involved and impractical April fool's jokes on Mother and us kids; one time pretending to fix us a surprise breakfast that turned out to be wax bacon and plaster eggs that he'd borrowed from a food display at the appliance store.

Since that Thanksgiving of 1951, I have never forgotten his parting words: "I'll be here, one way or another"—because that's the last time I ever saw my father.

On the first day of December, a little over a week after we'd celebrated Thanksgiving, Pop went for a walk by the woods edge, exercising his favorite bird dog. Pop and old Custer had spent fourteen years together and were the best of companions; the dog, like my pop, involved in the finding of quail. Pop was a kind but determined taskmaster when it came to dogs, and Custer was the finest-honed of all the dogs he'd ever owned, rock solid on point and honorable when hunting with other dogs. Pop always told everybody that he'd named her Custer because he'd cussed her so much, but the two of them had a unity and an understanding that was beautiful to watch. I still think about them walking the cold fields of December, making their winter plans and enjoying each other's company on that bright fall day. Pop had a heart attack and died the way he would most certainly have wanted to—working his dog.

It was because of this and the things that followed, that I finally wrote this book and let everybody in on my secret: I'm convinced this life isn't all there is to it, and all of our religions, myths and superstitions are just our scratching at the great door of the universe. I'll try to tell you about the rest of it, put together from the journal I worked so hard to keep during that long-ago winter of our fiddler ghost.

Chapter Seventeen

DECEMBER 6, 1951

OP IS BURIED NEXT TO MOM AND IT'S
very hard to write right now. At the same time I
know it's important to keep this journal, which
was Pop's idea. Writing these things down, per-
haps I can fill up the great empty place he no longer occupies in
my life. Lacey and I have been gone for nearly a week to Hannibal
for his funeral.

Pop's old friend and business partner Charley Day called Lacey
and I and my sister Marilyn in California; he told us Pop had
died, and I called the rest of our scattered relatives in Missouri.
It has been a hectic time, especially for Lacey but she made sure
to take care of herself and the baby and never got to the point of
exhaustion, thank God. Fortunately, Uncle Frank is the executor
of Pop's will and handled everything for us. Being a lawyer, he
was able to steer us through the handling of the business Pop
shared with Charley; his money affairs, disposition of his personal effects; our old house; the cremation and service arrange-

ments.

Pop, considerate to the end, left a very thorough will and Uncle Frank did all the rest. Charley got Pop's part of the hardware store in exchange for shares of stock for us since Pop knew that neither Marilyn nor I would want it, and unless I wanted the house, he would sell it. Divided between Sis and me will be the estate after bequests. Marilyn is on her way back to California and, like me, can't believe it's all over and Pop's gone. To live that long and have your lifetime summed up in less than a week is phenomenal, like a time-lapse in a movie. We had a memorial service with most of the town folks in attendance. They said nice things about Pop, including some funny ones you would have never heard at a funeral. I wonder if Pop heard them. I shook so many hands I'm still numb. I had to explain to dozens of older people that I'm not going to take over Pop's half of the store. The younger ones understood and nobody questioned Marilyn "that talented Clark girl" who is a behind the scenes force in Hollywood.

God, how we'll miss that big, warm man, who always seemed an anchor to my sister and me; a fine, cigar-smelling guy with a vast capacity for friends and small children, a capacious lap to sit on and an incredible depth of understanding in those laugh-wrinkled eyes. At least I have Hiram to let me know about other dimensions, but I can't share that with my sister. Her sophisticated lifestyle and career moves in Hollywood don't leave much room for ghosts. Maybe someday I can tell her.

Custer is with us now, Pop's marvelous old dog that understood every word Pop ever said to her and spent a lifetime serv-

ing the one person she adored. I should probably have put her to
sleep or whatever the veterinary word for dog killing is, but she's
as much a part of my memories of Pop as are his shotguns, hunting pictures, or any of the things of Mother's he'd left us. Custer
is lonely, confused and gray with age, and she'll live with us as
long as she wants to.

I'm confused, too, I don't understand why all the things you
love have to go just about the time you're old enough to appreciate them. Custer sits at my feet sensing my every move. It's as if
somehow what I do will bring back her dog-memories of a big old
suspendered guy with a dog whistle around his neck and a shotgun over the crook of his arm. He made her life a challenge and
a pleasure. I'm afraid I can't do that for her, but I can keep her
company. She still likes to go sit in the bed of Pop's pickup truck,
which we pulled home behind the Jeep. I think she's waiting for
him to come get her.

Hiram's existence has helped considerably. When we got back
from Hannibal, the ghost was waiting for us in our silent house.
Our neighbors had kept the house as welcoming for us as only
Ozark folks could. When we turned into the driveway from our
sad, exhausting journey, I saw smoke coming from the chimney,
and I had an immense feeling of relief. I knew the death I had
experienced was just a jog in the river of time, and our friend
Hiram was there to prove it. I felt so much better just seeing
smoke drifting down to Blessing Creek that I got a mental picture of Hiram chopping kindling to welcome us home. I hoped
that nobody else saw anything like that sight.

As soon as we walked in the door, Hiram said, "Welcome

231

home, my friends. The neighbors have been here to build up the fires and bring you food. I took the liberty of puttin' it in the oven to warm when I saw you come through Rolla."

"Hiram," I said, "*how* could you see us come through Rolla?"

"I really don't know how to explain it," said the ghost, "but I could have ridden with you, except you needed your thoughts and privacy, and I saw no need to ride in the vehicle you towed."

Lacey called out, "Hiram, where are you? I want to hug you."

I never cease to marvel at the sight of an invisible one-sided hug, seeing Lacey huge as she is, bending forward like a bowling pin about to topple. It was unsettling in a way, like watching someone performing before a mirror. I reached my hand out to meet Hiram's dry, firm, invisible grasp, and we shook hands solemnly. The kitchen smelled of sage dressing and baked ham, and the welcome smells of our familiar house were the best thing to happen to us since seeing the smoke from the chimney.

I brought Custer in from the truck cab and set her down on the floor to get used to things. She discovered Hiram immediately—how, I'm not sure—but she wasn't a bit frightened or awed and since she's almost blind, Hiram being invisible didn't bother her. Custer's life has been a matter of locating things that she couldn't see anyway.

"Your father's dog, I presume," said Hiram gently. "She must miss him a great deal."

"We all miss him a great deal," I said.

"I know," sighed Hiram. I could tell by looking at Custer that Hiram was petting her ancient head. "But now you know that missin' someone doesn't mean that they were—are, gone for-

232

ever."

"Hiram, you don't have to do anything but exist to help us a lot," I told him. "I don't know where Pop is, but at least we know he's somewhere. That everybody's somewhere."

I went to sleep last night with that comforting thought.

DECEMBER 7, 1951

HIRAM HAS BEGUN to materialize at odd times; it's going to be really strange the first time he does it when somebody is here. I worry since people are here a lot. Today, every neighbor was present for at least a few minutes to express their condolences, which in the case of Ozark people is usually in the form of food. The array of pies, cakes, cobblers, and other sweet stuff, makes me think my neighbors believe sugar is some sort of therapy for grief, sickness, or loss. The Smiths, Summers, Blacks, Pulvers, Terrills, Cartwrights, McClellans, and Farleys, have stopped by at different times to see if there was anything they could do.

Myrtle Summers, practical about everything to do with school, hired a substitute teacher while we were gone and consequently isn't worried about missing scholar-days. She has been very concerned about Lacey's welfare, as Virgie Black has been. Virgie remarked that she hoped "havin' a death in the family wouldn't work off on Miz Clark and mark the baby." It's all I can do to keep Hiram's hands off of her.

In less than a day, Hiram and Custer became fast friends and now are great companions. They've gone for several walks, which I think is good for both of them. Earlier today I saw Custer standing in the yard, wagging her tail at nothing, and I knew the old

233

man was talking to her. I watched a covey of quail scuttle through open ground under the apple trees, and it was pleasant to watch the old dog work them, freezing into a dog statue when she finally filtered out the scent and solved the puzzle. She runs into things occasionally, but it was fun to watch her cast about for a whiff of quail with her head held high and then low, as she figured things out. Hiram can't give hand signals, but then Custer couldn't follow them even if she wanted to. They work by whistles, strictly the vocal kind, since I don't think a chrome-plated dog whistle hanging in the air would be a good idea in case of unexpected company.

DECEMBER 9, 1951

HIRAM MATERIALIZED UNEXPECTEDLY today while Lacey was sitting by the fireplace and sorting through photo albums we brought back from Hannibal. She was chatting to him about the people in the old 1920s and '30s photographs, and the ghost showed an interest since these were the years he knew nothing about after Bessie's death. They represent the wonders of our modern age that came to pass, and he wanted to hear everything and see everything that had happened to the world since he'd left. Airplanes, electricity in homes, telephones, radios, automobiles, refrigerators, indoor bathrooms, hot water heaters, typewriters, batteries, washing machines, chainsaws and everything else we take for granted, he has never seen or imagined, and his interest is sharp and clever. But the truth of the matter seems that while he's curious to have a discovery or invention explained, he is like one of my pupils—satisfied with a simple explanation.

He has no interest in further detail unless it concerns music. He has no desire to ride in a car or fly in an airplane; but several days ago he had to examine Lacey's wire recorder in the same way he'd done with the record player and speakers. It perplexes us what turns him on like a light bulb, and sometimes it's unpredictable.

Nevertheless, Lacey was holding up a photograph, taken around 1900, of my great-grandmother seated at an old pump organ in her Victorian music room. I was sitting across from them with Custer at my feet, and I was taken with how lovely my wife looked, huge as she is, with her long red hair hanging about her face, her eyes sparkling with the firelight and the animation of sharing the pictures. All of a sudden, Hiram literally lit up like a bulb; he didn't glow or assemble, but instantly was in our presence as real and tangible as any person.

"Lacey, look," I said nodding.

She turned to see the visible Hiram puffing his pipe while he was looking over her shoulder, intent on the old photograph. He looked like a schoolboy watching a fishing bobber.

"Why there you *are*, Hiram," she said brightly.

Hiram, who had been lost in memories, immediately looked down at himself startled. "Why, bless my soul, so I am!" His interest in the scrapbook put aside, he said, "And just in time for your first violin lesson!"

Hiram fetched the fiddle and bow. He asked Lacey to stand facing him as he placed the fiddle under his jaw. Raising a brow and grinning, he leaned down looking at her, holding the fiddle only by his chin. As if he were a conductor, with his right hand he raised the bow in the air and twirled it. Lacey smiled and in concert with him, she turned around with her back to him, and he brought the fiddle around and positioned it under her chin. Slowly, she raised her hand, palm up, and placed it under the fiddle neck and tentatively arched her fingers over the strings. Hiram reached around and placed the bow in her right hand, as he held his hand over hers. I could see the splendid instrument intimidated her, but as he guided her hand, it captured her, eventually winning her confidence.

Hiram was delighted that she was an apt pupil and understood his every instruction. I grabbed my tablet, rapidly writing notes on his comments.

He said, "You have the artist's ear my dear, and the cello has taught you more than perhaps you know about drawin' the richness from a string."

The ghost fiddler was so enthusiastic, he didn't notice when he removed his hand from the bow, sunlight was shining though him like a lampshade. Asking Lacey's permission, he once again placed his right hand over hers and then gently positioned his left fingers over hers.

It made a lovely picture—the tall ghost providing background for her small head and shoulders as he talked. "If you will, let us play a tune of my time that you still know, for I have heard you hum it in the kitchen. 'Dixie'—a simple tune perhaps, but one that has swelled a million hearts.

"Let's play in 'D,' first position if it's comfortable. You see, bowin' is the secret to the notes the left fingers learn to select. The bowin' hand draws sounds out like nectar from a flower—

like so . . ." and he demonstrated with a great quivering chord. "It swells them and presents them to the voice of the Guarnerius, which opens its great wooden throat to sing."

Sing "Dixie" it did—in both their hands, with notes that raised the hair on my neck. *Holey moley!* I thought, wondering at the marvelous picture they made. I kept scribbling as the ghost explained harmonics, and Lacey anticipating him, played the notes. She'd learned rudiments of the violin in music classes but only marginally, just enough to show beginners in case she ever taught. But with Hiram's expertise and joy of sharing music, her face glowed with understanding. By the end of this first lesson she had learned to play two tunes, "Mississippi Sawyer" and "Grey Eagle," both square dance pieces.

Smiling broadly, Hiram said, "I am gratified that these survived, I heard both on your radio; the music was set into a configuration with banjo, guitar and mandolin, the narrator called it 'Bluegrass.' It sounds very like the mountain music of the Cumberlands, or any mountains in the South."

"It's named after Kentucky, the Bluegrass State," said Lacey. "My Daddy loves it. He says it's the true American music."

"Indeed," Hiram said thoughtfully. "In my time Kentucky was called the Tobacco State, but no matter." He hesitated. "I somehow think American music must come from a greater origin than one state since so many cultures are involved, wouldn't you?"

"Well, I always heard the banjo was African," Lacey mused. "Violins and mandolins were invented in Italy, guitars are Spanish, bass fiddles first developed in Germany, and those are just Bluegrass instruments. I guess if you want *American* music, you'd have to make all the instruments yourself."

"Out of hickory perhaps," smiled Hiram, "with strings of cougar gut." He laughed at Lacey's look. "No, Mistress, it has nothing to do with materials or country of origin I believe, but of the minds of people who express themselves with whatever instruments come to hand. The Jews have no country and created music for all lands. The Africans dragged here against their will, have restructured their own from racial memory. Perhaps all music is racial memory of some sort."

Lacey kept asking questions that interested him. "Why didn't our native Indians have a music that had influenced the invading settlers?" and "Why didn't Indians invent as many drums and musical instruments as Africans?" and so on.

Hiram didn't have answers for her questions but instead posed other ways of thinking. "Perhaps seeking American music is like seeking *American* culture, or *American* religion, or *American* eyes, as if in other lands, people's eyes are in their elbows. It seems to me that a glimpse of America's music would need a kaleidoscope orchestra."

Their conversation went for on a long time.

I MAY BE mistaken because I'm not a musician, but I sense the teacher in Lacey; she has the ability to pass on learning that I have recognized in my own makeup. I think Hiram sees this too; his careful explanations of his knowledge are not so much that he expects her to become a virtuoso, but that he wants her to recognize and appreciate the skills that make one.

I got a better look at Hiram in daylight than I ever had before.

He is a tall figure (apparition?—ghost?—spook?—haint?) nearly as big as Pop, but angular and imposing and has a rather commanding presence. Yet, his face is good-humored, and in the afternoon light, his eyes were kind and as blue as cornflowers, and his groomed white hair glistened. He had fine leathery skin the color of wheat straw and tan-looking hands with long artistic fingers, powered it seemed with veins. What runs in those veins or why Hiram should have a healthy tan is beyond my guessing.

If he is an illusion and I see him only as the way I picture him, then why does Lacey see the same person? If Hiram creates his own illusion as he does with his "holograms," why would he appear at odd moments? Especially when I thought his "mind" was so involved concentrating on the scene in my great-grandmother's music room. If Hiram knows more about this than we do, he can't or doesn't choose to tell us. Every time he disappears it's as if he blinks out like a bulb, leaving his pipe and a wreath of smoke hanging in the air. But when, as today, he takes the violin from Lacey's hands, it's as if he becomes a showman, if that's the word for it. It's as though he's a larger than life being; he fills the room and somehow makes it a stage with his presence.

I know he admires Lacey and perhaps because of her respects me accordingly; however, he focuses his *feelings* on Lacey—if I can use that word. When he plays for her, I watch the actual physical intensity he puts into a tune. I can almost feel his immense love for his music; it lights up his face and eyes. I believe Hiram is his own stage and must have been that way when he was alive. Imagining this man as a soldier is a lot like trying to

239

picture Cary Grant catching hot rivets on a skyscraper.

HE SPENT THIS afternoon telling Lacey about his music education. He told how his father, who had studied music as part of his early upbringing as a young gentlemen of his time, had sent him off when he was twelve to a music teacher in Knoxville. Sent there, he learned what he could of the classics: the violin creations of Mozart and Chopin; the almost mathematical inventions of Bach; and the thundering concertos of Beethoven. He had traveled to Knoxville by steamboat and stayed for six months boarding with his teacher in a huge old house filled with music and children. He said the best part of his instruction was that his teacher was a Jew—Jacob Stern. His teacher had emigrated from Bohemia and had actually heard the great violinist Paganini play there in 1831. "Herr Stern" as Hiram called him, had not only taught him to write music but more importantly, had given him an appreciation of the Guarnerius his father had entrusted to him and a fascination with the sounds it could produce.

Hiram said, "Herr Stern told me, 'Paganini also played one of these *Gesu* violins and thought it so fine, he never performed on another. I never thought I would hold a Guarnerius, much less a Gesu model and the hard part is to live up to such a fiddle.'" It was said kindly according to Hiram and with none of the condescension he expected from a teacher. He was to learn that Herr Stern, though a concentrated teacher, was no taskmaster but a gentle soul who let music speak for itself.

The most important benefit of this, Hiram added, was the

240

lesson in another culture his father had intended. He had never met anyone Jewish before and was amazed at Jacob Stern's musical family; the older children could play almost every instrument in Herr Stern's collection, and the younger ones were always learning. The big house was usually full of music, and laughter, and fragrant with Frau Stern's cooking. Since his lessons were day-long, Hiram learned about Jewish dishes and snacks Frau Stern saved for his "recess" times. His memories of this vibrant family were so much fun to listen to that I had a hard time concentrating on writing. Now and then, Hiram would pick up the fiddle and illustrate some rollicking tune he'd learned from his time with the Sterns, a tune as likely to be from Cremona, or Czechoslovakia, or Madrid, as anyplace else in that faraway continent.

I feel awkward trying to capture the vitality of Hiram's words as he described what he called his "adventures" with Herr Stern. Hiram said he had problems learning terminology such as *adagio* and *vivace,* Italian words for tempo and (a word he had to spell for me), *scordatura*—for the mistuning of a certain string or strings to play in another key without shifting a position, and *ricocheting* the bow—bouncing it off the strings. Prior to going to Knoxville, Hiram said he had learned to play by listening to fiddlers, most of them black.

He told us his teacher's lessons varied in nature and were never boring. This was partially because when Stern would mention some instrument like a *Ballaiaka* from the Ukraine, or a *Sitar* from Bombay, he would send one of his children off on a search to find the particular instrument; when they returned, he

241

would play it to illustrate his lesson."

As part of his education, Stern would take him around to meet other violinists. Hiram said, "I thought at the time, it wasn't so much to show my playin' but rather, to show my Guarnerius. Everyone wanted to play my fiddle, and I let them. But after a while, I began to see that I could play it better than they could, and I realized that Herr Stern wanted me to see *that*, as well. I was his star pupil and he was proud of me."

With his six months of schooling over, Hiram went back to his family's farm; but Herr Stern had left no doubt in his mind that music would rule his life. He practiced and played when he could, inviting every fiddler he met to swap tunes with him. He told us that he had memorized and transcribed over a hundred old Negro songs, work chants and ballads, and enough reels and jigs that he could play all night for dancers, without repeating one. By the time he was courting Bessie, he was nineteen and the best-known fiddler in Eastern Tennessee. He could play every stringed instrument available, including several African ones, like the thumb piano—little metal strips on a box resonator.

"When my father Ezekiel died in 1850," he said, "I had earned very little of the inheritance left to me and my brothers and sisters, for I was always off a'fiddlin' and had no real talent for crops or managin' livestock. I had to play for people, for I sensed that this was my gift."

Our ghost didn't sound the least bit apologetic for his lack of agricultural abilities, just a little sad. "Our older sister Peggy married well. The youngest, Sarah, died of cholera, the same disease that took my father and my mother. My two brothers were able caretakers of the land and when father died, I gave them my share, taking only a hundred acres for house and home and a handful of slaves, who I freed and hired to do my farmin' for me."

From his tone it was evident that this memory was pleasant for him. "Given my choice, I had picked a musical family who sang the day long and had the color and the rhythm of Africa in their words and movements. They were their own people and besides ritual songs, they created their own music as they worked, in the same way they adapted their religion to the Christian one, and their musical instruments to the ones existin' here. Whatever they touched became a thing of created music . . . like this . . ."

To our surprise, Hiram chose to illustrate by making a series of popping and clicking sounds with his mouth, accompanied by rapid hand slapping rhythms and a hummed tune that vibrated through his nose and lips.

What resulted from his efforts was a vibrant "hologram" of a young black man playing what appeared to be parts of his body—face, and head—with his hands, while the tune came from Hiram, from nowhere and everywhere—and the black man's bare feet kept percussive time in puffing dirt. It was a most startling performance with Hiram providing all of the sounds himself. At the conclusion of the tune, our hologram illustration vanished. Lacey and I applauded as we laughed along with a breathless Hiram.

"Oh my," he said, "that was great fun to remember young Obey in his prime, eephin'. I only wish I could have provided the other singer's chant and the high voice of the leader outlinin' the verses." When he caught his breath, he continued, "The colored family inspired my youth and my music, and as I had hoped, continued to work for me by free choice. This was Silas' family, and my inheritance was enough to pay them to build their own house and do farm work on my acreage, on shares."

Lacey asked, "What about your brothers, did they keep your parents' house and free their slaves, too?"

The voice of our ghost hesitated and became somber. "I am sorry to say that the house was unlivable, for no one dared to inhabit a place where cholera had struck. All clothing, furniture and house appointments made of cloth or leather were burned— the house fumigated with burnin' sulfur and left to stand until it was thought the disease dissipated."

As though the smoke from Hiram's pipe exemplified his sadness, he blew it away. "My brother Lucas, like me, had built his own house and he and his family escaped cholera. My younger brother Tab, who lived at home, survived it by some miracle. I was married to Bessie at that time and lived a mile away. Cholera was a sudden death and irrespective of age, race, or wealth. It was said that one could be hale and hearty at breakfast and dead by sundown. Tab came to us by horseback to tell us that our parents and sister were stricken and needed help. By the time we'd sent to bring a doctor and arrived ourselves, it was a house of death."

Lacey and I were silent.

"It was unspeakable tragedy," said Hiram with slow deliberation, "for my family had always been our joy, our inspiration, and our pride in accomplishment. My musical father's deep bari-

244

tone singin' each mornin' had warmed our childhood. My mother's readin' of the classics instilled in my sister the urge to write, which she did very well. Each of us children had the wish to become our best and live up to these gifted people, who were gifts themselves to all of us."

The ghost's voice was heartbreaking with memory. Silent tears ran down Lacey's cheeks, tears she didn't try to wipe away.

"The few house servants who lived through that dreadful plague were as destitute as we. For some of them, our family was the only one they had ever known and for all of them, the kindest in their hateful world of slavery. All of us were sure it was the worst time of our lives."

The irony in Hiram's tone crept in to tell us that this hadn't proved to be the case. "But that was a time of limited sacrifice, compared to what was to follow in a few years." He continued grimly, "What happened to Tab and Lucas represents to my mind, the truly unthinkable sorrow of our family, for it put them at war with each other. Tab felt as I did, that one person could never own another's mind, body, or spirit. However, he was bound in partnership with our brother Lucas, and he could not free his slaves." Hiram sighed deeply. "Tab gave up his birthright, brothers, sister, and all, to go join the Union army when the war broke out." His voice shook with the memory. "Lucas never forgave him. It was without a doubt the most rendin' wound that war could bring a family and the South—that settin' of brother against brother over values each held dear. And it wasn't just Tab and Lucas, a dozen families were sundered by the war in Hamilton County alone, each sure of rightness in the sight of God. I was forgiven my views, for I stayed with the Confederacy and my land and my people, despite my abolitionist nature."

Hiram stopped to calm himself and lit his pipe again. He stood over us to finish his declaration, pipe smoke like a flag. "I am a Southerner in mind and spirit still," he said gravely, "for the South gave me my music and left me proud of what I had learned on my own. But I was American more than Southern and not put here just to learn the music of other countries or only secular parts of mine. I needed to find our own music and play it—I hoped—for this entire land."

There was a long pause. "I know that sounds high flung and boastful, but I could have done it too, or at least helped do it," declared our ghost finally, "before this war came to destroy all kindness, all brotherhood, all the music of the inventive South, and replace it with drums and bugles and the noise of patriotism."

It was as if Hiram were back in those old-times, caught up in his emotions. He said *"this war"* as if distant cannons could be heard at Medley Springs.

Lacey was loath to interrupt him, but decided that this was enough sad history for the afternoon. I didn't blame her. Her mind was going in another direction.

She said, "Steve, if we can hear him, then everybody can. Let's record him!" She turned and asked Hiram, "Would you put some of that 'eephing' on my wire recorder? I think that's the most fun the baby has had today."

"Why yes, Mistress Lacey!" Hiram said, "and perhaps a bit of eeohin' thrown in. Forgive an old man's draggin' of y'all through my past."

While the two of them set about recording the primitive sounds of Hiram's yesterdays, I made notes of dates and names he had mentioned. Hiram was fascinated with the recording machine and no wonder; he had never heard himself recorded.

He declared, "This is the first time I have ever recognized my own definition of notes played back to me!"

On my next trip to Rolla, I must remember to order more wire because—God help me—we are recording music that has been sleeping nearly a hundred years, played by a dead fiddler who might have been a virtuoso. There's some real benefit to the children of Indian Glade though; for the first time I feel very much a part of the history I have been trying clumsily to teach.

Chapter Eighteen

HE NEXT TIME HIRAM BECAME VISIBLE
was a bombshell. I have to tell this from Lacey's
report because I remember I was at school trying to catch up on the work all the kids had
covered while I was gone. My substitute teacher was a well-mean-
ing lady in her sixties, who hadn't taken a lot of trouble to keep
up with advances in education and I'm sure the kids took advantage of her. When I called to thank her and say I'd be back on
Monday, she told me the kids' favorite phrase was "Mr. Clark
doesn't do it that way." Poor woman, she was experiencing what
every substitute teacher calls "Sink the sub."

In any case, I'd gone to the schoolhouse on Sunday and stayed
late catching up on eighth grade math so that I could teach it
next day, and Lacey was home with Hiram. When I got home, I
got the whole story from her in the kitchen. I listened while she
poured me a glass of wine and began fixing supper.

It had been one of those Ozark days that still amaze folks who live here—forgiving days in early winter that get up to sixty degrees and make a three-inch snow melt in an afternoon. Lacey had been in the side yard looking for a future location for a herb bed, when Pastor Tucker pulled into the driveway a little after three in the afternoon.

Pastor Tucker had paid us a previous visit in August to welcome us to the neighborhood on behalf of his church, The Standing Rock Holiness. It was one of the many country churches scattered over our end of the county, most of them Pentecostal and fundamentalist in nature, and she had met two other preachers on similar visits, always friendly but trolling earnestly for new parishioners. Lacey had informed them all that we were Unitarians—a gentle fabrication that at least kept us from being labeled "infidels"—and we had had no more solicitors. She was therefore a little surprised by this one.

Pastor Tucker was wide in girth and made up for his shortness by wearing cowboy boots and a Stetson hat that barely fit into his big Buick. Lacey told me that he emerged smiling and tipped his towering hat to her.

She said, "His eyes took in every square inch of me—the yard and the whole place—like he was fixing to auction everything off. He even looked like an auctioneer, with a belt buckle big as a headlight."

When she said that, I remembered the man with the flicking eyes. Soames Black, who had been there when the preacher stopped, had commented on the eyes. "That feller sizes a man's pile" he put it, "like a tax assessor."

Pastor Tucker had come, however, to assess our rumored ghost and to warn us that the God-fearing people of the area would not tolerate "conjured up spirits." He was polite enough, she said, but left her no doubt that our "demon" he had heard rumor of, came from talk among the pious. He offered Bible study and counseling as a cure for our "hainted dwelling" as he put it. Lacey, who is always forthright except for the Unitarian placebo she thought was kind, told the preacher that we hadn't "conjured up" anything and needed no counseling. Lacey had never lost her temper despite her impatience with anything approaching "mean-spirited ignorance," which she said he was a "walking crock of."

Lacey was livid. "The man actually told me 'all ghosts are demons, minions of Satan and put here only to deceive and harm,' like he'd *known* a bunch of them. And, while I was choking that down, he got started on all the stuff ghosts inspire people to believe—like evolution, science and psychology!"

"Uh-oh," I said. "Science? He's edging into *my* territory. Sounds like he's sour on education."

"Sour on it?" she snorted. "He's never been that close to it. His line of reason makes the Trolls sound like a gaggle of physicists."

"*Now Mother,*" I said in my best Soames voice.

"Oh hell, I can't help it," she groaned. "He was so sure of himself, rattling off scripture and stuff about 'familiar spirits' and how humans who try to communicate with the dead are evil people raising demons."

I steered her away from that. "Well you know we're not evil but he doesn't. He's just a good 'ol boy interpreting the Bible like it was written by old-timers who talked to God nonstop and were also born writers who took dictation."

"Well I think he's dangerous," she said, stirring a pot, "kind of a like a kid fishin' with dynamite, he's liable to blow up some old life form that cures cancer."

I agreed with her interesting view but didn't comment. My mind was on our ghost. "Where's Hiram? Did he hide out during Tucker's big lecture?"

"Oh no, he wandered in about the middle of it," she said Lacey-fashion. "I didn't get to that."

I carefully swallowed the wine that was halfway back up my throat. "No you didn't," I managed, thinking of George Burns and Gracie. "But please do."

"It was actually great, Hiram heard Tucker carrying on and decided to show up," she said smiling. "He came walking out on the porch with his fiddle and bow under his arm, just as solid and real as you are. He was even wearing that red plaid shirt your pop gave you and a Cardinal's baseball cap. He waved his pipe and said, 'Lacey, honey, your pot's a'bilin' over.' It was so natural and easy, I almost believed it myself. I shouted back, 'Thanks Uncle Hiram, I'll be right there. Mr. Tucker's just leaving.'"

Lacey grinned at my expression, which must have been stunned.

"Steve, I turned back to Tucker and Hiram raised his hand to wave, too, and looked so much as if he belonged here! I think the cap did it." She stopped for breath, "Hiram's just wonderful."

I thought Lacey was wonderful too and told her so. But I was still pretty upset. "I'm afraid of that preacher, Lacey. Preachers make a living putting ideas in people's heads."

"Oh Steve," she told me exasperated, "he's ignorant as a fishing worm. He was like a high school teacher I had who set in to teach us about the ancient Greek philosophers and began by calling Socrates, 'So-crates' and Aristophanes, 'Wrist-o-fanes.' Don't you remember how dreadful it was as a kid to have a teacher say something that showed they were teaching you stuff they didn't understand?"

I unfortunately knew the feeling, which was a little like the one I had teaching math, but my uneasiness wouldn't go away. "What on earth got into Hiram to show himself? I thought we had an agreement about that."

"Why don't you ask Uncle Hiram?" she said smiling to show me how comfortable she was with the ghost's new title. "I think he thought the whole thing out as well as we could—maybe better."

And sure enough, Hiram had. When he came down at Lacey's call, I saw what she meant about the red shirt and ball cap. He looked like somebody's moonshiner uncle who was here for a visit from maybe, Arkansas. On him, Pop's bib overalls were a little saggy, bleached out and just ragged enough to complete the image.

I was about to ask him if carrying the fiddle was why we could see him. When he set it down to shake hands—that answered my question. I found myself staring at an empty shirt and overalls, suspended as if on a dress dummy.

252

"Hiram, it's good—or was—to see you, but I thought you were going to keep a low profile."

Hiram shook my hand gravely and released it to pick up the violin. He was immediately his old, bright-eyed self. "It was time for me to be seen, my friend, I have seen that visitor's like before and he required misdirection. Besides, I have discovered that there is a sort of inspiration to holdin' my livin' Guarnerius that works dependably to make me visible."

"Well that's good to know," I said doubtfully. "But if you're Uncle Hiram now—much as that would be a relief to explain to folks—you'll have to carry the violin all the time."

"For now that's what I'll do," said Hiram, "which will be easy, for it's much like findin' a lost child to me, a constant comfort and companion."

Uncle Hiram smiled winningly at us. "I'll be Stephen's eccentric Uncle Hiram who is never without his fiddle. And this way I can play as much as I like without causin' questions amongst the neighbors."

"That's fine with me," said Lacey, putting an arm around him, "but you have to call me Lacey, not 'mistress' and how are people supposed to think you got here Uncle? Did you walk from Marion County?"

Hiram didn't even blink, "Why Stephen's cousin brought me. He dropped me off on his way to St. Louis, in case I could help with house chores when you are confined. It was late and no one saw his wagon stop here." Seeing Lacey's look of amusement, he hastily added, "His *vehicle* I meant, clearly."

The more I thought of it, the better I liked Hiram's idea de-

253

spite the number of things that could go wrong. If we were really headed for an inquisition by churchly neighbors, a "live" Hiram would solve a lot of our problems with his presence upstairs. Best of all, Lacey could relax a little; being constantly on guard had to be stressful for her, no matter how much she denied it. I could tell that Tucker's visit had scared her, and "Uncle" Hiram coming to her rescue had done worlds for her confidence. That was good enough for me.

"Thank you, Uncle Hiram," I sincerely told our ghost, "and welcome home. You were a lot more sensible than I would have been with that guy. I don't speak Bible very well."

"He did not either, I'm afraid," said Hiram absently, "but that reminds me, in the pastor's diatribe I heard him say that holdin' converse with ghosts encourages acceptance of such blasphemies as evolution, science and psychology. What, pray, might *evolution* be?"

"Uh-oh," I said.

"Uncle Hiram," said Lacey, "evolution will have to wait 'til after supper. I need to feed this man. Come sit with us and I'll fix you a *dram* of wine."

"Oh no, Mi . . . Lacey," he corrected himself. "I shall leave you to dine together. I must let music erase that fool's hateful thoughts."

He stopped at the foot of the stairs and stood musing. "I have been reflectin' on some of the music I have heard on your radio, of the sort that makes me think my state might be very close to heaven indeed. I have listened to pianists I only dreamed of and reed music that speaks of doors openin' and a rhythm that dances in a way only the Paganini of my time tried to capture." He peered at Lacey, "Are you familiar with a pianist called Shorty Nadine, or a lady by the name of Wynonie Harris, or people called Louis Jordan and his Tympany Five?"

"I know Shorty Nadine is actually a singer named Nat Cole," she said. "He changes his title when he plays jazz piano, but I'm not an expert on popular music, Uncle. I have heard 'Saturday Night Fish Fry' by Louis Jordan. You like that sound?"

"I like what it says to my ears," said Hiram. "It sounds like people searching for a way to express America by first expressing themselves.

"I am curious about this term, 'jazz,'" he added thoughtfully, "It sounds vaguely familiar. Where's it comin' from?"

"I'm pretty sure it's a black word," said Lacey. "I do know it refers to syncopated time and a hell of a lot of improvisation on the part of the musicians who play it. Pretty loose, isn't it?"

"Jazz," said the old man, as if to himself. "I thought it meant somethin' else." He shook his head, "Well my dear I shall continue my learnin' upstairs."

And with that, our new uncle trudged upstairs, fiddle under his arm. Uncle Hiram, I could see already was not only hooked on his headphones and his radio, but he was going to be a very thoughtful relative.

❖

DECEMBER 10, 1951

TONIGHT, WINTER WINDS are tearing at the old house again. Hiram and I have been sitting by the fire and listening to the howl of the storm around the eaves and talking about his ghostly world. I'd still like to be talking to him, but I want to write this down before it gets away, because I don't think Hiram will be here very long. He's like the spirit mentioned in the annotations to *Rime of the Ancient Mariner*, "one of the invisible inhabitants of this planet, neither departed souls nor angels," who are always on the move. Hiram has read Coleridge in his time and when I quoted the line to him, he nodded slowly remembering it. He smiled and said, "Well at least Coleridge never brought up demons. I don't feel the least bit demonic. *Plague take that preacher!*"

What an incredible guessing game this visible Hiram is; I never know just what to ask him. The ghosts I have read about are all like Hamlet's father, full of answers and supernatural knowledge and warnings of vengeance or retribution, but it's as if our Hiram just waits to find his purpose and even then seems good humored about it.

I know I should question him about things ghostly, because how many people have ever talked to a ghost and shared the information? But Hiram has no answers for me, so far anyway, only the occasional concepts he tosses out, which are as confusing as the fact that he exists.

Earlier this evening, while the fireplace burned like a blacksmith's forge from the draft sucking the chimney, he sat across from me, while Lacey was in the baby's room wrapping some gifts for Christmas. Custer was with her, interested in the new smells, I suppose.

Hiram was talkative, a mood brought on by the storm and the cozy fireplace.

Here's what I've gathered to put down that he said:

"Life ends but existence doesn't. I'm proof of that, I suppose. I should have known that before, watchin' the renewal of things every year on the farm. I thought that existence had to be renewed by nature, a plantin' of it like seed. But the evidence was right there before me all the time—livin' things get old, wear out and die, but the forces that cause life to exist never diminish at all. They only alter, takin' on other shapes and forms of life—as in music, and art, and new ideas, perceptions of minds that appear when their time has come."

Wow! I got that all in squiggly shorthand; I'm trying to read back to see if I understand.

I have to admit that this sort of premise is new to me, but across from me sits somebody or something with a violin on his lap. He's puffing his pipe, and the cold winds howling around the house are no more to him than the ticking of the kitchen clock. Just when I begin to think I have a grip on sharing a life with the concept of a ghost's existence, Hiram redefines both and whoops! It's back to the drawing board.

I think we're caught in the middle of some sort of miracle, and as Pop would have said, "I'm not chambered for that caliber." I'm going to jot down what Hiram did a while ago, just to see it in writing, the way you pinch yourself to see if you're dreaming or awake: Hiram, without setting aside his fiddle, put a log on the fire!

Lord, it sounds preposterous to relate that, but we were sitting there, Hiram on one side of the fireplace, me on the other, on the old hearth stool. A log fell in the fireplace and Hiram replaced it without moving. A big split section of white oak lifted itself from the wood box and carefully rolled itself onto the fire while the ghost stared at it with an air of total concentration, like a man carrying full glasses on a tray.

"*Good God, Hiram!* How did you do that?"

"I really don't know," said the old man honestly, "but I've been practicin' with little things. I decided to see if I could move anythin' so big with my mind. It's a great deal of work however I do it."

"*Levitation!*" I said in my amazement. "You mean, you just think that things will move and they do?"

"It's just somethin' to pass the time," replied the old man apologetically. "I concentrate on somethin' and move it in my mind just as if I were pickin' it up with my hands. I don't think I could move anythin' more easily one way than the other."

After months of watching pipes light themselves and wine glasses emptied into nothing, I admit I'm not too surprised by anything anymore. However, this does add another dimension to our ghost, of considerable significance: he can exist on two planes at once! I almost called Lacey to come see this new piece of amazement, but Hiram, having done it, was off on a side trip to literature. He skips and changes direction sometimes like a leaf in a March wind.

"I've been readin' your father's copy of *Walden*," he said, "and rememberin' the first time I read that remarkable book. Thoreau said, 'Time is but the stream I go a-fishin' in.' It seems to me that this is my case."

He was looking at me in what seemed a very strange and

258

intense way, as if he wanted to see what my mind was all about.

"I remember the quote," I said, "but I'm not sure I know just what it means."

"I've been thinkin' that perhaps I could show you," said the old man gently. "Would you like to see the school that I attended in eighteen-hundred-and-thirty-eight?"

"Of course, Hiram."

"It was also the church house," he explained dreamily and as he talked, he disappeared. I was alone in the strange but somehow comforting grip of his mind, like someone who has become used to hypnosis.

I sat on a bench at the rear of a log building about half the size of Indian Glade School. It had a rough puncheon floor and two glazed windows, one to a side. A thin, sunburned man sat at the teacher's desk beneath a framed portrait of Christ teaching some little children, one finger pointed up at the sky where cherubs were looking down benevolently. Before me, lined up on a church pew were the scholars of Hiram's time, three girls and four boys, all with slates upon their laps. I looked for Hiram and thought I recognized him in one of the youngest boys, a child of about nine with straw-blonde hair and eyes as blue as ice.

The children were wonderful, a regular history lesson of dress and deportment. Two of the girls wore pigtails tied with great ribbons. One, the oldest—maybe Hiram's sister?—wore her hair piled on top of her head in ladylike fashion. I stood up to see them better and nearly fell over the hearth stool, forgetting that I was still in my own living room. No one paid attention to my clatter, this was Hiram's world, and I was as invisible to them as he was in mine.

One of the small boys rose to recite something and the teacher smiled at him encouragingly. I marveled at the depth of Hiram's memory, every detail of the scene was clear except for the edges of my peripheral vision, which was a blur, as if I were looking through a frosted windowpane. On the teacher's desk was a world globe, a dictionary that looked more like a Bible, and a school bell of brass so much like the one I use that I had to look twice. The other thing on the desktop was a great, wooden clock-like machine. I watched the long-dead teacher call one of the boys up to his desk and had him take apart the machine. While the others worked their sums on slates, the little guy separated all the wheels, springs and cogs of the wooden machine, and spread the parts out on the floor. When he disassembled it entirely, the teacher gave a nod, and he began to put it together again.

Suddenly, I realized that Hiram was showing me the answer to Austin McClellan's inability to learn numbers or much of anything else. In a schoolroom of a hundred years ago, I was seeing how my ancient predecessor mined for the hidden talents of his students. With almost magical insight that little boy put the machine back together—and now, tonight I know what to do. Austin McClellan is going to disassemble my old lawn mower engine with Pop's tool kit, and we'll see what happens. God knows I've tried everything else on the child.

I wanted to call Lacey and share this scene with her, but I was afraid that like me, she'd forget where she actually was and perhaps stumble over something and fall. I don't know how long Hiram held that picture in my mind, but it was long enough for me to focus on everything that Hiram concentrated on: the quaint, handmade dresses of the girls with their puffed sleeves and quantities of lace, and the little boots that buttoned up to the ankle and then peeped beneath the long skirts as they moved. They were like tintype characters, the boys in their suspenders and homemade shirts and breeches that bloused at the knee, long woven stockings and brogan shoes. The ancient pendulum clock that hung behind the teacher's desk (a desk likely swapped on Sunday, I thought, for the pulpit in the corner), was there to remind teacher, preacher, and learners that time is something likely to get away from us if we don't keep an eye on it.

What a trip that was, the old schoolroom, the long-dead scholars, and their serious schoolmaster whose calluses and sunburn showed that his work didn't end at the three o'clock bell. There was an oak bucket on the bench beneath the coat rack, with a dipper handle sticking out, not very different from my double-walled cream can. Around the walls were portraits—etchings, I suppose—of Washington, Jefferson, Ben Franklin, and the other founders of the country, who might have been actually seen in the flesh by many people still alive when this phantom school was in session. The weight of history hung over these child-scholars, but their quaint dress was nothing to the timelessness of their eager faces. They looked like my kids, scrubbed and ready for each new day of learning. They were as real as a color movie.

There was a movement behind me and I felt, rather than saw, Lacey come into the room. I turned to warn her. "Honey, be careful where you step, it's one of Hiram's pictures. The school he attended when he was a boy."

261

"I see that—and look at the teacher, Steve. He's got that Clark *lets see what you got* grin Pop had. Is he one of your great-great-great-kinfolks?"

I hadn't seen that about him, I just saw a young man about my age with long sideburns, a collarless shirt, and a worn frock coat much frayed at the elbows.

When I looked again, making sure that Lacey didn't stumble over a chair, I saw the teacher take from the boy (who I thought might be the young Hiram), a slate with a figure written in chalk on it. The schoolmaster, sure enough, had that look Lacey had described, questioning eyebrows and inquisitive grin.

Hiram, concentrating on his illusion and lost in time, I guessed hadn't noticed Lacey and I staring curiously at his creation.

Glancing back at the clock on the wall, the teacher gave a great stretch and smiled at his students. When he said "dinnertime," I read his lips and watched startled as he did something my father used to do—he kissed his palm and patted his belt buckle. It was a gesture my pop said meant "a blessing on this meal." Lacey and I held hands and watched in stunned silence.

"Good God, Lacey, unless that was some kind of a coincidence I don't believe for a minute, schoolmasters run in the whole damn family!"

The image vanished and Hiram nodded over the re-lighting of his pipe.

I made notes of what I had seen, while Lacey and Hiram talked about children and schooling and of course, music. They are so fond of each other and Hiram does his best to wait on her. She went to bed a while ago and Hiram has gone upstairs to read.

I'VE SPENT THE last hours thinking about a few items I need to address: the Christmas party on the 20th at school; Christmas; our baby's (no name yet) birthday that could happen— God knows when; a preacher who has decided we are tools of Satan; a school board leaning that way; presents for my school kids (maybe a silver dollar for each of them from Pop's coin collection); a call or letter to Vera to tell her about Hiram, the thread that runs through all of our lives.

Mom—Vera waiting to drive over here to help with the baby will be surprised to find out she has an in-law by marriage— Hiram who is staying with us. There is no way to warn her over the phone, which would be about as secret as announcing it with native drums. The most important idea I must stay centered on is that the endless Möbius strip of time is a fact and that all of us, me, Lacey, Pop, Mom, the Donnellys, the Trolls, and maybe even the kids I'm daily teaching to cope with this life, have one thing in common: it's distinctly possible that we've all lived before.

Chapter Nineteen

OOKING BACK AT MY NOTES, I CAN almost go back to those days when we were so close to Christmas that the short days were never long enough to get anything done, much less everything.

❖

DECEMBER 15, 1951

LACEY, BIG AS a barrage balloon, has insisted on decorating the house with wreaths of greenery and ornaments. I depended upon Hiram to help her with reaching high places like our tree, which takes up the area between the piano and front entryway. We had brought home all of Pop's fifty strings of Christmas lights, and I managed to decorate the porch and eaves with half the outdoor ones with enough left over to wrap our twin firs. After thinking about it, I got Hiram to hold the ladder. Since his violin seems to be the only thing that gives him visibility, I had asked him to leave it in the house so we wouldn't have to worry about people passing by. We were lucky no one did because he was as excited about the lights as a child seeing fireworks. He insisted on giving me directions as I began at the top and slowly walked the string of lights around the firs. I even had him plug them in, since electricity is such a wonder to him and his sigh at the beauty of the firs lighted up at last, was worth all the effort.

Lacey came out to see our work and was so enchanted with the effect of our shining house in its forest hollow that she sent Hiram in to don Pop's bibs and a shirt and cap. "You know people are going to drive by to see this," she said sensibly, "we better get ready for company."

After the preacher experience, I knew she was excited by the idea of validating Hiram's presence and wanted to experiment some more. People did drive by and slow down to look, but no one stopped tonight. After nine o'clock, I unplugged the cord to all the outside lights leaving only our Christmas tree lights on. Lacey had gone to bed, and I was finishing my school work when Hiram came to sit by the fire and pet Custer's gray head, light his pipe, and study the glowing tree beyond the piano.

When he started talking, I put away my papers.

He began by saying, "What I least understand about my state is why I've been so alone." He paused for a bit and then continued. "If what has happened to me has happened to others who died, it would seem that I would have a goodly bait of company, appears to me. Surely the dead must be numerous."

"I've thought the same thing," I admitted. "There's an old

265

saying, 'There's a lot more layin' down than there is up walkin' 'round' that keeps coming to mind. Why wouldn't you have a connection with other ghosts?"

The old man was silent a while.

"I've a great notion," he said to make a point, "that spirits or ghosts, or whatever it is that I am, are not created to deal with each other, but only the humanity they can affect in some way. Perhaps they deal with promises not kept—debts not paid, things not said, a task not fulfilled."

He went on. "I've been rememberin' a great deal lately. Maybe my mind is tryin' to tell me more about why I am fated to be here. I must suppose it is an act of God's will and deal with it."

The old man reached to touch the violin that lay on the end table next to him, and with the touch, he was visible for a moment. "I know that passin' on the music was always my joy, but how can I play for an audience in my circumstance now? People like that parson already see the violin as Satan's instrument—as some thought even in my day. So for whom am I supposed to play? Mistress Lacey and you? Perhaps your unborn child? Or maybe only for the recordin' machine she captures me on. And why did I appear in so many lives before I was allowed to find my music again?"

"*So many lives?*" I asked. "You mean your return to Bessie and your sons? When no one knew you were there?"

"Oh no, I mean the many lives of others I have affected since my death that have had no explanation and are still a puzzle I work at."

Now I was certifiably confused but didn't want to disturb his

266

wandering thoughts.

"Music allows me to gather powerful, wordless images that immerse my mind," he went on, "such as the concept of a life for a life, which keeps peckin' at my thoughts. Is that familiar to you?"

"Well, I know about a tooth for a tooth, an eye for an eye," I said doubtfully, "they're in the Bible, though I don't like to think it's something God would say."

"I was readin' your copy of Kiplin's works, and I was struck by a line from *The Ballad of East and West*, which goes, 'A gift for a gift, said Kamal then, a limb for the risk of a limb.' It makes me wonder. I have such strange memories at times, of other situations, other battles, other places, as if I have given my life for a life more than once. I have no idea why this is so, but bein' here and recoverin' my music has enabled me to see some of the times I have appeared before to affect a life. It makes me wonder if I am now responsible for those lives I saved by doin' it. Would you be willin' to see one of these memories?"

"Let me make sure Lacey is asleep," I replied.

I went to the bedroom and Lacey was snoring gently, her long hair spread out on both pillows. When I came back, Hiram was visible and staring at the Christmas tree. The soft glow of lights shown on ornaments older than I was, passed down by my grandparents and Lacey's, and Hiram was fingering a little blown glass military trumpet that had once been mirrored silver.

"A strange Christmas ornament," he mused, "a battle trumpet on a tree of peace."

"Go ahead Hiram," I said. "Lacey is sound asleep."

267

"Don't be surprised by anythin'," said Hiram. "I don't always have control over these things once I start them."

For several minutes all I could hear was the crackling fire and thought that Hiram might have left the room. I stood up and the fireplace began to fill with a dense opalescent mist pouring outward into the room. Then everything disappeared, the tree, fireplace, all was engulfed by the mist; I remembered the last time this happened and braced my mind.

I found myself standing in the middle of a dark forest of firs or some kind of conifers that were facing a little opening in a woods. It was daylight but the gloom of the ancient trees shut out sunlight, except for what filtered down in spotted patches on a small clearing. It was as if I had actually been carried to this place. It was so real, I felt as though I could have leaned against one of those huge trees if I wished and walked out into that small clearing.

As my eyes got used to the light and shade of the woods, I saw a man. I was standing behind where he lay on his stomach in a patch of dark fir needles; he was looking through binoculars at a distant spot on the other side of the glade. I was looking there, too, and had to glance down to spot him when I saw him move a hand from under the fir boughs, which he had pulled over most of his body. A flat tinny-looking army helmet hid his face, the kind American and British solders wore in the First World War. He was wearing a brownish uniform of the same vintage and I recognized his gear: gas mask, field pack, bayonet and ammunition belt, canteen and the 30.06 Springfield rifle that lay beside him. He had a full tote bag next to him, which I supposed held hand grenades, or other explosives. He had to be an American because he wore those ridiculous legging puttees that were part of the uniform in those days. He was all alone.

Into my line of sight came a patrol of men in gray. I saw the body of the prone soldier tense as he watched them, and I became fascinated by what was about to happen. It was a German patrol led by an officer, I think, since I had no knowledge of what his German insignia indicated. There were bars on his collar and he was riding a large bay horse. In the sparse rays of the sun, I saw soldiers walking behind him in single file. They wore those unique flaring helmets that the Germans invented, and had fluted gas mask canisters hanging on straps from their necks. Each had a Mauser rifle slung upside-down for easier transport. Every soldier had several of those strange "potato masher" hand grenades hanging from his belt, and one man carried the barrel and receiver of a light machine gun. They were as real as my skin, which was crawling with the same fear the waiting American must have felt.

As they entered the glade, I could see the faces of the Germans—young faces, as innocent of hate as my schoolchildren. They looked like Boy Scouts dressed up for mock battle in a play and their leader wore a garrison hat, with his spiked helmet hanging from his saddle horn. As I watched, the troop came to a halt at a sign from the man on horseback, and the dozen or so boys took off their helmets, wiping their faces.

It was uncanny. I was standing within ten feet of the American solider, who lay motionless in the striped shade of firs, and I felt the danger he was in, as much as if it were me. The eyes of the patrol leader scanned every inch of the glade, seeking the enemy. An enemy who lay there before me wondering, I suppose, how far his grenades and ammunition could possibly go against a dozen men.

From deep within my memory I knew what was happening as well as I remembered *Treasure Island* or the death of King Arthur and wondered if I had read it.

Just as it seemed that the scanning eyes of the horseman would find the prone solider, the entire patrol turned in unison and looked at the opposite end of the glade from where I watched. A white-haired man riding a horse had ridden up on the group of Germans, apparently by accident. His uniform was probably French, I thought, since he wore no helmet, only a cockaded cap. I had the feeling he was a scout looking over the terrain for troops who would follow, unlucky enough to stumble on a squad of Germans doing the same thing.

In an instant, he pulled his horse about and put spurs to it. As he looked back to see what his chances were, I saw his face clearly. Even without a beard, it was Hiram. As the old man twisted his mount through the timber, the German patrol unslung their Mausers and began firing. It was eerie to hear nothing, watching that scene as rifles recoiled and ejected cartridge shells spun through the air. Pulling a Luger from his holster, the patrol leader set out in pursuit; his men followed, afraid to fire for fear of hitting their leader. Hiram had only to get into the thick woods and put a hill between them, but the German on horseback foresaw this. Stopping, he leveled his Luger and with both hands squeezed off a long shot as the scout's horse bunched itself to climb the steep bank. The horse, a big sorrel, fell carrying his rider with him, and the patrol ran toward them. In a moment, they were out of the glade and I didn't see them again. The prone man before me got quickly to his feet and, with shaking hands, put his field glass in its pouch. I looked at that familiar face and the gold ring on his right hand, and I knew everything.

It was my pop as he must have looked in 1918. It was so much my pop, I thought at first it was me; the resemblance was so plain. I saw Pop's heavy gold ring made from California nuggets that he'd worn since he was seventeen. And I knew, witnessing this remarkable sight, that Hiram was not only tied to the violin, the bed, and piano . . . he was tied inexorably, for some reason, to me.

THE IMAGES FADED and were gone. Hiram and I were alone in the living room before a cheerful fire. It was like returning from a different world, which I suppose in a way it had been.

"Good Lord, Hiram," I said, when I could say anything. "That was Pop, and you saved his life! When did you remember this?"

"*When* doesn't matter much to me," said the old man, who had lit his pipe and had returned to invisibility behind it. "Time bein' still such a puzzle. For instance, I know that I might save your life, too, or perhaps already did when I saved your father. But I do not understand about the time when these things occur. I must also have exchanged Kamal's 'gift for a gift' or a life, by not takin' the one of the soldier who killed me. Did you have a relative who fought in The War Between the States?"

271

That thought had never really occupied my mind, knowing I must have had several. My family had lived in Missouri for well over a hundred years, but the Clarks I knew weren't much for history, much less the Civil War.

The Donnellys, however, kept track of ancestors like a tribe of Mormons, and I remembered hearing Rabon mention a relative who had fought on one side or another.

I said, "Hold on a minute, Hiram," and headed straight for the bookcase to get the huge Donnelly family Bible that Rabon had loaned to us.

Printed in 1870, it was a huge old-fashioned book, which had room for pictures, marriages, birth and death entries in the front section. It was crammed with Lacey's ancestors' names in lists that marched through the years. I hadn't had time to more than glance through the old Bible, saving it for a time when Lacey and I could go through all the family records together—perhaps to add our generation and our new baby's name and picture to the dozens there. On the other hand, I did remember seeing pages of people in old uniforms, and it didn't take long to find the Civil War era near the front.

The third picture page I turned to told me all I needed to know, and feeling my hackles rise, I silently held out the great book for Hiram to see.

Dylan Donnelly had a page all to himself:

Born 1845—died 1896, age 51 years, 3 months.
Married Belle Simmons in 1866, to that union three
children: Matthew born 1867; Celia born 1868;
Roney born 1870. Dylan served with the GAR in

272

the infantry under the command of Maj. General
Joseph Hooker 1863-1864, wounded twice in action.
Buried at Doniphan, Missouri, April 7, 1896.

The words as meaningful as they were (since I had heard
Rabon talk about Grampa Roney), was not the reason I handed
Hiram the Bible. Above the words, in an oval cardboard frame,
was the young man the words described: Dylan Donnelly. It was
a boyish picture of a soldier, posing for a camera of that time, in
a new and shiny uniform and his rifle at parade rest. In the faded
copper antiquity of the tintype, the face looked confident and
proud, ready for the powder flash that would record him for history and for us. But I had seen him more clearly in the "hologram" the ghost had shown us, and I knew him well. He was the
Union solder who had killed Benjamin Springfield on that foggy
morning mountaintop near Chattanooga.

"I should have known," said Hiram, the great book suspended in midair above the hearth, while my unseen friend studied
the picture. "I reckon I have interfered with time, confoundin'
the order of things, and now time is callin' me to account. Well,
whatever the cost, I don't think I could have done things differ-
ently."

"Good God, Hiram!" I burst out. "If you had, Lacey wouldn't
be here. That soldier was her great-grandfather."

"True," said the ghost thoughtfully, "and I suppose, neither
would you or apparently myself—if I am here."

The concept was so shocking, I had an urge to wake up Lacey
who was better at multi-level thinking, but she was sleeping so
restfully. I restrained myself and instead tried to be helpful.

273

"Hiram, perhaps the account is paid up now. Maybe the music and your memories have come back to free you to go wherever you belong. You're different now, you know. Do you suppose the fact that our baby is coming is urging you to *create* yourself again?"

Hiram's head or at least his pipe nodded. "I'd like to believe somethin' of the sort, as much as I seem to have affected the past, I must believe that at least my musical soul was intended to survive into the future."

His voice became more cheerful. "Perhaps my music will have value to another generation of the family I seem to have inherited."

That was an interesting thought and it reminded me of Hiram's own children, and by this time, great—maybe great-great-grandchildren.

"What's happened to your family, Hiram—those two boys I saw in your picture, Harlin and Jacob and their families?"

The long silence that followed made me sorry I'd asked.

When Hiram spoke again, his voice was unutterably sad. "Jacob, my pride, my joy, and my hope for a future I was never destined to see. Ever since I produced the picture of my boys for you and Mistress Lacey, I have struggled to capture memories of them, all the while dreadin' to know the truth."

I had an uncomfortable foreboding and asked, "Jacob, your protégé?"

"Dead at thirteen, helpin' his mother fork hay from the loft. He fell and struck his neck on a manger and never moved again. I watched him fall and could do nothin' but fall myself, headfirst

274

into hopelessness."

I was overwhelmed with the enormity of such a loss for our poor ghost. *I thought, no wonder he had wandered the lonely corridors of memory, afraid to open a door all these years.*

Eventually, I gathered enough nerve to speak. "And Harlin? I know he survived because of his daughter Maudie."

Hiram sighed, but his voice was a little lighter when he answered. "Harlin was a good boy and as you would put it, a survivor. He helped Bessie with the farm as best he could, but his heart was never in it, and after the war he was always wanderin' off to play for a dance or a frolic at some mountain cabin."

There was no reproach in Hiram's voice and he told these things like an observer, which I suppose he'd been.

"Harlin loved to play music for people but lacked the genius that Jacob was born with. He liked other instruments as much as the fiddle and could play them as well. He liked to drink while he played, too. I suppose to drown memories and took his music to bear baitin's, cock fights, and rough dances where a fiddle was as apt to be cracked as a head and Bessie never let him touch my Guarnerius after I was gone, though Jacob played it all the time."

The old man spoke slowly as if he were reconciling his son's devil-may-care ways. "Harlin didn't mind, for he was never jealous-hearted about anything, a free spirit who took life as it came and one instrument was very like another to him."

This answered the unspoken question Lacey and I had pondered: why hadn't his children inherited the Guarnerius in its bedpost hiding place?

But Hiram wasn't done with his son's history. "Harlin mar-

275

ried but wasn't much better at that than farmin', for he was forever out of pocket as a young man. His wife died in childbirth as
did the child, while he was off to a backwoods fiddler's contest,
leavin' her home with Bessie."

The growing horror I felt listening to this made my flesh crawl.
How much could people take, back in the days he described?
How could Bessie remain sane through this unending cycle of
death and the destruction of hope?

Hiram's voice continued his deliberate tale. "The doom of
this family blow, added to childhood memories of death and dashed
dreams for Harlin, and he never played a fiddle again, although
he never gave up music. He also waited ten years to marry his
second wife, Sally—Maudie's mother. By this time, Bessie was
an elderly lady and unable to do much with the farm or her existence, except to persevere."

I knew the ghost, telling me this, was doing his best to do the
same.

"Sally bore Harlin three children, but though they liked their
father's music, none of them seemed particularly gifted. Though
Harlin and later my Bessie, when she went to live with them,
encouraged them to sing and play. My violin stayed in its hidin'
place nevertheless, for it was no knockabout play-pretty, and
Bessie treasured it as her one connection to Jacob and to me."

Hiram stopped and relit his pipe. "And now you know as
much as I have remembered, little enough for a hundred years of
history, but I have only received it myself in bits and pieces. What
remains of me is in God's hands."

"Hiram, thank you. I have no idea what happens next, but

276

you must think of us as family now, because Lacey and I do."

I reached out my hand and his unseen one grasped mine. We shook hands solemnly on that thought, and even though my hand grasped the invisible, Hiram's was as real to me as mine. His touch was as firm and reassuring as that of any human being, and I knew in the handclasp that whatever elements a man might lose in dying, love isn't one of them.

Chapter Twenty

REPARING FOR THE CHRISTMAS PLAY
and the party afterward was a lot of work and
fun. I could give it all the time the kids deserved
because Hiram was there for Lacey, more con-
fident in his role as visiting uncle every day. If someone came to
the door, Hiram grabbed his fiddle and answered the knock, looking like an old fellow whose hobby had been interrupted. He
played the part so well, even the mailman called him "Uncle
Hiram," and everybody seemed to accept his fiddle as easily as
his pipe, his cap, or the dog that was always with him.

LACEY LOVED PLAYING cello accompaniment to Hiram's
fiddle, and one evening I arrived home to hear the sound of
"Carol Of The Bells." They played so inventively that I stood in
wonder on the walk for a minute or two, caught in the sounds of
Christmas emerging from our fairy-tale house wrapped in snow.
The beauty of their lively duet mesmerized me.

278

After supper, Lacey said she had an idea how we could incorporate Hiram into the school Christmas party. She and Hiram had been plotting it out for days and had perfected a plan. At first I was appalled, but soon realized she'd thought it through better than I could have. Since our neighbors knew we had company anyway and that our guest played the fiddle, I realized that having him play for a crowd would be a clever way to establish his reality.

I have to admit that the idea of letting people who thought ghosts were Satanic, see poor old Hiram in a festive setting, which we could control, was fun. It appealed to my imagination but it was also dangerous, since we would be toying with a situation that depended on supernatural stuff none of us understood. But Hiram was so touchingly anxious to try and Lacey so confident, I gave in. One constant in Hiram's ghostly rule of appearance seemed to be the Guarnerius, which brought him to life with the immediacy of a light switch. It might be a chancy thing to depend on, but in view of what I'd learned about Hiram's history, life was based on chance anyway. So why split hairs?

AT SCHOOL, I told the kids that Lacey and my Uncle Hiram would play for everybody, and the kids liked the idea. They were so excited about the night, they would have agreed to anything. The kids were already so obsessed with the Christmas play, it's a wonder I got anything scholastic done.

Weeks before, we had drawn names for gift-giving and to top that, we also had a drawing to select the three students who would find and cut the school Christmas tree. This job was usually done either by the teacher or, in years before, one of the biggest boys, but I saw no reason to limit tree picking to age or gender. The three kids who won the drawing were a perfect cross-section of my school—Mildred Cartwright age eleven, Cissie Smith, eight, and Austin McClellan. The older kids declared disgust with the idea that two girls and a first grader could ever manage to find a good tree, much less bring it in. Given their choice of where to find a tree, the three children chose the north side of Blessing Creek where the cedars march up terraces of stony bluffs to the Indian Glade plateau.

Cedars are the Ozark Christmas tree—strange to me, who grew up in an area of pine and imported fir, but native to them. I gave Austin the saw to carry and sent them out at recess to bring in our tree, hoping for I don't know what. About a minute before recess was over, what we got was one of the loveliest, fattest and most Christmas-tree shaped cedars I'll ever see. My small crew dragged it to the snowy entryway, and we cobbled together a tree stand and put it up immediately. The schoolroom smelled like the woods, and we quickly put work away for the rest of the afternoon and practiced our play.

My sister Marilyn had decided to be a real Santa Claus for Indian Glade. She had sent me a letter back in October, asking for all the ages, gender, and various personalities of my children, and the week before Christmas, a huge box of presents had arrived. After a preliminary viewing by Lacey and me (not the presents, just the wrappings), we put everything back in the box and put it under the school tree. Each day until Christmas the child with the best day's effort got to feel his present, weigh it, poke it, fondle it, and shake it. It was absolute bribery, and they loved it. Austin McClellan bribed into education by getting a two-cycle lawn mower engine to disassemble, couldn't believe he was also getting a present the size of a breadbox.

I CAN REMEMBER those days before that long-ago Christmas almost without consulting my journal because they sparkle so with time. My Lacey was glowing and vibrant, fairly humming with the excitement of having her first child in a time when the world was in the mood for celebration. Nothing fazed her; I watched her in awe as she bustled and wrapped things, fixed amazing meals that made no sense—like hot dogs with peanut butter and summer potato salad—and insisted on doing all our laundry in Pop's washing machine in the cellar. She did all this with incredible energy, climbing stairs like a monkey and laughing when I worried. At least Hiram had been through this before and he was a calming influence for both of us.

"A woman bearin' a child," he told us during one of their pauses in rehearsal, "bears the future with all of its promise and quirks. She is two bein's and in two places at once and can be excused for any odd behavior."

"And what *odd behavior* would that be, Uncle Hiram?" asked Lacey, pretending to chew a bite off his bar of bow rosin.

That was also the day I remember when Hiram said one of those things that let us know how much he appreciated our being there for him.

"Do you remember the musical term *rubato*, Lacey?" he asked her musingly.

"Like *adagio*, and *presto*, and *andante?*" she inquired. "I know they are tempos, Uncle. *Rubato* is where you use one note more expressively than the next, even when it's the same note."

Hiram nodded appreciatively. "Herr Stern told me that *rubato* was stealin' emphasis from one note to give it to another, as *ta-DA*, the musical flourish. He said the word meant 'robbed time.'" The old man's eyes crinkled in humor, "Nowadays, I apply that term to my playin', for all my memories represent *robbed time*." His face turned solemn. "I cannot tell you how much playin' music with you has meant to me."

"Same here, *Uncle Rubato*," said Lacey grinning, "we're gonna knock 'em dead at the schoolhouse. Present company excepted, of course."

Somehow I couldn't really worry much about Lacey when it came to coping, and seeing how fond she was of Hiram, I was glad we were making him part of our lives.

ON THURSDAY NIGHT, I presented Hiram and Lacey to open the festivities, to a packed schoolhouse. Hiram was wearing an old suit of Pop's—it hadn't fit Pop for twenty years—and a shirt and tie of mine. He looked very distinguished, very much the violinist in that outfit, and the assembled families couldn't take their eyes off him. Neither could I, but for a private reason—I was afraid he'd disappear. Lacey had given him a meticulous haircut and trimmed his beard so neatly that he looked almost professorial. A tall, imposing presence that was so unlike the ghost I knew that after a while, I began to relax for the first time in a week. Lacey had a good time showing off my "Uncle Hiram," who we had decided would be supposedly married to one of my pop's sisters.

The only time my stomach plunged in these introductions was when I saw that the Terrills had brought their preacher along, the dreadful Pastor Tucker. Hiram smiled, shook the man's hand firmly but no more firmly than he held onto his fiddle with the other. Hiram looked him over from head to foot the same way the preacher looked at others, as if he was "sizing his pile," too. Lacey couldn't resist taking a shot.

"This is the man who made me boil your oats over, Uncle Hiram," she said sweetly and was pleased to see Pastor Tucker turn brick red. He wasn't used to being taken lightly.

The audience, besides the entire school community, included to my astonishment, the Trolls, who arrived at seven o'clock, scrubbed, perfumed, and amazingly sober for the Christmas "doin's." They brought presents, too, in the form of orange candy peanuts and a sack of hard candy that would have taken teeth out of a corn-sheller. The Burdeys were on their best behavior that night and tried to limit their vocabulary to what they thought was fitting language, something that must have galled Clive. I was glad to see Clive and introduce the family to Hiram, who had a hard time keeping his face neutral. I knew it was all he could do, not to ask about Pus and his wonderful flying dog.

The Trolls made up, in some ways, for Pastor Tucker, who scarcely concealed his disapproval of them and whose eyes darted about like a cat in a room full of mice. The man was looking for evidence of sin and when his eyes fell on Hiram's violin, they glowed like coals. I half expected him to say "A-Hah!" But Hiram looked too dignified and respectable to mess with in that company. I was quite sure Pastor Tucker had invited himself to the party to make sure that the Christmas play didn't offend any of his religious taboos.

At last, when everyone had found a place to sit or stand, I tapped the hand bell with a ruler. Behind the curtain, I heard my actors giggling and shushing each other. Hiram and Lacey took their places—Lacey seated with her cello and Hiram, tall and impressive, standing at center curtain.

I spoke to the audience. "Thank you all for coming folks. Before we present our play, a scene from Dickens' *A Christmas Carol*, we have a special treat for you—my wife Lacey on her cello, and playing the violin, my uncle Hiram, to bring you a 'Carol Of The Bells.'"

I don't know what those rural folks expected to hear, but what followed was the most amazing rendition of that song I had ever heard—no words, but the voice of the violin singing merrily as a choir, and the bells chiming everywhere with the *pizzicato* of Hiram's fingernails picking tinkling bells out of thin air with either hand. The cello took up the snowy pipe organ harmonics to the tune. It ended with Lacey bowing a long haunting chord, while Hiram plucked three parting bells from the great hollow voice of the Guarnerius. The audience was stunned. I saw Clive Burdey's lips move in a silent "Gawwwd day-mmm!" The other listeners looked at each other in wonder before they began to applaud.

Even Pastor Tucker had to applaud slightly, though I could see it was out of character for him and he didn't look happy.

Hiram and Lacey took bows and moved to the side when I promised the audience that they would play again later.

The school play included a wildly condensed version of the Crachit's Christmas dinner. It turned out to be like all school plays from time out of mind; it was funny and touching with all the kids doing things their parents expected and treasured. I kept an eye on Pastor Tucker; I was afraid he was going to stand up and object to the ghost part, but he managed to control himself. As a matter of fact, he was the only person that brought a camera, and during the play I noticed the flash of his camera, which at the time I thought ought to be pretty funny and cute. I decided that maybe the dour preacher might have a soft side after all.

Some of the children were nervous and forgot their lines; they stood gaping like fish until children in the wings would "whisper" their lines. Every one knew each other's lines and they were as interchangeable as parts for a Model A Ford. Some of them getting carried away, fairly shouted their parts. Cissie Smith playing Tiny Tim with super-charged energy, nearly brained Bob Cratchit (Cleavis Farley) with her crutch while climbing onto his shoulders, and the curtain got caught on the Ghost of Christmas Present's (Betty McClellan) cornucopia, exposing a couple of costume adjustments backstage and a lot of tittering Cratchits.

Aside from all these expected mishaps, the play was all anyone could have wanted. After Cissie Smith said, "God bless us every one" and my young actors had taken their bows, they had their picture snapped, and we closed the bed-sheet curtains. Lacey and Hiram played "Silent Night" and "Oh Little Town Of Bethlehem," while the children "struck-the-set" and made room

285

for the cast and family party around the Christmas tree.

We had an overflow crowd and needed every square inch of the space left around the little cedar, which was festooned with the children's handmade ornaments: strings of popcorn, paper chains and cutout snowflakes. I'd used Pop's truck battery and had attached it to a couple of six-volt strands of lights, to illuminate the tree. The children, so proud of having their very own lighted tree, had to explain to each of their folks how we had done it.

My sister's presents were so surprisingly right for everybody; I was in awe at her insight. I watched the children open them very carefully, saving both string and paper. It was very different from the Donnelly household where wrapping flew into ripped piles as everybody tore into their gifts with Irish abandon. I took mental notes for Marilyn who would want to read about it in detail.

Oran Cartwright got a crystal radio set to put together. Little Austin McClellan got a small one-cylinder steam engine that really worked, with a tiny candle for power. Betty McClellan got a nurse's uniform with first-aid kit. Irene Farley received a candle-powered carousel with angels holding little tinkling bells. Cleavis Farley and Ruby McClellan got sturdy pocketknives with bone handles. Cissie Smith got a doll with two changes of costume, and so on, until Lacey and I could see that Marilyn, using only imagination, had made every kid feel special.

The presents were exactly of the right proportions. Although they represented a lot more thought than most of the families would have taken, they blended in perfectly with the small gifts we all gave each other and didn't overwhelm anyone. I blessed my sister Marilyn a hundred times for being a distant Santa to children she would never see and for imagining so well their needs and dreams.

The older people seemed to enjoy themselves as much as ever at a school "doins," even though they started out a little less comfortable, a fraction less outgoing than they were before the ghost rumors.

They said it was the best play they had ever seen and everyone complimented Lacey and Hiram's music, but I felt a disturbing distance involved in the evening. I know no better way to put it than to say that a sort of formless agenda existed in that room that Christmastime shouldn't generate.

Remarkably, Hiram was the one who finally brought the party around to what it should be, and I was first to realize it. Hiram's good spirits were simply too high for me to lose my own, and gradually took over the old school room. It was as if he had saved up goodwill and his southern charm for all those years, to spill over onto these children. Parent by parent, I began to sense the uneasiness dissolve as the old man came up with story-tunes he played and sang with his deep southern accent. He sang about a little tailor who tried to shoot a "carrion crow" with his bow and arrow but killed his cow instead, and half a dozen funny songs like "Froggy Went A-Courting," which had the kids in stitches. He led them in "Good King Wenceslas" and "Jingle Bells," giving Franny Terrill the job of jingling the sleighbells, which "Uncle Hiram" remembered to bring from home. Soon most of the children gathered around that fascinating old man to sing Christmas carols, chatter to him and show him their gifts. Uncle Hiram became the hit of the party, making his violin meow and bark, trill like a dozen different birds, sound like a baby, and even sing a few words the kids guessed. This left me free to go to the big Charter Oak stove and make a great kettle of popcorn, which Lacey and some of the other women rolled into molasses balls and passed around to everybody.

I have a feeling it was the longest anyone had ever stayed for a schoolhouse party, entertained by the very ghost I was likely to lose my job over. If any of them were suspicious of Hiram's presence in the first place, they had no time to question him about anything. It was as if Lacey and I had hired an entertainer just for them. Before the families left, all of the men took time to shake his hand and said the usual invitation, "You'ns all come see us now,"—with exception of Pastor Tucker who herded the Terrills before him like sheep before a storm.

"Thank you for taking pictures, Pastor Tucker," I said. "Could you make some copies for the schoolhouse?"

"Definitely, Mr. Clark. We'll be seeing you," were his parting words. I believed him but wondered if "We" was in the royal sense, which I wouldn't have put past him, or meant his whole flock of ghostphobes.

The rest of the folks left more slowly, the children wanting to hold onto every minute of this shining night. They were now actors, and no one at home would be liable to forget it.

All the women were polite to Hiram and solicitous about Lacey, taking time to give her last minute compliments on her music, advice about the coming baby, and directions for her to follow.

Eventually the Trolls left (jump started or pushed, of course), Soames and Virgie after them, and last, the Summers family's taillights disappeared, leaving us alone. I heaved a weary *job-well-done* kind of sigh.

"Hiram," I said, "you were incredible." The ghost chuckled knowing my stress for the past four hours.

"I fear I'm a born performer," he said, "and the chance to play for young people again kept ticklin' my memory for tunes. I do appreciate your trustin' me to entertain. And what a pleasure it was to play in your company, Mistress Lacey!"

"Uncle Hiram," said Lacey, "I wasn't playing all that well. It's getting hard to reach around the 'Buford' to bow those far strings."

Last week, she'd been trying different joke-names for the baby and I have to admit "Buford" was an improvement on "Bucky-Bob," "Wilameeny-Sue" and "Little Rufus-Earl," all of which she made-up from her Ozark memory bank.

I looked around at the lack of mess, not a scrap of paper on the floor, paper cups and napkins all burned in the stove, and all coffee things and leftovers taken home by the ladies who had brought them. I thought the only feast schoolhouse mice would get out of this would be flakes of popcorn, fragments of candy, and the shards of walnuts fallen into ancient floor cracks—walnuts that Mrs. Summers had patiently cracked for everyone from the basin that she kept all evening in her crow-black lap.

The most amazing thing about the evening, we had actually introduced Hiram into a gathering of people who didn't believe he could (or should) exist, and he turned out the most believable and lively person there.

As I banked the stove with ashes and went around blowing out all the lanterns—turning off the mantle lamps, and putting Pop's truck battery in the Jeep—I thought about Myrtle Summers. Closing the schoolhouse door behind us, I remember smiling, thinking the old lady had an ability to haunt any room she was in that by comparison, put our sociable old ghost in the shade.

As I locked the door, it wasn't the cold that made me give a little shudder; something told me that despite passing this first test of Hiram's believability, our problems weren't over. I kept hearing the threat in Pastor Tucker's parting words: *We'll be seeing you.*

Hiram was in high spirits even though he was crammed in the back of the Jeep with his fiddle case and Lacey's cello. The Christmas music had inspired him to talk about the music in his head.

"Do you have much supply of music paper, Mistress Lacey?" he asked. "I have a great notion to put some musical ideas down."

Lacey chuckled. "Uncle Hiram, you sure drove your ducks to the right puddle. I've been carting around music paper for four years wondering if I'd ever need it. A hundred sheets be enough?"

To our amusement, Hiram appeared to think about that. "Why I believe so," he said leaning forward eagerly to put his head between us. "I am thinkin' of devisin' a suite of music that Bessie inspired me to do some day—composed of waltzes, dance tunes, and colored folk's songs of old-times. Perhaps you might help me remember how to construct notes again."

Lacey said, "You bet, Uncle, and I have a book or two that

will help."

ONCE HOME, HIRAM and I changed clothes and got busy building up the fires and taking out ashes. Consequently, it was a while before I could sit down, have a drink and recap the night in my mind. Lacey, in a quilted flannel robe, drank some warm milk to keep me company. She looked tired, but her eyes were shining with memories of the evening and the fun of watching Hiram come to life for the children. She wasn't sleepy and brought up what was on both of our minds.

"Steve, what's the master plan for Christmas? Are we going to just play it by ear and see what happens?"

It was something I had already been thinking about for days.

We decided improvisation was about as sensible as anything we could do. Rabon and Vera would want to be here for sure, but Rabon only for Christmas day. He always had inside construction work to do in the winter and crews to supervise. It was certain that Vera would be here to help after the baby's birth, but for Christmas she wouldn't stay any longer than Rabon. The baby was the unknown factor, and Doc Brant's suggestion that we let Santa bring him was as real a possibility as tonight, or New Year's night for that matter.

"So we'll give them Hiram's bed on Christmas Eve and put Hiram on the couch?" I asked.

"Right," she said, "and we'll keep it simple. I don't think this is the time to introduce my folks to Hiram. If people stop by and bring him up—God forbid—we'll make up a story for Mom and Dad. He's *your* uncle."

That agreed on, Lacey called up to our ghost who had gone upstairs to wipe and polish his violin. In deference to us, Hiram walked downstairs carrying fiddle and bow to be visible.

"Uncle Hiram, music paper is in one of the closets upstairs, along with a chromatic harmonica I used in school, and there's a composer's handbook with all the tools to write a symphony, I expect."

Hiram smiled and bent to kiss her hand. "I cannot thank you enough, my dear child."

A queasy thought came to me. "Uh, Hiram," I said carefully, wondering if I'd read too many ghost stories, "have you ever tried writing anything down?" I seemed to remember something spooky about ghostly writing that disappeared, and I didn't want to dampen his excitement. He was ahead of me, though.

"You remember I saw myself in your mirror, Stephen," he said. "Also, I played 'Elizabeth's Waltz' to Mistress Lacey's recordin' machine, and she played it back for me. Surely music in written form should be as existent as that played."

That got Lacey's attention. "Yeah, but Hiram that was your fiddle, your spirit-Guarnerius that makes us see you. It doesn't mean a pencil will do that."

Hiram looked perplexed. "I would think it's the music rather than the instrument that makes it possible, Mistress. For you first saw me seated at the piano before I even remembered my fiddle. If I am but a musical bein', wouldn't writin' my work be as effective as playin' it?"

Lacey, preferring action to what-ifs, went to her writing desk and grabbed a pencil and tablet. She slapped it down on the small table beside the couch. "Let's find out, write 'my name is Hiram.'"

Hiram laid the fiddle aside as we watched the pencil move over the surface of the tablet. It remained utterly blank.

"Whoa!" said Hiram, but he said it calmly as though he were talking to a horse.

"Okay," said Lacey, "try 'my name is Benjamin Springfield.'" The result was the same. Lacey didn't seem discouraged, "Steve run get some music paper and let's see if he can compose."

When I finally found the thick package and brought it down, it appeared that Lacey had thought out the situation as well as anyone could. She picked the top sheet and quickly scrawled a music staff and clef sign and handed the pencil to Hiram.

The pencil flew across the page and this time left a flurry of black spots with posts and tiny flags.

"*Voilà!*" sang Lacey. "Uncle Hiram is a musical reality, sort of a song about to be played or sung or something. Now we know what makes you tick, Uncle!"

"Wait a minute, Lacey." I had just had a jarring thought. "Remember the preacher's camera? Was he just taking pictures of the kids? What if he took a picture of Hiram and there's no one there?"

"But Steve, Hiram never put the fiddle down. He was visible every minute."

"But would the camera see him?" I asked.

"*Ohmigod!*" said Lacey. "I was so glad everybody was seeing him, I never thought about it."

I remembered the camera Lacey's folks gave us last year; it

293

was packed away somewhere. "Do you have any film in the camera?" I couldn't believe I hadn't thought of the film evidence before, but neither Lacey nor I were camera people.

"I think some came with it," she said slowly, "if it keeps that long. Are you going to take pictures of Uncle Hiram?"

"I have to try," I said. "Maybe it's like the scales we tried to weigh him on or the tablet you gave him. Maybe a camera is also the wrong tool to measure Hiram with."

"I don't think you can take a picture of music," she worried, "and that's what Uncle Hiram seems to mostly be. I can't believe we got so careless."

"It's okay kid," I told her. "We were thinking about the children and the parents and the music, and Hiram looked so natural."

After a bit of searching, I found the little Kodak Brownie in a box under the eaves. I was relieved to find a flash attachment, bulbs and a container of film. I left it up to Lacey to load the film and put a flash bulb in the reflector.

"Hiram, play 'Dixie,'" I said.

The ghost, wearing Pop's coveralls and house-slippers, tucked the violin under his whiskers and did just that. I went through the roll of film, taking pictures of Hiram, Lacey, the tree, the fireplace, the kitchen and while I was at it, using up every flash bulb. When I ran out of bulbs, I turned on lights and hoped for the best.

I did think, now that my mind was working again, to have something or somebody beside Hiram in each shot so that the pictures wouldn't look too strange to the person developing the

294

film, in case Hiram didn't register.

"I don't know where the Medley Springs drugstore sends film to be developed," I told Lacey, "but I hope I get these back before the preacher gets his. Maybe he'll wait 'til after Christmas to send them."

"In your dreams," said Lacey sourly. "I bet Rectum Tucker has developing stuff in his basement in case he catches people in mid-sin."

"You mean *Reverend Tucker*, I think," said Hiram mildly.

"No I don't," snapped Lacey.

Chapter Twenty-One

RIDAY MORNING WAS A FINE, BRIGHT day to begin the last day of school before our Christmas holidays. I got up before it turned that way; I had to make a fast trip to Medley Springs before dawn to put our film through the mail slot at the drugstore. It was a quick trip at that time of the morning and I took Pop's truck to make it faster, trading it for the Jeep when I got back.

Only the northern slopes of the hills still had patches of snow and for the first time in my life, I hoped it wouldn't be a white Christmas. I felt guilty about wishing it, remembering how Pop felt about sleighbells, but Lacey was awfully near term, and we were twelve miles from Medley Springs. A Jeep, no matter how sure-footed and dependable, was no comfortable way to get Lacey there. Worse, her folks would have to drive across the Ozarks in Christmas traffic, and a big snow at this time would make any trip a bobsled ride.

296

I drove the Jeep slowly on the road under the bluffs, thinking about the children and how excited they had been Friday night opening their gifts. I wondered if Austin had taken his little steam engine apart yet, or if the big boys had *poked* pocketknives already—*poking* being a funny Ozark term for knife-swapping. The best thing about teaching, I thought, was the kids. If teaching good behavior meant staying flexible, honest and curious, they taught me right back with things like "poking" knives.

As I drove up the long lane to the schoolhouse, I eased my mind about them. The kids could save up their sledding and snow games for a couple of days I thought, until "Buford" got here, and God knew, with January and February coming, there would be plenty of snow to play in. But still, I remembered the magic of Christmas snow when you were little and thought Santa's sleigh depended on it to land on your roof. I sighed. I also made a small wistful wish that Hiram would show up on the film I had delivered. It wasn't quite a prayer, my mother had warned me against wasting those on trifles or matters of convenience. Prayers, she thought, were for events that cracked the bones of the soul.

I PULLED UP to get my always inspiring first sight of the school, there were already kids on the playground and a fine, ropy curl of smoke from the chimney. This meant that Orin and Buck had already warmed the little room, filled the wood box and put paper in the privies. Coming through their woods-path from the Farleys' were the bobbing the heads of the rest of my scholars—Farleys, Terrills, Smiths and McClellans, and all was right with my small world.

I said a silent thanks to the God who looks after schoolteachers, for a day that would at last get back to normal, and pulled in to park in my usual spot, which in summer would have been under the shade of the huge oaks.

The normal part ended right after lunch. Hiram arrived while I was reciting my fifth and sixth graders for any sign of memory concerning fractions.

Betty McClellan, who had come up to my desk to use the pencil sharpener, spotted the visitor through the west windows. "Mr. Clark, the music man is here."

"It's your Uncle Hiram," added Mildred Cartwright from the blackboard.

All attention focused on the door, which rewarded our patience with a polite knock. All eyes turned to me. I walked to the back of the room while my mind was wildly sorting emergencies and how I would handle them. I swung the door open a foot and peered out.

"The baby?" I guessed.

Hiram nodded. He stood on the top step and took off Pop's cap with an old-fashioned respect. He wore what he had on when we first saw him, except for adding a denim jacket of Pop's, and having his fiddle case tucked under his arm.

Before I could say anything else, he spoke. "Stephen, my friend, I am sorry to interrupt your school, but Mistress Lacey is goin' into her confinement."

I couldn't believe his formality, until I realized he had rehearsed this speech all the way here.

"Give me a minute, Hiram," I said. Turning to the children, I

298

asked them to excuse me for a moment, while I talked with my uncle outside and then stepped out and closed the door.

"Hiram, is she in labor? Has her water broken? Has she called the doctor?"

Hiram shook his head to the first two questions and smiled at the latter. "Mistress Lacey is indeed a competent woman, Stephen. She waited until she had experienced several pains before she decided to confide in me. She's used your speakin' contrivance to the doctor's office, and he has requested that she come in."

I had questions but no time. "Hiram, can you take over? I'd dismiss school, but the kids need supervision while they get their books and clothes together. The big kids know how to shut down the stove and close the school house."

"I can take care of that," said the old man. "You might remember I went to one of these myself. Introduce me to the children again and be off."

I opened the door and Hiram followed me into the warm room. I made it quick because I was a first daddy, anxious about Lacey.

"Kids—Uncle Hiram. Uncle, these are my kids. Guys behave; do whatever he tells you. I've gotta go, I'm having our baby." The laughter caught me as I grabbed my coat. "I mean Lacey's. There'll be school tomorrow, whatever—teaches." There was more laughter but I closed the door on it. I ran to the Jeep, my mind full of pictures of Lacey groaning in pain on the floor.

IT WAS only a mile-and-a-half trip, and a few minutes later, I practically smashed through our front door to find Lacey calmly

299

sipping a cup of tea and looking over the pages of Hiram's stack of sheet music. She looked to my amazement like someone thinking about taking a nap. Beside her, like an afterthought, was a little suitcase packed with a few necessities.

"Sorry about sending Hiram, honey, but push came to shove," she said as she reached up to give me a kiss. "He was the most practical person to send and he's probably teaching 'em *do-re-me* by now."

"*Jesus, Lacey!*" I exclaimed, lifting her gently to her feet. "Don't worry about Hiram; let's get you to the doctor!"

I pulled the Jeep out of the way and backed Pop's truck out of the shed to warm it up, while I fetched blankets and a pillow from the house. The truck was almost luxurious in comparison to the bare-bones seats of the little Jeep, but a poor place to bring a baby onto the world.

I even thought about bringing hot water, but Lacey drew the line at this level of paranoia and said, "Steve, For God's Sake, this isn't a covered wagon and I'm not gonna have 'Buford' in a corn row. We're only goin' in for a check up."

On the way, she did her best to calm me down. "Just drive like you're hauling eggs, Steve, and I'll be fine," she said. "Mama told me it took her twenty-four hours of this to have me, and I've only had half a dozen pains."

Oh my God! I thought, Half a dozen! She's going to have the baby in this truck and I'm going to have to deliver it! I worried about leaving Hiram at the schoolhouse, but not much. There are times in life when you just deal with things and hope for the best.

When we got to Doc Brant's office, we were taken right in,

but he wasn't nearly as impressed by Lacey's labor pains as I was.

"Maybe tonight—maybe tomorrow," he said, "maybe next day." He said this after an examination that only took five minutes. "Tell you what, Lacey, if you have a good book to read, why don't you spend the night over at our hospitality suite?" His good-natured face crinkled in a grin, "I'm not superstitious much, but the old-timers like December 22nd for a birth date, and you might deliver a future Madame Curie and put a notch in my belt."

I'm sure both of us wore the same startled expressions and he chuckled.

"What's December 22nd," asked Lacey, "besides three days before Christmas?"

"Oh, it's what they call the Winter Solstice," said Doc, dialing the phone number to the little hospital. "One of those things where the sun—to our eyes anyway—quits moving south in winter before it starts moving north again. It hangs there a spell, and folks say that was the big winter celebration back in the ancient days before Jesus made it into Christmas. . . . Hello! This is Roy Brant. You got a birthin' suite ready for Alacia Clark? She's half a mind to have a baby."

He hung up grinning. "They're all fixed for you, Lacey. They've even got a phone so you can call up everyone you know while we wait for you to get serious about birthing."

He was so confident and at ease about this incredible happening that I felt my nerves begin to relax a little. My leg muscles, from the tension of the drive, as taut as Lacey's cello strings, began to feel more natural, and my breathing was back to normal.

As we drove over to the little doctors' clinic, I finally had time to think about Hiram again.

"Jesus, Lacey," I said, while I was unloading her suitcase and carryall purse from the pickup, "I wonder if it was a mistake to leave a ghost in charge of my kids."

"Well, sweetie," she said, "you were the one who told them you believe in him, so why don't you just do that!"

It was a good thing to say and I didn't remind her that at the time, Hiram had been just an idea I vouched for, not a specter wearing a feed store cap.

"You're right," I said. "It's just that I got a picture of Hiram getting absent-minded and laying his fiddle down to help Franny Terrill tie her shoes. . . . He'll do fine."

The nurse, a lady named Billie, was waiting for us and took Lacey back to her room, which, except for the hospital bed, looked homey; there was a chest of drawers, a reclining chair, a rocker by the window, and cheerful wallpaper. There was a bedside table with a telephone, a little dressing table with a big mirror, and three paintings on the walls of flower gardens in Medley Springs, one of them beside the courthouse. Adjoining the room was her own bathroom and another small bedroom for a visitor. The only concession to her room's purpose was a shiny tile floor and an antiseptic smell to the air. When Billie told us she had "fixed up" the room herself, I knew Lacey was in good hands.

Billie was a big motherly lady with arms like a farm hand and eyes like jewels. She told Lacey she had three kids herself, had helped deliver twenty-six babies and said, "There isn't much to it except for the waitin' around," then added, "and as for you," she said looking at me with a mischievous twinkle, "go home and wear out your own floor. This'uns just been waxed. She'll call you when she needs something."

IT WAS AMAZING to look at my watch, once back in the pickup, and realize that I had only been in Medley Springs for an hour. Lord, the children still had an hour of school left, unless Hiram had sent them home.

I drove fast as I safely could, all the time running through my mind scenarios I could imagine with Hiram. I knew he was a good and kind spirit, or I would have never trusted him with my kids, but the things that could happen when you dealt with another plane of existence were something beyond reason. What if Hiram decided to tell about his own school days and came up with a hologram. Jesus, the man was a born performer by his own admission. What if he decided to let Oney "eeph" for them, or laid down his fiddle to write something on the blackboard—at which point he would simply disappear like a magic trick! This kind of thinking, mostly caused by worrying about Lacey, had nothing to do with my unease about Hiram. When I pulled into the clearing by the school, I saw the flag still whipping in the north wind and knew my students and Hiram were still there. I sighed with relief.

I walked up to the door and cracked it open like a visitor, not believing someone hadn't heard me arrive, until I realized that everybody was singing. Their eyes were on Hiram, who was fiddling and singing the verses to "Oh Susannah," while the kids

303

sang the chorus.

Lacey hadn't missed it far; on the blackboard were the notes of a scale my kids had never seen, marching up the steps of music lines, and Hiram was teaching a music lesson, the first they had ever had. I was entranced.

Closing the door quietly behind me, I sat down on the bench next to the water bucket and listened. Hiram was indeed a performer and he held those kids' attention like a circus ringmaster, his eyes going from face to face as he sang the silly verses, playing them on his fiddle and directing his untrained chorus with his bow. The children enthusiastically sang with him whether they could or not.

I felt embarrassed that I ever worried about this incredible old musician losing his audience or his determination to play for them. He was like the figurehead on a timeless ship, forging ahead no matter what. What moved me, knowing the song, was that he made the old fiddle sing like a young soldier's cheerful letter home, and I found myself singing along on the chorus.

At the end of the song, Hiram waved his bow at me. "Ah, Mr. Clark, I see you are back again! We've been havin' a pretty good time learnin' the cheerful nature of music."

The children turned, surprised by Hiram's announcement, and little Franny Terrill, of all children, came running and took my hand trustingly. "Teacher, notes are like numbers, only more fun and Uncle Hiram's teaching us to count them."

"Hmmm," I told her, smiling, "it looks like I've been leaving something out of our lessons. How about the rest of you, do you think we need some music lessons around here?"

Every hand shot up, even the eighth graders, though Cleavis Farley had told me last week that his mind "was full as a corn crib and I cain't chamber one more thing."

"Will Mr. Hiram be teaching us music?" asked Ruby McClellan.

"I expect you'd have to ask him," I said, raising my eyebrows toward Hiram. The kids all looked at him but most were too shy to ask a strange adult any such thing.

Hiram understood this and spoke right up. "If I am allowed, perhaps I could come one day a week and we'll learn notes together and practice singin' parts. I must tell you, however, I'm not sure how long I will stay here in this neighborhood."

The "yays" and clapping from the kids were proof enough my kids needed music. I also knew from Hiram's "if I am allowed" that he referred to a more sublime permission than mine.

"Okay kids, let's do that. Indian Glade now has added an art, uh, music department and if you guys take it seriously enough and work at it, I'll add it to your grades."

That taken care of, I told them that I had taken Lacey to the hospital, that she was fine, and we would have to wait for news. I also warned them that I planned to leave when I got word, but that there would be a substitute teacher coming to take my place.

They were too polite to groan, but their faces did it anyway. My previous sub, Mrs. Thompson, had not brought out the best in enthusiasm with this bunch.

Mavis Farley raised her hand and asked, "Could Mr. Hiram substitute?"

I grinned at her. "No ma'am," I told her, "Mr. Hiram doesn't have a teaching degree—in this state anyway, and your teacher has to have that before you kids can get grades. You do want grades, don't you?"

That worked, since all the children took more pleasure from their grade cards than I ever did from mine as a child. It was a measuring stick they could use to cope with the huge world outside the Ozarks, a world they trusted me to explain.

"Now, since we don't know how long we'll have Uncle Hiram to teach us, why don't we have him play something else for us? How about something from history, Uncle?"

Hiram plucked at his strings and thought. "Tell you what," he told the children, "here's an old story about a man travelin' through Arkansas tryin' to find someplace to spend the night, and he comes upon this old fiddler sittin' under the drippin' porch of his shack."

He lit into "The Arkansas Traveler," a tune most of them knew, but none of whom had heard Hiram's version. When he stopped each verse for the conversation between the traveler and his unwilling host, Hiram changed his voice comically, from the traveler's polite southern drawl to a rustic Arkansas twang that had the kids in stitches.

"Whah don't you mend yo' roof, sir?" asked Hiram the traveler, and Hiram the hillbilly replied, *"Why, win hit's a'rainin', I caint o'course and win the sun's a'shinin', hit don't leak!"*

I watched in wonder as Hiram created this imaginary dialogue, his face taking on the expression and mannerisms of the rascally old Arkansawyer. He did it so well that when the traveler takes the fiddle from him to play the second part of the tune, he

306

captured the look of amazed joy on the mountaineer's open-mouthed face so exactly that the kids roared, and I did, too.

I think that with this hypnotizing performance, I really understood for the first time the fierce dedication Benjamin Springfield had felt for his music when he was alive. The fire that had refused to die with him was even now inspiring the children of Indian Glade School to look for what music could say to them. I made up my mind at that instant that whatever happened to Hiram, my school kids, while I taught, would also hear music in this room where they came to learn.

Chapter Twenty-Two

IRAM AND I ARRIVED HOME AROUND dark, having given the smaller Smith and McClellan kids a ride in the truck bed to their mailbox roads. The children loved the Jeep, which everyday seemed smaller to me. In the fall, most of them had waited at the school road just to pile in or on it and ride the bumpy quarter-mile to school. Since I couldn't carry them all, I had to make up one of those Occam's razor rules, which make the simplest way best: I only carried the smallest kids. It only worked because nobody wanted to be small enough to qualify. Today in the truck, Hiram got to ride up front with me because he was old and a guest, and nobody fussed.

We pulled into our driveway and I had actually remembered to leave the porch light on. Custer, barking in the shed, was pathetically glad to get out and welcome us. Once inside, I made a call to the little hospital, and Billie told me in so many words to get a grip and let nature take its course. She said *she* would call *me*, because Lacey was trying to have our baby. So, Hiram and I busied ourselves with the stoves and fireplace and soon had the place feeling cozy. It seemed appallingly empty without Lacey and I had no appetite for a supper I'd be eating alone. I made a drink and sat by the fire worrying while Hiram, to keep me company, sat looking over his pages of music manuscript and hummed to himself. He had a marvelous hum, sort of like the bass strings on Lacey's cello. I nodded to it, waiting for the phone to ring and trying not to think of the other people on the party line as thoughtless and uncaring cretins keeping it busy.

"You should probably eat somethin', Stephen," said Hiram, after I had made three trips to the woodpile to fill the already over-flowing bins, and two to the phone to check it, which of course just burred with its noncommittal dial tone.

"Babies, and in particular this one, will wait to make the grand entrance—and the overture has only begun," said Hiram.

Through my haze, I caught the key words. "Why *in particular* this one?" I asked, sitting up to stare at a pipe lighting itself. Hiram had laid the fiddle in its case and was gently tilting the rocking chair across from me.

"Because I think it may be perhaps the reason I am here. This baby, to be born at the year's turn, could be cause for my existin' nearly nine decades beyond my time."

"Aren't you presuming a lot Hiram?" I found myself saying, even though I knew it was just my frayed nerves speaking. "This baby is going to be his own person, not just a vehicle for your musical plans. It's *our* baby, Hiram, not yours!"

The minute I said it I was ashamed, but I was still irritated.

The idea of anyone planning a career for an unborn baby was as offensive to me as signing one up to go to Harvard. For all we knew, the kid might want to be a blacksmith, raise bird dogs like Pop, or live in the woods like Thoreau.

Hiram, however, took no offense. "It is only my *hope*, Stephen," he said in a soothing voice, "not my plan. I have no presumption to outguess the stars. But I have waited though three generations of my own line to find someone to hand my musical gift to and have ended up here after all."

I asked him dryly, "Exactly what is your gift, Hiram, that makes you so sure you can pass it on like a hair color or good teeth or an inborn talent?"

His answer humbled me. "It is not *my* gift, my friend," he said quietly, "and I am sorry I would let you think I was so vain. It's the gift of the cosmos, the knowledge that music is a universal language spoken by most livin' things but understood by few humans." He sighed, thinking he hadn't said it well. "I reckon I see music as just love, Stephen. Love for life. Love for expression. Love for beauty and harmony and all the things I believe God's sent a poor spirit of a human to try to pass on."

"I think I understand, Hiram," I said, "but you have to know I want our child to operate on free will and curiosity. If music becomes his life work, that'll be great, and we'll do everything to help, but he won't be one of those princes who has to wear the crown, like it or not."

Hiram surprised me with a chuckle. "If a Supreme Bein' directs me," he said, "looks like he would have told me like Hippocrates told the first physicians, 'First, do no harm.' I apologize for my insensitivity my dear friend who is already callin' his unborn 'he.'"

We both laughed, which felt good, and before I could say anything else, the phone rang. It got me up quicker than any alarm clock and I made it to the kitchen before it could ring again and said, "Hello, this is Steve Clark."

"Mr. Clark," said Soames Black, in his slow, unmistakable voice, "I hope I didn't catch you at supper."

I hastened to say he didn't, but that I was expecting a call from the hospital.

"Well, I understand Mistress Clark is in the way of havin' a baby," he said, giving me a good idea of how private a party line is, "but I'm afraid we are bound to have a meetin' of the school board tomorr'. Hit's about a complaint that's perty serious and you should be there to speak your piece. I've called Miz Thompson to take up school tomorr', cause you know Myrtle, school has to keep if it snows two foot."

I tried to keep my voice very controlled and neutral. "Soames, I don't know when this baby's going to get here. If I can, I'll come to your meeting, but right now, the baby's more important. What's this all about?"

"Maybe foolishness," he said with an inflection that put it somewhere between rumor and plague. "The Terrills claim you're a'harborin' a demon, and let him teach the scholars dev'lish music."

"Uncle Hiram?" I said when I could say anything. "*Devilish?*" In my gut, I knew the preacher had the pictures and Hiram wasn't in them. I said the first thing that popped into my head. "Soames,

311

my uncle taught them how to put notes on a blackboard, and sang 'Oh Susannah' and 'The Arkansas Traveler.' That's *devilish*? Hiram walked to school to tell me about my wife and offered to stay with the children while I checked on her. You've met him, Soames! Does he look like a demon to you?"

"Mr. Clark," said Soames patiently, "I don't even believe in no sich of a thing, but the board is duty bound to hear out any complaint about a schoolmaster, with him present to defend hissef."

"And how about Uncle Hiram?" I asked. "Do you want him present, too?"

There was a silence while Soames thought that interesting premise out. "Well," he said at last, "seems to me if a preacher aims to set in on school biness, you kin have a fiddler set in on it, too. Neither one got no biness there in the first place, to my notion, unless they have chirren in school."

I felt a small sense of relief. At least Soames wasn't buying the complaint, out front anyway.

"What time do you want us and where?" I sighed. "If the baby comes tomorrow, you may have to hold your trial without me, Soames, because I intend to be there when my child is born."

Soames sounded shocked. "Why plague on't, hits not a *trial*, Mr. Clark, just a hearin'," he protested, "and a man's place is by his wife when she's birthin' a baby. We just need to git this complaint settled and out-the-way before reg'lar school takes up agin. You call me when your child is borned and you kin take an hour, and we'll git this hearin' scalded whichever place you wants to put the scaldin' barrel."

312

Jesus, I thought, scalding hogs was some Ozark way to describe the complication of the baby's arrival, Christmas, my "hearing," Vera and Rabon's visit and Hiram's ghostly presence in our lives, all to be dealt with in an allotted chunk of time.

"Mr. Black," I heard myself say, "I'll tend to your business, just as soon I have tended to our own." It sounded terse, I knew, but not as terse as I felt. "Why don't we do this at Walt Bangert's office in town and do it right? Walt's the one who warned me not to let religion into my teaching. I think he'd be the one to consult about 'devil worship' in my school, don't you?"

I could tell this startled Soames because he was speechless for a bit, but the idea pleased him. "Well now that should suit ever'body," he said in his slow drawl, "nobody more down to earth than old Walt. You want to call him, or you askin' me to?"

I knew a vote of confidence when I heard it and returned the compliment.

"I'm asking you, Soames," I said. "Tell him the situation. Set your 'hearing' for sometime tomorrow afternoon. I'll be with Lacey tomorrow anyway, whatever happens, and I'll call if and when I can get away and we'll go from there."

"Mr. Clark, I 'preciate it," he said slowly, "and I'll be glad to put this away. Most folks thinks you're a fine teacher for the chirren and I don't mind sayin' that's been my own opinion—up to now anyways. But my job's to see nothin' don't git in the way of their learnin'."

I hung up the phone, exasperated, but sure I had at least one board member on my side.

Hiram's voice was sad when I went back to the living room.

313

He had apparently heard both sides of the conversation, which didn't surprise me, since nothing about Hiram did that much anymore.

"That is a good man, Stephen, and I am so sorry to have caused you grief in a time of happiness. Thank you so much for invitin' me to appear on your behalf at this witch trial."

"Oh hell, Hiram," I said, recovering my drink and cigarettes and sitting down to pet Custer's grey head, "you're family now, even if you are a ghost, and we believe in you. If I have to tell them the whole truth, I will."

"I would hope that won't be the case," said Hiram mildly, "since I have begun to find myself so comf'table as an uncle and not a spirit to be explained to people who would not understand a word. The Pastor Tucker has no doubt found evidence that I do not exist in some sense and we must deal with that, I suppose."

"Good luck arguing with a photograph, Hiram," I said. "If you're not in it, you're not of this world, and Christians make up their own rules."

"Hardly that," said Hiram gently. "They take them from a Bible that they earnestly believe, even though it applies to so little of mankind or the universe, of which human writers were so ignorant. I tried to follow its teachin's myself, Stephen, while I lived. It is called the Good Book for a reason."

"So what do you propose we do when we appear at the Good Book Witch Hunt?" I asked, using his term for the hearing.

"Why I intend to behave as you would want an uncle to," said Hiram reasonably, "and conduct our defense accordin'ly."

He was so matter of fact about this major disaster that at least part of my gut relaxed a little. It was as if a small voice told me that whatever happened tomorrow, I was all right tonight and could get back to worrying about Lacey and the baby.

When the phone rang again at eleven o'clock, I was ready for it.

It was Billie the nurse. "I do believe our Lacey's getting down to it," she said cheerfully. "She's having five minute contractions. If you want to see how this is done, doctor says you can come in if you drive slowly and watch for deer."

"Watch for deer?" I said stupidly.

"On the highway," said Billie patiently. "Doctor likes husbands to be there, but not to work on. He says tell you it'll probably be an hour or two, so don't hurry."

"My God it's coming!" I said when I'd hung up. "The baby, Hiram, it's getting here tonight after all! Jesus, get in the truck!"

It never even occurred to me to leave our ghost and I think Hiram was touched by that, since we had previously argued.

"I think I had better stay, Stephen, to watch over things and mend the fires. This is your big night, not mine. Custer and I will keep the home fires burnin' and await your return. And we'll all deal with the witch hunt tomorrow."

"Oh, of course. Good thinking Hiram. If any one calls . . . never mind. We'll figure out Vera and Rabon later when we have something to tell. And Hiram, thank you!"

Heeding Billie's advice, I washed my face in cold water, combed my hair, and even remembered to get extra cigarettes and a cup of coffee to take along. A book would have been out of the question—like trying to kill some time reading Sanskrit.

315

I could make better time in Pop's truck, but I decided to take the Jeep, in case of snow.

I was reminding myself more of Dagwood Bumstead every minute—a bumbling cartoon character I had grown up with, who was always late and disorganized. At last, I headed for Medley Springs, trying to drive slowly and put my thoughts together. I also remembered to watch for deer.

OUR BABY WAS born at 12:05 a.m. I was right there in cap and gown to watch as my daughter came into the world—Billie handing her to me as soon as Doc Brant had made sure she was equipped with everything a baby would need to get by. I didn't get to hold her long, but long enough to raise my eyes and whisper, "Here she is, Pop, proof life goes on."

Lacey, exhausted but very much herself said, "Let me see who I've been packing around all this time." I carefully laid the baby in her arms, where she examined the little face with care. "Red hair, blue eyes, a Clark chin," she said admiringly and added "a Donnelly temper," as the child cried, protesting this new and surprising world. "It's okay, little one, I know, you need a name." She looked up at me smiling. "I believe she'd like Elizabeth, that suit you Pappy?" she asked, knowing the answer.

"It sure beats Buford," I said, unable to take my eyes off the two of them, these two beautiful creatures to share my world with.

"If Hiram can pass his music to her," said Lacey kissing the tiny mite of life, "it'd be fine with me, Steve, but I always loved the name Elizabeth anyway," she grinned, "and it would please the old man so."

"Elizabeth it is, honey, as fine a name as time could come up with."

Billie arrived and I was ushered out of the room so that she could tend to Lacey. Another nurse, named Dot, had showed up to weigh and measure Elizabeth, after which Doc Brant stuck his head in to give last minute advice.

"I'm going to the house directly," he told me, "and I'd advise you to do the same thing. Men don't have much function around here, and women do better work."

"You're trying to get rid of me," I said.

"Lacey needs a good spell of rest, she's got milk to produce and the girls will take care of the baby." He stretched mightily. "If you want to, you can lay down here," he said, reading my mind, "but unless you've got tits full of milk, you're in the way." His kind face broke into a smile. "I just delivered my first Solstice baby! Probably be a movie star or maybe the next Louisa Mae Alcott. Go rest up, son," he said, "we'll call if you're needed."

I went back in to say goodnight to Lacey who had been tidied up but looked worn out. I kissed her and told her I was going home to tell Hiram, but would be back in the morning.

"Steve," she said sleepily, "I 'spect Uncle Hiram knew before we did. Now you watch out for deer."

At the door I turned, remembering, "Did you call your folks?" I asked.

"I did," mumbled Lacey, "but you best call and tell 'em I came up with Elizabeth. They'll be wondering if they bought the right color snowsuit for Christmas."

"I sure love you," I told her, but she was asleep. That was all right; I figured she knew the love part already.

I WAS WIDE-AWAKE and brimming over with happiness all the way home and honked at two deer I remembered to watch out for, their eyes shining by the road. "Hi you guys," I shouted, "I'm a Daddy!" They galloped off, maybe to spread the news.

Hiram had the Christmas lights on when I turned the last curve, and I saw the big fir trees glowing in the yard. He was waiting at the door when I drove up.

"Congratulations, Stephen!" he said, pumping my hand. "I am so happy for the two of you!"

Lacey was right, of course, our ghost had anticipated my news, and I didn't mind at all. But Hiram, ever the southern gentleman, had to assure me that he hadn't invaded our privacy. "I caught your excitement and joy," he said, "the moment the happy event occurred, and Custer woofed with the awareness that something had happened. She stood with her ears cocked as if she heard her master's voice."

I thought of my little prayer to Pop and knew that it had somehow muddled its way through the cosmos.

"We have a daughter, Hiram, and Lacey has named her Elizabeth."

He might have been a ghost with insight beyond ours, but when his eyes filled up with tears, I knew he hadn't known this.

"Oh my dear boy," he stammered, "my dear girl, how kind . . . how kind of you both."

"She's got Lacey's red hair," I told the old man, "but other-

318

wise she just looks like, uh, a baby, I guess, all pink and round-faced and glad to be here." I suddenly remembered her grandparents. "I've got to call the Donnellys!"

I went to the phone, never even considering the time of night. It was time to wake the world up anyway; I was a father and felt very much like Paul Revere. Rabon, who was ever ready for emergencies on the job, answered on the first ring.

"Grandpa," I told him, "this is Steve. A new Queen Elizabeth has been born. Tell the court."

Luckily, I had held the phone away from my ear knowing Rabon's enthusiastic vocal range. I was ready for his huge "Whooo-Ha!" which of course woke Vera. I spent the next few minutes telling them about the baby's weight, and Donnelly temper, and how Lacey was, and how my Uncle Hiram had arrived to help me keep house until she came home. The fact that I had never mentioned an Uncle Hiram before didn't even register with those two, who had between them enough uncles for a platoon. The baby's name was as taken for granted as the baby herself.

The things I had always admired most about my in-laws were the generosity of spirit that Lacey had inherited, and their opinions that people should be allowed their own choices, friends and quirks. Vera, who hadn't liked her own name much, had picked her daughter's "Alacia" out of a fairy tale, and Rabon's mother had been "Flannery," so Elizabeth sounded lovely to both of them.

Our parting arrangement was that they would be here for Christmas unless the weather became dangerous, and Vera would stay a few days to "help with Elizabeth," as she already called her—no Donnelly ever referring to a child as "the baby" once she had a name. I found that comforting.

I also got some satisfaction out of the two clicks I had heard on the line while talking to the folks, meaning that my middle of the night call had gotten two or three neighbors out of bed to share my news. For the school board ones, it gave me additional pleasure to know they would have to make a trip to town tomorrow to share my day in court. I was tempted to wake Soames Black to tell him that he could have his trial any time he wanted to, but it seemed too petty a thing for the new Elizabeth's father to do, and besides one of the clicks was probably his anyway.

The thought, however, brought me back to Hiram's predicament and mine. I went back to the living room and in the glow of the Christmas tree lights, Hiram was carefully wiping off the maple back of his violin. He looked as unperturbed as a man turning an old tool in his hands, and his pipe smoke drifted lazily toward the fireplace. It made me relax a little to see this gentle-eyed old man, who perceptibly wasn't worrying much about what tomorrow might bring. He had of course, sensed my thoughts and set his pipe down in the pewter bowl Lacey had found for him.

"I know it sounds presumptuous of me, Stephen," he said, "but you have not eaten, and I would advise doin' so before you take up worryin' anymore. I took the liberty of lookin' in your icebox and made you a ham and salad-greens sandwich. There's milk in there also and I poured you a glass."

All of a sudden, I was starved. I brought everything, including some potato chips into to the living room, and sat noisily munching, while Hiram smiled in approval.

"Thanks, Hiram," I sighed at last. "I was forgetting that an army moves on its stomach."

"I believe *travels* is the proper term," he said, "but no matter. I believe the army I was in had little enough to put in ours, accordin' to your history book, which says it caused General Lee's surrender." The ghost's voice became more serious. "But I can see you are thinkin' in military terms about tomorrow, my friend, and I must suggest you leave those to me. Inept soldier as I was, I still understand the nature of men's battles better than most."

Something about Hiram's voice told me that further questions wouldn't gain me much and I withheld them. In my heart, I knew that the thing worrying me was—not lying to people about Hiram—but getting caught at it. With all my guilty feelings about it, the truth would have been as impossible to tell then as it was now, and I would have to depend on Hiram to protect us from the consequences of taking him into our lives. We had given it a lot of thought, Lacey and I, and we believed in him, and as Galileo told the inquisition, "I could do no other."

"Hiram," I said, getting up to begin turning out the Christmas lights, "this has been a very long day, and you're right; I need to give up making plans and just go lie down."

"I will be happy to turn out your lights," said Hiram cheerfully, "electricity being a fine thing to control. And I will see to Custer as well. I will try not to wake you."

I went to sleep to the gentle rustle of music paper and the soft chords of his violin and the only light I extinguished was my own.

321

Chapter Twenty-Three

WAS AWAKE AND HAVING MY FIRST CUP of coffee when the phone rang. Lacey was up and as excited to be a mother as she was the night before. It was the kind of call we made to each other when we were courting, and her voice finished warming me up.

"You coming soon?" she asked in a silky voice, "your daughter's been asking after you."

"Hiram and I will be there within the hour, if not sooner," I said.

There was no way I was going to tell her about the hearing until the last minute. We spent our time talking about Vera and Rabon's excitement and hung up, so she could eat breakfast.

I immediately called Soames, told him the news and agreed on one o'clock for the meeting at Walt's office. I asked if Walt had been much perturbed by this disruption of his schedule, and Soames said, "I don't reckon he's much dis-comfitted, Mr. Clark, he spends most of his time untanglin' schoolhouse fusses as it is. This new law agin' teachin' scripture in schools is a'goin agin' custom and settin' the hair on a lot of church folk."

Another fine hog butchering metaphor to add to education, I thought and wondered if Mrs. Summers would approve. It reminded me to ask who would be present at the meeting.

"Well, the board, of course, and Preacher Tucker and the Terrills. They wanted me to have my boys there, since they said they saw hainted goin's-on at your place, but I know fer a fact how deep those lads can git their bill in a jar, and I told them no. Same for anybody else talkin' to hear their head rattle. This is school biness, and there'll be no preachin', like the law says, and no blackguardin' nor hocus-pocus neither."

That was encouraging. How was Pastor Tucker to do his ghost-bashing without preaching?

I thanked Soames and turned to see Hiram descend the stairs. "Am I presentable for Mistress Lacey?" he asked, with no reference to the hearing.

All I could think was that he was the least likely ghost anyone could imagine. He wore a pair of Pop's Levi's jeans, a blue plaid wool shirt with string tie and a western-cut leather sports jacket Mother had given Pop years ago. These, with fringed low cut moccasins and Pop's small-crowned and dressy-looking Stetson, made him look for all the world like someone waiting to go on stage at the Grand Ole Opry. The fiddle case under his arm didn't hurt the impression.

"My God, Hiram, you look like a country star!" I laughed. "Lacey will want your autograph.—Wait." I dashed into the bed-

323

room and got a pair of Pop's aviator-style shooting glasses out of a drawer in the dresser.

Hiram put them on and the image was complete. Even with the beard, or maybe because of it, Hiram might have been a director in Hollywood, an actor dressing a part—anything else but otherworldly.

WHEN WE GOT to Medley Springs, Lacey was the ultimate proof that Hiram had acquired a rural reality. She was sitting up in bed reading a copy of *The Saturday Evening Post* when we arrived. Her eyes lit up with delight to see me, and happy surprise when she saw the old man holding his Stetson before him.

"Well, my crown in heaven, Hiram!" she crowed, "just look at you. You fixin' to play for your new niece?"

Hiram laid his hat on the bed and bent to take her hand and raise it to his lips. "I came to pay homage to you both, Mistress Lacey," he said, gently, "and offer the young lady my humble services."

Billie, who had followed us in, couldn't get over Hiram's silver beard and hair. Looking at him, she said, "Lacey, would you like me to bring in Elizabeth?" In a moment she was there with our daughter wrapped in a flannel blanket and handed her to me. Hiram bowed and lifted Elizabeth's little fist with his forefinger and kissed it.

"Madam, welcome," he said softly. Elizabeth reached curiously to feel his whiskers. Her eyes were wide-open, huge and very dark blue, and I couldn't look at her enough.

I placed her in Lacey's arms and we talked for a while, until

324

Billie took Elizabeth back to finish her nap we'd interrupted and left us alone.

Then it was time to tell Lacey about our hearing and Pastor Tucker's complaint to the board of directors. Lacey's independence, added to her new motherhood, gave her face a look I loved.

"How dare that bug-ignorant outfit attack God's way of doing things!" she stormed. "I may not know what you are, Hiram, but I've got sense enough to know there's no harm or meanness in you, and you're as soft a creature as Elizabeth." She had angry tears in her green eyes but they weren't helpless ones, and I felt good seeing them. "You tell them whatever story you think will smother the fire, Uncle, and we'll back it up."

When we left for Walt's office, she was smiling again. Her parting words to me were all the encouragement I needed.

"Tell them what God told Noah, Steve," she said.

"Two of everything?" I asked.

"No. He also said, just use whatever you find on earth and don't be more trouble than you're worth."

"Sounds like a country song." I laughed.

"And Hiram looks like a country singer," called my wife.

EVERYBODY LOOKED SERIOUS in Walt's office when we arrived, but all of my board members were polite when they congratulated me on our new baby. Jeff Farley, with his blonde hair brushed neatly, was the only one who pumped my hand with an encouraging grin. Myrtle Summers was there with her son Sonny, in addition to the Terrills, who to my surprise had brought T.J.

with them. The little boy looked very uncomfortable and didn't want to look at Hiram or me. The preacher, in suit and tie, sat at the end of a row of several chairs, which Walt had assembled in a loose circle for the board.

Walt, who had worn a rusty old suit for the occasion, got right down to business. "Now, way I understand this, we're here to listen to a complaint made against the schoolmaster of the Indian Glade deestrict," he said, "presented by par'nts of scholars of the Indian Glade school. That'd be you, Mr. And Miz Terrill. Do I have that right?"

Standing up, Bailey Terrill nodded and said, "Yessir, Mr. Superintendent, this's our boy T.J. and this here's . . ." he turned toward Pastor Tucker as if to introduce him, but Walt interrupted him.

"That'll be fine, Bailey," he said. "I know Preacher Tucker. Now I have to tell you'uns-all that the only testimony that will be admissible in this proceedin' is from the par'nt of a scholar or board member of the deestict. None other applies."

He wagged a big finger at the completely stunned assembly.

"With all respect to the visitors, Preacher Tucker, and Mr. Clark's uncle, and Sonny Summers," he said solemnly, "these proceedin's are school biness, and I cain't allow outsiders to contribute opinions or comments to our proceedin's. I would ask our visitors to take seats elsewhere in the room."

The look on Pastor Tucker's beefy face was worth the entire trip. Not only was he not allowed to preach, but apparently he was going to have to leave the burden of his testimony to the stolid Terrills, who looked at each other in dismay.

326

The Pastor shot to his feet, his face flaming. "Superintendent, I must protest!" he shouted, "I am a man of God and I have come to protect all young minds from this . . ."

Walt's hand and voice stopped him in mid-sentence. "Whoa!" he ordered. "Not one more word sir, or I'll put you outside. I have warned you that these are school proceedin's and no outsiders are to be heerd from. Now if you would please take a seat elsewhere."

I could almost hear the wind go out of the preacher's sails as he reluctantly left his seat and went with Sonny and Hiram to the back of the big office. Hiram preferred to stand by his chair, but the preacher sat as far from both of them as he could. His look at the Terrills as he sat down was as commanding as he could come up with under the circumstances, and I could tell he was about to explode.

"Now, Mr. and Miz Terrill," continued Walt when everybody was seated, "I would like you to tell us all exactly what you object to in Mr. Clark's teachin' performance."

Bailey Terrill, inspired by his preacher's look, got hastily to his feet. "Why, Superintendent, the man believes in spirits!" he said. "And told my chir'den he did. He told all the chir'den, includin' little T.J. here, he b'lieved in ghost-es." He looked over at his preacher earnestly, "and Pas...uh, we have evy-dence he has a familiar spirit hisself."

Walt took all this in, his face impassive. "I see," he said slowly, "and did Mr. Clark instruct his scholars to think that they should believe in ghost-es, too?"

Bailey's brown furrowed. "Well he might as well have," he

327

said finally, with a questioning look at Tucker. "Them kids b'lieve anything he tells them."

"Well let's ask Mr. Clark," said Walt turning to me seriously. "Mr. Clark, did you teach your scholars a belief in ghost-es?"

I stood slowly and spoke with all the deliberation I felt. "Mr. Bangert," I said, "some of my students, talking about Hallow-een, asked me if I had ever seen a ghost. I said I believed that I had, but wouldn't expect everybody to—sort of like seeing shapes in clouds. If I remember correctly, I warned them that people perceive what they choose to and advised them to think for them-selves."

Walt stood a moment considering that, his eyes deep into mine. Then he turned back to the Terrills, his eyes lowered to T.J. "And you young man, I take it you were a witness to what Mr. Clark said. Could you tell us, in your own words what you understood him to say."

I didn't look at T.J., so that no one could accuse me of intimi-dating the child, but heard Walt urging him to speak up. Finally, I heard his thin little voice mumble something, which the pa-tient Walt asked him to repeat louder.

"Teacher said some sees ghost-es and some doesn't," piped T.J.

"Thank you Mr. Terrill," Walt told him gravely. His eyes ran over the assembled board when he asked, "Does anyone here challenge the teacher's statement as he has recalled it?"

There was silence until Jeff Farley finally put up a big hand. "That's what my chirren says he told 'em," he said, "and my kids ain't bad to lie."

Walt took this in, and nobody seemed to have anything to add.

"But ask him about his familiar spirit," demanded Bailey leaping up excitedly, "the one right there, he had a'teachin' dev'lish music right in the schoolhouse!" He pointed an accusing finger at Hiram.

Hiram was standing like an interested observer while his hands were busy lighting his pipe, his fiddle case and western hat in the chair next to him. The board members turned to look at him and he nodded at them with his brows raised quizzically, as if he was politely amazed that anyone would doubt his country style reality.

Walt shook his jowls uneasily at Bailey as he said, "I don't believe that *familiar spirits*, whatever that means, comes within the jurisdiction of the board of education."

He raised an eyebrow at me. "Mr. Clark, do you have anything to say to this accusation of teachin' music of a religious nature?" He asked me accentuating the last words carefully.

I stood, sending a silent message to Lacey—*Do or die, kid, here goes*—and began: "Mr. Bangert, and members of the school board," I said, "I allowed Uncle Hiram to stand in for me while I went to take my wife to the doctor yesterday. I thought rather than dismiss school unexpectedly, it would be all right to have an adult supervise them until I got back." I saw that at least I had everyone's attention, even the hostile stares of the adult Terrills and the mildly disapproving look of Myrtle Summers.

"Uncle Hiram is an accomplished musician," I continued, "and he took it upon himself, since he's not a teacher, to give my

329

kids a music lesson. When I got back, he was teaching them to follow notes and playing old tunes for them on his fiddle. I could see no harm in that."

"Satan's own instrument!" cried Bailey standing up to interrupt. "We don't send our chir'den to school to learn to caper around to lewd and carnal music. It's agin' scripture!"

"*Tell it brother!*" said Pastor Tucker, who had moved to a corner in the back of the room to escape Hiram's pipe smoke and Sonny's random chewing tobacco squirts at Walt's spittoon.

Walt rose, his face red with indignation. "Let me make myself clearer to you'uns all," he said slowly and ominously, his eyes traveling across the room. "We are here to determine pos'ble misconduct on the part of a teacher, not to discuss any sort of religious believin's. The lawmakers of this state have decided in a court of law that religious teachin's must not be involved in public schoolin' of no kind."

Walt had his "dander up" as Lacey called it, but his next words were calmer as he tried to apply reason to the touchy subject. "Your believin's about the value of music are your own, and may be stated or argied about among your own board when it comes to teachin' it, but this office, to my understandin', specifically forbids my allowin' religious predj'dice or church belief to interfere with schoolin', and I aim to do the job I was set here to do."

It was a long speech and Walt mopped his face.

I had an idea and spoke slowly. "Mr. Bangert," I asked, "would you mind if I asked T.J. Terrill what they learned from Uncle Hiram yesterday in my absence?"

Walt shook his head and sat on the corner of his desk to wave permission.

"T.J.," I told my second grader, "please stand and tell us all what Mr. Hiram did after I left him to watch over school yesterday."

T.J. got up obediently with a nervous look at his parents, and stood scratching, and rolling his eyes like any eight-year-old faced with a recitation. "Well he taught us some words I never heard before, umm, *doe, ray, me,* was some of them and ummm, *so* and *la* and like that, and some others that wasn't real words, but names for ummm, little eggs he drawed on the chalkboard."

T.J. added considerable foot twisting to all this, and I urged him on gently. "You're doing fine," I told him. "What else?"

"Well, he played a sound on his vy-lin for ever egg he drawed," he said, "and had us sing the sounds he played." He scuffed one shoe on the other one and snuffled loudly.

"He told us to call it a vy-lin, though I knew t'was a fiddle. Dad don't like us to listen to music much, but I couldn't see nothing wrong about it, iff'n t'was in school"

"Me either," I said to encourage him. "What else did he do?"

"Well ummm, he played some tunes like little kids sings, 'Ring Around Rosie' an 'Way Down Yonder In The Paw Paw Patch' an 'Pop Goes The Weasel' an stuff like that, an ummm, 'London Bridge Is Fallin' Down' an 'Weevily Wheat,' an ummm, all like that."

"Was that all he did?" I urged.

"Well," said T.J. concentrating mightily, "that's all I remember, 'cept he got us to sing a nigger song, too." He glanced at his dad hopefully, knowing he was supposed to testify against Hiram,

331

but not sure what was expected of him. "Mr. Hiram called them 'colored.' He said it was a colored children's song they made up," he explained, then stood looking at me, sweating the result of this confession.

"Do you remember the song?" I asked, smiling at his anxious face and remembering that few of my students had ever seen a black person, except in picture books.

"Yeah it was easy," said T.J., and before his parents could protest, he jumped up, "you just go, '*head, shoulders, knees 'n toes—knees 'n toes,*'" he squeaked the tune shrilly, touching all the places as he named them, "'*and eyes 'n ears 'n mouth 'n nose, head, shoulders, knees 'n toes.*'" On the last *toes* he tripped over his shoelace laughing and was jerked to his feet to be dusted off by his embarrassed mother. Bailey didn't look amused.

"Thank you T.J., that looked like good exercise, too," I told him, "so you know where all your parts are."

"Well it doesn't look like Uncle Hiram did much damage while I was gone," I said cheerfully to my board members, "and when I came back, he was playing 'Oh Susannah' and doing 'The Arkansas Traveler' for them. It made me wish I could teach them the music scale and a little American music myself, but I don't play."

Bailey erupted from his chair, incensed. "You weren't harr'd to play, you was harr'd to teach, Mr. Clark!" he stormed, "and we don't pay a school tax to learn our chir'den foolishness. I'm a good notion to move my chir'den to a deestrict where Christians has some say over what's taught and what isn't!"

I had hoped he was going to say something biblical and get

332

under Walt's guns again, but the superintendent had apparently heard all he wanted to know about Terrill's opinions concerning education.

"Now you look here, Bailey Terrill, you may send your chirren to any deestrict that'll accept 'em, but the law is the law here in Burke County, *Missoura.*" Walt emphasized each of his *laws* with a slap on his desk. "A lot of them schools won't have any art classes," he said, "or music classes or whatever else you think's foolish for chirren, but I can *garntee* you they won't have no religion, teach no religion, nor allow no religion, because it's the U-S-of-A law called separation of church and state."

"I don't charge my mind with sich as that," began Bailey, but big Walt had the floor and was holding it. "Course you don't!" he gritted, "on account of folks like you has brought it on."

His voice descended to a rumble. "Why, you think I'm some sort of infy-dell, Bailey? When I taught school, we said a little prayer to take up books, and I said grace over the chirren's noon dinner. Old Preacher Hobbs and his wife came by ever second week and did chalk-talks with flannel sceneries and Bible stories. Chirren loved 'em," he sighed. "Wasn't no church persuasion about it in those days, folks just respected God. And pert-near ever school had music of some kind. But you and folks that thinks different to you, has changed all that."

Walt's voice had lowered some as he calmed down and old Myrtle was listening and nodded, remembering. "Indian Glade used to have a py-ano before mice et the felts" she said, "and all the scholars learnt the scales and shape notes. We never had money to keep that py-ano from fallin' to staves."

Soames Black shook his big head sadly. "It was fine to hear music there t'other night. I purely hate that the Terrills has tuck umbrage at Mr. Clark's uncle."

"We b'lieve that man ain't his uncle at all!" said Bailey, recovering from Walt's lecture and getting down to the bombshell he wanted to drop. He spoke with an ironbound confidence. "We believe," he said with a hesitant look over his shoulder, "that man ain't even a man at all, but a critter from the dark side, come to work evil on this commun'ty!"

All heads turned to look at this strange description of the old fiddler they saw standing by a folding chair, his hat politely off in company.

Hiram obligingly lowered his tinted aviator glasses and peered over at us with his mild blue eyes. "Pardon me, was I bein' addressed?" he inquired in his soft Nashville accent.

The whole effect made Bailey's statement seem so ridiculous that even Walt's hard expression relaxed momentarily.

But Walt was no one's fool. "Mr. Uh, Hiram," he said, "I know I have told you that your testimony would not be required in these proceedin's. But may I make an exception to this rule by askin' your full name sir?"

Hiram gave a polite nod. "Hiram Walker," he said distinctly.

My heart didn't know whether to plummet or leap to this amazing statement, but thinking of Lacey's glance at the whiskey bottle that gave him his name, I threw my lot in with hers.

Walt considered the name gravely.

"And are you indeed Mr. Clark's uncle, Mr. Walker?" he asked with seemingly only distant interest.

"Well sir, actually no," said Hiram with much reluctance. "I'm sorry to say I am not."

Out of the corner of my eye, I saw the preacher and Bailey exchange looks of triumph, and saw Soame's jaw stop chewing, and a look of bewilderment on Jeff Farley's honest face.

I held my breath.

"Then how'd you come to be called 'Uncle Hiram' by Mr. Clark?" asked Walt, a stern note creeping into his words.

Hiram put his glasses in his shirt pocket and looked at Walt with candor. "I was very close to his dad, Jack, in the First World War, and the Clarks sort of adopted me, Superintendent. You know how companions in arms become, sir—or if you don't, I must tell you—closer than brothers."

I watched this amazing interchange in expressionless wonder. So Pastor Tucker had taken the trouble to check my lineage with my Hannibal relatives, and Hiram came up missing. And all the time I thought he had pictures, with Hiram missing.

"Mr. Superintendent," came Pastor Tucker's strident voice, "since you have allowed the supposed Mr. *Walker* to say something, may I speak?"

Walt turned toward the preacher and nodded, "As long as it has to do with the establishment of Mr. Walker's credentials and nothing to do with your religious views sir, you may have your say."

"I notice, Mr. Walker that you are never seen without your accompanying box of tricks," said Pastor Tucker, with the craftiest look at the violin case I had seen so far. "I wonder if you would be so good as to step away from it a minute and stand for

335

us in the light of day."

My breathing stopped as Hiram stared musingly at the preacher. He was caught, I knew, for even Lacey and I, his believers, had never seen him away from the tools of his music, and without them, he might be only the ghostly product of anyone's imagination.

But Hiram, after picking up his fiddle case, with an inquiring look at Tucker to be sure this was the "box" he referred to, laid it down and walked a little stiffly up to Walt's desk and stood, hands folded, for everyone's inspection. As he passed me, I saw the least indication of a wink in an eye as blue as a chicory flower, and I stood stunned, waiting for him to disappear. Instead, he gave the board a front, a side, and back view, and ended facing them again.

No one spoke, so Hiram did.

"I'm sorry I have caused my friends the Clarks any problems," he said softly. "For the past several years I have been somethin' of a drifter and seemed to belong nowhere. Hearin' my old friend Cracker-Jack Clark had died, I decided to call on his son and find out if a visit would be welcome there for old-time's sake." Hiram's eyes moved from face to face, giving everyone a chance to search his own. "Not only did they take me in," he continued, "but I was made to feel a wanted and useful guest, which for a lonesome traveler of my years, was a blessin' from God. I am so proud they chose to call me Uncle Hiram."

He waited a bit to see if anyone had further questions, and when they didn't, with a small bow to Walt, our old ghost turned and walked with the same careful gait back to his chair, almost as if he favored an old war wound. Altogether, it had been the best performance, even without that near limp, I could have imagined. At no time had he even referred to himself as a living person, but his story seemed impossible to disprove.

Even the disbelieving preacher sat as if thunderstruck that a demon could actually admit that he had been blessed by God, without dissolving on the spot.

Fed up with all this, Soames Black stood and put on his hat. He bit off a piece of his plug of tobacco and stowed it under his stained handlebar mustache. "Seems to me, Walt, we're perty much done here, unless you got more to say. I need to put a blade on the tractor before it snows agin."

Bailey Terrill got up, too. "You'uns still haven't satisfied the biness of a false teacher a'teachin' my chir'den pagan music," he stated firmly. "And if I take our two out, you don't have enough chir'den for yer deestrict to pay for a school." Obviously, Pastor Tucker had been helping with the math, aware of the narrow dollar margin the school operated on.

Mrs. Summers looked appalled. "Can he do that Walter?" she asked. "Shut off our funds in the middle of school year?"

"No," said Walt, "Mr. Terrill will have to get a lawyer to file an action with the board of education, and I don't believe they will allow him to send his chirren out of the deestrict. But if the Terrills are proved qualified to home school their chirren, I'm not sure you would get state funds for the two of them, that's all."

Walt looked sadly at the Terrills. "All you folks are a'doin' is causin' a hardship to your chirren and the community served by the schoolhouse," he said gravely. Then turning to the board members, said, "But if music is what all this fuss is about, I have to tell you folks of the board that this is not a required subject of a one-room school curric'lum, and certainly not a cause to disrupt the regular education of chirren."

His glance went back to Hiram. "I would suggest that Mr. Walker, whatever his musical skills, not be allowed to exercise them at Indian Glade School House. And that the rest of you show charitable allowance to Mr. Clark, who as far as I can see, only used Mr. Walker's services in an emergency."

He surveyed all our faces, ending with the Terrills. "Does that satisfy you Terrills?"

A look at Bailey Terrill's face was proof that he was far from satisfied, but the prospect of hiring a lawyer to tackle the State of Missouri had done a lot to temper his zeal.

"I want it put down on the record," Bailey growled, "that I believe this teacher is unfit to teach my chir'den."

"By reason of what?" asked Walt, sounding surprised. "Lack of trainin' or proper credentials would you say?" His voice was mild, but had a hard core. "Abusive to chirren? Or maybe too soft on discipline? What would you like the record to say?"

Bailey dreaded getting Walt's lecture about religion again. "A bad influence over small minds," he said, "and consortin' with gypsy characters."

"*Small minds!*" said Walt, his voice touched with wonder. I half expected him to roll his eyes upward, but he was more controlled. "There will be no record, Mr. Terrill," he said judiciously, "for which you should be thankful, considerin' that your state-

ments today could be taken as slanderous and said in front of witnesses. I would advise you to say nothin' else to this gatherin'."
He looked up at the clock. "Mr. Black," he told Soames, "I hope this meetin' has been useful."

"I believe it has," said Soames nodding. "I reckon we can sort it out from here. I'm glad Teacher wanted to have this done in your office. I'm not a great hand to know the rules."

The Terrills left first, preacher in tow, and little T.J. bringing up the rear. The child looked miserable, and I felt sad for him. Hiram slipped away too, leaving me to say good-bye to everyone and thank Walt Bangert.

"Tell your uncle I wish I could hear him play," he said solemnly shaking my hand. "And I hope he knows most folks down here show more hospitality to a stranger. I'm glad you took him in."

"Me, too," I said, "and I thank you. I'd begun to think maybe I was in the wrong profession or maybe the wrong place."

Jeff Farley shook my hand, relieved. Even Myrtle seemed happy I had survived the inquisition.

Chapter Twenty-Four

MET HIRAM IN THE COURTHOUSE HALL, coming from, of all places, the men's restroom. He looked so natural that it took me a moment to remember that ghosts don't use restrooms, a thing I had been too worried to think about when he had also used it on the way in.

He waited until we were in the truck to explain. "I thought it best," said the old man sagely, "to keep some part of what seems to be my musical soul upon my person durin' that interview with people who don't believe in me." He smiled, "I tried Mistress Lacey's harmonica, in the mirror, and it worked, so I put it my britches pocket. It was so long, it kept bangin' my knee."

And our ghost laughed for the first time since I had known him. It was a fine, full laughter, the kind I have always thought God created humans to do. I laughed with him in relief. Except for music and maybe tears, it was the most human trait Hiram had expressed.

"Do you reckon we can head off the photographs, as well as your excellent superintendent headed off superstition?" he asked.

"You *are* a superstition," I reminded him, "but let's find out. We seem to be on a roll, as gamblers put it."

We drove around the courthouse square to the drugstore. It was an ancient building, with a new chrome front and an orange Rexall sign that shook in the winter wind. Inside, the grey haired pharmacist put a shoebox full of film packets on the counter and asked for my name. He was shuffling through the envelopes when the phone rang. As he turned to answer it, I thought I saw sudden movement—a rippling of the envelopes in the box, as if a little wave had run through it. When I turned around puzzled, Hiram was a dozen feet away looking through a display of magazines.

The pharmacist hung up and turned back to me, "Now that was Clark? Was that a rush order? Them's separate, you know, costs fifty cents more."

"Yes sir, I wanted to get them before Christmas." I told him, and his hand went to the end of the box where two envelopes were separated by a card from the others.

"That's them," he said, "one for you—one for Tucker."

"Just the two?" I asked idly, opening my envelope as if to make sure the negatives were there.

"I believe that's it," he said. "The only rush orders we had and they just came in."

I paid him, bought two rolls of film for baby pictures and Christmas, and then Hiram and I went back to the truck.

"The other pack was for Tucker," I told him on the way.

341

"I know," said Hiram, "and I thought about purloinin' it but could see no way to avoid involvin' you."

"We'd better look at ours," I said grimly and took the stack from the envelope. The first picture I saw made me heave a great sigh of relief. It was the shot of Hiram playing "Dixie." Even in Pop's coveralls he was a striking old man, his blue eyes shining with the fun and emotion of the old song and his expressive hands perched like graceful birds on the fiddle and bow. However, the next picture was disaster; it was one Lacey had taken of Hiram seated. He had laid the fiddle aside to light his pipe and it was a picture of coveralls molded realistically around nothing, with a pipe above them, smoking in midair. It looked like a clever store window display, and my heart sank. The rest of the pictures were varieties of it—coveralls in various poses with a fiddle suspended by them, Lacey or me standing beside them and no evidence that Hiram existed, as far as the camera lens was concerned.

"Hiram," I said, "you were only visible to the camera while playing. I don't think our troubles are over."

"I was about to say the same thing," he answered. "Look." His eyes were on the sidewalk several parking meters down, where Pastor Tucker had just stepped from his Buick, his ten-gallon hat pulled down against the wind. The preacher looked neither to the right nor left, but headed for the Rexall, leaning like a sailor in a gale, his cowboy boots tilting him precariously.

Hiram, watching him, said something so surprising that I looked at his stately profile in wonder. "What a lonely man he seems, despite his bluster," he said sadly. "I think there is little of

342

joy or music, in his beliefs or his soul." He turned to see me staring and added humbly, "He wears no weddin' ring, Stephen, and thus has no way to measure the happiness of life he sees. I would like to know him better."

I had nothing to say, since the idea of knowing people like Pastor Tucker *better* was the last thing that would have occurred to me in view of his intentions.

"Excuse me a moment, I'll be right back," said Hiram's voice quietly, and suddenly I was alone in the truck with a pile of clothes and a Stetson hat beside me on the seat.

"Hiram?" I said aloud, and looked to see if the door to the drugstore opened, but nothing moved but the wind tugging furiously at the Rexall sign. A moment or two later, the door opened and Pastor Tucker emerged, a bright film package in his hand. What happened next was predictable; the wind snatched the huge hat from the preacher's head and he grabbed at it. The unsealed envelope flew away from his hand, to cartwheel down the sidewalk and burst open, scattering pictures. Tucker went for the great, tumbling hat first and almost caught it when it lodged for a second or two on a parking meter pole, but then it was off and rolling and soon in the street. I saw him glance back for a second at the pictures peeling off the scattered stack, but I guessed that the hat was more important. He chased after it, finally recovering it lodged against a car wheel half a block away. By the time he made it back to the drugstore, his pictures were pretty well distributed, most of them still tumbling across a vacant lot between the drugstore and a small café.

I had to feel a little sorry for the man myself, watching his balding head bob as he tried to chase down the pictures, which, one at a time, stayed pinned to something long enough for him to retrieve them. The search never led in our direction because of the north wind. My eyes were still on him when I saw two pictures and an envelope of negatives paste itself inexplicably to the passenger window of the truck. When I opened the door, the Stetson rose and my seat full of clothes inflated. Hiram was back.

"I suggest we visit Mistress Lacey and Elizabeth again," he said, picking up his pipe, as if our conversation had just been interrupted for a minute. I had the motor started and was backing the truck out before he finished.

In this part of the Ozarks, winds change suddenly and the preacher's eyes were starting to look everywhere for missing items. In a minute's time, we were on our way to the doctor's clinic, leaving Pastor Tucker to his finger-numbing search.

"Did you get them all, Hiram?" I asked.

"Oh my no," he said, lightly. "It would have been a shame to deprive him of our playing of 'Carol Of The Bells,' which was so becoming to both of us, that I was rather tempted to keep it for Mistress Lacey." He held up the small envelope of negatives. "However, I do have what you have explained are the originals of those, and two photographs that I would rather he not see."

At the first stop sign, I glanced over and saw why. One was a picture of Jeff Farley shaking hands with a tailor's dummy with no head, and the other, a group of children gathered around a fiddle suspended before them and the bow standing on end two feet above it, which I supposed was Hiram gesturing a story to life.

344

Finally at the clinic, it took an hour to catch Lacey up on everything. While I was talking, I loaded the camera and took pictures of Elizabeth and Lacey. Billy stopped in to take a picture of the three of us, Hiram politely declining to be included. Lacey, who was up and walking, was ready to go home. Doc Brant, who had stopped by to check on Lacey, gave orders that new mothers and babies were to stay at least thirty-six hours for observation, and he told Lacey that she could take Elizabeth home next afternoon, the day before Christmas Eve.

Doc met Hiram, scanning him with the thorough glance doctors always seem to have for older people. Noticing his violin case, he smiled warmly, "I see you play the fiddle," he said, "keep that up and you'll live to be a hundred."

"Thank you sir," replied Hiram smiling and bowing, "that's a goal few men strive for."

"And fewer are happy with," added Doc, looking at him shrewdly," but my grandpa always said, 'music and whiskey are the keys to long life.'" He turned back to me, "Well, come get these girls tomorrow and bring a lot of quilts, this wind's off the North Pole. Now, you all have a Merry Christmas."

Looking at my small family, I knew we were already doing just that.

ON THE WAY home, I stopped and filled the truck's gas tank, trying to think ahead to everything we would need. It seemed too cold to snow by Ozark rules, but the sky had darkened early, and the wind, which had whipped slate-grey banks of clouds over us all day, was finally beginning to calm.

Once home, Hiram and I let Custer in, built up the banked fires and turned on Christmas lights to make the house cheery. It was after I'd had a drink and was sitting by the fireplace with my grilled cheese sandwich-supper on my lap that Hiram startled my thoughts.

He was sitting in the rocking chair, his invisible hand stroking Custer's old ears, when he announced that he was going to pay a visit to Pastor Tucker.

"Tonight?" I choked, "You mean *now*, Hiram?" Fresh from memories of that formidable man, I couldn't imagine Hiram wanting to ever confront him again, much less pay him a neighborly visit.

"Well, I thought I'd wait a while," said the ghost's voice, "until he's settled in for the night. I must picture where he lives and how best to get there."

"Jesus, I know where he lives," I told him grimly, "over by Standing Rock on Dry Valley, near his church. But Hiram, surely you don't intend to go over there!"

I stared at the ghost's pipe, which was all I could see of him, and laid my tray on the floor. "Don't tell me you are going to appear like the Ghost of Christmas Past and scare him into being a nice person?" The concept tickled me. "My God, Hiram, the man probably handles snakes, speaks in tongues and has a shotgun loaded with silver buckshot for demon visitors!"

"None of those have aught to do with me," said Hiram mildly, "and they are only defenses of ignorance." He waited for his words to sink in. "Isn't ignorance the thing you seek to defeat in your teachin', my friend? Have you read much of Oliver Wendell

346

Holmes?"

"Some," I said. "I suppose you did."

"He was a much quoted authority of my time," said Hiram, "and I remember one of his premises, 'The bigot's mind is like the pupil of an eye—the more light you pour on it, the more it contracts.' I fear Tucker's mind is of that sort, and must be approached from its dark side."

I sat looking at the chimney-curl of smoke calmly rising from his pipe. "That's a pretty big target," I told him, "but just how would one do that?"

"I'm afraid one wouldn't," said the ghost, "but *two* might. I would like, since you know where it is, to picture it in your mind and take me to the pastor's home tonight."

Before I could protest that I had only driven by the house on the highway, he said, "Close your eyes and drive to it in your mind, I don't need detail."

I squinted and concentrated. It wasn't all that hard to picture the highway since there was a long hill leading to a curve, and just around it, a green metal bridge over Dry Valley. Past the far end of the bridge was a tall granite formation that was easy to picture—Standing Rock. Just past it, the road curved in my mind, and nearly at the top of the next hill was a little white church, and across the highway, set back from it in a grove of trees was the pastor's house. I had just formed the picture when Hiram said, "Let's take a look at it."

Even though, by this time, I was used to Hiram's holograms, I was still startled to find myself in one of his three-dimensional projections of a place I'd never been. . . . This time a room I would have never set foot in, under any circumstances: Pastor Tucker's living room.

I breathed a sigh of relief that this was what Hiram meant by *a visit*, and sat frozen as Hiram's mind walked around looking at walls, and the few pictures on them, mostly artist's concepts of The Last Supper, Jesus, or horses.

The next thing I noticed was that there was no Christmas tree, no decorations of any kind, and the walls were stark and the room barely lighted, except for one corner, where the light came mostly from a table. There, Pastor Tucker sat beside his telephone among a litter of papers, an ancient typewriter, literature, and the scattered pictures he had retrieved from the drugstore. Looking, as I supposed I did through Hiram's eyes, it struck me as a monastic cell, devoid of warmth or any attempt at a pleasant atmosphere.

To my dismay, the fat man, dressed in a bathrobe, looked up and stared directly at what I could only suppose was us intruding, and my hackles rose, but he soon looked back down to type a line to what I suspected was a sermon. Hiram's vision left the room and gave me a ghostly circuit of the house: moving through a sparse dining room, a kitchen as innocent of charm as a ship's galley, an unused room full of stored furniture and boxes and, finally, to a bedroom lit only by a night light. I felt like a burglar and must have groaned with the strain, when Hiram spoke aloud to me. "We're only here to learn," and then added, "look."

He had moved close to several pictures on the wall near the bed, and at more in upright frames on a dresser. I have no idea how Hiram lighted these, but as he moved from one to another, each one became as visible as in daytime. One in particular interested him the most; it was a family photograph taken, no doubt, during the Great Depression of the '30s: a father and mother and half a dozen children in front of an unpainted Ozark shack. The father was unshaven and looked as grim as the face of his bony, exhausted wife who was holding a new baby. None of the children were smiling. It was a picture of despair, like the shots of the Dust Bowl poverty in *Life Magazine*, I'd seen as a kid.

I looked for Pastor Tucker, but no one in that family was fat-faced. It was only when I saw the next picture, of a teenager on a horse, that I recognized the biggest child I'd seen standing behind his father in the one before. In the second photo was the same serious kid, in a cowboy hat and leather chaps, holding a guitar. It was our preacher in a happier frame of mind than I had ever seen him, but I recognized his coon-black eyes and, already, that appraising look.

There was one more picture on the wall that Hiram spent time on. Tucker, maybe in his twenties, in any army uniform, was standing by a very dark young girl holding a baby, on a porch with wrought-iron railings. It was hard to tell if the girl was black, or Creole, or perhaps American Indian—her features being a little of all these—but she was beautiful, with long black hair that shone like a crow's wing. She stood gracefully with Tucker's arm around her, and the baby held so that the camera could catch its features. The dark little face was solemn, its eyes big as an owls.

Hiram muttered a soft "hmmm," but then he went to the ones on a dresser top and there was nothing to do but follow along. There were two rodeo pictures of Tucker cut from a news-paper, one of him roping a calf, the other, playing his guitar and singing in front of a string band. That one had a caption: YOUNG COWBOY MATTHEW TUCKER *Entertains for Rodeo.* So, our preacher had a first name and, maybe, a black wife, as unlikely as that would seem.

In an ornate frame were the parents from the first photo, apparently taken in better times but just as grim, the father hold-ing a Bible in a stiff pose. Then, Hiram's gaze, and of course mine, went immediately to the pictures next to it; Tucker, this time in western cut civvies, with the dark skinned wife and the child we'd seen on the wall. The child was no longer a baby, but a skinny little kid of maybe five, who stood between his parents, and looked at the camera lens thoughtfully, with eyes so like his father's, there could be no doubt this was Matthew's son.

Finally, Hiram fastened on a picture of a dark young man in cap and gown. The face, despite the black searching eyes I'd seen on our preacher, was open and friendly. I pointed this one out to Hiram and remarked on the resemblance, and he sighed.

His voice was soft with wonder when he spoke. "Who would have thought it," he breathed, "Tucker's a man who once could see love beyond race. And now apparently can't *see* at all." We looked at the young man's photograph a long time, and at last we turned away.

"One more thing," I heard him say as I found myself looking numbly over the preacher's shoulder at his cluttered work table. The title of the sermon protruding from the typewriter was in caps, CASTING OUT THE DEMONS. I heard Hiram mutter,

"Merciful heaven, man, it's Christmas!"

Centered in the space to the right of the old Underwood, between phone and Bible, was a photo of Hiram playing for the children of Indian Glade, to which Pastor Tucker had added with his pen, horns and a tail. The Bible lay open to the book of Matthew—which I thought seemed fitting—with several long-hand notes from other chapters dealing with biblical warnings about demon spirits.

"Thank you, Stephen, and excuse me," said Hiram, and though the hologram remained of the preacher at his table, I sensed that I was alone, back in my own house.

Chapter Twenty-Five

HE VIVID HOLOGRAM CONTINUED TO
surround me, I could hear the clack of the type-
writer and even heard the preacher's furnace
come on, the first time I had ever heard sound
with Hiram's mental pictures. Unmistakably, our ghost was becoming multi-dimensional, which was proved when I heard a
chair from the hologram dining room dragging across the floor
to Tucker's horrified gaze, and saw it come around to the other
side of the table. The preacher shot to his feet and looked for a
wire attached to the chair. He lunged around the table to stop it,
but the chair kept coming, bringing him with it.

"What's happening?" he asked the chair, "Oh My God!"

He stared and came to a conclusion; he ran back to his own
side of the table and grabbed his Bible.

He shouted, "Begone Satan, Unclean Spirit, in the name of
Jesusss Christ-tuh!"

I watched the chair stop, spin slowly and turn to face him.

"*Mortal, it's Merry Christmas!*" roared a sepulchral voice. "*Named for Christ, who you wouldn't recognize if you met him.*"

Looking at the man's stricken face, I was sure he was about to crumple and fall. The voice continued, so supernatural it filled the room. Tucker's eyes searched desperately for it, but it was a voice far beyond hidden speakers or tricks and came from wherever he looked. While the preacher stood tilting, an unseen force seemed to push him down into his chair.

"*Sit!*" it ordered in the tone Pop used to use with Custer. "*And listen!*"

This said a dozen miles from Tucker's house, Custer lying at my feet looked up wonderingly at this order and got creakily into a sitting position. I petted her back down, my eyes mesmerized with the scene Hiram was sending me.

The voice from the hologram was stentorian, the sound of doom. "*Your father was a mean-spirited creature, Matthew. Abusing your mother and bullying discipline into all you Gospel-named children. You escaped him by joining the army.*"

Tucker's purple face remained speechless. The words deepened and seemed to come from above Tucker's head. His eyes looked up pitifully, though he was afraid to move.

"*Escaped him to pattern your behavior on him later,*" the voice inquired, "*like blaming music because you couldn't feel it?*"

Having no one to look at beside Matthew Tucker, I was hypnotized. His bulging eyes didn't know where to turn as the voice suddenly lowered, seeming to come from a well.

"*And you couldn't play music for people after they discovered you had none in your soul and just did it to get attention.*" Here the voice nearly quivered with anger. *"The most dreadful misuse of a gift you have shown, until now when you have decided to deny God's music to others!"*

When next it spoke, the voice seeming to have made its point, became gentler. *"This time you have drawn MY attention and it's time for you to mend your ways. Where is the love you showed that black girl you married, who sang like a bird until she saw your father in you, and left to save herself and your child?"*

At this, the pastor's color changed from brick to white, but the voice wasn't done.

"Your son, did he flourish in better hands and actually love the music you abandoned? Does it comfort you, deciding music was evil, to wish had riddance to both?"

The voice stopped, but it was as if the big pastor was gagged and only his jaw worked. His lips moved silently.

"What?" demanded the presence.

"Are you God or Satan?" Tucker asked in a helpless whisper.

"Confound it! You don't listen! I am neither! I am what is left of Christmas, poor human," shouted the voice. With a jolt, the chair pulled up close to the table. *"I'm not here about God; I'm here about His work, a part of which is Christmas!"*

The presence's voice, which had never been remotely like Hiram's, was now gentler. I could see the preacher's quavering face brighten a bit, and the big artery in his neck slow, with the first hint of mercy.

"I am sorry for your childhood, Matthew," said the voice, *"but sorrier for you, now, never searching for warmth or light or music in that grim book from which you only pull the darkest pictures."*

Tucker looked dazed, like a man in a doctor's office told he has something inoperable.

"*But there is always hope,*" added the voice, "*and this is the time for it—a time when the spinning world has given itself another chance at the light. You might give yourself another one as well.*"

Tucker struggled for words. I could see that the unseen voice had so accurately picked the details of his life apart, that all defense seemed useless.

"What now?" Tucker asked humbly, his face beaded with sweat. "I can't change the past. What is it you want from me?"

"*Not the past, numbskull!*" thundered the voice again, shaking the walls and making Tucker shrink and turn pale again. "*Humans can only affect a future. With what biblical name did you burden your son?*"

The preacher hesitated. "Jeduthun," he said weakly.

"*Jed-yu-thun,*" said the ghost carefully, sounding each syllable. There was a very long silence. "*Well at least a musical name. There's hope for you yet, and for him.*" The ghostly voice became almost cheerful. "*And is he a musical soul?*"

Tucker nodded, anxious to please. "He graduates from the Juilliard School of Music this year," he said, and then added hurriedly, "It was all his mother's doin'."

"*A school of music. His mother certainly,*" said Hiram, sounding to me at last, more like the congenial ghost I knew, and making me wonder if Tucker would recognize the change in tone from stern to interested.

But the man was beyond doing any analyzing. He shrunk when Hiram asked, "*Can she still abide the sound of your voice?*"

355

"Corey calls me every Christmas from wherever she is," said Matthew defensively.

"*Certainly, with her kind heart, she would,*" said Hiram, "*and you would know how to reach her, too, anxious as you are about your son's progress in his career?*"

The sarcasm came through to me as clearly as I was sure it did to Tucker.

"*Listen,*" said the measured voice stern as an obituary, "*to the first step of your new chance at humanity, Matthew. You will begin, as old Jeduthun did, by considering music as holy, written, and translated gospel. You will leave it to the people who create it and who will appreciate and change it through time.*"

The ghost's voice was as deliberate as a judge passing sentence, and Tucker bowed his head like a man hearing one.

"*Honor God's music, Matthew! You will not preach against it, criticize it, or take advantage of the ignorance of people in your flock by interpreting it for them. Let humans hear music in their own way.*"

I watched as surprised as Tucker, to see the piece of paper in his typewriter turn and un-scroll, wad itself and plop into a wastebasket. The silence that followed was impressive.

"*As your second step,*" said the voice serenely, "*you will telephone Corinna right now and humbly beg permission to talk to your son, who will be there for Christmas.*"

Tucker's eyes, just recovering from the ghostly episode with the typewriter, began to bug again feebly in protest, but the voice was inexorable.

"*You will ask for him,*" it went on, "*and you will ask him with all*" *your heart to forgive you for mean-spirited neglect and implore him to pay you a visit during this Christmas holiday."*

"He won't come!" exclaimed Tucker appalled. "He hates me!"

"Somehow I doubt that, Matthew," said the voice calmly. *"People, whose souls soar with music, seldom find time or room for hate. Now pick up that instrument, Matthew. I must repair music,"* said the voice, *"and to do so, must start repairing your life."*

Tucker's face contracted trying to puzzle this out, but it was obvious he had given up any control at all.

Fearful, wondering, but driven by the relentless voice from another dimension, the preacher reached to pick up the telephone and began to dial with trembling fingers. In a moment, I heard his hesitant voice finally say, "Merry Christmas?" to whomever it was who answered.

WHEN MY HOLOGRAM disappeared at last, I sat waiting, until I sensed at Custer's tail wag that Hiram was with us. I fetched our ghost a glass of wine to welcome him home. I couldn't make up my mind if I was disturbed or proud about the visit we had made; though intrusive and uncomfortable as it been for me, it certainly had results for him.

Hiram was festive and took his harmonica from its case so I could see him. "Have you heard of a Juilliard School of Music?" he asked. When I told him it was thought to be the best school of its kind, he chortled, "Imagine what determination that woman must have had to come up with such an education for her son."

"Determination and greenbacks," I added. "She must have done pretty well and maybe he got a scholarship. I expect it would take both."

Thinking about the woman Hiram had called "dark" brought me back to the boy's name. "What was this thing about 'Jeduthun?'" I asked him. "You seemed to know the name."

Hiram smiled warmly. "One of King David's soldiers turned musician, as told in the book of Chronicles," he said, "back in the times when music itself was prophecy."

The ghost chuckled at the look on my face. "I know, Stephen, but in my time the Bible was an almanac for life, impressed on children, and I was intrigued that Jeduthun composed for all instruments and choirs of that time, somethin' that in my heart, I hoped to do myself some day. I was overjoyed to find anythin' that spoke of the music I loved, in that grim old book, and I held onto his name."

He toyed one-handed with the harmonica and played a little riff without setting his wineglass down. "Who would have believed that pompous fool would pick Jeduthun, David's musical genius, as a name for a child? Perhaps fate picked it for him."

We sat thinking, but my mind was too tired to wander far. "Tomorrow's a big day, and I think I'd better rest up for it," I told him. "I hope Vera comes loaded with food."

I was going to say more, when the phone rang. I looked at Hiram, who merely raised his eyebrows, and I went to answer it.

"Merry Christmas?" said Tucker's voice sounding like a student answering a test question. "Mr. Clark, this is Matthew Tucker. I am sorry to call so late, sir, but would it be possible to speak to your Uncle Hiram?"

His polite tone was so foreign to the man I knew that I thought for a moment—*My God he's recognized his ghost for Hiram and is calling to blast him with scripture.* But something in the tone told me better.

"I heard him practicing earlier," I lied carefully, "and I don't think he would like to stop and argue scripture with you, Pastor."

Tucker hastened to assure me that argument was the last thing on his mind. When I'd made him sweat enough, I said curtly, "Let me see if he's still awake."

I laid the phone down and walked past Hiram to the foot of the stairs where I yelled, "Uncle Hiram, can you come to the phone?"

The old ghost, ten feet from me, laid his harmonica aside and took his time. It was at least a minute before I saw the telephone rise.

"Yes?" I heard him say, "To whom am I speakin' and why?" with just the right old-man crustiness of the musician disturbed.

I wondered how many of my neighbors' phones had reacted with a short ring of their own when mine went off, and whose owners were following the conversation. Sometimes, I thought, a party line could be more useful than any other form of gossip.

The talking was pretty one-sided, with Hiram's comments mostly limited to his southern flavored "yessuh's and "nossuh's," a neutral "You say his name is Jeduthun?" and a final, "You have a good evenin', suh."

When he finally hung up, I couldn't wait.

"Scrooge is starting to mend his ways?" I asked as Hiram retrieved his harmonica.

Hiram said, "I borrowed from Dickens and caught a guilty old man alone with his conscience and with no audience." He smiled, "I wish we could have heard both sides of his conversation with Jeduthun. I think his son was so smitten with his daddy's change of tone that he's comin' just to be sure if it's real. He's comin' down here after he's had Christmas with his mom and step-dad because Matthew used me for bait."

I was a little confused. "Used you for *bait?*" I repeated.

Hiram's eyes were shining with what I could only think was pride. "He actually told his son that he had made his peace with music and had heard an amazing fiddler in the Ozarks. He told the boy he wanted his opinion, which you and I both know is the way to any child's confidence. Then naturally, he had to win his way to mine."

"Hence the call," I nodded sagely, having fun because Hiram was. I said, "Would you like to have—I guess you'd call him *Jed*—come here? On the other hand, I'll be glad to take you over to Tucker's house. Whatever seems best, oh Ghost Of Christmas Present."

"I thank you," said Hiram grinning. "We can talk about that tomorrow. Now go to bed my friend, you must rest for your daughter's first day at home and her first Christmas Eve on Earth."

I WENT to sleep, first to the sound of Hiram's familiar tending of the stoves and kitchen, and then the faint and lulling voice of his violin. I thought of Lacey and our Elizabeth, of my school-children, and of the future, and dozed off finally, wondering for the first time, in my sleep, how long that lovely fiddle sound and

Hiram himself, would be part of our world.

Chapter Twenty-Six

F THE DAY BEFORE HAD BEEN HECTIC, it was just a rehearsal for Sunday, the day be fore Christmas Eve. I slept until I heard the sleepless Hiram stoking the morning fires and then got up and had a hot shower and coffee. I made an early call to Lacey. I was anticipating the trip to Medley Springs to bring my family home, and she was as excited as I was. The weather seemed to be holding, even though the skies still looked the color of hammered lead, the thermometer on the back porch register- ing in the twenties. It was all one to me; I'd have gone to get my family in a blizzard. To Hiram's amusement, I started the truck every hour to warm it up and made a dozen trips to Elizabeth's room to make sure it was warm, feel for drafts, and see that the small electric heater was working.

While I bustled around, Hiram sat at the piano having fun with some tunes he'd invented for his "Elizabeth's Suite," the top of the old square grand piled with notes apparently made to himself. It seemed to me, listening with the part of my mind I had to spare, that he was an accomplished pianist as well as fiddler. I marveled at the music he came up with, flavored so much with jazz-like and ragtime improvisations. It made me realize how much black music had affected his youth. This morning it was sort of like having Scott Joplin tinkering in the living room with bright little tunes that somehow would stay in my head all day. Occasionally, he would stop playing and I would hear the harmonica wail some frill he had invented for the score. It made me realize that whatever else Hiram might be, he was a musician beyond the ages, and the very spirit of everything he played on any instrument and brought to life.

I left before noon to pick up my girls and found Doc Brant as well as Billie there. Doc was giving Lacey some final instructions and doctor wisdom. He seemed pleased to include me.

"Lacey's breast-feeding your daughter," he said jovially, "will save you a lot of floor walkin' and burned bottles, and she's doing you both a greater favor than you can know. I do believe this little lady is one of those classic mothers we all imagine ours to be."

He shook my hand warmly and hugged Lacey before leaving for his office. When I tried to pay our bill, he would have none of it and said that could all wait for the New Year coming. As he headed out of the room, he said, "Now you go home and have a good Christmas and don't call me up every time the child hollers. Babies need to holler. Think of it as practicin' up to sing."

Once in our warm truck and heading home, Lacey sighed happily, "Steve, let's let Doc deliver all our babies, he acts like

363

we're doin' him a favor."

All the way home, when I'd glance over at her, her expression was like someone restfully looking at palm trees instead of winter woods, little Elizabeth peacefully asleep in her lap. I used the opportunity to catch her up on Hiram's impersonation of a Dickens' ghost and the seeming change he had made in the bleak preacher, all things I couldn't tell her on the phone.

When she heard that Tucker's son had actually attended Juilliard, she took in an excited breath. "Oh my God, Steve, did Uncle Hiram know how important that would be to someone from down here?"

I considered that. "I don't think they had a Juilliard in his time," I said. "But the idea Tucker's kid went to *any* music school, tickled him. He gave Tucker a lecture on respecting music that would have done your heart good."

"Oh, Steve, honey," she said looking at Elizabeth under the curl of quilt, "I love that old man so much, and I feel so sorry for him, but it'd just kill me to let him put some genius load on Elizabeth. Maybe she'll want to grow up to be an actress or a clothes designer, or hell, maybe a backup singer, for that matter."

I assured her that Hiram and I had already had that discussion, and I had told him that no one was going to plan out Elizabeth's future like an architect's drawing. She nodded, satisfied and went back to her palm trees.

Once home, the old man was waiting to welcome us, but, as usual, went upstairs to let us put our new lives together as soon as he'd made sure nothing was needed. It occurred to me often that Hiram must have seen butlers in his day and picked up on their withdrawing sense; he was always available, never in anyone's way.

We rearranged everything around Elizabeth. We put her crib in our bedroom, set up her little bath tub, and a big brass kettle jar-topped vaporizer in the bathroom, and Lacey organized all the baby food on the kitchen shelves for the day she'd start needing it. Looking at the array of bottles for water, orange juice, and just in case, formula, I began to understand the huge difference breast-feeding was going to make.

Interrupted by a phone call in the middle of sterilizing nipples, Lacey picked up the receiver; it was Vera and she sounded desperate. It turned out she had caught a cold and didn't dare come give it to Elizabeth. She was sending Rabon with gifts for everybody and would come as soon as she was feeling like a human. The poor woman sounded so congested and miserable, my heart went out to her, and at the same time, I rejoiced that she wasn't on her way here with whatever she had. She and Lacey talked for an hour, and Lacey promised to send home a "picture gallery" of Vera's first grandchild and not let Rabon break her in half.

It was a fun conversation to listen to, reminding me that Vera and Lacey both took every obstacle in stride and talked to each other like old friends, the sort of good feeling talks Pop and I always had. My mind wandered to the preacher whose tragedy, I guessed, was that he and his son had never found words to speak the same language.

When Lacey hung up the phone, she grinned, "Momma's fit to bite herself, but she knows she's got years to dote on Elizabeth, and she doesn't want to be remembered as the one that first gave her the crud."

I laughed. It was like the Donnellys to refer to every unknown ailment as a simple *crud* and dismiss it, a serenity that with Lacey, made everything seem right.

The rest of the evening was like that, somehow peaceful despite the many visitors dropping by to see the newest resident of Blessing Creek. Lacey was both proud and protective, with a friendly but instinctive *look-but-don't-touch* in her eyes, which kept Elizabeth from being exposed to all the company's germs. The Farleys brought a home-cured ham, the McClellans a cooked venison roast wrapped in bacon, the Smiths, pecan and mincemeat pies, and Soames and Virgie came with a pretty handmade Gibson basket, decorated with bittersweet and holly and full of jars of home canned fruit. They didn't all come at once, thank God, and the parents didn't stay long, saying they had left their children home to mind the fires and each other. Everyone asked about Hiram, and at some point in each visit, he came down, his violin in hand, to offer season's greetings, bow to the ladies, and shake hands with the men. He was wearing Pop's brightest red shirt and a green tie and told them he'd been upstairs writing a Christmas song for our new baby. I could see a new regard for him in our visitors' eyes and that the word about his wandering "history" had gotten around. Ozarkers love the *lost sheep* concept and apply it to anyone needing their endless hospitality.

Soames Black was especially cordial and even the suspicious Virgie's forebodings seemed to have been laid aside for the occasion. "Now you come by Christmas and bring your music," I heard her tell Hiram. "I've got a sister who's partial to the cord-deen. She's a widow lady," she hinted hopefully.

Hiram, to my shock, promised to come. "I don't have an accordion, ma'am," he told her gravely, "but perhaps a harmonica or two would please her."

Elizabeth's first court appearance, as I liked to think of it, ended before dark. With Hiram upstairs, the three of us spent a blissful evening together. Elizabeth was in her crib by our bed, the baby's room being too far away for at least several weeks. I wasn't sure that the baby's room wouldn't always be too far away, it felt so good to listen to her tiny breathing.

CHRISTMAS EVE, before sunset, Elizabeth's grandfather arrived. Rabon drove up in his van-like truck, so overloaded that for a moment I thought he planned to move in. It wasn't until all the shouting, back slapping, hugging, introductions, and baby handling were over that Rabon and I went to unload, and I realized that most of the contents of the huge van were gift wrapped things, plus the typical Donnelly overkill of food that came with all of their family get-togethers.

"I like your uncle!" commented Rabon, pitching out packages with his usual fervor. "He is a By-God-Southerner from the ground up, and I love a man who hangs onto the tools of his trade!"

He had noticed that Hiram hadn't laid down his harmonica while he shook with the other hand, and I was happy with Raybon's interpretation.

"Glad you like him, Rabon," I said. "He's the last of a dying breed. He's been teaching Lacey old fiddle tunes and has written a whole symphony he calls 'Elizabeth's Suite'."

I didn't mention that the Elizabeth honored was Hiram's long-dead wife. Rabon grinned with pleasure. "Damn!" he said, "what a Christmas present! All I got her were alphabet blocks and a gizmo to hang over her crib."

Hiram insisted on putting away the food Vera had sent for Christmas dinner, and for supper served us McClellan's venison, baked potatoes, and a salad. The harmonica in his pocket solved so many problems. I began to relax and watched the old ghost in wonder as he worked two-handed, wearing an old apron of Lacey's.

I was sure men didn't cook in his time, and helping him carry groceries beyond the refrigerator's capacity to the old built-in winter icebox on the porch, I asked him where he learned this stuff.

"I liked to help Bessie," he said, "and besides, bein' cook will give me an excuse not to eat with you. Southern cooks seldom sit, you know, always seein' to company's needs."

I had noticed this with Vera, who every year would take over the kitchen herself, lock, stock, and barrel, and flit over every speck of food like an anxious waitress.

"What'll you do tomorrow?" I asked. "It's going to be pretty awkward if you don't eat Christmas dinner."

"Why, I've been invited out," he said, "and after I've helped serve dinner, will ask you to carry me over to the Black's house to suffer through Virgie's widowed sister. I'll tell them I ate here."

ALL THE PRESENTS that would fit, like mine for Lacey, hers

for me, and ours for Elizabeth, Hiram, and the Donnellys, were piled under the tree, the rest mounded in what I can only call "Donnelly stacks." Sort of like haystacks but less tidy. After laying out or putting away all the Christmas dinner things to be cooked in the morning, Hiram took over the entertainment of Rabon, which was mostly a matter of getting his attention away from his granddaughter long enough for her to be changed, fed, or held by anyone else. What saved Rabon, from missing Vera too much to enjoy himself, was the phone. He talked to her for thirty minutes holding our daughter up to it and encouraging her to say words she wouldn't speak in a lifetime; "Bess it's time, Lizzie wants to say, Hi Gamma Vera, I look like a 'lil bitty angel, don't I Gamma?" over a hundred-fifty miles of phone wire.

Lacey witnessed all this with perfect serenity but at last gently unhooked Elizabeth from Rabon's big arms and put her firmly to bed. "You call her 'Lizzy' once more, Daddy," she said over her shoulder, "and you're off limits 'til she's my age."

By the time we all went to bed on Christmas Eve, I was pretty sure I had everything worked out. Four drinks and a dozen fiddle and cello and harmonica tunes later, the early rising—and already homesick—Rabon was tucked in Hiram's four poster. Despite his protests, Hiram had insisted on taking the couch, where he could tend the fires if needed.

"Merry Christmas, Lacey," I whispered as she turned to check on Elizabeth and hug me."

"You always know just the right *thang* to say!" she told me, and the two of us were asleep in each other's arms before we could say another word.

369

Sometime in the middle of the night I awoke, so aware of a new life, I guess, I had to see her to believe her, and after I'd checked on Elizabeth, I went into the living room to see if Hiram was reading. He was gone. His violin case and harmonica were both on the shelf of the end table, along with his pipe and the bowl Lacey had given him for an ask tray. The book he had been reading from Lacey's library, *Compositions of Nicolo Paganini*, was on the couch, and on the other end table were the neatly stacked sheets of Hiram's own compositions, which made a surprising pile. But no Hiram.

I walked carefully through the whole room. I took small steps making sure I didn't knock over any gifts, and walked around behind the lighted tree and then the piano, to look out the windows to the porch.

For some reason I couldn't accept that Hiram could be gone, not on Christmas Eve, and I can't describe the empty way my heart plummeted. Then, I saw by the lights on the fir trees, a major miracle. It was snowing—great white flakes of snow, spinning easily down, as big as silver dollars. The ground was already covered and there was no wind to disturb the gentle fall of the white, silent stuff. It had already covered the fir tree lights in gauze and was a Christmas dream of a snow. I was so taken with the magic of it that it was a minute before I saw Custer sitting on the top step of the porch, leaning familiarly on nothing. Beside the old dog, a bare place on the porch floor told me where our ghost had gone. He'd just found a good speechless companion to be with to share the quiet, falling snow.

I don't know how long I stood watching and remembering

that empty-gut feeling I had when I thought Hiram had wandered off again. With my heart full of thanks for everything, I at last tiptoed off to bed to think about what would be my daughter's first white Christmas morning.

I WOKE TO *"Holy mother o' God, people, look at this friggin' snow!"* from upstairs and the sound of Rabon's feet on the stairs. *"Merry Christmas, everybody! Jesus Christ, snow!"* He shouted and then remembering his new granddaughter, "Oh shit, I'm sorry, Lacey honey. Is the baby awake?"

"She is now, Daddy," called Lacey with her usual morning good cheer, "and just in time for you to change her."

"Good morning, Hiram," said Rabon, ignoring his daughter's joke and walking into the kitchen. "Got any coffee around here?" Hiram had been ready for this all night and at the first waking sound, had put the percolator on a gas burner.

"Goddamn snow!" boomed Rabon from the kitchen. "I'll need a load of firewood in the van to stay on the road."

"Relax, Daddy, it won't last long," said Lacey coming out of the bedroom. She added, "Elizabeth needs to see it!" Then she walked to the front door holding our daughter up to see the snow, which, though the flakes were smaller, was still falling like a curtain and weighing down the boughs of the firs.

What we could see of the yard and the woods around us was a fairyland of shapes; the fence around the spice garden was an elfish lacework. Elizabeth regarded it all solemnly with eyes that seemed as big a Lacey's. She was so attentive that I remember thinking she was going to expect every Christmas to be white

371

from now on.

I won't even try to explain what opening presents was like, except that all we missed was Vera's glee and laughter. Our main gift—and I remember it well—was from Hiram, the last person we would have imagined to come up with one. It was a hand copied "Elizabeth's Suite," bound in a piece of tanned cowhide that he'd found in one of the sheds. He had glued, tooled and varnished it himself. It was fifty sheets thick and had orchestrations for strings, wind instruments, piano and tympani, neatly noted. The dedication was to "Alacia and Stephen Clark, who believed in the spirit of this music, which will forever be Elizabeth's."

It's a measure of the way that I have always looked at Lacey; she didn't cry or even make a fuss over this stunning gift that meant more to her than words could have said. She just beamed at him, pressed the thick manuscript lovingly to her breast and got up to hug our old ghost and kiss his cheek. All she said was— "Uncle Hiram, you *are* Christmas." To which the old man shook his head but smiled and looked at us all happily. It was his turn to be amazed when Lacey handed him gifts from both the Donnellys and us.

All we had given him was another set of fiddle strings and a boxed assortment of harmonicas, but the imaginative Vera, inspired by her daughter, had found Hiram albums of orchestrations he might like—works of Verdi, Aaron Copeland, and Dvorak—and his face became a study as he looked through the boxed records.

"This is another world of music," he told Rabon humbly, "and

372

I don't know how to thank you and your wife for thinkin' so much of me."

Rabon, speaking for Vera whose own love for music had shaped her daughter's, said, "You've been making music for the kids and lookin' out for them—you're family." It was said gruffly, but with a warm tone that left no doubt it was heartfelt.

Lacey was enchanted with the Stainer-copy violin I had found for her, an old one I had bought at the music store and brought home for Hiram's approval and which he had refurbished and re-strung. As usual, she surprised me with books I'd wanted but never asked for and amazed me with a handmade sheepskin hat laced with hide strings, and like Robin Hood's, stood cocked at a jaunty angle. I have no idea how she worked on that hat without me knowing, but it was simply a Lacey hat and I knew my school kids would love it. As soon as she had called her mother and we had all talked on the phone, Lacey picked up her fiddle, along with Elizabeth and took her to her crib, where she played her a lullaby that only mothers know, and soon Elizabeth was asleep.

The snow slowed and finally stopped around eight o'clock that Christmas morning, leaving about five inches on the ground and the wind was beginning to shake it off the timber. After breakfast, I went out to start the Jeep. The snow was already starting to melt—Ozark fashion—but I knew the Jeep was the only vehicle that would move that morning and I had to take Hiram to the Blacks. When Rabon went to the bathroom to shave, I called Virgie and told her I would bring Hiram by after dinner if that was all right, and the old woman was delighted. I could imagine her constructing her own scenario with Hiram and her widowed sister. I remember muttering to myself when I hung up the phone, "Greater love hath no man, Hiram."

Hiram spent the morning cooking Vera's big turkey in the gas oven and peeling potatoes for mashing. Vera had seen to it that the only thing the meal would lack was her. Hiram had her vegetables already cut up, dressing ready to mix, her cranberry salad in the icebox, and her two pies waiting for placement in the warming oven along with a pan of her perfect rolls. While Elizabeth napped, Lacey spent time in the kitchen watching the gravy and setting the table for four, though she knew Hiram would never sit.

When Hiram noted the fourth plate, she said, "Uncle, on Christmas, expect a stranger," and pulled the aproned Hiram over for a hug, and the old man held her tenderly.

Hiram served dinner with a constant bustle that rivaled Vera's, only lighting down to tell Rabon that he had eaten while cooking. After the huge meal, I took him and his "music," (as Ozarkers call musical instruments), to the Jeep.

The road to Blacks, unspoiled by a single tire track, was a Lewis and Clark adventure. The snow altered the appearance of the road so much that I had to inch along in places where the center of it could be anywhere. Only the moving water of Blessing Creek, on my right, and bluffs on the left, defined where the road had to be, and we were forty-five minutes getting to the ford that led to the Black's driveway. There, however, sat a man who appeared to be dressed like Santa Claus, on a tractor. Having just bladed the Black's road, Santa was apparently on his way to clearing the one we had just come over.

"Merry Christmas!" he shouted and waved us to cross the creek. When we came up beside the tractor and stopped, I could see that Santa was actually Carney Black, sporting new "Christmas plunder" in the form of a down-lined parka in the fire engine crimson everybody called "deer season red." By the time we climbed out of the Jeep's canvas doors, Carney had already uncorked a flask from a side pocket and offered it to us.

"Now you'll be Teacher's Uncle Hiram," he said, pumping Hiram's hand, while he offered me the bottle. "Jesus, I'm sorry you give me and Vance a turn that time we saw you in the house and didn't know who you was! Shit-o-dear, we caused a ruckus!" He roared with laughter.

"Pleased to make your acquaintance, sir," said Hiram in his polite way, and when I handed the flask to him, he took a small sip. "I apologize for start'lin' you boys."

"Aw hell," said Carney, "we're the ones sorry, comin' home drunk and getting Ma wound up. She's been wantin' that old house to be hainted ever since I was a button—and us goin' along with it!"

We talked a little more before Carney went back to his tractor to "finish bladin' before supper," and I drove up to the house. It looked remarkably tidy in its covering of snow. I went in with Hiram to take the Blacks Lacey's Christmas gift, an ornate box of chocolates she had known they would all like. The place looked the same but smelled wonderful with the dinner they had just eaten and the windows were still opaque with steam.

Virgie greeted us very warmly. No one could have guessed that a month ago she would have liked to see Hiram burned at the stake. We met her sister, Magnolia, the accordion lover, whose bosom resembled one, and Vance's girlfriend, a plump country girl named Judith with huge green eyes (mostly for Vance) and a voice like a kitten. I joked a little with Vance, who was helping Judith with the dishes and chatted with Soames a while before reminding them that I had company myself. I felt a little bad about leaving Hiram to the wiles of Magnolia, but left knowing that by the time I came to get him for "suppertime" he would have charmed his way into the whole family.

I came home over the bladed path of Carney's tractor and met him coming back to clear the creek road toward the highway. The sun had come out and the snow was melting. Turning into our driveway, I discovered he had also cleared it. Rabon had already moved his van into the bladed space; he was ready to head home the minute he had done what he came to do. Lacey's description of him as a "bug on a stove lid" was fairly precise.

For the next hour, we took enough pictures to convince Vera that we had captured every expression, angle, feature, and dimension of her granddaughter. We also gave Rabon a wire recording of Hiram playing parts of "Elizabeth's Suite" and the little Christmas song he had written for her, called "Christmas Bells." The ghost had wanted to send a thank you note to Vera, but knowing that wouldn't work, he dictated it to Lacey before dinner and had her sign it for him. Packed up with these, most of the dishes he had brought, half the food, and all the presents meant for the Donnelly family, Rabon took off in time to make it home before nightfall, if the highways were all clear.

Chapter Twenty-Seven

EDUTHUN TUCKER ARRIVED THE DAY after Christmas. True to Soames' forecast that it was too early for snow to stay, the roads were mostly clear. It was a good thing, because the young man pulled up in a foreign car built way too close to the road for Ozark oil pans.

The car was the least surprising thing about Jeduthun Tucker. When he climbed out of it, he just kept coming—tall and rail thin, with hair as long and black as his mother's had been in her picture. When all six-foot-five of him had emerged and stood looking at the front door, I could see that he had no coat but was wearing a fingertip length one-piece shirt of a very dark blue with a high-embroidered collar and sleeves, and black slacks. It was his face that got my attention. In the years since the picture we'd seen, he'd become nearly my age—early twenties, grown a mustache and had a short goatee, and with his swarthy skin, looked like a Muslim prince from a child's storybook. He reached back into the car's tiny back seat and brought out a white violin case. He came striding up the walk eagerly, taking off dark glasses he'd worn against the snow glare. His jet black eyes, bright as a guileless child, met mine as I opened the door to welcome him. It was startling to see such childlike eyes on such a big face.

"Hi, I'm Thun Tucker!" he greeted me, with a dazzling smile, and held out a hand as long and dark as everything else about him.

"Excuse me for not calling first, but knowing your run in with Pa-Pa, I figured I'd show my own face, and take my chances."

His voice was mellow, and when he laughed, it had the richness of black men's mirth, almost a form of music. His diction seemed uninflected with any region of the country, except for the French sounding *Pa-Pa*, accentuated like ta-dah! I supposed his careful speech was a result of his years at Juilliard.

I welcomed him in, noticing he naturally ducked doorframes and protected his violin case with his gangly arm, so much for expecting a "Jed" from a high school graduation picture. He was definitely used to being tall.

"And how is your father, Thun?" I asked when I got him seated in the biggest chair we had. His eyes, which had searched the room, landed with delight on the piano and then he laughed when he saw our big speaker cabinet.

"Pa-Pa's having an epiphany," he said, "some private audience with God. But whatever it is, suits me. Last time I saw him, he wanted to stomp on my fiddle. This time he wants me to meet a fiddler. I couldn't resist. Besides, Ma-Ma said, 'do it!'"

Lacey came in to greet our company and like me was a little

flabbergasted at his size. "Thun," she said, "as in thunder? You're sure big enough."

"Well, when you're black anyway, it beats *Jed*," he said good humouredly, "and nobody's gonna buy Jeduthun, which was Pa-Pa's choice of names."

When Hiram came downstairs at Lacey's call, he took the "Thun" name in stride, and they shook hands cordially, at the same time sizing each other up as I would suppose specialists at anything do—swordsmen, fiddlers or auctioneers.

I went to make drinks and came back to find them already deep in conversation begun by Lacey, who was curious to find out how Matthew Tucker had ever managed to come up with a son who qualified for Juilliard.

Thun was happy to oblige; his deep voice vibrated with enthusiasm. "My Ma-Ma's name is Corinna Le Beque now." He told us, "She's Creole and started out as a Fontaine, which is a big music name down in New Orleans."

Listening, I caught the first down-South inflection in his smooth voice; he pronounced it *Naw-lins.*

"She met Pa-Pa after the First World War back in 1920. The army'd sent him to New Orleans to guard the port and he just stayed on after the war, breaking horses, fixing cars, playing guitar in small music joints." He continued, "Ma-Ma sang with a band. It was love at first sight, according to Ma-Ma. This Missouri hillbilly wanting to sit in with a bunch of Cajuns and Dixieland horn players, trying to learn jazz and blues, just to be near her. It was a lost cause, but she loved him for trying. Man with no soul for it, trying to jam with wailin' Cajuns and Creole soul brothers—did not have a clue."

Lacey was having a good time and she turned to glance at Hiram to see how he reacted to "Dixieland" and "blues" and "soul," words he couldn't know.

Hiram was attentive and puffed his pipe approvingly. He had been listening to his new records all morning through Lacey's earphones; energized, he was ready to talk about music or anything concerning it. He beamed at Thun, eyes shining as they did when he fiddled "Dixie" or watched Lacey play.

Thun's attention being on those two, I was able to sit to one side and make some notes while they talked. I'd get up now and then to tend the fire or look in on Elizabeth.

I don't know how long they talked about Jeduthun's growing up, but it was a long story. How Matthew and the Creole girl Corinna had married and had Thun, and how they went about trying to make it work. They had stayed together for fifteen years, with her finding more and better jobs, bands, and opportunities, until she at last got a recording contract with Gulf Breeze Records, when Thun was fifteen. Matthew, unused to women outdoing him, had become withdrawn and less supportive of his wife's career with every year. Finally, falling back on his own selling abilities, he tried selling musical instruments, then cars, then real estate, without much success.

The marriage broke up when Thun was in high school making straight A's in music and with his own little jazz band ensemble for school competitions. His tuition scholarship to Juilliard came as no surprise to anyone, but it didn't please Matthew, who saw music as the dissolution of his family and demanded that Jeduthun get a real job. When no one listened, he filed for divorce, sure that this would bring them around. When it didn't, he moved back to Missouri, blaming the break up on Corinna's music, which he said had made her forget the "subservience" demanded of women by the Bible. His one inheritance being his father's religion, Matthew seized upon that to sell, and became ordained through a mail order course.

It was fascinating to hear Thun; his voice was never judgmental or bitter. I got the feeling that this was a result of Corinna's patient teaching and he quoted her as saying, "Blame never bought nobody's breakfast." A year after the divorce, she remarried, this time to her Artist and Repertory man at Gulf Breeze Records, Julien Le Beque, who financed Thun's move to New York City and Juilliard.

When Hiram questioned Thun about what he intended to do when he graduated, there was no hesitation.

"There's a new time coming in music," he told Hiram, "and I want to be ready for it. Many people up North think it's all coming from the South. Mostly black artists making the jump— getting past all the middle of the road stuff, you know, crooners and ballads, and big band soup to slow dance to, dumb-cute cookie cutter songs we call *white bread*." He grinned hugely at Hiram's attentive face. "We're past rhythm and blues. As my friends put it, we're hot to *get down*."

Hiram had devoted the past months listening to the radio and record player, and he was anxious to have this explained.

"Get down to what, exactly?" he asked.

Thun grinned. "I'm not sure, but nobody else is either and

that's what makes it so exciting! All these cats searching for it, they got a word—*dig*, like it was under the ground somewhere. It's mostly a black thing—like jazz."

"Why would *cats dig* music up?" asked Hiram with interest.

"*Cats* is a jazz term," said Thun, "black word for music people. It's like *get down* and *riff* and *scat*. It's just our speech for our music. Jazz is what black people invented from playing white instruments, and a lot of us were a step better at them than they were—a giant step toward a new sound." Thun explained this carefully, unsure how much this old white man knew. "Back in slave days," he said with a grin, "white people wouldn't let us have African instruments. So, we learned to play white ones. With us it came out free form, no rules to learn—people improvised."

"I see," said Hiram solemnly, "much as my friend Silas did with the piano—playin' in what he called *ragged time*. Much as Paganini did with the violin."

Thun lit up like a sparkler. "I don't know Silas," he said, "but Paganini! That's who cranked me up!" He crowed, "Imagine a guy from those days who'd dare to flatten his bridge, file it down so he could play four-note combinations and chord from every position. I bet the critics wanted to fry his ass. My theory professor told me, 'Invent with the voice of the violin and you can invent choirs and cathedrals around it.' Shit, Paganini did better than that, he invented an attitude!"

Then they were off and running. Language ceased to be a problem, if it ever was between those two. Out came Thun's fiddle, a brisk little Stainer, and he whipped off a Paganini theme

382

that Lacey had told me was from one of his concertos. Hiram forgot to puff his pipe, so intently was he fixed on Thun's fingers and flying bow arm. He knew that Thun wasn't showing off, just expressing a thought he couldn't put into words about Paganini's construction of notes to let Hiram know how deeply he appreciated the man's inventiveness.

The next high point of the evening was the opening of Hiram's own violin case and the awesome silence that followed the removal of the ancient Guarnerius. The look on Jeduthun's face as Hiram drew the bow over the strings to play one of the Paganini caprices, I thought was going to make Thun cry. Instead, he laughed with delight. It was Hiram that impressed him, not the fiddle.

What followed, according to Lacey who was better equipped to understand it, was one of the most colorful and vital exchanges of musical ideas she had ever heard between two musicians.

At one point, Thun would go to the piano to illustrate some polyphonic theory. At another, Hiram digging out a harmonica, doing his best to explain how he saw the path blacks had used improvising tunes into blues and jazz. Thun borrowed Lacey's guitar to accompany one tune, which led to his explaining "bottleneck" guitar to Hiram. Then that got them into using "slide" bass notes and then using the bass for percussion. This led to Thun playing a walking bass for Hiram on the piano, while our ghost improvised a blues tune on the guitar. Hiram amazed us with his proficiency, since we'd never seen or heard him play Lacey's guitar.

Lacey's description might be more accurate, but my interpretation of that winter afternoon was of two music lovers meeting across a century and finding no problem with time or tools.

At Hiram's suggestion, they finally went upstairs to keep from waking Elizabeth. Lacey and I just sat and looked at each other, listening to fiddles and the guitar talk and exchange views overhead.

She sighed happily. "My God, who'd a thunk it? Uncle Hiram takin' to jazz like a fish to water!"

"Maybe music is *all* water," I told her, "just different fish swimming around in it."

She smiled. "Why, you silver-tongued devil! You should try writin' a book."

"Maybe I will someday," I told her.

Upstairs, Thun was explaining "scat" to Hiram, who was retaliating with a black recital of syncopated "eephing" and "field holler" nonsense words and "bluesy" things that Ella Fitzgerald would have had fun with.

SUPPER CAME AND went. I took a turkey sandwich upstairs for Thun, who would only take a bite now and then between tunes and comments. It got very eclectic sounding to me. Hiram would play some improvisations on his fiddle from a guitar tune Thun had improvised, and Hiram would say, "It could use tonkin," or "fertilize that chord," or "that needs to soak," terms that Thun seemed to absorb without question. They were already friends.

Close to midnight, when they finally came downstairs, neither Lacey nor I needed to be told that Hiram's long search was

384

over. Thun hugged us both as though he had known us for years, but his parting with Hiram was less dramatic. It was as if they would be seeing each other tomorrow.

It was only after Thun had gone, and we all sat watching the fire crackle sending light flickering around the ceiling, that Hiram began to tell us what I have kept to myself for fifty-five years now. I can still see the old ghost in the rocking chair. It was his favorite place to puff his pipe and think about his fate, his eyes searching time, his hands fingering the old violin on his lap.

He told us, "Who knows where music goes? Thun spoke of a new concept of syncopation he called 'rock,' which his generation is toyin' with, a black concept no longer satisfied with soothin' sounds for the mind. *Rock* will go directly to heart and bone and will *rock* the foundations of whatever we thought we knew!"

We realized the old man was speaking to himself, and neither of us commented.

Hiram mused: "Thun talked of guitar chords that could be held out, stretched electrically and rolled like buildin' blocks of sound, a configuration of levels impossible to imagine in my time—and just now becomin' a reality in his. *Just think!* A bass note that can stand and quaver long enough to erect a musical staircase. Instruments that can hold an echo, and drums that are allowed to pulse and roll like Africa . . . *the force and emotion of it!*"

The ghost leaned forward to look at us, his eyes staying on Lacey. "*Rock* will sound strange," he said to her, "a departure from expected ways of listenin' from our comfort in predictable patterns—from our satisfaction with the past."

Lacey asked doubtfully, "*Rock* is the music of the future?"

"*A music* maybe," he said slowly, "I don't think there is any such thing as *the* music anymore than *the* people, or *the* invention or, for that matter, *the* religion. From what I have seen, I think people keep reinventin' everythin', includin' themselves, but despite the evidence, are more amazed by what they have done so far, than what they seem likely to do. —It has been strange to observe."

We sat in silence, watching the fire eat at the logs.

Soon, Hiram knocked out his pipe and chuckled softly. "Thun thinks this new 'rock music' will replace the old, but I think he knows better. Music does not replace itself like a lizard's tail, only growin' from its own roots. I am anxious to spend time in his mind and perhaps do what I was intended before I move on. I think I will go with him to this Juilliard place and help him invent the future of the music he believes in."

Neither Lacey nor I spoke for a minute, knowing that if this could be explained, Hiram would get around to it.

At last, Lacey asked, "Will you need clothes, Uncle Hiram, to travel with Thun?"

"No, Mistress Lacey, I will need nothin' of this earth anymore, I think, includin' my violin. I must leave everythin' here that has served its purpose, includin' . . ." and here he gave a final tap to his pipe and laid it in its bowl, "this pipe with which you welcomed me into your world. It has been a treasure."

I protested, "*But Hiram, your violin!* That's the real treasure! It's probably priceless, and besides, it's what brought you here. You said it was your soul, and its music enabled us to see you and believe in you!"

Hiram chuckled again fondly, "Music is the soul that brought me, the same that the original Jeduthun carried over from three-thousand years ago. I have learned now that violins are only love-carved wood, Stephen."

"But what do you want us to do with it Uncle?" asked Lacey practically. "Should we send it on to Maudie's children?"

"No," said Hiram. "They would only love it for a triflin' worth that has nothin' to do with its true value." His tone was firm. "It belongs to this musical family who gave me strength to pass music on. Play it yourself, my dear, or teach Elizabeth, or put it back in the bed leg for some future Paganini, perhaps in generations to follow," he paused pondering that. "Or, if hard times should beset you and your children, sell it or barter it for what you need more, if it's worth anythin' today. I would only ask that it go to someone who will play it lovingly."

Lacey asked, "But why don't you give it to Thun? He would treasure it."

Hiram's answer told us he had thought about this carefully. "The last thing Thun needs to treasure is anythin' that might divert his ambition right now. The Guarnerius speaks of age and music done, while his mind is busy inventin' new sounds, perhaps even an instrument ears have yet to hear." The old ghost smiled at her, "I'd like to see him do that and I'll perhaps be allowed to whisper in his ear without him knowin' I'm there."

The idea that Hiram was leaving us was almost more than Lacey could bear, and when he moved to put his fiddle on the table, she reached for him.

"Not yet, Uncle Hiram," she cried and hugged him. "Elizabeth needs to say good-bye as much as we do."

She went to the bedroom, brought back our daughter, and Hiram held her a moment, then kissed her tiny hand.

"Farewell, Mistress Elizabeth," he said seriously, "and may you always find your own way in this world." Elizabeth with her quiet blue eyes on his face seemed to be listening with a smile.

Hiram, standing to put her back in Lacey's arms, extended his hand to me. "Thank you, Stephen," he said formally, "for your trust, your kindness and your belief. Since you are as much a born teacher as I was a born musician, may I leave you, too, with somethin' to pass on?"

"Good God, Hiram!" I said. "What a question!"

He smiled. "Of course, it is just that your history books choose to miss the point about the South and you are a teacher. Please remind your children that the war I died for wasn't about makin' the colored slaves equal Americans at all, and no one did." Hiram's eyes took on that perplexed look I had seen so often, not as if he didn't know what to say but how to say it. "That war came about because of the way the South saw the rigid Yankee way of government, the stiffness of their language, their music and their religion, their do-or-die way of livin'. We seceded from the Union peacefully, to maintain our easy goin' culture, and I believe we would have one day shamed ourselves out of slavery. Tell your children, please, Stephen, to forgive the South her stubborn ways, and appreciate her music.

"Consider it done," I told him.

Turning to Lacey, he said, "And you child, with your love for music that brought me back so I might pass it on, I leave you all I have to give, and I will carry you in my heart. Could we play one last tune together, you and I, with my hands guidin' yours? Perhaps, it would be fittin' to play 'Elizabeth's Waltz.'"

Lacey, trying hard against tears put our Elizabeth into my arms and I took her to her crib. When I came back, I had the camera with only one exposure left on the yellow indicator. Lacey had taken the fiddle and bow from his hands as Hiram stood behind her as in her first lesson. His long fingers overlapping her small ones, he tilted his whiskered cheek against the top of her head lovingly, as they both began to play. I finally got my mind to work and took the last picture. Before my eyes, old Hiram began to fade with the final bittersweet chord of the old song from the history that had killed him; our ghost was gone.

For a moment, Lacey just stood there letting the emptiness sink in and then I took the fiddle, gently, to free her hands and let her cry. I felt my own tears wet the case as I put the Guanerius away. I'm not sure if either of us knew what the tears were for, but when you cry, it doesn't matter.

After we had talked a while and said good-bye to our friend with a heartfelt midnight hug, we went upstairs together and Lacey turned the spindle while I turned the base of the bedpost. We slipped the cased fiddle back into its old hideaway where it had waited for Hiram so long.

"We'll get it when it needs us or when we need it," she said, "and Hiram trusts us to know." It was the kind of plain comment coming from Lacey that would be engraved on stone for us both. Hand in hand, we went downstairs and understood that in this world, at least, only time tells us anything.

Epilogue

ELL, IT'S GETTING LATE, BOTH IN HOURS and in years, and I see that my story is done, nearly sixty years after its beginning. I never intended to write a book, anymore than I'd try to write a symphony, those things being more in my children's line of work. I just wanted to tell a story and I'll be damned if it didn't turn into all of these pages, like some old codger's wanderings.

Of course, I *am* an old codger now and can wander where I please. Not too far, of course, physically, because it would worry Lacey, and I'm not too good at getting around anymore. She's the one who drove us down to Blessing Creek so I could revisit the old house we've kept so long. I needed the memories to finish this story, which has so obstinately become a book. The house on Blessing Creek is still a good one, much built onto and altered over the years, to accommodate three children and seven grandchildren's lives. More important with any house, I think, it sits where it belongs.

So far, three generations of Clarks have used it to recover from illness, divorce, hard luck, and death, or just as a place to come to think beyond our blinders. (In the old days, these were the eye patches horses wore to make them look straight ahead and miss all the fun.)

Just sitting here on the back porch this afternoon, looking up the hollow, dabbed with autumn colors until it resembles a textured Van Gogh, reminds me that no one in our family has ever looked straight ahead, but always around, to see what else was happening. As with horses, this has caused a lot of unexpected divergence in planned journeys from A to Z, which never came out that way.

I should tell you about the kids.

Liz, our oldest, whom you've met as Elizabeth, is fifty-five now, and became a concert violinist on her own at twenty-three, with no pressure from Lacey or me. She's played first fiddle with four symphony orchestras in ten countries. She's had two husbands now, but her real marriage seems to be to travel and music, and Hiram's Guarnerius is her only child. We know our old ghost would have not only observed, but also approved.

Ben is the middle one, fifty-three, and the real writer of the family. Stories about Hiram got him interested in The War Between The States (Missouri had more battles than any state but Virginia), and he has written two books about it, plus a couple of good novels about other things. He and Suzy had three girls, all grown and married, and Ben is now a successful literary agent in New York City.

Our youngest, Rabon, is forty-nine, and his middle name is Jack, to honor both grandfathers. When Grandpa Rabon died at seventy-nine, two weeks after Vera, he left a trust fund for each of his grandchildren, and Rabon used part of his to buy the old Indian Glade schoolhouse acre from the state and the eighty acres around it from Vance and Carney Black. It still stands, for any old scholar to visit, the door never locked. Rabon surprised us with a little brass plaque he'd made for the door, which visitors probably think is a misprint. It says, "In memory of Uncle Hiram, who was born in 1829 and in 1951 moved on."

Rabon never attended the old school, but he liked the concept of it and stories we told about the history of it. He has it repainted every few years and always tells the painter to respect the words carved in the little entryway from the long-ago scholar; *Schoolteachers is sons of bitches all.*

Rabon is an architect who actually designed a school of this type for autistic kids, though it is a much larger building. The basis of the school has the same "family" premise; kids of different ages help, watch out for, and teach each other. He has a house in Medley Springs and one in St. Louis and has four children, three boys and a girl.

Since I began this story with Lacey and me, I'll come full circle.

I taught my last day at Indian Glade in 1954, which was the year all these places began to be consolidated into large "R" (for rural) schools around Burke County. "R" schools are fine places that still exist—with good lighting, climate control, lunchrooms, a school nurse, and the latest in computer technology for children. They have music and art departments, good libraries, and the best teachers the county can find, with no Myrtle Summers to keep her black watch on scholar-days and budget.

They're pretty much a dream come true, and yet—be careful what you dream for. I tried to teach at one for a year but missed the democratic mix of things too much—the "flingin'" of knowledge at different age kids, to see who picked up what and the chance a teacher had in one-room days to personally implement the results.

I went instead, to teach at Medley Springs High School where most rural students at the time were graduates of one-room schools and felt free to ask any questions they liked, with side trips that were more fun than the answers. Over the years, I did my best to apply what I had learned about one-on-one teaching and eventually got my masters in education. I ended my teaching career when I retired as principal of that school in 2001, feeling pretty good about my years of teaching.

I'm not sure if I could be called a success, but I had taken Pop's advice, which was, "Find something you like to do and see if you can make a little money at it." Pop gave so little advice; it was always memorable. The only other piece of advice I remember was to finish anything I started and tidy up afterward, which in this case would be telling you what has happened to the people I wrote about.

The children I taught at Indian Glade School are now scattered like quail and some are dead. Ruby McClellan and T.J. Terrill died in the Vietnam War; Sandra Pulver, killed in a car crash when she was in her twenties; Buck Smith died of lung cancer at forty. They were real people, these first students of mine and the real world happened to them. I kept track of them as best I could.

Little Austin McClellan dropped out of high school and went to work for a car dealer as a mechanic, and now owns an automotive garage in St. Louis. Oran Cartwright and Penny McClellan married and raised cattle. I taught three of their children over the years, in high school. The one who became a nurse was actually Irene Farley, who, incidentally, helped deliver a grandchild of ours. All the rest of my scholars have passed beyond my knowledge, moving away to other states, and I hoped, taking some of the Ozarks to places where its unmeasured pace will come in handy.

The years have taken their toll of most folks who figured in "Hiram's Year," as Lacey still calls the few months he was with us, the greater part of them never making it to the turn of this century. Carney and Vance Black, now old men like me, are still here, but Vance was in a care center last time I heard, a victim of Alzheimer's. Carney runs the huge Black farm with his sons and sons-in-law.

The Trolls, Clive and Beulah Lou-Lou, moved south to West Plains, Missouri, in 1956 and sometime in the '60s, Clive blew them both up while "ciphering" gas from a farm storage tank. I only learned of this when Travis T. died in 1977, and I read of them in his obituary. Travis T., in turn, had parked his truck where a train wanted to go. So I guess their deaths were all Troll tradition.

Matthew Tucker, forever changed, in true Dickens' fashion, by his visitation from Hiram, had mellowed a lot in his views. He

395

remarried in his sixties to a widow from his church, who happened to be Virgie Black's sister, Magnolia. I do know he limited his usual scathing "Church News" diatribes in the *Medley Springs News*. We had read his muted mutterings on so-called science and evolution, but never a word about ghosts, spirits, or demons. However, he did make pleasant comments about church music, which he began to play again and even went so far as to learn to play the accordion.

But that makes me take a little side road to my summing up, which anyone getting this far shouldn't mind. It's about a trip we made to the old funeral home in Medley Springs when Matthew finally died in 1972. I've never attended funerals much, even back then, but Lacey and I both went to the Tucker visitation the day before, on the chance that we'd see his son.

We'd had two phone calls from Thun in the twenty years since we'd seen him, one the week after he'd left our house, wanting to speak to Hiram. I had told him then that Hiram had moved on, left no forwarding address; the only thing I could say that would make sense to him. The second call was five years later when Thun produced the first of his long list of hit albums for Gulf Breeze and wanted Hiram to know about it. Lacey took the call and told Thun that we hadn't heard from Hiram, but she suspected that he knew about the album already. She said it was easy to tell that to Thun, because she believed it herself.

We'd read in the Medley Springs paper that Matthew Tucker's son (as well-known as Phil Spector by this time), was producing an album in South Carolina but intended to fly back. I had wondered if we ever met again, what he'd be like, if Hiram's passion had passed to him and even wondered if he'd even remember us from our one meeting.

Sure enough, Thun made it back, and he was pretty easy to pick out at Stokes Funeral Chapel, since Medley Springs had only two black families back then, and none of the Standing Rock Holiness persuasion. He was there to greet Matthew's mourners in the lobby of the funeral home by the guestbook, and we caught him alone.

"Steve and Lacey Clark!" he boomed, and grabbed us both as if we were the people he had come to see. I asked if his mother had come too and he smiled.

"Ma-ma's in Hollywood doin' a voiceover," he said grinning, "and she advised me not to come either—scandalize all the honkies." He beamed at us warmly before getting serious. "I had to come!" he said. "Pa-Pa's the one who sent me to meet Hiram, and Hiram was a real head trip for me. He turned me on then, and still influences the way I think. Is that weird or what?"

"All that music he knew about?" asked Lacey smiling.

"Oh, hell no!" said Thun, "All the music he didn't know shit about but wanted to learn. It was like he'd been blank for fifty years. Didn't know Armstrong, didn't know Thelonius Monk, never heard of Brubeck, or Kenton, and thought Duke Ellington was English royalty. I remember at the time, I just stared at him. I said, 'Hey, Uncle, where've you been? These dudes are the Movers, man!'" Thun had a fat chuckle over that. "You know what he said? He told me, 'Perhaps, but *movers* movin' toward or away from what?'"

Thun sighed, remembering.

"'Moving toward or away from what?' got me thinking. It was the curiosity that old man had, that *what-if?* thing that woke me up. If this old dude who latched on to Paganini, dug him, and could make the leap to ragtime, orchestras, and jazz, wasn't hearing anything seminal happening yet, there was someplace we needed to go. I didn't want to miss going."

The lobby of the funeral chapel was a poor place to talk. People kept coming up to sign the guestbook, looking up at Jeduthun with confusion and wondering if they'd come to the right viewing.

"I'm pretty useless here anyway," said Thun, "Ma-ma was right, I look like a Swede in a tux at a *fais do-do*. Let's go outside a minute, unless you want to go look at Pa-Pa."

Lacey assured him that she'd had enough wax museum experiences with our own families, and we went around to the back of the building where someone had thoughtfully put a bench and a pair of folding chairs.

Thun got to the point right away. "Hiram's gone for good, I guess." he said, lighting a cowboy-looking cheroot.

"Well, yes," I told him, appreciating the *gone* synonym, which left me the chance to use it again. "As far as we know, he's been gone for years now. But he told Lacey and me, he was going to try to keep an eye on you, you know, your work before he—uh—left."

"Maybe he did," laughed Thun. "I got his vibes every time I'd go a new direction with a rock group I thought could do chart material. I was tempted to call you a lot of times, see if I could run the old guy down, but I was always covered up. Besides, he'd told me he was a wanderer, never stayed anyplace long."

Thun shook his head, remembering. "I wanted to thank him, but I wasn't sure what for and I'm still not. It wasn't ideas exactly, I always flashed on stuff myself. It was bigger than that . . . his concepts, maybe drive, I dunno. I only spent a few hours with the man, but he jolted my ass. You know what I'm saying? It was more like he's been with me for years, doing bluegrass, zydeco, jazz, hard rock, heavy metal, whatever was happening."

Thun waggled his cigar. "He was larger than life. He was, like, a force field, booking for someplace that you could go, too, if you wanted, or else get the hell out of his way." Thun laughed richly. "Wait, that's kind of what they said about *me* in *Variety* one time."

Lacey laughed, too. "I read that when our daughter Elizabeth brought the article home from college," she said, "and they were right about you. But with us, Uncle Hiram was just a gentle old man who thought America needed its own music, however or whenever you whittled it out. I think he'd be proud of what you've done so far."

"Well here's to him," said Thun, doffing an imaginary hat, "and I hope he knows there's a lot of heavy people whittlin'. Which reminds me," Thun had a half puzzled, half humorous look, "did you two ever find something a little spooky about your Uncle Hiram? Like he could put thoughts in your head? Words or maybe just concepts?"

"Thun," I said, "Hiram could put complete pictures in our head, and did. You referring to anything special?"

"Damnedest thing. I was workin' with another producer on a

sound track for a film a while back, a young guy from Savannah—maybe twenty—and he said 'Need's tonkin',' which was what Hiram called a big hook on a percussion track, like maybe a cowbell or blocks. I never heard anybody else say that." He grinned. "Gave me a little shiver. A year later, when I was mixing an album with a rock'n'roll producer from LA, he came off with another Hiram, 'Best let that soak.'" Thun looked at Lacey, "I said 'Hey, you know Hiram?' and the dude says, 'What's a Hiram?'"

Lacey smiled serenely. "I guess Uncle Hiram's part of the language now, as well as the music."

I guess we talked to Thun for a half-hour, catching up, but he kept an eye on his watch and when Lacey noticed, explained.

"I'm not staying for the funeral. Pa-pa's new family can handle that. I've got to get a flight back to Muscle Shoals. But I'm glad I got to see you and thank you for . . . well, letting me borrow your uncle for a night."

"You're welcome, Thun," said Lacey, "but we just borrowed him too, you know, maybe for a lifetime. Have a good trip."

THAT WAS THE last time we saw Thun, but over the years we've seen pictures of him and gotten packages from him, new albums he's produced or played on. Once, we received a video cassette labeled "Where's Hiram?" which startled us, but turned out to be a sort of audio twist on the "Where's Waldo?" theme and was all jazz improvisation by a group of masters that Thun had put together for the fun of it. It was mailed from Vero Beach, Florida, where I guess Jeduthun Tucker has perched for now, still trying to find the definitive American music for us all, somewhere in the space between Oregon, New Orleans, and Carnegie Hall. We wish him luck.

But for Lacey and me, up in our seventies and not sure of the music our grandchildren are listening to, wherever it goes is fine and comforting because we are sure we, in some strange way, had something to do with it. And that brings me to the end of this story.

Like most old people, we spend a lot of time reminiscing and we have decided that when it comes to music, we can allow ourselves a favorite sound to go with the big picture over the mantel. The best picture I think I ever took was with the last film in Lacey's Brownie, enlarged and put in an ornate frame by Liz, years ago. And the sound to go with it is that wonderful waltz that so captures the old South that Hiram knew, scented with magnolias and rich with time's never-ending memories.

We copied "Elizabeth's Waltz" from the wire recorder years ago, and now, along with the lyrics Lacey learned from Hiram and sang herself, it's on a disk, all electronically cleaned up, digitally accurate and enhanced, brighter than ever. We listen to it sometimes on summer nights when lightning bugs perform their waltz in our trees, but especially at Christmas, which for our family is a time of remembering our Christmas spirit, the visitor we set a place for still.

The picture is old Benjamin Springfield at Hiram's ghostly best, showing Lacey how the spirit of music could always find America . . . anywhere. But the lyrics printed beneath the frame tell more. They tell why people like us will always believe that ghosts are gentle souls . . .

ELIZABETH'S WALTZ

We'll waltz to every southern breeze
Under the stars on summer nights
We'll spin in our circles beneath the lights
Elizabeth and me.

Waltzing beside a southern sea
Fireflies and dancers all have gone
The love we are sharing will whirl us on
Elizabeth and me

(Bridge)
Led by the violin
Lost in a misty haze
Weaving the maze we're in
Spinning through all our days

When all we know is swept away
You'll find our love a dancing star
To light up the night where the waltzers are
Elizabeth and me.

And now they belong to you.

Afterwords

I was over twenty years writing this book, which is a grossly inefficient way to write, but I had to wait to find out how it ended. Most people, who set in to write books, manage their time better and so did I with my first two, one of which even became a movie three years after it was published. "Hot damn!" I thought at the time, "Now that's the way to write for a living!"

But ghosts have a different schedule, and before I followed Hiram, I had to follow a musical life myself for several years, and write a book (Home Grown Stories and Home Fried Lies) about that and other Ozark happenings. My ghost didn't care. Having already wisped around the universe for a hundred and thirty-odd years, he wasn't a bit jealous of time, and for all I know spent some of it watching Andy Griffith reruns, and expecting Dan Randant, my publisher, to remind me that Hiram still waited in the wings of an unexplored stage for me to finish what I began so long ago.

So now I'm done, though I'm sure Hiram isn't. His ghostly waltz still hums in my head, and I hear his unseen touch in such unlikely places as TV soundtracks, car radios, and rap music on boom boxes. I hear him on "Prairie Home Companion" and the "Late Night" shows, and at Bluegrass festivals, as well as on Public Broadcasting concerts that celebrate old music. Most fun of all, I hear his meddling with commercials, his "soakin'" of movie scores and his "tonkin'" of things that need a rhythmic punctuation.

I also suspect he has meddled with my hearing, which these days mushes every instrument but a fiddle, which still comes through loud and clear. For all I know, he has arrived at the Music of America he was seeking and is long gone to wherever ghosts go. I however, wouldn't bet on it.

—M.J.

Acknowledgements

Books are like orchestras, the result of a lot of people helping to make a creation real. I will try to thank them all, but their efforts are beyond words.

Thanks to my old friend and publisher, Dan Randant, a musician himself, who kept an old score of mine and inspired me to reinvent it. Dan has kept a faith in his fellow man that continues to renew my own.

Unending thanks to my wife Diana, also a musician, who made it possible through her endless research and patient detail, to bring the past to life and make it real again. Diana's belief in the book and in me was the foundation I built it on, and her ghostly cover illustrates the amazing range of her artistry, skills, and dedication. I'm simply grateful to Diana for being all she is.

Our combined thanks to Bee Walker, who spent a lot of her valuable time proofing, editing and taking this book a personal way, which I hope has made my often-awkward language readable to others. Bee is an Ozarkean, and is therefore to be trusted.

Thanks to Kevin Cook, a writer friend, who worked to reproduce the original book for evaluation. His enthusiasm and help have earned our gratitude.

Special thanks to Byron Berline, the incredible fiddler from Oklahoma, who introduced me to the first Guarnerius violin I ever heard, forty years ago — playing of all things, "Hamilton County" from Hiram's Tennessee, and raising a world of echoes to match my goose bumps from that ancient instrument.

Thanks to Denise Bonis, a concert violinist who came to visit us, and stayed to charm "Elizabeth's Waltz" out of my head and make it a living reality for others to hear.

Thanks to my daughters, Carole whose artistic insight as "first reader" was as important as her enthusiasm and Valerie, who as a writer herself has constantly reminded me that capturing things on a page is what we do.

I have to thank every violinist who ever touched my memory with a soulful instrument that leaps time like a painting, carrying the listener with it. Every fiddler, like Vassar Clements, Joe Stuart, Kenny Baker, and my Missouri friends, the Goforth brothers, John Hartford, Howe Teague, and a dozen others whose lives intersected my musical career. And thanks to whatever ghost inspired an old hearing-impaired guy who doesn't hear thunder well, to compose "Elizabeth's Waltz" as a tribute to all of the fiddlers now gone.

And finally, I must thank my Ozark friends and neighbors who have throughout my life, supplied an inspiration for me to save their words, their music and most of all, their unfailing belief that a sense of humor is essential to being human. That, after all is what has allowed them put up with me for all these years.

—M.J.

ABOUT THE AUTHOR

Mitch Jayne has varied his writing career with years spent in teaching, in radio, and as a professional musician (bass fiddle) and songwriter with The Dillards. He has authored three previous books: *Forest In The Wind*, *Old Fish Hawk*, and *Home Grown Stories and Home Fried Lies*, and has written about the Ozarks for newspapers, periodicals, and radio, most of his life. While in California with the Dillards, he wrote TV material for Dick Clark Productions, and appeared a number of times with his group as "The Darling Boys" on the Andy Griffith Show.

Mitch and his artist wife, Diana, live in Eminence, Missouri, where he writes a humor column for a number of Ozark publications and gives talks on Ozark culture, humor and language.

For more information
and to hear and buy the music,
visit www.fiddlersghost.com